Praise for the Christiansen Family Series

When I Fall in Love

"[*When I Fall in Love* is] an exquisite romance. Profoundly touching on the topic of facing fears, this book is a true gem."

ROMANTIC TIMES

"Readers who are already enamored of the sprawling Christiansen clan will feel even more connected, while those new to Warren will be brought right into the fold."

BOOKLIST

"Warren has a knack for creating captivating and relatable characters that pull the reader deep into the story."

RADIANT LIT

It Had to Be You

"*It Had to Be You* is a sigh-worthy, coming-into-her-own romance highlighting the importance of family, the necessity of faith, and how losing yourself for the right reasons can open your heart to something beautiful."

SERENA CHASE, *USA TODAY*

"This character-driven tale with a beautiful love story . . . gives excellent spiritual insight and a gorgeously written look at what it means to surrender and let go."

ROMANTIC TIMES

"Susan May Warren delivers another beautiful, hope-filled story of faith that makes the reader fall further in love with this captivating and intriguing family. . . . Powerful storytelling gripped me from beginning to end . . . [and] lovable characters ensure that the reader becomes invested in their lives."

RADIANT LIT

"This is one author who is only getting better with each book, and I cannot wait to find out which character we are next invited to meet in this Christiansen family."

FICTION ADDICT

"A gem of a story, threaded with truth and hope, laughter and romance. Susan May Warren brings the Christiansen family to life, as if they might be my family or yours, with her smooth writing and engaging storytelling."

RACHEL HAUCK, BESTSELLING AUTHOR OF *THE WEDDING DRESS*

Take a Chance on Me

"Warren's new series launch has it all: romance, suspense, and intrigue. It is sure to please her many fans and win her new readers, especially those who enjoy Terri Blackstock."

LIBRARY JOURNAL

"Warren . . . has crafted an engaging tale of romance, rivalry, and the power of forgiveness."

PUBLISHERS WEEKLY

"Warren once again creates a compelling community full of vivid individuals whose anguish and dreams are so real and relatable, readers will long for every character to attain the freedom their hearts desire."

BOOKLIST

"*Take a Chance on Me* is the first of six books in this new series from prolific author Susan May Warren—and I couldn't be more excited! I've already fallen in love with the Christiansen family . . . and I can't wait to see how Warren brings true and lasting love into the lives of Darek's two brothers and three sisters."

SERENA CHASE, *USA TODAY*

"A compelling story of forgiveness and redemption, *Take a Chance on Me* will have readers taking a chance on each beloved character!"

CBA RETAILERS + RESOURCES

"Warren's latest is a touching tale of love discovered and the meaning of family."

ROMANTIC TIMES

ALWAYS ON MY MIND

SUSAN MAY
WARREN

Christy Award–winning author

Always on my Mind

a Christiansen Family *novel*

Tyndale House Publishers, Inc.
Carol Stream, Illinois

Visit Tyndale online at www.tyndale.com.

Visit Susan May Warren's website at www.susanmaywarren.com.

TYNDALE and Tyndale's quill logo are registered trademarks of Tyndale House Publishers, Inc.

Always on My Mind

Designed by Jennifer Phelps

Edited by Sarah Mason

Published in association with the literary agency of The Steve Laube Agency, 5025 N. Central Ave., #635, Phoenix, AZ 85012.

Always on My Mind is a work of fiction. Where real people, events, establishments, organizations, or locales appear, they are used fictitiously. All other elements of the novel are drawn from the author's imagination.

Library of Congress Cataloging-in-Publication Data

Warren, Susan May, date.
  Always on my mind / Susan May Warren.
    pages cm. — (Christiansen family)
    ISBN 978-1-4143-7844-2 (softcover : acid-free paper) 1. Man-woman relationships—Fiction. 2. Minnesota—Fiction. I. Title.
  PS3623.A865A79 2015

  813'.-6—dc23   2014036475

Printed in the United States of America

22   21   20   19   18   17   16
8   7   6   5   4   3   2

For Your glory, Lord

ACKNOWLEDGMENTS

WHEN I'M IN THE MIDDLE of a story, it's always on my mind and it's a little dangerous to be around me. You never know when I'll corner you in the kitchen to work out a scene or call you to ask for help with "just one tiny detail."

I rely on my circle of supporters more than they realize, I'm sure. But with each story, they show me that they are not going to abandon me. That they'll stand by me and throw me ideas (or critiques!) when I need them. I'm so grateful.

Their sacrifice doesn't go unnoticed, so my deepest appreciation goes to:

Rachel Hauck, who worked through every scene with me, faithful on the other end of the phone. I couldn't write a book without her.

David Warren, who sits down and works through all my character kinks (and the male POV! What a gift!). Thank you for your brilliance.

Sarah Erredge and her cute husband, Neil, who learned that even he can be pulled into brainstorming.

Peter Warren, my wonderful, crazy middle child, who inspired Casper's wild, adventurous heart.

Noah Warren, who has Casper's sensitive, loving personality and is my last brainstorming victim left at home. You are a treasure!

Andrew, my Thor. Life with you is always exciting.

Karen Watson, who always knows just how to round out a story and make it stronger. Yes, I mean it—you are brilliant.

Sarah Mason, for her amazing editing skills. You make this feel easier than it is.

Jesus, who shows me every day that I belong to Him and that He loves me.

And to my amazing readers—you bless me with your encouragement. As I write, you are always on my mind. Thank you for reading the Christiansen Family series!

THE AREA OF
DEEP HAVEN
AND
EVERGREEN
LAKE

Two Island Lake

The Garden

Evergreen Resort

Gibs's house

Evergreen Lake

Pine Acres

N

GUNFLINT TRAIL

HWY 61

DEEP HAVEN

Minnesota

Lake Superior

My dearest Casper,

It's not easy to be the middle child, the one who is neither the oldest—the responsible legacy bearer—nor the youngest, pampered and cherished just because he is the last. The middle must both follow and lead, must know how to soothe wounded pride and embolden others to greatness. The middle child must know how to love.

You, Casper, possess this beautiful gift. You are an amazing middle child, carrying both the dark hair (I'm sorry, Son, but you are most likely destined to lose your glorious locks early) and pensive blue eyes of your father and the heart of your mother—compassionate, sensitive, and seeking to nurture others.

Unfortunately that heart I gave you makes you feel more deeply, wound easily, and—sometimes to your detriment— love without reserve.

I wish you truly understood what a delight you are! From the moment you arrived, hearty and charming, you won our hearts. I remember you standing in your crib, mesmerized by Darek, coddled by Eden and Grace. You cried when they cried, laughed at their teasing, and even when they hurt you, you followed them.

Then the others arrived and you decided to love them with everything you had. Despite the age difference between

*you and Amelia, you tried to understand her. Most of all,
I know watching Owen rise in fame couldn't have been easy,
but you bore it, cheered him on, believed in him.*

*If only you could see your own light, the one that shines
out past the shadows your brothers cast over you. You try so
hard to fit into their lives, to hold up your unspoken promises,
believing for some reason that you are second best. And that
if you don't accomplish or find something extraordinary, you
will be forgotten.*

*You are the epic middle of the story, Casper. That
delicious, rich, charming, sometimes-challenging, always-
compelling middle that holds the family together. You are
the life of the party, the spark that draws us close. Your belief
that there are some things worth fighting for inspires us, and
your courage to seek the precious in life is like the heart of
Christ.*

*This is my prayer for you. That you would see how much
the world needs you. How valuable you are to God, to us.
And that you would no longer see yourself as second best but
as someone worth finding and cherishing.*

*Do not let the world steal away your tender,
compassionate heart. It is precious in God's sight.*

And mine.

Your loving mother

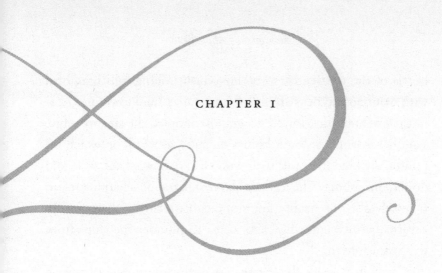

CHAPTER I

A MAN STUCK IN PARADISE should have someone to share it with.

Especially on New Year's Eve.

Casper Christiansen angled his skiff along the shoreline toward the littered beach of Cay Comfort, the moniker given by the locals to this wash of beachfront in Old Port Royal, a tiny key off the island of Roatán, Honduras.

The island time forgot, the perfect place for a person to hide. To listen to his regrets. To figure out how to find everything he'd thrown away. Like his future. His self-respect.

And if that man could find the treasure hidden in the east end of the island, he might even return with the pride he'd left behind in Minneapolis the day he found out his brother had a too-intimate history with the woman he loved.

Casper had followed the rumors of treasures away from the

1

hustle of the west-end resorts. Here lush, rolling hills brambled with bamboo and dense ferns fell into the sea, and towering coconut palms and thick-leaved sea grapes canopied the creamy-white sand beaches. Locals built homes on stilts, as if still on watch for pirates, the kind that stole their women and dragged chests of gold doubloons ashore. The legends claimed marauders had fortressed themselves in the nearby limestone cliffs, securing their gold in caverns before venturing back to sea to plunder the ships from the Spanish Main.

Casper had spent the better part of four months, in between diving for Fitz Hanson's archaeological dig, plotting out exactly where pirates like Captain Morgan had secured such treasures.

And tonight, while the rest of the world celebrated New Year's Eve, he'd unearth old Morgan's treasure, start a new chapter of his life.

Casper raised his hand to a bronze-skinned ten-year-old perched at the end of his *cayuka*, fishing wire fastened around an old detergent bottle. He wore a *Life is good* T-shirt and cutoff jeans, his hair long like Casper's.

The child waved back. "Grouper for you tonight, Mr. Casper!" The afternoon sun glinted off his smile.

Casper gave him a thumbs-up. He'd eaten enough fish to grow fins.

Past the boy, the ocean stretched beyond the curve of the bay, the aquamarine water so glassy it begged him to reach out for the sea anemone shadowing the ocean floor, run his fingers through the schools of blue tang and creole wrasse scattering among the shoals.

But he knew better. Fertile rumors of shipwrecks and sunken treasure, along with the hypnotizing ocean, lured a man into the turquoise depths and the dangerous labyrinth of coral latticed along the edge of the bay. Beyond the wall of jagged coral, deep in underwater caverns, squid and moray eels lay in vigil, preying upon men lured by the hope of gold doubloons and fueled by the yarns perpetuated by locals eager for tourists.

Casper, however, had sorted the truth from the lies and knew why treasure eluded hobby enthusiasts scouring the sea.

They were searching in the wrong place.

Casper angled his skiff out from shore, away from the tangle of mangroves that scarred this part of the island. Yellow-naped parrots and lime-and-scarlet macaws sang from the shadows beyond the nest of vegetation, deep in the tropical forest, home to geckos, frogs, lizards, and ancient iguanas the size of a man.

A tepid wind off the sea combed his hair, the air salty, drying his lips, his skin having turned leathery from his daily work at the *Valiant* wreck site.

Dig director Fitz Hanson seemed to believe the entire island—and its hidden treasures—belonged to him. If he knew what Casper did on his days off, he might fire him on the spot, send him packing back to snow-encrusted northern Minnesota, where, according to his mother, winter had turned bitter and angry, plunging them into subzero suffering.

Casper supposed he should feel guilty—in fact, yes, he did. But not because he was enjoying his days in the cerulean-blue ocean, his nights watching the moonlight trace a milky finger over the waves.

No, his guilt sank into his bones, had claws. In the quiet of the night, the memory of his fury could shake him awake, fill his throat with regret.

He'd caused a rift in his family that he didn't know how—or even want, sometimes—to fix.

A white-faced monkey squealed at him from a gnarled banana tree before scampering away. Casper steered the motorboat into the quay, where he'd first located the trail of set stones leading to shore.

The stones betrayed the telltale sign of a foundation, a mooring site for sloops such as the type Welsh privateer Henry Morgan might have utilized.

And according to Casper's research, this little inlet just might contain Morgan's lost treasure, the one first unearthed over seventy-five years ago by infamous adventurer Ziegler Hanes. Tale had it that, once upon a time, a river ran through the forest into the bay. Along this river, pirates lugged their treasures to a cave embedded deep in the tangle.

Ziegler Hanes had thrashed through enough mangroves to discover the cave, explored it, and unearthed three chests wrapped in chains. These he cut open, then dragged one by one out to his ship, under the onslaught of a hurricane. Finally leaving behind the last chest, he'd nearly wrecked his ship escaping the island to nearby British Honduras.

Which meant the last treasure chest could still be here. Right here, in fact, if Casper had his calculations correct. And so what that he'd spent the past two months unearthing nothing but pop cans, metal wire, dented buckets, and rusted buoys? He'd nearly lost his heart once digging up what seemed like the find of the century, only to discover an ancient refrigerator.

Yet, deep down, Casper knew the treasure waited just for him.

He moored the boat and retrieved his machete, a portable shovel, his metal detector, and headphones.

He trekked into the green, remembering his steps, hacking at forest until he reached a clearing, his last search grid. Low-hanging sunlight streamed through the coconut palms, mottling the ground as he switched on the metal detector and fitted on his headphones.

Treasure hunting isn't going to give you a future, Casper. If you want to accomplish something in life, you have to work for it.

He shut his father's voice from his head. With sweat dribbling down his spine, wetting his long-sleeved shirt, the mosquitoes nibbling at his legs, and the no-see-ums dive-bombing his neck, yeah, he could consider this work.

He got a hit and spent ten minutes with too-eager enthusiasm unearthing a rotted tin can.

Blowing out a breath, he drew his arm across his forehead. His stomach clenched, empty after this morning's plum jam on bread.

Is that what you want? To be a treasure hunter?

He shook away Raina's voice, but she never escaped far, haunting him just beyond his thoughts.

I'd like to find something precious, yes.

Six months ago, he thought he had, in Raina.

He swallowed, needing a drink, something cool against his parched throat.

An hour later, Casper set the detector down and pulled the headset off his ears. He'd uncovered another tin can and a cup. A real haul. Maybe his pal Doug was right when he suggested Casper head home when the new interns arrived in two weeks.

He hadn't exactly discovered a lost fortune. And he'd spent most of his time helping Fitz haul old cannons, tin plates, and the occasional charred wooden beam from the ocean floor.

He felt more like a day laborer than an archaeologist.

So you're like what's his name—Indiana Jones?

Raina again, and for a second, he let her settle there, remembering her in his arms under a northern moon. The way she ran her fingers through his hair, made him believe that he could be happy in Deep Haven, discovering a life with her.

Slinging the metal detector over his shoulder, he turned it on but kept the headphones around his neck as he trekked back. He swung the detector loosely over the ground, following a tumble of rocks that could have been a stream, perhaps.

Or maybe he was simply afflicted with an overactive imagination. The ability to tell himself a good tale, make himself believe it.

Like the fact that he could have a happily ever after with a woman who clearly saw him as second choice.

See, there she went again, tiptoeing into his brain and perching there.

Yeah, pitiful man that he was, he could admit he still thought about—even cared for—Raina Beaumont. Probably more since he'd escaped the family drama and soaked himself in the sun day after day.

Casper nearly missed the shrieking of the detector as he stepped out of the jungle, fifty feet down the beach from his skiff.

The needle bumped into the red and he dropped the detector, grabbed his shovel.

The sun hung low, an orange fire glowing over the horizon. As the trees slung shadows across the beach, he dug furiously against the onslaught of twilight.

His shovel hit metal. Falling to his knees, he worked out the sand and ran his fingers over what looked like a rusty piece of chain.

For mooring a boat.

Casper sat back, his heart sinking.

Except . . .

He looked closer. The chain seemed hand-hammered, the edges of each link rough and not engineered.

In fact—he pulled the rest of the chain from the earth, found the end. His pulse caught at the sight of an ancient padlock, broken open.

He examined it, his mind turning through his research and landing on the story of Hanes and his third chest of doubloons.

Abandoned under the storm's onslaught, the chain had broken off.

Casper got up and began to run the detector in a grid around the chain, back into the forest, where the mangroves had taken root.

The detector shrilled and he dropped it, retrieving his shovel and beginning to dig.

The now-milky twilight pressed shadows into the divots of the soil as his hand fastened around plate-size pieces of broken metal. He leaned into the hole and cleared away the sand, his breath short as he touched the rough, rotting top of a box.

Sweat blackened his hands as he cleared away the dirt, trying to lug the box from the sand. It refused to budge. Casper attacked the hole with his shovel, widening it enough to wiggle the box lid free.

What if—?

He crawled his fingers along the edge, hoping to find the bottom of the lid, but as he handled it, the box creaked and the lid broke free, off its hinges.

The archaeologist inside halted him.

But he knew what manner of men haunted these islands. If he left the box here, by tomorrow it would be looted.

As sweat dripped off his chin, saturating his shirt, Casper eased the broken lid open.

Muddy water filled the inside.

He held his breath as he plunged his hand into the murky contents.

Silt sifted between his fingers. He worked them deeper, found the edges, then the bottom, his fingers scraping against wood, then . . . rock.

No.

Oh no. He felt around the hole in the bottom of the box where the elements had bashed it against rock, destroying the wood.

And the storm had washed away any doubloons, any looted spoils from the Spanish ships sacked by the legendary pirates of the Caribbean.

Casper pulled out a handful of gray mud, watching it leach out of his grip.

Around him, bats awoke, blotting out the darkening sky, screeching. Monkeys screamed back, and mosquitoes sawed in his ears.

He closed his eyes to his audience.

Happy New Year.

If the fifty waiting guests were depending on Raina Beaumont to get the bride to the altar, located in the fireplace room of the posh Summit Hill mansion, they should pack up and head home before the snowstorm buried them all for the weekend.

Because Raina hadn't a clue how to answer cute Gina McCune, despite the look of desperation in her young and worried brown eyes.

"What would you do?"

Pearl Jam's "Just Breathe" threaded out into the hall, signaling the processional.

"I . . ." Raina glanced toward the front, connected with Michele, the bride's mother.

Oh, boy. They wanted *her* advice? Did no one notice the fact that their wedding coordinator sported a pregnant belly under her not-so-little black dress? Not that anyone could guess that the father had ditched her long before he even knew about her condition. Still, she hardly felt able to dispense wisdom.

Maybe, however, no one noticed her swollen ankles or the way she bumped around the room like a tank. Probably today's activities—the decorating crew, the cake delivery, the flowers—simply distracted everyone from her cumbersome girth.

Even her boss, Grace Christiansen, had refrained from ordering her to sit, put her swollen feet up, breathe through the occasional Braxton-Hicks contractions.

But given that the elite bash counted as Grace's first major wedding-catering gig, perhaps Grace didn't have time to spare a thought for her assistant's grand mistakes in life.

Raina and the bride had to figure out their futures on their own.

Gina blinked, fast, hard, staring at her bouquet of blue hydrangeas and white roses. "It seems right, but it's the rest of my life. And . . ." She glanced through the half-parted double oak doors to her groom, Kalen Boomer, tall, blond, and swarthy, a hockey goalie for the St. Paul Blue Ox. He stood next to the green-tiled fireplace, beside his best man and the pastor he'd imported from his hometown. Kalen clasped his hands in front of him and stared at the floor.

Gina turned back to Raina. "How do I know I want this? I mean, yes, I love Kalen—so much it hurts sometimes—but how do I know that we'll be happy ten years from now? That he'll still love me?"

Raina opened her mouth, glancing past the petite bride toward the massive dining room, holding the delicious reception

Grace had created. Garlands of white pine boughs wrapped with twinkle lights hung from the windows, the chandelier, the wainscoting. The collection of round tables glittered with gold chargers crowned with red glass plates over an ivory tablecloth, the room fragrant with the scent of cinnamon-stick favors wrapped at the head of each plate.

Raina held her breath, willing Grace to appear with some pithy words of wisdom. Her roommate always seemed to have something profound for Raina over the past six months as she struggled to figure out the rest of her life.

"What I wouldn't give to just . . . *know*. To see the future and know I'm making the right decision. Some sort of lighted path," Gina was saying. "I mean, look at you. You're happy and married and have a baby on the way . . ."

Oh. So someone did notice. And probably thought Raina had removed her wedding ring to accommodate swollen fingers. It wasn't like she'd had a deep and personal conversation about her marital status with Gina over the past three months, and Grace had handled all but the most recent in-person planning sessions.

Gina's eyes grew glossy. She drew in a breath.

If Raina didn't conjure up something, this entire thing could trek south in a heartbeat. A sudden image of the bride escaping through the kitchen, upsetting a tray of champagne shrimp, flashed through her mind.

But frankly—good question. How did anyone make a lifelong decision like marriage? Or whether to be a single mother or give up her child for adoption?

Likely any advice Raina gave the bride would only turn out to haunt the poor girl. Besides, sweet Gina seemed to have done everything right, her future nothing but sunny.

As far as Raina peered ahead, she saw only darkness.

She tried a reassuring smile but clearly managed to scare the bride because Gina's eyes filled.

Then—"Shh, honey."

Raina turned to see the bride's mother slipping through the doors. Tall, elegant, blonde, and not a hint of the Asian descent evident in her daughter, she appeared to be in her early fifties and still wore her wedding ring, despite her recent widowhood.

"Mom—sorry. I'm just having a second of . . . Well, how do I know this is the right decision?" Gina turned to her, and Raina stepped back, watching the moment she'd always longed for herself.

A mother's advice.

Michele took her daughter's hands. "We don't know what tomorrow will bring, but you can't live your life fearing the what-ifs. Kalen is a wonderful man, and he becomes the right decision the minute you say, 'I do.' The bigger question is, are you ready to make that decision?"

No. Raina wanted to scream it out for Gina—or maybe herself. With only six weeks left . . .

Her hand slid up to press against the baby's foot, lodged just below her ribs.

"Yes." The shadows cleared from Gina's expression. She peeked through the doors, a soft smile lifting. "Yes."

Her mother held out her arm. "How about if I walk you to meet your groom? Your father would have preferred to do it, but I know he's watching."

Now a tear ran off Raina's chin. She forced a smile and held open the doors as Gina and her mother headed down the aisle.

Gina met her groom, and Raina slid off her shoes, watching

them exchange vows. As the ceremony progressed, she picked them up and headed to the kitchen.

The holiday dinner aroma could knock her over—roasted beef au jus, garlic mashed potatoes, freshly baked wheat dinner rolls. In her last trimester her appetite had returned with the ferocity of a wildebeest.

Grace managed the kitchen—and her small staff—with the skills of a general. Raina watched her and for a moment wished she could be assembling the spring salad rather than manning the front lines.

But she simply couldn't move with the same speed as before. Maybe after . . . when . . . what?

She hadn't a clue what her life might look like by spring.

Grace glanced up from where she stood plating baked Brie and crackers—appetizers for the guests. "Is the ceremony almost over?"

"Ten minutes or so. How are we doing in here?"

"Perfect." Grace glanced at Ty Teague, down for the weekend from Deep Haven, helping out as a server. He looked debonair and festive, wearing a tux and white gloves, his curly dark hair freshly groomed. "We might actually pull this off."

"Of course we will," Raina said. "I wasn't sure for a moment, though."

Grace met her eyes, stricken. "Why? Oh no, did she have cold feet again?"

"You knew about this?" Raina barely stopped herself from reaching for one of the plump shrimp curled around a champagne glass filled with spicy cocktail sauce. "She nearly didn't walk down the aisle. Started asking me if I thought she should get married. As if I know."

She moved aside for Ty and Nash—one of Grace's culinary

school recruits—to deliver the appetizers to the parlor, where the reception festivities would begin.

Grace finished plating the next Brie appetizer, then picked up oven mitts. She opened the oven. "She's just hurting over her father's death. It's hard—losing him so close to the wedding."

"Yeah. Sad. I get it." Sort of. After all, Raina had lost her father too. But he'd been in jail. And she hadn't exactly kept in touch.

"And she's their only child. They really thought he'd beat the cancer this time—hence why they hurried the wedding. Kalen only met her this summer." She checked the lasagna, then returned it to the oven. "Nearly ready."

Grace pulled off the hot pads. "I met her dad once, about three weeks before he passed. He was so proud of her—and really liked Kalen, which is saying something. He was so . . . I don't know. *Possessive* is not the right word, but . . . doting? Maybe because they had to fight so hard to adopt Gina—I think they went to China three times before they finally brought her home. Gina said she was four, and by that time, she needed six operations to fix her leg. They spared no expense on her. I think she even graduated from Princeton."

Grace directed Aliya, one of her favorite assistants, to start bringing the salads to the dining room.

Raina picked up two plates. "She never mentioned her leg."

Grace held open the door. "Yeah, she was born with a deformity or maybe was injured in birth. Anyway, she's fine now."

Raina set the salad plates on the chargers. Glanced toward the wedding. "Beautiful, in fact."

Grace touched Raina's hand, gave it a quick squeeze before she went back to the kitchen.

Raina slipped her shoes on and headed to the double doors just as she heard the pastor announce the couple.

No hint of regret creased Gina's face as she held hands with her groom and walked back up the aisle. They disappeared for a moment into the parlor while the rest of the party exited, then returned to dismiss the guests. Raina directed the crowd toward the parlor for appetizers.

"You look pretty tonight, Raina."

The voice startled her, and for a split second, in that place where she parked her dreams, she heard the deep tenor of Casper Christiansen complimenting her.

When she turned, the man talking to her could be mistaken for him, with dark-brown hair, long behind his ears, and kind eyes.

Except, no—this man had a beard and brown eyes and, well, belonged to Grace. "Thanks, Max," Raina said.

Maxwell Sharpe slicked up well in a black suit and silver tie. "My girl in the kitchen?"

"Yes." She reached out to touch his arm, stopping him. "But you are assigned to the parlor. You're a guest, not staff."

He made a face at her, and for a second she thought he might disobey—after all, hockey players didn't exactly mind their manners.

But he surrendered to her words and disappeared to celebrate with the guests.

And Raina surrendered, just for a second, to sinking down on the arching dark oak staircase. The piano and cello from the ceremony continued to play, and "A Thousand Years" lilted out.

She ran her hands over her stomach, listening to the laughter from the parlor, the sweet music echoing into the hall, and drew in a long breath. Her throat ached. See, a girl with this many hormones flooding her body had no business at a wedding. It only conjured up too-tangible images of the man she'd driven away. The man she could never have. Not after the wounds she'd raked into his heart.

And now just the flash of memory could stir up Casper's smile, the feel of his summer-toned arms around her, and if she didn't get herself under control, she just might end up in a puddle.

She pressed her fingers under her eyes, shook him from her mind. He'd left—and who blamed him, anyway? She had to move on.

Ty came out, carrying glasses of champagne. He glanced at her, frowning, his sweet brown eyes suddenly concerned. She shook her head, smiled, waved him into the parlor.

"Raina, dear, thank you for your help in keeping Gina calm." Michele emerged from the room, and Raina made to push up from the stairs. "Oh no—you sit. You have to keep that little bundle safe." Michele slid onto the stairs next to her. "If my Steven were here, he'd be offering to rub your feet. He did that for all three of my pregnancies."

Raina glanced at her.

"Oh yes, I was pregnant. Lost the last one at six months. I was never able to carry to term. But God had other wonderful plans." She stared into her champagne, golden and glistening against the hall chandelier. Outside, the wind blew snow against the windowpane, rattling it. "Steven tried so hard to hang on until this day. Would have, if not for the staph infection. He went so fast."

Michele forced a smile. "Such a beautiful wedding, despite the storm. I think we might have a few overnight guests."

"It's still early, and Grace has dinner ready—"

"And it smells delicious." She touched Raina's hand. "So have you and your husband picked out any names?"

Raina shook her head. Didn't correct her. After all, what could she say? *I have no husband? This baby is the result of a one-night stand?* The enormity of her stupidity could take her breath away.

"Nothing?"

"I . . . can't settle on anything." Starting with whether she'd be the one naming her baby.

"You never know when that baby might want to show up."

"As long as it's not tonight," Raina said, her hand running over her bulk as the baby decided to shift.

Michele laughed. "Yes. That might add too much excitement to the evening. Happy New Year, Raina. I predict next year is going to be wonderful."

Raina managed a nod as the bride's mother joined the party. No, the baby wasn't coming tonight.

Which meant she could figure out the rest of her life tomorrow.

CHAPTER 2

"SERIOUSLY, DUDE, the chest was empty?" Doug slid up to the bamboo bar where Casper perched, nursing a tepid Coke, his calamari appetizer soggy and cold. Behind him a local band plunked out a Bruno Mars cover—"Just the Way You Are"—the rendition slow and sloppy and drawing a slew of couples wrapped in love pretzels onto the dance floor.

Tiki torches lit a path to the beach, where the velvety-black surf rolled onto shore, perfect and romantic and heartbreaking.

"That's just about the most pitiful thing I've ever heard. You find a bona fide treasure chest and it's nothing but mud."

"It's not funny—"

"It's hilarious, bro." Doug gestured to the bartender, who slid a foamy beer in front of him. He lifted it to honor Casper. "To finding the treasure of the century—not!"

"I'm leaving."

"I hope you're going back there with a torch and your detector, because by tomorrow morning, the place will be crawling with treasure hunters."

"It's gone, Doug. I scoured the area until I could barely see my hand in front of my face. I'm telling you, if there was any gold left, it's been washed out to sea or maybe stolen before—I don't know. But it's not there." He slid off the stool. "Happy New Year."

"You're really leaving? The night is young." Doug glanced past Casper and grinned, raising his beer. Casper followed his gaze, and it landed on a couple of tourists in bikinis holding drinks in hollowed-out coconuts garnished with umbrellas. The brunette winked, her hair loose in the wind, and for a moment Raina appeared, smiling at him.

Casper turned away, back to Doug. "No, dude, the night has come and gone. According to my watch, it's after midnight."

Not that the partygoers had any intention of winding down soon. On the beach, a bonfire blazed, locals dancing in the undulating light, the sparks like fireworks as they snapped, crackled, and popped. From other beach bars and decks, a cacophony of sounds—blues, reggae, pop—serenaded the New Year.

Casper had no taste for the celebration. In fact, he should be home playing Monopoly with his family, eating his sister's homemade pizza.

He dug a fistful of lempiras from his pocket, left the bills on the bar. "Thanks."

The barkeep nodded.

Doug stopped Casper with a hand to his arm. "Fitz was looking for you today. Said he needed to know if you were going to stick around after the new recruits join us in a couple weeks."

Six months ago—maybe even six weeks ago—a quick yes would have shot to Casper's lips, his hurt fresh and volatile. But a man didn't spend Christmas away from his family without feeling the wounds reopen, without taking a good look at them.

Without realizing that perhaps a few of them had been self-inflicted. And today's debacle only told him the truth.

He couldn't find a treasure if it washed up onshore in front of him.

Maybe answers—healing—could be found not in running but in returning home. Diving into a different life. "I dunno."

"Well, if not, he needs you to train someone else," Doug was saying, glancing now and again at the girls by the bar.

"How hard can it be to slop out the boat?"

"Hey, you got to work on the last cannon lift—"

"I got to hold the line and shout, 'Ready, bring it up!'"

"No one said archaeology was glamorous work, Casper."

"I don't need glamorous. But I do need to be . . . I don't know . . . actually needed." He shook himself out of Doug's grip and headed out of the bar, into the night.

"Casper, are you leaving so soon?"

He turned at the voice and knew Doug had sicced pretty Martha Queen on him. Half-Trinidadian, half-Asian, the petite diver could steal a man's breath away with her amazingly smooth coffee-brown skin, those chocolate eyes. If he didn't already have Raina occupying too much of his brain, he would have let sweet, smart, beautiful Martha get a foothold inside.

"Hey, Martha."

She'd caught her curly black hair back in a tie-dye hair band, but it flowed out in thick, tantalizing corkscrews. She wore a pair of Army fatigues and a pink T-shirt, the smell of coconut oil lifting off her skin. "Stay," she said, her voice light. "It'll be fun."

Maybe. Yeah. Right now, he could appreciate a little distraction. Even just a walk down the beach with a pretty girl.

Or . . .

Casper blew out a breath. No. He wasn't Owen, and the memory of his brother's indiscretions and the destruction he left in his wake sent a chill into his smile. Besides, until he got Raina out of his head, any late-night romantic stroll would only be wasted on him. "Nah, I'm headed home."

Martha caught up with him, tugged on his shirtsleeve. "Then I'll walk with you."

He glanced at Doug, who lifted his glass to him. Oh, brother. But short of being rude—

Besides, she lived only two doors down from him, in the grouping of tiny houses Fitz rented for the staff, and on a night like this, maybe she could use some protection. "Okay."

He headed out to the beach, kicking his toes through the cool sand. Stars littered the sky, fell into the black ocean. He could make out the *Mayan*, Fitz's ship, docked at the wharf, the lights in the portholes like eyes.

Martha walked beside him. "Doug says you found a treasure chest."

"Nice. By morning, the entire village will know."

"I think they already do." She had taken off her sandals; they dangled from her fingers. "I heard it was empty."

"Yeah. Of course it was." He watched as a couple ran into the surf, laughing, hands entwined. They fell into each other's arms.

"Are you going home after the New Year?"

He didn't answer. The scent of the bonfire seasoned the air, the beat of drums and Bob Marley on the breeze. Waves whispered against the sand.

"I think you should stay." She touched his hand then and stopped him, stepped in front of him. The wind caught her fragrance and twined it around him. She pointed to the necklace he wore. "That's a good idea—to put one of the copper coins Fitz gave us on a lanyard."

He'd really made the necklace for Grace. Or . . . okay, yes, Raina. But she'd probably think the trinket silly.

Now Martha touched his cheek, smiled. "Casper, I don't know why, but there are shadows around you, darkness. You're in the most beautiful place in the world, on the night of new beginnings. Isn't it time to cast them off and start over?"

He stared at her, his chest a little hollow.

Then she rose up on her toes and kissed him. Sweetly, softly. He closed his eyes, letting her, tasting pineapple juice on her lips, a hint of her lure in the air. He slid his hand to her shoulder, and the urge to surrender, to lose himself in her affection, even for a moment, stirred inside him.

Yes. Maybe he should let it go, move on—

His cell phone vibrated in his shirt pocket and he jerked away. Martha startled.

"Sorry. Uh—" Casper fished out the phone, looked at the screen. "It's my sister. She wants to video-call me."

"Answer it," she said, smiling as if undeterred by the distraction.

Oh, boy. He tucked his heart back into place, then answered the call.

Grace's face appeared on the screen. "Casper! Happy New Year." She wore a Deep Haven sweatshirt, her hair pulled back, her face scrubbed clean, her blue eyes warm, and homesickness nearly knocked him over.

"Sis." He glanced at Martha, but she seemed content to stand there and grin at him. "I expected you to be out with Max tonight."

"Actually, I catered a wedding for another one of the Blue Ox players. And I wanted to call and tell you because . . . well, okay, I miss you."

He swallowed the crazy boulder lodged in his throat. Aside from a few e-mails to his mother back in Deep Haven, he hadn't done more than text his sisters since his escape to Central America last fall.

His voice nearly cut out, but he dragged it up, tried to right himself into something casual, easy. "Me too."

"I'm so jealous. You're standing on a beach in paradise, and I'm here, dressed in my sweatpants and wool socks."

"Where, exactly, are you?"

"It's my new apartment. Wait; I'll show you around." She got up, held her phone away, and gave him a tour of the apartment. He made out a small kitchen, the quilt that used to cover her bed folded over a chair, a flat-screen TV on a flea-market table.

Grace appeared back on the screen. "I know—humble digs. But I have my own catering company, with three more gigs coming up in the next three months, and I'm working at a bar and grill in St. Paul. I'm doing it, Casp. I'm really catering for a living."

"That's awesome, Grace."

"So. How do you like Roatán?"

"It's . . ."

"It's gorgeous and he nearly found a treasure today!" Martha leaned into the conversation, Skype-bombing. She looked at him and winked.

He managed a return smile.

"Who's that?" Grace asked, almost too brightly.

"Uh . . . my friend Martha."

"We're celebrating the New Year!" Martha said, and he wondered just how many pineapple drinks she had consumed. In fact, he should walk her straight home.

"Yes, you are," Grace said, laughing. "What's this about a treasure? I always knew you'd strike it rich someday."

"No—I didn't—"

A cry on the other end made him stop. Grace turned away. "Raina, are you okay?"

Raina?

Casper's heart skipped and stopped in his chest.

Grace was living with Raina? And then, as if he needed a reminder of exactly how much he missed her, Grace moved out of the camera's view.

And from the shadows, across the room, he saw her. Or part of her—most of her was covered by the sofa back. But the lamplight illuminated her enough for him to see her beautiful, long, silky black hair.

He longed for a glimpse at her amber-brown eyes, but he got instead a very inspiring view of the ceiling as Grace set the phone down.

Raina's voice came again, high and panicked.

His own panic sparked, right behind it. "What's going on? Grace?"

"Don't worry, Raina. Everything will be fine—just stay calm." This from Grace before she picked up the phone. "Sorry, Casp; I gotta run. Uh—Happy New Year. Love ya."

Then Raina's voice filled the background, calling Grace's name as she clicked off.

Raina?

"Is she all right?" Martha made a face. "That didn't sound good. Maybe she had a little too much fun tonight."

"She's fine. I'm sure she's fine." Casper pocketed the phone. *Just stay calm.*

It wasn't Grace's words so much as her tone.

No one up there in snowy Minnesota was staying calm.

Martha laced her fingers into his, stepped up to him. "Now, where were we?"

"We were going home," he said.

Apparently, denial had her number and decided that tonight Raina had to face the truth.

She was having a baby.

Not this moment, thankfully, but soon—very soon if the terbutaline didn't work its magic, calm her uterine muscles, and stop her body from laboring.

She lay in a quiet semiprivate room, the predawn silver grays streaming through the window of the birthing ward at Methodist Hospital. An IV dripped fluids into her body—as if she didn't feel bloated enough. And exposed. And cold. And . . . alone.

Grace, it seemed, had left her sometime in the last hour. Raina had awoken from her catnap to find the orange vinyl recliner empty.

Not that she blamed her best friend/roommate/labor coach for wanting some real shut-eye. Grace had stepped in like she'd promised, bundled Raina into the car, and hustled her to the medical center. She'd filled out the forms, updated the staff on Raina's medical history, held Raina's hand, and kept Raina's emotions in a tight, coiled ball instead of exploding into a messy, ugly debris field of panic.

Except now Grace had vanished, and the panic threatened to edge its way out of Raina's chest, into her throat.

She put a hand to her mouth, leaned her head back against the pillow. Closed her eyes.

Then, instead of the words of the doctor, reassuring her that they'd stopped the contractions, or even Grace's voice, reminding her that she wasn't alone . . . she heard laughter.

The high, ebullient voice of Casper's new girlfriend leaching out through the phone. *It's gorgeous and he nearly found a treasure today!*

Yeah, she bet he did. Probably in the form of some tall, thin, blonde beach bunny who—

No, that wasn't fair. Casper wasn't his brother Owen, and he deserved to be happy. Deserved to start over.

Deserved to forget her.

Raina's eyes burned, and she ran her hand across her cheek, catching the tear.

Footsteps, then the curtain rolled back. She opened her eyes to the sight of her OB doctor, Natasha Mortensen, her auburn hair in a ponytail, her hazel eyes bearing the night shift hours. "Good morning, Raina," she said, keeping her voice low.

The woman in the opposite bed had delivered sometime in the early hours, right before Raina arrived, and—lucky her—had slept the night through, her husband perched in the recliner beside her bed.

A sweet, normal, perfect family.

Natasha set down a file, then unwound her stethoscope, placing it on Raina's belly. "Good heart tones." She stepped over to the monitor and read the printout of the baby's heartbeat. "The baby seems to be free of any distress. And you haven't had a contraction for two hours. That's good."

She examined Raina, then pulled up a chair. "Okay, here's the news. I'm going to keep you here a little longer, just to make sure the contractions don't start back up, and then I'm sending you home to rest. You're at thirty-four weeks, so the baby is nearly full-term, but I'd like to see if you can hang on at least another week, maybe two." She patted Raina's arm. "Two weeks to catch up on all your Netflix shows before this little bundle arrives. But you'd better start picking out names."

Natasha stood, squeezed her arm. "I'll see you back here in two weeks. No sooner—got that?"

Raina managed a nod as Grace walked in with an answer. "Aye, aye, Doc."

Grace set a bag down on the bedside table. "I had to run out and score you some breakfast and a cup of decaf joe. What did I miss?"

Raina just stared at her. Oh, what she wouldn't give for Grace's calm under pressure. The way she could look at life and pull out the silver lining, believe that everything would work out. She clearly hadn't lived Raina's dark life.

"Bed rest for two weeks." Raina lifted her shoulder. "Then I have to figure out what I'm doing."

Grace opened the bag of food. "I found a Panera down the street. One broccoli quiche just for you." She pulled out the quiche, a napkin, and a fork. "And two weeks of forced bed rest? Think of all the books you can read."

Raina stared at the quiche without an appetite. "I'm so stupid."

"Huh?" Grace sank down into the recliner.

"I . . . I can't get it out of my head. That girl last night— Casper."

"Oh." Grace stared at her coffee, took a sip, then looked out the window. "Yeah, he did seem to be . . . okay."

"More than okay. He's moving on, and frankly, I don't blame him. I mean, it's not every day you get your heart broken by find-ing out the woman you like—"

"I think he was in love with you."

"Which makes it even worse—although I think we can both agree it was just a summer romance."

"Casper takes things pretty seriously, Raina. I mean, yeah, he was the family troublemaker when we were kids, but he's also the guy who shows up when you need him."

"And I hurt him. No, I destroyed him."

Grace leaned forward. "You didn't lead him on. You didn't know you were pregnant—"

"With his brother's kid! From a stupid, brainless mistake. Why did I—?" She pressed her hands over her eyes. Swallowed. Found her breath. "With everything inside me, I wish I could go back to that night, to that girl sitting on the pier with Owen, and warn her. Tell her to use her head instead of being charmed by the romance of the stars and the fact that your youngest brother is very handsome."

"And charming. And broken. I'm so sorry for the way he behaved."

"*We* behaved. And look what it caused—your brothers brawl-ing over me at your sister's wedding, Owen vanishing, Casper taking off like Indiana Jones in search of lost treasure, and you having to babysit me."

"I'm hardly babysitting you, Raina. In fact, I fear I worked you too hard tonight . . ." A wry expression washed across her face. "I'm sorry."

"No. I have to work. I mean, I can't freeload . . ." She paused, took a breath. "And I have to face the truth. I am having a baby I can't take care of, bringing it into a world without a father, without a family. I know I would make a terrible mother—"

"Raina—"

She held up her hand to stop Grace's words. "My own mother died when I was nine, and even before that, she wasn't around much, with fighting the cancer. The thought of being a mom is . . . Well, I can't wrap my brain around it. Really, how could I take care of a baby? My child deserves a better life—a bigger life. Something stable and safe."

"What if Owen—?"

"No." Raina tried not to interject emotion into her answer, but it still came out fast, hard. Final.

Grace seemed nonplussed. "Right. Okay. But what about Casper? He doesn't even know you're pregnant. Maybe if he knew . . ."

"No." This time the word emerged softer. "Imagine that conversation. You thought Casper lost it when he realized that Owen and I had . . . I mean, yes, it happened before I met Casper, but I don't think that made it hurt any less. Now imagine his face when I tell him I'm having his brother's baby. Even if he could look past that to a future with me, I highly doubt he's going to want to raise Owen's child. Or that he should."

Grace's mouth tightened into a grim line, truth—or agreement—in her expression. "What if you stayed with me?"

"Grace, be serious. You have a life to build with Max." Raina shook her head. "I think I have my answer." She ran her hands over her belly, finding a foot, an elbow. "I keep thinking of Gina. And her mom. And her life. I think I've been holding on to the wild, impossible hope that Casper might show up, forgive me, and . . . I don't know—figure out a way for us to be together. But . . ." She swallowed again, her eyes watery. "I am a fool."

"Raina . . ." Grace reached for her hand, but Raina drew it away.

"Even you would agree that it's better for Casper to move on." Grace sighed.

Raina nodded despite the dagger in her chest. "Which means that I need to also. I don't know how, but I have to give this baby a better life than I had."

Grace frowned and began to shake her head.

"You know this is the best thing for everyone, especially the baby. She needs a home with two parents who love her and can provide for her and . . . No more denial or hope of the perfect happy ending. At least for me. But I can give it to my baby."

She ran her hands over her face again. Yes, this was the right decision. "You need to go home, Grace, and get some sleep. When you come back, would you bring the adoption file with you? The one the agency sent over? I need to pick the perfect parents for my child."

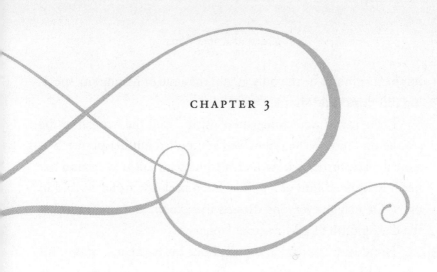

CHAPTER 3

CASPER KNEW HE HAD the tendency to gamble big, to throw himself into the hope of finding something priceless, but this time he
might really get hurt.

He stared out the window as the plane touched down between
the grimy snowdrifts that edged the tarmac. The sky hovered low,
a chilly pewter gray, the early afternoon sunshine imprisoned
beyond a wall of clouds. When a few of his fellow passengers
began reaching for their parkas, he realized he'd packed his jacket
in his checked bag. Not thinking clearly as he boarded the puddle
jumper off the island fourteen hours ago in ninety-degree weather.

In fact, he'd had one thing on his brain. One person. His one
consuming thought over the past two weeks.

Thankfully he had a sweatshirt crammed into his backpack,

but he just might be the only guy in the state of Minnesota sporting flip-flops. And shorts.

"I take it you went somewhere warm," said the woman in the seat behind him as she unbuckled and pulled out her phone. She wore a black turtleneck sweater, a white scarf knotted around her neck. Reminded him of his sister Eden back when she worked in obits. Or maybe everyone dressed like gloom and doom during the dark month of a Minnesota January.

"Honduras," he said and pulled out his backpack. Shoot, his phone had died somewhere over Texas and now he'd have to pray that Grace was at home when he showed up at her apartment.

Hopefully she'd feed him too.

And hopefully—okay, he more than hoped it—Raina would be there. Willing to listen. Willing to forgive him . . . maybe simply willing to start over.

That's all he wanted: a reset. No dragging up the past, just a clean, fresh beginning where Owen didn't lurk in the shadows, haunting their relationship. Certainly after all these months they could shake off his specter.

"Well, you'd better get something on those bare feet because according to my phone, it's a toasty twelve below." The woman shouldered her bag and stepped out of her row, grabbing her carry-on.

Casper followed her out through the Jetway and into the bustle of the Minneapolis–St. Paul airport. He stopped at a Caribou Coffee and tugged out his sweatshirt, pulling it on before heading to baggage claim. He smiled wanly at a little girl holding her mother's hand, gawking at his attire.

His duffel bag shot out of the chute and landed on the carousel. He picked it up and lugged it to the car rental desk.

He hadn't planned on returning in the middle of winter—thus

his motorcycle, still in storage, would have to stay tucked away. The female rental clerk also eyed his clothes, his long hair, and his bandanna hat, a smile on her lips. He pegged her around twenty-four—his age—and when she handed him his folder, she suggested he put on some pants before venturing outside.

Maybe he should have listened, because by the time he boarded the shuttle bus, his legs had lost feeling.

As he rode out to the rental lot, he took a good look at his sanity and considered that he'd left it on the beach in Roatán.

No. Raina's voice had imprinted on him that night two weeks ago and still hadn't vanished. The strange panic in it gave him the answer to Doug's question and the strength to give Fitz his notice.

His resolve only deepened with each day he trained his replacement, so by the time Casper shook the sand off his feet, he'd already returned to Minneapolis. Already held Raina in his arms, at least in his mind, his heart.

He let the Prius warm before he pulled out of the lot, reviewing his winter-driving techniques before edging into traffic and heading toward Minneapolis. He noticed the Mississippi had frozen nearly solid, the highways coated with salt. He'd forgotten the misery of winter in Minnesota.

I'm not in love with you, Casper!

Raina's shout through the reception hall before Jace and Eden's wedding suddenly echoed back to him, reaching out to sink brutal fingers in his chest as he took the exit for I-35W, toward the Uptown area.

But he'd seen her face before she said those words. Seen her beautiful brown eyes fill, her wretched expression.

Yeah, she'd been lying. Trying to protect him. From Owen. From their secret.

According to his sister Eden, Grace lived in an Uptown apartment building, just two blocks off Lake Calhoun. Hopefully she'd forgive him for not calling to warn them, but he didn't want to spook Raina, send her fleeing. He exited the highway onto Lake Street and tried to calm his racing heart.

In fact, he might be sweating. When he stopped at a light, the past continued to bullet through his brain, as fresh as yesterday.

There you are! . . . What did you do to her, you jerk?

His words the moment he'd seen Owen, only a few short hours after his kid brother had shown up for Eden's wedding, cocky and selfish. And only a few short hours since Casper had assembled all the puzzle pieces of why Raina had rejected him.

In the wake of his own words, Casper's fist found his brother's face. He didn't care that, as Owen got up, he wiped blood from his fattening lip.

And then, as Casper's world crashed around him, Owen shrugged. *Shrugged.* "I don't know what you're talking about," he snapped. "I never hurt Raina. We . . . So we hooked up."

Casper nearly came at him again. Instead he'd left before he dismantled his brother.

It had taken him the last five months to put himself back together. To see how it all laid out.

Clearly Owen had met Raina at their brother's Memorial Day wedding. Somehow they ended up together. He didn't want details, refused to let his brain linger there.

It wasn't until after Owen left town that Casper met Raina. Sweet, tough, beautiful Raina, stranded on the side of the road in the mud. He'd invited her to be a part of his dragon boat crew, a competition he'd fought to win—with her at his side.

And yeah, he'd fallen for her, hard and fast. Apparently she had that effect on Christiansen men. But he'd believed her when she kissed him, believed the affection he'd seen in her eyes.

Believed that yes, he'd at last found what he'd been searching for.

Then one day . . . she simply walked away from him.

He'd finally figured out why.

Guilt. Somehow she thought she'd betrayed Casper. And frankly, he'd thought it too, after the incident with Owen.

Except he couldn't blame her for what happened before they met, and as that truth sank into his brain, his anger had worked free.

Leaving behind only regret.

He read the street signs, slowing as he drew up to a three-story brick building. He turned at the corner, found the lot around back, and parked.

Yes, maybe he needed pants. At the very least real shoes. But he'd get them later—after seeing Raina. And Grace. Right—Grace first.

He got out, went around to the front door, and got into the building by holding the door for a resident encumbered by a bag of groceries.

He hooked his foot around the inner door, reading the listing for the apartments on the security system in the foyer. He found Grace's on the second floor and took the elevator up.

The place bespoke a green lifestyle—plants near the elevator, clean white hallways with bright windows that overlooked the snowy patio, a covered whirlpool, and Adirondack chairs.

He stopped at her door and blew out a breath.

Swallowed.

Knocked.

And closed his eyes when he heard the voice. "Grace, seriously? Of all times to forget your key!"

Raina.

He smiled, pressed his hand to the door. He couldn't wait to see her reaction. But just in case she wasn't ready for guests, he said, "Uh, actually, no. It's . . ." He took another breath. "Casper."

He waited for the door to fling open, stepping back so he could catch every nuance of her expression.

Yeah, baby, it's me. Back from the high seas.

He actually let those words float through his head and wanted to roll his eyes. He let his crazy smile dim. No need to scare her if she wasn't quite on the same page. Yet.

The door didn't open.

He stepped forward again. "Raina?"

"What . . . ? I thought . . . Aren't you supposed to be hanging out on a beach somewhere?" Her voice sounded tight, almost . . . angry? Or maybe just surprised.

"Yeah . . . or . . . no. I came back. I'm done." He added a softness to his voice. "I came to see you."

More silence. Then, "I thought you were Grace. I'm . . . in my robe."

See, this was why he didn't just let her fling open the door. He had sisters—he got it. "No problem. I'll wait."

More silence. A darkness began to settle deep in his gut. "Raina?"

"Grace isn't here."

Huh. It seemed she hadn't moved. "Okay."

"Can you come back later?"

Oh. He put his hand on the door, lowered his voice further. "Well . . . maybe we could talk?" He wanted to wince at the soft

36

pleading in his voice, but he already appeared desperate, standing here in his flip-flops, looking nearly homeless.

"I . . . This isn't a good time."

The darkness webbed his chest. But what did he have to lose? "Raina, please, could we just . . . ? I am so sorry for what happened, and I've been doing a lot of thinking and—"

"Casper?"

He turned and spotted Grace stepping off the elevator. A bag of groceries hung from her hand. "I can't believe it!"

"Hey, Sis."

She ran toward him, flung herself into his arms.

And just like that, he didn't feel like the underdressed homeless guy in the hallway. He twirled her around, then put her down.

"What are you doing here?" Thankfully, when Grace said it, it didn't sound like an accusation.

"I . . ." He glanced at the door.

"Oh, Casper." Grace's voice softened, and she shook her head, sadness in her expression.

He frowned. "What?" Oh no. He never considered the idea that Raina might be dating someone else.

But of course she was—and why not? Beautiful, amazing Raina had moved on. Forgotten him, and now he'd made yet another colossal mistake. "I should have called." Understatement.

Grace shook her head. "Let me call Max. He'll let you bunk there."

She wasn't even going to let him in to talk to Raina? He hadn't seen that coming.

Grace took out her phone. But a sound emerged from the other side of the door, something akin to a moan, loud and long, and it stilled them both. He caught Grace's expression and went cold.

What—?

"Grace, is that you?" Raina's tone dredged up the memory of the New Year's call.

"Is there something wrong with Raina?"

Grace's jaw tightened, but she pocketed the phone, put the key in the lock. "Casper, just . . . stay calm."

Stay calm?

She opened the door. "Raina, are you okay?"

"In here!"

He peered over Grace's shoulder and guessed the sound was coming from the bathroom.

Grace turned and handed Casper the bag of groceries. "Stay here."

Not on her life. He set the bag on the counter and followed her to the bathroom, not caring if Raina was in her robe—or less.

But nothing in his brain prepared him for the sight of her sitting on the floor in a puddle of water, her face contorted in pain.

Pregnant.

She looked up and met his eyes even as Grace grabbed a towel and asked, "What happened?"

Raina looked away, holding her belly.

Her *pregnant* belly. Casper just stared at her, his brain scrambling. How—?

"My water broke. I think the baby's coming."

Grace hooked her arm around Raina's waist, helped her to her feet. "Then we need to get you to the hospital."

Casper stepped back as Grace wrangled her through the door, toward the bedroom. "Casper, there's a bag in the family room. Get it and a bunch of towels."

He couldn't move. Just stared at Raina as she struggled, one hand to her back, groaning. She stopped suddenly, bracing her hand on the wall, breathing hard.

Oh. My.

Grace breathed with her. "You're doing well."

Casper rested his own hand on the wall. Tried to breathe.

The contraction passed, and Raina hobbled to her room.

Pregnant.

He stood there, hollow.

"Casper." Grace had returned and now stopped in front of him. She reached up and touched his cheek. "Can you help me get her to the hospital?"

His mouth closed and he nodded. As he stared at Grace, however, the truth took root, burned through him.

He didn't have to do the math, didn't have to use his sleuthing skills to figure it out.

The woman he loved was having his brother's baby.

Of all the times for her wildest dreams to walk through the door, fate had her hunched over, waves of pain suffocating her, immobilizing her.

In fact, she could barely see straight.

Another contraction swept through Raina, and she crumpled at the end of her bed, onto her knees, breathing through it—or trying to.

She might be levitating from the pain.

Then, just like that, the fist released and left her sweaty and gasping on all fours in the middle of her bedroom.

Yeah, that was pretty. She felt like a beached whale, awkward and cumbersome. She collapsed onto the floor on her side, willing it all to go away.

Willing Casper to go away. She glanced through her half-closed eyes to where he stood in the hallway, starting at his tanned bare feet, fresh off the beach, and working her way up.

Oh, he couldn't see her like this. Not when he stood there dressed like the free-spirited renegade she'd fallen for, his body bronzed and fit, those blue eyes on her, tearing her apart. One glance at him and it all came back—their summer romance and the fact that she'd fallen so hard it took her breath away.

And his words through the door—hauntingly sweet, sad, and wanting to . . . what? Whatever the reason he'd returned, seeing her had to knock it out of him.

For her part, she'd heard his voice, and suddenly the contractions she'd ignored most of the morning roared to life.

"Raina, c'mon, you have to get up." Grace's voice slid through her despair.

"No."

"You can't deliver your baby on your bedroom floor. We have to go."

No.

"Raina," Casper said softly. His voice still had the power to stir hope and a sweet, forbidden heat inside her. A low tenor, solid, capable. The man who'd made her feel—what seemed so long ago—cherished.

Or at least not alone.

She heard him kneel next to her, smelled him—distinctly male, the saline hint of the sea on his skin. He put his hand on her arm. "Let's go."

No. She couldn't bear it—the thought of him touching her,

seeing her with stringy hair, soiled and fat, coiled in pain. She jerked her arm back. "Go away, Casper."

The words burned through her, but she swallowed any attempt to soften them, opened her eyes, and steeled herself against the sight of him.

If anything, up close he'd only managed to become more devastatingly handsome, with a ragged beard and his chocolate-brown hair curling out the back of a red bandanna.

He frowned, his sea-blue eyes filled with a concern that could make her weep, especially when he reached out for her again. "Let me help you up."

She shook her head, pushed up from the floor. "No. Please, Casper, leave me alone."

The next contraction rolled over her, and her body betrayed her. She whimpered, collapsing back to the floor.

"Hardly. Grace, get me a blanket. Raina, relax. You have to breathe. The baby needs air. Breathe."

She'd breathe as soon as her body decided not to turn inside out.

By the time the contraction released, she was crying. She barely noticed as Casper draped a blanket over her.

"It wasn't this bad before," she gasped.

"Before?" Casper said.

"She went into preterm labor a couple weeks ago. She's been on bed rest ever since," Grace said as if Raina couldn't speak for herself. Or maybe she couldn't because another contraction gripped her, and this time she felt her entire body begin to shift as if the baby had moved inside her.

"I think we're running out of time," Raina said when it ended. She opened her eyes and found Grace. "Okay, let's go."

She was shaking, however, and groaned. Probably that was all Casper needed because suddenly he slid his arms under her and picked her up.

As if she weren't the size of a small Volkswagen.

And Raina, thanks to her pitiful state, uttered barely a protest. He curled her to his chest as Grace tucked the blanket in around her.

Oh, she'd forgotten the heady sense of being in his arms, the solid planes of his chest, the cotton and surf smell of him, the way he could make her believe she was safe. She hated herself a little when she reached up, grabbed a handful of his sweatshirt. "Please don't drop me."

He gave her a look then, his expression so pained or perhaps horrified that she had to close her eyes. "Never."

He carried her from the apartment into the elevator, Grace trotting behind with Raina's bag.

"Your car or mine?" Casper said.

"Mine," Grace said. "I'll drive; you hold Raina."

Raina didn't argue. A contraction hit, and she clung to Casper, this time trying to relax, grateful for his grip on her.

"Breathe, Raina. Just in and out." He demonstrated as if he'd taken the preparing-for-childbirth classes with her.

For a second, regret filled her throat. What if he had? What if she'd told him about the baby instead of pushing him out of her life?

Except, well, the baby wasn't his, was it?

She closed her eyes and breathed.

When they got to the car, he lifted her into the backseat, climbing in beside her. Grace added the bag to the trunk of her Altima and then ducked into the front.

"Don't have this baby in my car," Grace said as she pulled out.

Raina tried to laugh, but the entire thing seemed so wretched that she could only offer a sad rumble.

Casper tucked her sweaty hair behind her ear, and she looked at him, her lip caught in her teeth.

His eyes were wet. "Why didn't you tell me?"

"What exactly could I have said that would have made any of this okay?"

He glanced away, a tear hanging off his chin.

"I . . . I didn't mean for this to happen. I wish—"

"I know." He looked at her then, a softness in his eyes. "I know."

She couldn't bear it, even as the next contraction rose through her. "You shouldn't be here. I . . . You shouldn't have come back."

And then, as Grace drove toward Methodist Hospital, she focused her breathing, concentrating through the pain. *Don't have the baby in the car.*

They drove up to the emergency entrance, and Casper got out, went hunting for a wheelchair. He returned with wheels and a nurse.

He lifted Raina from the car and set her in the chair as Grace pulled away to park. The nurse wheeled Raina into the emergency room bay with Casper jogging to keep up. He helped as Raina levered herself onto a gurney.

He reached for her hand, but she pulled it away. "I meant it, Casper. You shouldn't be here. I'm not your problem—"

He stared at her as if she'd slapped him. "Problem—what are you talking about?"

The nurse began to take her vitals, checking her pulse. "The on-call OB is on her way. Do you have a particular doctor you see?"

Raina gave her the name, then leaned back into the pillows, breathing hard.

Somewhere in that time, Casper had taken her hand. When the contraction released, she let go and noticed him rubbing his fingers.

"See, that's what I'm talking about. You're always stepping in, trying to fix things. But you can't fix this, Casper. You can't fix . . . *me.*"

He frowned and she blamed her hormones, her pain, for the sudden flux of anger. "Don't look at me like that. I know you, and you can't stand to fail, to see someone you care about hurt. Sometimes you just have to walk away, Casper, and let people deal with the choices they've made."

"Raina, I'm not walking away from you. Not again. I get—I really get—why you didn't want to tell me about this. But the fact is, you can't do this by yourself. You're having a baby!"

"Yeah. Owen's baby! Have you not figured that part out yet?"

He closed his mouth, and a muscle pulled in his jaw. So maybe he had. He took a breath, ran his hand behind his neck. Swallowed. "Does he know?"

She looked away as the OB doctor came in.

"Miss Beaumont. So lovely to see you again. And this time nearly full-term."

"I did my best," Raina said, another contraction coming on.

"You did great. And is this the lucky father?" She turned to Casper. "Dr. Natasha Mortensen."

Casper's eyes widened. He stared at the doctor's outstretched hand. Took a long, shaky breath.

Right then Raina got the answer to the question she feared asking.

He might have been thinking about her, might have even gotten on an airplane to see her again, but Casper Christiansen had no desire to step in and claim this child as his.

Nor should he.

Because then things would really get complicated.

"No, he's not the father," Raina said, her voice sharp. "The father isn't in the picture and never will be."

Casper frowned, a darkness in his expression.

"Okay then," Dr. Mortensen said after a moment. She reached for some gloves. "Raina, do you want him to stay?"

He looked at her, and she'd have to have been blind not to see the words written on his face.

She closed her eyes. "No."

Dr. Mortensen turned to him. "I'll ask you to step out while I check to see how far along we are in labor."

Casper seemed not to get it for a moment.

"Casper, leave," Raina said. "And don't come back. I got this."

His eyes narrowed. "Fine. Have it your way." He shoved his hands into his cargo shorts and stalked away, down the hall, out of the ER.

Out of her life.

Right where he belonged.

Dr. Mortensen stepped up to the gurney. "Ready to have this baby?"

CHAPTER 4

CASPER NEEDED TO FOLLOW his own advice to Raina—*breathe*.

He just needed to step out of this moment, calm his heartbeat, and figure out how to fix this.

He paced into the waiting area, headed over to the window, and stared at the grimy parking lot. Snow sifted from the gunmetal sky, a wispy layer of white over the black-edged snowbanks.

So Raina was having a baby. It didn't have to change—

He drew in a breath, the truth like a knife. Owen would always be lurking on the sidelines, poised to show up, to be a father to his child. Which would leave Casper where, exactly? The favorite uncle?

Except Raina's words kept pinging through his head. *The father isn't in the picture and never will be.*

What did that mean?

"Casper."

He turned at Grace's voice. She'd emerged from Raina's exam room, holding a bag filled with her clothing. "We're heading up to delivery. She's ready to give birth."

Already? "I'll meet you there."

Grace held up her hand. "She doesn't want you there."

"I'm not going to be in the room, Grace. I'll just wait. Make sure she's okay."

Her expression of compassion only made it worse. "I'm so sorry you had to find out this way, Casper."

"She should have told me." He knew his words didn't make sense, heard the arguments ringing in the back of his head. But he couldn't help the steel taste of betrayal that lined his throat.

"Maybe. But it wasn't really any of your business. For the record, I argued with her—told her to tell you. To tell the rest of our family, but she swore me to secrecy. You can't imagine . . ."

"Grace—wait. She said that . . . that Owen isn't going to be in the baby's life. What did she mean? Was he a jerk about it?"

Grace sighed. "It was her business—her choice. I begged her to tell him, but—"

Her words hit him quick, sharp. "Are you telling me that she never told him?"

"It's not like Owen would have stepped up."

"He might have!"

"He's not you, Casper." She shook her head. Drew in a long breath. "Listen, I know you care about her, but you left, remember?"

His mouth tightened at that. "Yeah, I remember. But now I'm back."

She headed over to the elevator and punched the button. He followed.

"Seriously, Casper—"

"I'll leave once I know everything is okay."

Her face softened. "Okay. I'll come out as soon as the baby is born."

They got onto the elevator. He stood there, watching the floors light up. Then asked, "Did you know she was pregnant before I left?"

Grace sighed. Nodded.

"And you let me go."

"I thought it would be best. She didn't want you to know, and you needed to get her out of your system."

He had no words for that, seeing Grace stand in the crossroads between her friend and her brother. When the doors opened, he headed over to the waiting room. Marmalade orange– and coffee brown–patterned sofas lined the walls, the wooden tables covered with *Parent Today* magazines. A couple in their midsixties sat vigil on the sofa, watching *Jeopardy!*

"I gotta go, Casper. I'm her delivery coach. I called Max to come and get you. He'll take you back to my place to pick up your car."

"Tell Raina . . ." Except his words died there. Tell her what?

Grace gave him a soft look. "I know. I'm so sorry." Then she disappeared behind the swinging door.

He stood there, an interloper, sure that the eyes of the elderly couple hung on him.

He found a chair in the corner and sat, tucking his hands between his knees, suddenly cold.

And hungry.

And foolish.

He leaned back, pulled up the hood on his sweatshirt, tried not to look like the guy who'd flown two thousand miles for a woman who didn't want him.

He closed his eyes and wasn't sure how much time passed before Grace's fiancé gave him a nudge with his foot.

Max took up a little too much space in the room, looking every inch like the superstar hockey player he was with his long brown hair, a scruff of beard, leather jacket, black jeans. "Hey, Casper."

Casper got up, met Max's hand. "Thanks for the ride."

Max gave him a wry smile. "Not the best way to find out about Raina, huh?"

Casper shoved his hands into his shorts pockets. "Yeah. That's what I get for not calling ahead. I thought I'd surprise her. Whoa, surprise!"

Max didn't laugh at his caustic humor, his expression solemn. "Dude, what is it about this girl?"

Casper's sarcasm died and he sighed, ran his thumb and finger against his tired eyes. "I don't know. I ran away, trying to forget her, but I can't seem to get her off my mind. Apparently I needed a taste of cold reality . . . except . . ." He shook his head. "I'm such a fool. I'm still thinking . . . she needs someone, and what if that someone was me? I love kids, and—no. That whole idea is stupid."

Thankfully Max didn't have a moment to confirm his words before Grace came through the door, grinning.

"Max!" She flung her arms around her fiancé, and he kissed her, so much love in his expression when he let her go and smiled at her that it sent a pang through Casper.

"So?" Max said.

"It's a girl. Beautiful. Dark hair, blue eyes—adorable."

"How's Raina?" Casper asked.

"Tired, but okay." Grace grabbed Max's hand, looked at Casper. "Want to see the baby?"

"Really? It's okay with Raina?"

She nodded. He braced himself to hold back from the crazy plan forming in his head. But what if he let Raina recuperate, come home, settle in with the baby? What if he convinced her to give him a chance to prove himself—that maybe, in time, he could get past this? They could build a future together—Raina, the baby, him . . .

He refused to call himself foolish, to admit he hadn't really thought it out, and went right to . . . hopeful.

Grace led them down to the nursery, away from the delivery room. She stopped at the large window and pointed at a bundle swaddled in a pink blanket. "That's her. Number four."

An unfamiliar warmth curled through Casper at the sight of the fattened baby face, the cherub lips, the dark hair twining out the top of the bundle. A perfect replica of her beautiful mother. He pressed his hand to the glass, his chest on fire. "She's amazing. What's her name?"

Max had stepped up, wrapped his arms around Grace, his lips against her hair. Inside the nursery, an infant began to wail.

Grace sighed. "I don't know. Raina is going to let her parents name her."

Casper stilled. "What are you talking about?"

Grace gave him a sad smile. "This is the last time we'll ever see her. I already called the agency. Raina's giving up her baby for adoption."

"What?"

"Casper, please. I've talked to her until I'm wrung out about this. I thought, with her living with me, she'd see it would be okay, that Mom and Dad would be thrilled despite the circumstances, but she can't see that far. She's convinced herself that the baby would be better off with different parents and . . . I don't know. Maybe she's right. She believes she's all alone, despite what I tell her. You have to agree, it's for the best—"

But his body turned to ice. "Have you *lost your mind*? No. I don't have to agree." The words began exploding through him, even as he looked back at the infant—his niece. His parents' *granddaughter*. Owen's child. "I don't agree *at all*. Grace, what are you thinking? Owen doesn't even know he's a father. And Mom and Dad—you're going to steal their grandchild from them?"

Grace's eyes had filled. "You forget it's not my decision. It's Raina's."

Raina's.

Casper turned and headed down the hallway.

"Casper!"

But he didn't stop, just headed to the nurses' station and inquired after Raina's room number.

Grace hadn't caught up to him before he found Raina's room. He took a breath even as he heard feet racing toward him, then knocked.

Max had him by the arm when Raina said, "Come in."

He shook Max away, but Grace's voice slowed him just a step. "Casper, consider Raina's position."

"I've had enough of considering Raina's position. She can't do this to our family." He shoved into the room.

He didn't mean for his voice to sound so dark, so raw and angry, but he didn't amend his words when he saw Raina looking drawn and fragile in the bed. She wore a white bathrobe, the covers over her body, and sipped a drink from a hospital cup.

Okay, it did sucker punch him, just a little. A fragment of the heat left him, softened the sharp edges of his thoughts. Still, he marched up to her bed. "You can't give up this baby, Raina."

"Sorry, Raina; he just came in—"

Raina held up her hand to Grace, her dark eyes on Casper. He knew that look. It had accompanied the few times she'd shoved him out of her life. She folded her hands over her body. "I can, and I am."

"And what about Owen?" His voice shook, but he lowered it.

"What about Owen? He has no interest whatsoever in this child—or me, for that matter," Raina said.

"That's not true. You just have to give him a chance."

"To what—make a bigger mess out of this? I don't love Owen, and he doesn't love me. We aren't going to get married and live happily ever after, Casper." A tear snuck out, trailed down her cheek.

He watched it, fighting the urge to care. Clearly he didn't know this woman at all. "Maybe not, but the fact is, you can't ignore all the people you are hurting. My parents, Owen—"

"And none of them are going to raise this child. None of them can give this baby—my baby—the home she deserves." Her voice shook now, her breath fast. "I have nothing to offer her. I don't even have a place to live. I'm . . ." She swallowed, looking out the window, another tear slipping off her chin. "I'm not ready to be a mother. This is the right thing to do."

"No—"

But Grace's hand on his arm stopped him. "Casper. It's not our decision."

Raina didn't look at him.

"It should be," Casper said quietly. He stepped away from

Grace, toward Raina, his voice steel. "You can't just erase what happened, Raina. You have a baby—a baby who will be loved by my family. But once you sign the papers, it's done, and you can't go back." He ran a hand over his mouth, realizing for the first time that his face was wet. "Please don't do this. You're not alone. You have us, and God will help—"

Her face turned dark. "God will help me?" She gave a sharp, brutal laugh. "That's rich. Casper, here's truth for you. God doesn't love everybody, despite what Sunday school says. Sure, He loves people like you and Grace, who grew up in a home with two parents. He probably even loves Owen, despite his sins. But God—no, He doesn't love me. God doesn't even notice me. I am *nothing* to Him. So don't start preaching to me about how God is on my side and will make things all better. That fairy tale is long over."

He stood, stunned. Had nothing but, "Then consider this. You will always regret this decision."

"The only thing I'll regret is letting you for an instant back into my life. Go away, Casper. You can't fix this. No one can, not even *God*. So just . . . please, leave me alone. Go back to finding lost treasures and forget about me."

He stared at her, the way her jaw tightened, the flash of chill in her eyes, and for the final time realized that, yes, she was right.

There would be no second chances for them.

"You got it, honey." He turned and shoved past Grace and Max, out into the hall.

There he punched the elevator button and waited for Max to arrive. They got in together, Max stony.

When the doors opened to the lobby, Casper marched out. He didn't stop in the entryway but charged right into the night, where the frigid air turned his bare skin to ice. He lifted his eyes to the stars, then closed them.

And stood there, letting the cold turn him numb.

Casper's voice embedded in Raina's head and drove her from bed to wander the hallways. *You can't just erase what happened, Raina. . . . Once you sign the papers, it's done . . .*

As the lavender threads of morning tore through the hospital shadows, Raina found herself at the nursery.

She perched at the window overlooking the babies, wrapped like gifts in duck-printed flannel blankets, their wrinkled, old-man faces furrowed in slumber.

One woke, frowned, and began to wail. A nurse came in, scooping the infant up before he woke the rest of the babies.

Raina's baby lay asleep, her dark hair peeking out of the swaddling. Her *Layla*—yes, she'd named the child and tucked it deep inside like a secret.

Raina traced her outline against the glass.

You can't go back.

What if she took Layla home? Tried to build a life for her?

You have a baby—a baby who will be loved by my family.

Stupid Casper. He had no business conjuring up hope, brittle and sour in her chest. She had no doubt the Christiansens would attempt to embrace the baby. After six months with Grace, she'd seen enough of the family to believe that she wouldn't be alone.

But for how long? What happened when Casper got tired of playing uncle and met a woman who didn't remind him every day of her sins, his mistakes? And Owen—he certainly wouldn't show up to change a diaper.

Even if he did, the last thing she needed was a marriage steeped in bitterness and founded on duty. Yeah, that was a recipe for happily ever after.

But if she stayed single, she doomed the baby to the same lonely, poverty-stricken latchkey childhood she'd endured. And what if something happened to her? What if, like her mother, she got cancer and left this earth with her daughter only nine years old?

Who would take Layla then?

As for God—right. He would hardly rush to her side to help.

A food service attendant trundled a cart of breakfast down the hall, past her. Her stomach recoiled at the smell.

Raina pressed her forehead to the cool glass.

You will always regret this . . .

She shook Casper's voice from her head and followed the food cart back toward her room.

She might not be keeping her child, but it didn't negate the fact that she'd given life to another human being. And given the gift of motherhood to a woman who longed for a child.

Yes, that thought could almost temper the urge to curl into a ball and weep.

Sunlight cascaded in through the windows, the sky blue for the first time in weeks. A golden layer of snow blanketed the landscape, soft and ethereal as she entered her room.

She climbed into bed, drawing the covers up. Leaned back into the pillows, her body still sore from yesterday's quick birth. She closed her eyes, heard the knock at the door.

Breakfast. "Come in."

The door eased open. "Good morning, Raina."

She opened her eyes to Dori Marcus, her social worker from

the adoption agency. In her late twenties, she wore a crisp green jacket and her dark hair boy-short. Put together, confident.

As if she knew all the right decisions.

"Are you ready to get this paperwork done?"

Dori didn't say the words directly—it seemed that perhaps the social workers at Open Hearts Adoption Agency were schooled in the delicate art of convincing a woman to surrender her child into the arms of another. In fact, ever since Raina had contacted the agency, they'd treated her with a sort of gentleness, as if she might spook, change her mind.

She couldn't turn back now. "Yeah, I'm ready."

"Perfect. Irene and Michael are here and ready to take the baby home."

Raina tried not to let those words sting. She swallowed and opened the file of papers Dori handed her.

"Just so you understand, this is a temporary agreement until the judge signs the formal papers in sixty days," Dori explained. "You'll sign the formal relinquishment before then. The waiting period gives you a chance to think through your decision before it becomes permanent."

"I've thought it through—I don't need to wait."

"Of course not. But it also gives the adoptive parents a chance—"

"They're not going to give her back, are they?"

Dori shook her head. "It's just a precaution so the state can monitor how they are doing with their new child."

"Please tell me I picked the right people." Raina stared at the file, pulling out a picture of the couple. Rail-thin and academic, with a manicured life, Irene O'Leary seemed the perfect woman to make the right choices for Layla. And Michael, handsome, broad-shouldered, dark curly hair—well, he reminded her a little of Casper. Loyal. Committed.

At least the Casper she'd known before he learned the truth. Yesterday, and before.

Dori touched her arm. "The O'Learys have been trying for years to have a child. They will adore the baby."

"Then let's get the paperwork over with." Raina pulled out the custody papers. "Where do I sign?"

When Dori didn't answer, Raina looked at her.

"I just need to confirm verbally, one last time, that this choice is of your own volition and that you have thought through all your options."

All her options. And those were exactly . . . ?

"Yeah. I know this is the right decision." But her words pinged off her, even as she steeled herself against them.

Please, let this be the right decision.

She held her hand steady as she signed the papers. Closed the folder. Took a breath as she stared out the window.

Dori didn't move. "Did you have a chance to hold her?"

"I don't want to hold her."

"Just to say good-bye? It might help."

And that's when the terrible roaring in Raina's chest began to fill her ears. Her throat. She shook her head, kept staring out the window at the airy blue sky, the wispy cirrus clouds.

Dori paused a moment—too long for Raina's liking—and finally left.

Raina held the covers to her face, muffling her ragged breath.

She'd known it would hurt, just didn't realize the depth of the searing wound upon her heart. She imagined Irene and Michael picking up Layla, dressing her in some pink sleeper, maybe with doves or bunnies like the ones she'd seen at Walmart. They'd add a stocking cap, bundle her in a snowsuit, and tuck her into her carrier.

They'd bring her out to their Lexus or perhaps a minivan they'd purchased just for their new family. Then they'd drive home to the perfectly attired nursery, with a shiny new crib, a layette with pink ruffles, and a spinning mobile of angels to watch over her. Irene would rock her to sleep, Michael standing guard, and after Layla dropped into gentle slumber, they'd stand peering over her crib, holding hands. Smiling.

Grateful. Yes, please, let them be grateful.

Raina's breath rippled out, her face wet, and she got up, went to the bathroom, and showered.

It seemed the best place to drown the noise of her weeping.

She finally got out, weakened and hollow, and dressed, staring at herself in the mirror—her sunken eyes, her wet, thick hair. Her body, padded from pregnancy, seemed doughy, still full.

You will always regret this . . .

No. She *refused* to live the rest of her life with regret lining her thoughts. She had to figure out a way to keep going. Start over.

Even forget.

She was packing her bag when she heard another knock. "I'm not hungry!"

"Oh, shoot. Then I'll have to eat this bagel myself," Grace said as she entered.

She set the bag down on the table just as Raina turned. Her expression must have betrayed her.

Grace's smile fell. "So you did it?"

Raina nodded.

Grace took two steps, then pulled Raina into her embrace. Raina hung on, refusing to cry. Not anymore.

She gritted her teeth and pulled away. Smiled. "Time to move on."

Grace raised an eyebrow.

"My aunt Liza wrote a week ago asking if I could house-sit for her in Deep Haven while she goes to some art colony in Arizona for the winter."

"She doesn't know—"

"No, but it's a good idea. I'd have a place to stay, to recuperate. Figure out how to start over."

Grace took her hand. "You could stay in Minneapolis, you know. No one is kicking you out."

Raina shook her head. "I have to break away from the past few months, figure out how to shake free of my mistakes." She turned and zipped her duffel bag. "I just need time, and then . . . yeah, maybe I'll be back. I can sublet your place when you and Max finally elope."

"Huh?"

Raina dredged up a smile. "You know you're itching to go back to Hawaii and tie the knot. I'm surprised you're not planning it for the midseason break Max has coming up."

Grace wore an enigmatic expression.

"You are! I knew it."

"I don't know—it's just . . . We don't want to make a big deal about it, and with the publicity Max has gotten since he did that PSA about Huntington's, it might turn out to be a media mess. He's got that golf tournament in Hawaii, so we just . . . I don't know."

Raina touched her hand. "It's perfect. At least one of us gets our happy ending."

She pulled away, but Grace held on. "Casper is still in town. He's staying with Max. I know you two fought, but . . . maybe . . . ?"

"I don't want to see him. I meant it when I told him to go away." She sighed. "Being with him will only remind me of this past year. I have to figure out a way to steer clear of dangerous men—or at least the kind with adventure in their devastating blue eyes and charming smiles. The next man I date—if ever—is going to be boring."

She smiled, trying to coax one out of Grace, but it didn't work.

"Listen. I love your brother, or I thought I did. But it won't work, Grace, and you know that. What I did will always be between us. He should just go back to Central America and become a treasure hunter. That's what he wants, anyway—he is just caught up in our summer fling. He needs to move on."

Grace winced but didn't chase her words. "What if you run into my parents in Deep Haven?"

Raina lifted the duffel bag onto her shoulder. "Deep Haven isn't so small that I can't avoid them for the next few months. And if I do, I'll smile and keep pushing my grocery cart. They don't have to know anything. Ever." She stopped then, testing Grace's expression for agreement.

Grace sighed, nodded.

Raina headed toward the door.

"I think you have to wait to be discharged," Grace said, picking up the bag of bagels.

"I'm done with waiting. I've waited nine months to put my mistakes behind me. I have to move forward if I have any hope of breathing again."

CHAPTER 5

EVERGREEN RESORT WOULD NOT go under on Darek Christiansen's watch. No, he planned on wresting a heat wave of business from winter's frigid grip, even if he turned into a snowman doing it.

Darek chipped the last of the ice off the stairs to cabin one, dumping salt on the steps and decking before returning to the main path. Electric lanterns hanging from wooden poles lit the trail as if winding through a Narnia wonderland. Although, in another hour, it might be termed a dark and stormy night.

The sun, long obscured by low-hanging clouds, lent peaked, waning illumination to the graying day, and the descending blizzard blotted out anything beyond twenty feet ahead of him. Wind howled, the snow like blades on exposed skin, the air so frigid that frostbite lurked with every passing minute.

The kind of night that compelled a man to stay home, curled in front of the hearth with his wife and seven-year-old son.

But not Darek. Because only he remained to rescue Evergreen Resort from the black hole of bankruptcy.

He pulled the scarf over his nose and mouth, dampened with the moist air of his own breath, as he scooped another shovelful of snow from the walkway to cabin two. With the drifts already three feet high, his shoveling added another layer to the mountainous piles.

More than once, he'd longed for the towering, shaggy evergreens that used to cordon off the property, creating an enclave of winterland joy. But after the forest fire a year and a half ago, the replanted trees would take years to mature.

By then, perhaps, Darek would have gotten it through his thick skull that Minnesota in January did not make for a fantastic vacation spot. As if to confirm it, the weather had to turn brutal the first three-day weekend of winter, Martin Luther King Jr. weekend. Darek took a chance on opening for the holiday, and his ads in the Minneapolis newspapers had netted him four reservations from hearty folks who loved to snowshoe, ski, and snowmobile.

And the newest rage—snow biking.

Darek had five fat-tire snow bikes in the newly built garage, just in time for his weekend guests.

If they made it through the storm.

"Darek!"

He heard her voice rise above the wind, turned, and recognized his wife, Ivy, bumbling along in the snow, unsteady on her feet despite the cleared path. She wore his green Army surplus jacket, a pair of his mom's mittens, a bright-orange knit cap, her UGGS, and still looked like the most adorable snowman he'd ever laid eyes on. He sank his shovel into the snowbank and crunched toward her.

"Ivy, what are you doing here? What if you fell?" He tried not to immediately press his hand on her belly, where his daughter—or maybe another son—grew.

She caught his arm, steadying herself, breathing a little hard. "I hate to say this, but you'll have to shovel all over again on your way back to the lodge." She looked at him with those pretty green eyes, a wisp of her red hair peeking out of the hat. "But don't go any farther to cabin four because they just called and canceled."

Well, he should have expected at least one cancellation, with the storm originating in Minneapolis. He had no doubt the highway was a giant skating rink. "Okay. I'll check the heat and water in the rest of the cabins—"

"And the reservation for cabin two also canceled."

Oh. Shoot. But once the storm cleared, the snow would be pristine.

"And the folks from cabin three called and said that they were coming up tomorrow. But that they heard the report and it's forecast at sixteen below. They quoted the weatherman as saying, 'Skin can freeze in five minutes in that kind of weather.'" Ivy lowered her mittens from her air quotes and gave him a sad expression. "Sorry, honey. I think they might cancel too."

"Perfect."

"I know. I brought some soup for you—it's on the stove. You just need to heat it up whenever you're ready. Tiger and I are going to pack up and head home."

"Ivy, I don't think . . . What about the roads?"

"I'm a northern Minnesota driver now. I'll be fine." Then she tugged on his scarf and pressed her lips against his, cold and sweet, and he wanted to wrap his arms around her and sink into the snow, add a little heat to the chill.

He grabbed the collar of her jacket, leaned down to steal another quick kiss. "I'm sorry—I have to stay here until the guests for cabin one arrive."

"Maybe all night in this weather," she said, pulling his scarf back up. "Your parents escaped just in time."

He knew she meant the weather, but her words could easily refer to their timely exit out of management of Evergreen Resort.

"I imagine they're sitting on a beach in Florida, watching the ocean roll in."

"I doubt that. If I know your dad, he's fixing the sink in your aunt's rental, and your mom is painting your cousin's room or even helping him find a job," Ivy said.

"They'll miss having him around. They really got attached to him this fall." In fact, his cousin's moving in with the family temporarily had ignited a new warmth between his parents, something he hadn't realized they lacked.

"It was smart to plan the trip to Europe to see Amelia right after Florida. Your mother won't have time to struggle with the empty house."

That and finally—*finally*—Dad would get to see the world. Starting with this trip to Europe, where John and Ingrid would renew their vows and visit their youngest daughter, studying abroad.

No, Darek would not let the resort go under on his watch. After thirty years at the helm, his father deserved to walk away and enjoy his golden years. "I'll call you later. Are you sure you're going to be okay driving home in this storm?"

"Do I wish I already lived in that beautiful house you're building for us just fifty feet from here? Um, yes. But we don't yet, so I'll be fine driving home in the storm." She patted her tummy. "But we'll all miss Daddy."

He put his hand over hers. "I'll be home as soon as I can. Kiss Tiger good night for me."

Darek watched Ivy disappear along the path, wanting to run after her. But his guests would arrive, he'd get them tucked safely into their cabin, and then he'd hustle home to his snug rental house in Deep Haven and curl up next to his delicious pregnant wife. Now that he'd moved them out of the tiny apartment into a real house, in anticipation of the baby, his life seemed to be falling into place. Until the cold snap of the century.

Grabbing his shovel, he trekked over to cabin three and re-cleared the path to the door. Leaning his shovel next to the door, he opened the cabin, expecting heat radiating off the tiny stove he'd lit two hours ago. The cabin had a furnace, but the stove added ambience and warmth for the guests—and prelighting it gave them a welcome-to-the-north-shore feeling.

His mother's tradition that he intended to continue.

Except no homey glow emanated from the stove, and the cabin's air contained a below-forty-degree *brr* and reeked of gas. He toed off his boots and padded over to the stove, discovered it on.

Which meant propane saturated the room. He turned it off and opened the window, gulping in some of the bracing air.

Then he headed to the furnace, located in a closet next to the bathroom. Climbing on all fours, he peered inside and discovered the pilot light off.

But if he lit it, the place just might explode.

Yeah, that would add a toasty glow to the evening.

He got up and went to the faucet to turn on the water, just to keep it running while the place aired out. Last thing he needed was frozen and burst pipes.

Nothing trickled out. Too late. But he didn't have time to total the repair bills in his brain. For now he'd have to move tomorrow's cabin three guests to cabin two.

He made a mental note to turn off the main water supply for cabin three in the lodge before a possible crack flooded it.

He refused to assign blame, but the person heading up the insulation of the pipes had been Casper.

Who wasn't around for Darek to interrogate. Or strangle. But what if the kid had forgotten to heat-wrap the pipes?

Probably now that Casper had his own life, turning into a high seas explorer, he couldn't be referred to as a kid anymore, but Darek still saw Casper as the thin, gangly kid who shadowed him. Casper knew how to fish and hunt and could take care of himself, but he always seemed to be right there at Darek's elbow. Pestering to help.

Darek hoped Casper hadn't overhelped him right into a plumbing nightmare.

On his way back, he'd shut off the stove in cabin four and make sure cabin one still put off a homey warmth. He pulled his boots on again and trudged out to four, not bothering to clear the path.

The stove glowed, the place toasty, but he checked the water and the pilot light just to be sure before closing it up. He turned off the stove and went to check cabin two.

That fire had gone out also. He opened the windows and drew in a breath of relief when water trickled out of the faucet. At this temperature, the pipes could freeze overnight. In fact, he should check all the cabins, turn on all the water, just in case.

He checked cabin one and found it warm, the water flowing

freely, the furnace burning. The perfect north-shore welcome for weary travelers.

He hiked to cabin two, shut the windows, and relit the pilot light. He turned the stove back on, the heat chasing out the cold.

It might be warm enough for guests by morning. Although, at sixteen below, he had his doubts. Besides, who wanted to spend even five minutes outside in that cold?

Maybe he should have built that sauna.

In cabin three, he found that the propane had escaped, so he shut the window and relit the furnace. It flickered on, but he didn't relight the stove. The cabin was uninhabitable until he thawed the pipes.

Night finally fell like pitch, no stars, just his flashlight beam illuminating the icy snow that bulleted his face as he trudged to the lodge, his brain finally working through the list of to-dos.

He'd have to open the attic in cabin three, search for a leak, repair it. Then he could thaw the pipe and wrap it in heat tape and insulation.

The way it should have been done in the first place.

Darek had worked up a decent steam by the time he reached the lodge. He stared at the empty lot, drifted with snow, and realized he'd have to plow again before the guests arrived.

He made his way to the garage, his empty stomach knotting, nearly tasting Ivy's soup—maybe pumpkin. He loved her pumpkin curry soup.

He flicked on the overhead light in the garage. The place still smelled new, recently drywalled and heated. He parked the resort trucks on one side; the other he used as his workshop. A Wood-Mizer portable sawmill gleamed under the hanging bulbs. A table saw and chop blade in the back, next to the workbench—recent additions that helped him finish the trim, the kitchen cupboards.

After a year of rebuilding, he'd figured out why his father spent so much time in his shop. Darek liked to create things, to solve problems. To provide.

Except, on days like today, he considered that it might have been easier to be a firefighter or a . . . well, just about anything else, really.

Maybe Casper had it right, seeking his fortune on a tropical island.

Except Casper was nursing a broken heart. And Darek knew exactly how that dug into a man, festered.

No, better to be in a frozen tundra, a warm welcome waiting for him, than in paradise, suffering.

He opened the garage door and climbed into the cab of his pickup/plow. Backed it out. Closed the door.

He reached the end of their long drive, scooping out snow and ladling it off to the side, and turned around in the road, noting that the snow had nearly obliterated Ivy's tire tracks, then headed back, his wipers fighting to clear the glass, the defrost on high.

He peeled off another layer of accumulation, adding curls to the snowbanks. His blade churned up ice, growled against the dirt of the lot.

He finally parked the plow outside so he didn't get trapped and climbed out.

The heat of the cab had thawed him, turned his scarf soggy. But as he stood in the cleared lot, the storm seemed to ebb, and for a moment he saw past the swirl of white to the darkness, the glowing lights of the cabins, the illuminated walkway to each one.

Narnia, indeed. And someday, with hard work, he would put his family's resort back on the map.

His stomach growled as he returned to the garage to grab his shovel, except something hung on, nagging . . .

A swath of light cut through the darkness, and he turned, peering and waving at the approaching guests. See? True Minnesotans, not afraid of a few snowflakes.

A truck pulled up, the lights blinding him, and parked next to his plow.

"You can park over here!" Darek gestured to the driver.

The guest got out and walked around the truck, hunched over, hands tucked into his sweatshirt.

"Nah, I'm good—gotta leave room to clear the lot." The man wore a baseball cap, a pair of shorts, and hiking boots. "Hey, Bro."

Darek stared, taking in the sight of a tanned Casper, dressed, of course, like he belonged on some Caribbean island, with his hair curling out from under his hat. "Casper!" He reached out for a handshake, then pulled him into a hug. "What are you doing here?"

Casper stamped his feet, his hands returning to his sweatshirt pocket. "Freezing."

"Yeah, well, have you ever heard of pants?"

Casper opened the truck cab and pulled out his duffel bag, a backpack. "I left them all here." He headed to the house. "Mom and Dad inside?"

Darek followed him. "Nope—they're in Florida. What are you doing back?"

"Nice. Not 'Hey, great to see you. I really missed you—'"

"Great to see you. I really missed you. What are you doing here?"

Casper pushed open the entry door, and Darek followed him inside. The sweet smell of pumpkin curry soup rose up to welcome him, and the instant heat, the quiet eye inside the storm, had him aching to turn around, get in the truck, and go home.

Casper dropped his duffel and backpack on the floor as if he were arriving home from college for a weekend instead of suddenly appearing after his nearly six-month vanishing act.

"Casper, seriously, what are you doing home?"

Casper unlaced his boots, pulling them off. "Where did you say Mom and Dad were?"

Huh. Okay, fine. "Florida. And then they're going to Europe to visit Amelia."

Casper frowned. "Amelia's still in Prague? I thought she was coming home for Christmas."

"Were you paying any attention at all to her conversations this summer? Amelia's in Prague taking photography classes and touring Europe for the entire year."

Casper raised an eyebrow.

"Right. Okay. Well, she's staying until June, Mom and Dad are going to Paris to renew their vows for Valentine's Day, and I'm here, hoping our one and only reservation shows up tonight."

Casper picked up his duffel bag. Made a face. "One reservation, huh?"

"Yeah. Listen, I gotta go out to check on the rest of the cabins. Then I'll be back and . . . I'm going to be asking questions."

Casper's eyes narrowed. "It's not exciting. My time was up, so here I am."

But Darek recognized a lie in his words, the way Casper's jaw tightened, the stress in his eyes.

"Light a fire. We still have to wait for the guests in cabin one to show up."

"Darek, I have news for you—"

"Don't say it, Casper. Just don't say it. They'll be here."

Casper stood over the stove, drawing in the fragrance of curry, cinnamon, onions. If he didn't know better, he'd think that perhaps Grace had raced home to have one of his favorite meals waiting for him. He ladled some into a bowl and put it in the microwave to warm.

Something soothing to welcome him home. To quiet that hollow sense of failure that had dogged him as he traveled north, all eight hours of a normally five-hour trip.

It didn't help that the lodge was empty, missing even the exuberant greeting of Butterscotch, the family dog. Grace had broken the news of Butter's recent passing.

A reminder that life could never really be the same again.

It had taken four days of holing up at Max's, licking his wounds and trying to find some wheels, for Casper to sort through his options: Return to Roatán to keep swabbing the decks and doing underwater grunt labor for Captain Fitz. Stick around in Minneapolis and try not to pick up the phone to call Raina or, worse, show up on her doorstep. Not that he would.

He couldn't get past the mistake—*her* mistake—of giving up her child and how that irrevocable decision could tear so many people asunder.

Go away, Casper. You can't fix this. No one can . . .

He still waged war with her in his mind. But her last words always won. *Just . . . please, leave me alone.*

Absolutely. Which meant he had to steer clear of her. Until he figured out where to do that, he pointed his new-to-him truck north.

Harboring a secret that felt like a live ember in his chest.

Certainly Darek would have something he could build or repair—didn't the resort always need extra hands? Yeah, here he'd make himself useful, even if he had to fall in behind Darek's shadow.

Here he'd somehow figure out a way to forget the fact that he'd wasted the last five months of his life.

He brought his duffel bag upstairs to the bedroom he'd shared with his brothers. Owen hadn't slept in the bed under the dormer window for four years, at least. And Darek had moved out long before that. So Casper's memories dated into his early teenage years, wrestling matches on the shag rug, trying to avoid knocking over one of Mom's homemade rock lamps or busting a hole in the hand-me-down dressers. Owen's posters of "Boo" Boogaard still hung on the wall, and Darek's firefighting manuals were tucked into the bedside bookcase as if time had simply stopped.

Maybe, for Casper, it had. Because while everyone else in his family seemed to move forward—Eden and Darek married, Grace engaged and opening her own business, Amelia finding adventure in Europe, and even Owen fleeing his past, certainly, but maybe joining up again with the Jude County Hotshots and finding a new place in the world—only Casper seemed stuck.

And returning home as if he hadn't anywhere else to run.

Except he didn't, did he?

He dropped the duffel on the floor, his legs cold. He probably should have purchased pants in Minneapolis instead of borrowing from Max.

He dug out a pair of sweatpants from his dresser and returned to the kitchen. Stirred the soup and put it back in the microwave.

Outside, the snow hurtled against the sliding-glass door, an angry snarl of frigid temperatures that would scare off even the hardiest of tourists. And Darek knew it.

Casper moved over to the fireplace, where he built a small tent of kindling, newspaper, and his mother's favorite waxed pinecones. He lit it and warmed his hands over the blaze. Then he added some hickory logs and closed the grate.

He returned to the microwave, retrieved the soup, and found a lone bagel in the freezer.

He thawed it, toasted it, added butter. Set the dinner on the counter and pulled up a high-top stool. Dug in.

The soup had a delicate hint of cinnamon, the sweet bite of yellow curry. Maybe Ivy made it. He dipped his bagel in it, took another bite.

Yeah, home. The perfect place to figure out how to cool off, how to live with the mistakes of others.

And his own. Because as he finished off one half of the bagel and savored the soup, he thought back to the night when he'd realized Raina had slept with Owen.

The night he'd spent driving around Minneapolis on his motorcycle, the need for speed kicking in, fueling his anger.

His jealousy.

It stirred to life in a blaze that erupted in a full-out brawl right there in Eden's wedding reception venue.

Owen had left, angry and belligerent, and well, Casper fled too, the hurt pushing him beyond forgiveness.

Which left Raina pregnant and alone.

And now left him and Grace bearing her terrible secret. He

supposed he should be thankful that his parents—especially his mother—weren't here to force it out of him. Just being around them, seeing their love for Tiger, would tear him in half.

He'd have to forget Raina. Forget the baby.

Stop trying to fix everything.

He was sopping up the remainder of his soup with his bagel when he heard the door open.

"Casper!" Darek poked his head into the house. "Turn the water off in cabin three! Hurry!"

Casper slid off the stool. "What?"

"Downstairs—the water main to the cabins—turn off cabin three!" He shut the door.

Casper raced downstairs to the half-finished basement. Long ago used as a rec room and storage space, it also housed the water main and electric breakers for the resort. He stepped into the chilly utility room, found the water main, and turned off the flow.

Then he ran upstairs, opened the closet, and found his dad's Carhartt pants. He pulled them on, along with a pair of Sorels, then grabbed a hat and work gloves.

The cold could steal his breath with one swipe when he stepped outside. Snow pelted his face, knifed down his collar. The lamps lit a path to the cabins, and he crunched through the drifting snow as he ran toward cabin three, set off from the path, close to the lake.

The lights from the front windows streamed out over the deck, into the night, and he could hear yelling.

He scrambled up the stairs and threw open the door. "Darek?"

Oh no. Inside, water flooded the new wood laminate floor, the freshly laid Berber carpet, the source a waterfall cascading down the formerly pristine, ocher-painted walls.

"Up here!"

He didn't bother with his boots, just slid across the floor to the pull-down attic stairs. "What can I do?"

"Did you shut off the water?"

"Yeah, but it has quite a way to travel from the house—"

"Get me more towels!"

Towels. But Darek had emptied the bathroom, and the hall closet contained nothing, so Casper tromped into the bedroom and pulled off the blanket from the queen bed. He wadded it into a ball and climbed the stairs. "Here!"

A flashlight illuminated the attic space, bright and sharp, Darek straddling a pair of joists, wrapping a long pipe with towels. When he looked up, Casper handed him the blanket.

Darek took it, his jaw tight. "Thanks."

The insulation seeped with water, and Casper could hear it trickling. "What happened?"

Darek turned to wrap the blanket around the pipe. "The pilot light went out, and I had to open the window to let out the propane and—shoot, Casper, why didn't you insulate this better?"

Huh? How was this his fault? "You're putting this on me?"

Darek worked to wrap the pipe, his hands shaking. "I wish I could take off whenever I wanted. Search for treasure. I hope you struck it rich."

Nice welcome home, Bro. "No."

Darek finished wrapping the pipe. "Get me another blanket."

Casper pursed his lips as he climbed down, ripped the next blanket off the bed. He handed that to Darek. "It's not going to help. The insulation is already saturated. We'll have to tear it all out, tear out the ceiling, the walls, put up new Sheetrock, replace the floor, the carpet—"

"Shut. Up." Darek raised his hand, not looking at him. "Just stop talking."

Oh.

Darek was breathing hard, and now he leaned back. He wore a two-day beard, fatigue around his eyes. He looked at Casper, a chill in his expression.

And Casper got it. "This isn't the first pipe broken, is it?"

Darek's face hardened. "Cabin six."

Oh. Now Casper really put the pieces together. "You *do* blame me."

"I left on my honeymoon and asked you to finish insulating the pipes. I trusted you, Casper."

His brother's accusation felt like a blow to his Adam's apple.

Darek climbed across the joists toward him. "It must be nice being a treasure hunter. At least then I'd have something to blame when I didn't find gold."

Casper stared at him, not sure how he should respond.

"How long are you sticking around?"

How long—? "Why, is there a time limit?" Casper climbed down the stairs.

"I just want to know if we can count on you. I mean—you get into a fistfight with Owen, then ditch everyone at the wedding, vanish for the better part of five months, and show up like everything's fine?"

"Now? You want to have this conversation now?"

Darek followed him down the stairs. "I'm just saying, are you back, or is this another pit stop? You can't have it both ways—either you stick around or you don't."

"I don't know, okay?" But as he watched Darek survey the damage, his face paling when he sank a foot into the pond that used to be their carpet and the water pooled at the edges of the hand-tooled baseboards, a little heat went out of him. "I'm sticking around. At least until summer."

Darek said nothing. He unwound his scarf, pulled off his hat, and tossed them onto the sofa. Sweat dribbled down the side of his face, his dark hair matted. "No lost treasure, huh?"

"No. I mean, yes, but—it's a long story."

"Bummer. We could use a strike-it-rich moment right now." His tone didn't sound like he was kidding. He walked over to where a puddle formed on the floor from the ceiling drip. "Did you know that we've had the coldest winter on record so far, and it's not even February yet?"

Casper went to the kitchen, pulled out a saucepan, handed it to him. "I swear to you I insulated those pipes, Darek. But it's fifteen below outside—pipes freeze at that temperature."

Darek said nothing as he set the pan on the floor. Then he went into one of the bedrooms. Came back with the remainder of the bedding and threw it on the laminate, sopping up the mess.

"Ivy's pregnant."

Pregnant. That's right. He'd completely forgotten the news his mother had e-mailed. He found his voice, wrestled it into something easy, cheerful. "Really, that's great. Congratulations. When is she due?"

"April."

"Boy or girl—?"

"I dunno. Listen, here's the deal."

At his tone, Casper looked up from where he helped mop the floor.

"I can't pay you. So if you're going to stick around, you have to get a real job."

Casper recognized Darek's grim look. Something his father had worn during the lean years. The years when he worked with a skeleton crew and recruited his children to fill in as outfitters, trail guides, and maintenance. "What's going on, Darek? What aren't you telling me?"

Darek walked to the sofa and grabbed his hat, his scarf. "I had this brilliant idea to move up the opening to New Year's weekend. We got the place up and running . . . for two guests."

Ouch.

Darek looked at him. "I'm glad you're home. Really. I just need to know that I can depend on you."

"You can."

Darek held his hat for a moment. "Dad used to say that you have to go out and make something good happen; you can't just hope for it. Success isn't magic—it's hard work."

"I know."

"Good. Because it's time to make a choice. Treasure hunting or a real job." He pushed past Casper.

"Where are you going?"

"Back to the lodge for more towels. And then I'm going to have some of that soup my wife left me."

CHAPTER 6

Two weeks of hiding and finally the sun had decided to emerge.

Slate-gray skies, blue-mercury temperatures, jagged icicles hanging from Raina's porch, the mighty Lake Superior tossing blocks of ice onto the snow-crusted shoreline—it had all trapped Raina inside her aunt's house, drinking hot cocoa, reading books, and trying to figure out how to put herself back together.

She'd hoped that day after day she would feel just a little more whole, a little less fragile and stripped as if she'd left half of herself somewhere.

Instead, the hole seemed to burrow clear through her, the pain deep and embedded in every breath.

And the nightmares, the ones where she stood alone in a room, a baby wailing beyond an impenetrable cement wall, became more vivid.

There didn't seem to be a night that she didn't wake in a hot, tangled mess in bed, after throwing herself again and again at the fortress.

She needed something—anything—to help her move forward. A job. A plan. A hint of a future.

She'd purchased a local newspaper at the grocery store, scoured the ads, and found a listing at Wild Harbor Trading Post. It sold kayaks and fishing gear as well as outdoor clothing, but the thought of working there only dredged up memories of paddling with Casper in last summer's dragon boat race.

The last happy moment in her dismal, chilly life.

A listing for a Meals On Wheels driver demanded a working, dependable vehicle. Hers worked, but at these temps, *dependable* might be sketchy.

Which meant she'd have to answer the ad for nursing assistant at the local care center. She could probably figure out how to change bedpans and transfer patients from bed to wheelchair.

She donned her powder-blue parka, a pair of earmuffs, and mukluks, wound a pink scarf around her face, and braved the subzero temperatures for a walk to the care center. How else was she going to get her figure back? But she felt stronger every day, and soon she'd fit into her old jeans.

The care center perched on a hill overlooking the lake. Raina found the entrance and, armed with the paper, approached the front desk. "I'm looking for the manager," she said, pointing to the ad.

"She isn't here, but go ahead and fill out an application," said the nurse, who handed her a clipboard.

Raina took it to the nearby reception room and sat on the sofa. *The Price Is Right* played on a television nearby, a small congregation of elderly in wheelchairs, some with trays, watching the show. In a patch of sunlight, a woman stared out the window. A man with a feeding tube slumped at the table, eyes unseeing.

Despite the plants by the door and the cheery-pink scrubs of the nurses, the place reeked of age and despair.

Raina couldn't take even a hint of despair. Not right now.

She returned the still-blank application to the desk and headed back out into the cold.

Now what?

She shoved her hands into her pockets, ducked her chin into her coat, and walked toward Main Street.

Down the hill, ice locked the harbor and someone had cleared a skating area. It gleamed clear and shiny against the brightness of the day. The smell of smoked fish seasoned the air, and the snow crunched under her boots. If she blew out her breath, it crystallized a moment, reflecting the sun before shattering.

Maybe Pierre's Pizza would take her back. But the thought turned to acid inside her. No, Pierre's stirred up too many memories of cooking with Grace and eating pizza with Casper. Back when she thought she might have a chance of living happily ever after.

The better of her wretched options would be a job at the Wild Harbor. She headed down Main Street, then cut over a block.

She passed a brick building on the corner. A row of bottles in a display window caught the sun, sparkled. Blue, like the frigid ice thrown onshore.

Below them, on another shelf, she spied a collection of figurines. Unicorns and rabbits, some of them crystal, others milky white.

She stepped back to read the store sign. The building seemed caught in time as if it had been erected during the frontier or lumberjack era of Deep Haven. A brick facade, with a false front and hand-lettered, faded words across the top: *Deep Haven Collectibles.*

In the door, she spied a faded, warped Open sign strung on red yarn. Above that, tucked in the window of the door, a yellowed scrap of paper. On it, scrawled in block print, were the words *Help Wanted, Inquire Within.*

She opened the door. A bell jangled overhead.

The store stank of dust and neglect, the layout bearing the markings of a hoarder with towering racks of collectibles, from figurines, faded *Life* magazines, and crystal glasses to a row of gumdrop machines, a shelf of chess pieces in the form of Chinese warriors, and stacks and stacks of bundled newspapers. She barely fit down the narrow aisles, the displays made from doors on sawhorses, old wooden milk crates, and upended buckets.

Odd that she'd never noticed this place before. She picked up a glass basket with ruffled edges and ran her fingers over the bumps along the glass.

"That's milk glass," a voice said.

Raina turned to see a brittle-thin elderly gentleman dressed in a brown sweater vest and woolen trousers, with thick white hair above his ears, sparse on top.

"Very old. Very expensive."

"Can't be that old. Maybe the fifties." Raina held the basket to the light. "See this pattern? It's called hobnail. The Fenton company started manufacturing it in the early fifties. Also, see the color? If it was original milk glass—which, by the way, was made with arsenic—it would fade along the edges, turn almost translucent. This is more opaque, which dates it as younger. I'd guess this to be worth around $30 at most."

She put the basket back and picked up a water bottle. "Now this is a barber's bottle, the kind they used to wet hair. See the translucent edge? And the hand-painted poppies? This would probably sell for about $100 on eBay."

The proprietor had come around his desk and now took the bottle from her hand, examined it before replacing it on the shelf. He peered at her. "How do you know all this, young lady?"

"My grandmother used to have a collection of milk glass. Had her own display room—probably a hundred or more pieces. She taught me how to value it."

"This particular piece just came in. It's part of an estate we're cataloging."

Raina walked to the door, peeled off the handwritten ad. "Is this filled?"

The man pulled his spectacles off his head and looked at the paper. "That's been there nigh about fifteen years, I think."

"So . . . are you still looking?"

"Do you know how to run a computer?"

"I can manage."

"Good, because my grandson gave me one for Christmas and I haven't a hope of a duck in a snowstorm of figuring it out. I turned it on and counted myself a genius."

She liked him. He had an aura to him, something sweet and gentlemanly. "Raina Beaumont." She waited for the usual response of *I know a Beaumont—Miss Liza, the local potter*, but the man said nothing about her name and instead took her hand.

"Gustav Hagborg. Local picker and collector. People around here call me Gust."

"Nice to meet you."

He shuffled behind the desk, pulling up a chair. Raina didn't know where to move without knocking something over. "Now, what do you know about the picking business?"

"I . . . um—"

"My grandson Monte calls it estate picking, but I like to call it the unseen treasure business. It's all junk to the owners, but it becomes a find with someone who sees its value. Right?"

She shrugged.

"Take that piece you're holding. Used to belong to Aggie Wilder. She had an eye for antiques—used to come in and browse. We'd sit and chew on old memories." He shook his head, memory playing on his face as he pulled off his glasses, ran a thumb across his eyes.

"Did you know her well?"

"Her husband, Thor, was one of my best friends."

"Thor?"

"Thorsen Wilder. Died, oh, thirty years ago, maybe." He leaned toward her. Winked. "I always had a thing for Aggie, but she never loved anyone but Thor. She did know how to beat a man at bridge, though. And she could dance . . . oh, my, she knew how to dance. Used to hold parties in her backyard under the starlight, even after Thor was gone."

Gust settled back in his chair.

Raina had the strange sense that she might be intruding. "Do you . . . ? Are you still—?"

"Yes, yes, you're hired. That's just fine. That's perfect, actually. We've been working on Aggie's estate for her granddaughter in Minneapolis, cataloging it before the property goes to auction. Monte's been pestering me for someone to help him dig through the homestead." He held out his hand to shake hers. She found it bony and strong. "I think you're an answer to prayer, my dear."

He stood, gesturing for her to follow him.

Raina stepped over a crate of old signs and followed him down a hallway to a back room. There, in a tiny office crammed with a metal file cabinet and a matching desk shoved up against the wall, a laptop computer sat open, the Windows icon spinning.

He held out the chair for her to sit down. "Let's make a deal. You teach me how to run this thing, and I'll teach you about how to turn trash to treasure."

The blue-skied day, the sharp brightness of the sun against creamy mounds of snow, the vast sheet of pristine white across the lake—it all begged Casper to tear off his oxford and tie, grab his fishing pole and Clam ice hut, and escape to a quiet place. He could nearly feel the tug of a walleye on the end of his line.

"So you think these skis are the best for backcountry touring?" The man inquiring held a pair of Fischer Orbiters and looked like he might be more suited to lounging in front of a wide-screen than tromping through the bushy, untamed wilderness of northern Minnesota. Balding and carrying an extra fifty pounds in front, he wore an oversize ski jacket over a pair of suit pants and dress shoes as if he had left the office in a hurry, still undecided about his vacation north.

Casper met too many weekend wilderness enthusiasts—in fact, Evergreen Resort had built its legacy business on these city folk who developed an itch to explore.

At 1 p.m. on a crisp, beautiful day, Casper understood that itch far too well. He tore his gaze away from the wide picture windows at the back of Wild Harbor Trading Post, showcasing the view of the frozen harbor, and onto his customer.

"Yeah, the Fischer is a great choice." Casper took the ski, black and yellow, still fragrant with fresh wax. "It has a wider body, so you get more stability going down the hills and more traction as you trek up. It's a fantastic cross-country ski. And it comes with a one-year warranty."

"What do you think of these, honey?" a voice called across the store.

Casper's gaze tracked over to the man's wife. Similarly built, she had her eye on a pink ski jacket and black pants. She wore a parka, jeans, and a fleece headband over her dark hair. She held up the jacket to her husband.

"Pretty," he said and turned back to Casper. "What bindings would you recommend?"

Raina had hair like that. Smooth and silky—

"And do they come with boots?"

Oh. He found a smile for the customer and sorted through the options. "Fischer makes a great binding—the Magnum. It's an all-purpose binding for backcountry skiing. The steering plate is contoured, so you have better control and turning in the rough. And these here—" he reached over and grabbed a pair of track boots—"are the matching boots. Again, all-purpose, warm. They have a wool liner and a built-in gaiter. And the top zipper helps for easy slip-on. I myself have a pair of these and love them."

That last bit was nearly true—he'd taken the equipment for a spin just a few days ago with Ned, as part of his sales training. He'd also watched videos on all the products, tried out the line of demo snowshoes, and taken a snow bike out for a ride. He already owned much of the accessory gear—the Nordic socks, the all-weather gloves, even the backcountry trackers.

Ned Sutton had taken one look at Casper—attired in a clean

pair of khakis, a dress sweater he'd dug out of his closet, and one of his dad's ties—and offered him the job. It helped that Casper and Ned had trekked nearly all the back trails during their high school days.

Dude, seriously? You're back—and willing to get a real job?

But what choice did he have, really?

"And where's the best place to go for—you know, beginners?" the man asked. He glanced at his wife as if he was referring to her.

Casper played along. "We have a trail that overlooks Deep Haven called the Pincushion Trail. It's well-used, so it's groomed and gives you a fantastic view of the lake. As for others . . ." He walked to the desk, to the pile of brochures, and handed him one. "Here is a complete guide of trails in the area."

The man took it, shoved it into his pocket. Handed Casper the skis. "We'll need a set for the wife, too. And anything else she wants." He winked at Casper, who didn't know what to do with that.

But he fitted them for skis, boots, bindings, poles, and even that outfit, as well as hats, mittens, and face guards.

"You can stop back in tomorrow to pick up your equipment from the shop."

Ned clamped Casper on the shoulder as they left, packages in tow. "You're my hero. Or maybe my secret weapon." Ned wore a black vest emblazoned with the Wild Harbor logo. With his nearly white, curly blond hair and football build, Ned had charmed his way into the hearts of too many girls in high school—was probably still leaving broken hearts scattered around Deep Haven. Hanging with Ned had cemented Casper with a similar reputation, although he'd never been the kind to take relationships casually.

Which clearly led to today and Casper's struggling to assemble the pieces of his shattered pride.

"You know, you have a future in retail if you want it." Ned's father, who purchased the trading post twenty years prior, had recently left the management in his son's hands while he headed to warmer climates. "I need a good manager, and I think I'm looking at the perfect candidate."

"I dunno, Ned." Casper headed back to the ski-fitting area, where the man and his wife had tried on boots, and closed up boxes. "I've never seen myself as a manager."

"Maybe it's time to start. You can't be a treasure hunter forever."

"Archaeologist."

"Whatever. You're good at this. Think about it." Ned checked his watch. "And take a lunch break, will you?"

Ned disappeared to the front of the store to help a customer while Casper returned the boxes to the back room, located upstairs. Speckled, graying pictures of fishermen docking their boats and hawking their catch lined the store, the place filled with legacy and legend. Sometimes, when he worked late, Casper could hear the voices of the past, feel the hum of adventure and conquest, of courage bred into the early voyagers, and feel like he hadn't completely betrayed himself.

You're good at this. Think about it.

Shoot, he didn't want to be good at this. But maybe if he wanted to start over, get the past out of his system, find his footing, he'd have to embrace a new kind of life.

He jogged downstairs to the office and grabbed his jacket. "I'm going to Pierre's. Want a slice of pizza?"

Ned shook his head as Casper stepped out into the bright sunshine. Frigid wind off the lake bullied its way down the collar of his jacket, and he zipped it up, bracing himself against the subzero temperature. His dress pants did nothing to protect him, so he hustled down the street, away from the lake, cutting through the park on his way to Pierre's. At least he'd worn his hiking boots instead of silly dress shoes.

He ducked into Pierre's Pizza and added himself to the line.

"Casper, you're back!" This from Claire, who now managed the restaurant. She and her husband, his brother's friend Jensen, worked as caretakers of the resort homes across the lake from Evergreen. The homes untouched by the forest fire two summers ago.

Pixie Claire wore her short dark hair back in a blue bandanna. As Casper approached the counter, he noticed the baby shape under her apron. For the love of pete, he couldn't escape this sudden bloom of pregnant women. "I see congratulations are in order."

"Oh, I still have about five months left." She ran her hand over her tummy. "But Ivy and I will have school chums."

He managed to keep his smile intact, but frankly, everywhere he turned, something reminded him of Raina. Of the baby.

"How long have you been home?"

"Just a couple weeks. I've been helping Darek repair one of the cabins. We had a pipe burst and had to gut the place."

"Oh no—"

"Yeah, but he knows what he's doing. He hopes to have it ready for Valentine's weekend."

"I have no doubt he's glad to have you home. If anyone can help him fix the place up, it's you."

Right. "Well, I'm working at the Wild Harbor too."

She raised an eyebrow. "Really."

"No judging. A guy has to earn a living."

She laughed. "Casper, the day you settle for a suit and tie is the day I stop singing love songs. We all depend on you to live the wild adventure we can't have."

He knew she meant it as a compliment, but her words dug into him, turned the day sour. "The only adventure I'm after today is two slices of pepperoni."

"Right," Claire said and boxed up his lunch, put it in a bag. "By the way, the Blue Monkeys are playing at the VFW for Valentine's Day. I hope you'll come."

"Absolutely," Casper said. "Great to see you. Say hi to Jensen."

The wind swirled in off the lake and grabbed at his collar as he stepped out of Pierre's. He tucked his head down and headed back to the store, turning at the corner to stay out of the wind.

If anyone can help him fix the place up, it's you.

See, that was his problem. He just kept meddling, thinking he could somehow show up and solve everything. The curse of the middle child, perhaps, this idea that he had to fix it, had to keep the peace.

In fact, the meddling could be a sort of adventure too. Sheesh, he should have seen that.

His meddling would die—right here, right now, today. From now on, Casper Christiansen minded his own business. Punched in at work, grabbed a hammer when asked . . . but no longer would he show up like some Oliver Twist, hands extended, practically begging for more of other people's problems.

And he'd make a fantastic manager for the Wild Harbor Trading Post.

He was standing at the curb, about to jaywalk between two cars, when he saw someone emerge from the antique store on the corner. In fact, he'd thought the place closed, so the figure caught his attention.

He stilled. Backed up for a better view.

A powder-blue jacket, a pink scarf, white puffy earmuffs—it

could be any tourist bumming around town. But for the long black hair, braided down her back.

He ducked into the nearest alcove—that of the historical society—out of sight and peeked around the edge.

She'd stopped at the corner, looking both ways before crossing, and he got a good, perfect, breathtaking view of her face.

High cheekbones, a smattering of delicious freckles over her nose. Pensive amber eyes that could drill through him, make him forget his name, his destination.

He pulled his head back, tasting his thundering heart in his mouth.

Raina.

Back in Deep Haven?

He peered around the corner again and spied her headed down the street. Ready to run smack into him.

Please, Casper, leave me alone. Yeah, bumping into her would really scream *moving on*!

He ducked inside the historical society, moving away from the door.

"Casper Christiansen, what on earth are you doing?"

Running? But he turned at the voice and found Edith Draper standing in the foyer. A display of grainy black-and-white pictures under glass depicted a brief overview of the history of Deep Haven, and on the wall, brochures and maps showed the evolution of the area from the days of the early voyagers to the present.

Edith Draper might be the one person who'd lived through every era in Deep Haven. She wore a sweatshirt with the words *Far north of ordinary*, the Deep Haven logo underneath, and a pair of black pants, her white hair styled and neat. Glasses dangled from a chain around her neck.

"Hello, Mrs. Draper," he said, watching out the window. "I . . . I was cold?"

"And now you're just lying to me." She stared out the window. When Raina walked by, Edith clearly saw how he turned his back to her, just in case.

"My, my, we have a situation, don't we?" She raised an eyebrow. "And who is that young lady?"

"No one," Casper said. His gaze fell on a box of books and clothing. "Is that a nautical compass?" He picked up the round brass object nestled in what looked like a genuine fur *shopka*. He opened it. A cord attached the lid to the body.

"It's a sundial compass," he said. "Wow, I've only seen a couple of these. In fact, Fitz, our dig director, had one."

Edith came up to inspect it. "We didn't know what it was. It had all these strange hash marks over each number—"

"See, it has an internal magnet to orient the sundial, and then the shadow that is cast by this cord gnomon falls on the number and tells the time." He closed the lid, turned it over. "There are instructions on the back. And . . ." He peered at etching on the side. "These must be the initials of the owner. T. D. W."

Edith reached down and pulled out the fur cap. "A voyageur cap!"

"It's amazing how warm these are. My dad used to have a couple made of rabbit. This one looks like it's made from beaver. You untie these flaps here, and the ears fold down, as well as the nape in the back." He demonstrated, then handed the hat back.

Edith took it, considered him. "Your mother mentioned your love of history, but I had no idea. You know, we need some help around here—"

"I have a job."

"Good, because we can't pay you. But maybe this will interest you." She tugged on his arm and led him to a storage closet off the main display area. "We've had a shortage of help recently."

He stood there, staring at the collection of books, maps, shipping and fishing memorabilia, clothing, shoes, utensils, photographs—and for a moment he couldn't breathe. "Where did you get these?"

"This came from the Linnell estate in Hovland. Evidently Carl Linnell worked for the government, and when they purchased the land up in Mineral Springs, intending to tear most of the old buildings down, he couldn't bear losing all these artifacts. So he saved them. His children donated them to us, but we don't know where to start."

He walked over to a box and pulled out an ancient tuxedo with silk lapels, torn at the shoulder. "Interesting acquisition from Mineral Springs, a voyageur trading town."

Edith leaned in, raising an eyebrow. "My thoughts exactly. It seems that a smart young man who loves history might enjoy cataloging these finds and maybe even tracking down their history."

She pulled out a wallet-size date book. Stuck her finger through a hole in the pages.

Casper took it and opened the cover. The writing appeared nearly unintelligible, the ink smudged with water and the elements. And the hole seemed to tear through the pages as if . . . shot?

He closed the book. Took another look at the memorabilia. Maybe the best way to forget his past was to dive into someone else's. And it wasn't like he'd run into Raina buried in memorabilia at the historical society. "Mrs. Draper, I would be delighted to help you."

She smiled. Patted his cheek. "Young man, you're the answer to my prayers."

With any luck, his dad didn't even have to know about the disaster in cabin three.

Not that Darek would lie to him or even not tell him . . . eventually. But news of trouble at the homestead was the last thing his father needed during his second-honeymoon trip to Europe.

Besides, Darek had handled it. And with the addition of a brand-new electrical socket and ceiling light fixture to replace the one shorted out by the flood, he'd managed to overhaul and rebuild the cabin in three hardscrabble weeks.

Just in time for Valentine's Day. And if the website bookings were accurate, they just might be full.

Love to the rescue.

He grabbed his wire clippers and tape and climbed the ladder to the socket. The low afternoon sun flooded into the room, turning it amber and stirring the scent of the new wood floor, the freshly laid carpet, the rehung and painted Sheetrock.

The door opened. "Knock, knock."

Darek smiled down at the sight of his wife entering the cabin. She wore her dress coat, UGGs, and carried a white deli bag.

"Hey there, handsome."

"I'll be right down."

"Take your time. I have to sit for a second." She slid onto a chair. "I can admit, I never thought that I'd consider five degrees a heat wave."

"You're an incubator. Everything is doubled." But she did look a little red-faced. "You okay?"

"Yep. Tiger's outside building a snowman, I think. Boy, that kid has energy." She pulled off her hat, loosening her long red hair. "He talked nonstop from school. I swear, he could be a lawyer someday."

"One in the family might be enough." Darek finished tying the electrical wires together. "I don't need to be outsmarted by two of you."

Ivy laughed. "Hardly. I think you do just fine, Mr. Christiansen. Look at this place. It's gorgeous. If anything, it looks better than before. Can I book it for Valentine's Day?"

He came down the ladder, set the wire cutters on the counter. Crouched in front of her. "You have other plans on Valentine's Day."

Then he touched her face, leaned up, and kissed her.

He could never quite get enough of the taste, the wonder, of kissing his wife. His second chance. His reminder that yes, God loved him. Forgave him for the mistakes of his first marriage.

She cupped her cold hands around his neck and leaned into the kiss, and he lost himself for a long moment with the taste of her, coffee on her lips, the smell of vanilla on her skin.

Yes, she'd be very busy on Valentine's—oh no.

He pulled away. "Wait. Valentine's Day is a Friday. I have to be here for the check-ins." He made a face. "I'm sorry, honey."

Her smile fell. "What about Casper? Couldn't he work?"

"Oh, babe . . ."

"You don't still blame him for the pipes, do you?"

He didn't know what to think. Once he'd unwrapped the pipes, he'd found the insulation eaten away—or maybe it had never been applied. And yes, heat wrap encased the pipes, but not double layers like Darek instructed. Or thought he had.

"The resort is my responsibility."

"The resort belongs to your family. That includes Casper. Maybe you should let him help—"

"I have been. We re-drywalled the place, and he helped run new pipe, and I let him paint the ceiling and the walls—"

Ivy was smiling.

"What?"

"You are so funny. I happen to know that you hovered over him every time he picked up a hammer or Spackle knife or paintbrush."

He opened his mouth, but she put her hand over it. "Don't even start. I have text messages. Voice mails. Photographic evidence." She pulled out her cell phone, scrolled to a photo, and held it up. Casper, white-faced from sanding Sheetrock, with Darek behind him, his mask pushed up onto his head, his own hair white. Yeah, for a couple hours there, with Casper helping to shoulder the repairs, the resort hadn't felt quite so strangling.

"I concede to the prosecution. But still—Casper's got a job, and I can't ask him to give up his Friday night."

"Because, what, his calendar is booked?" She raised an eyebrow even as she tucked the phone away. "Is it just me, or has he suddenly become a homebody? Are you sure he's okay? He seems . . . I don't know. A little broken?"

"He's fine."

"And what about—? Well, do you think he's over Raina?"

"Probably. It was just a summer thing." Darek got up, picked up the fixture from the counter. Balancing it, he climbed the ladder.

"It didn't sound like a summer thing, the way you described the fight between him and Owen."

"I wasn't there until the tail end. Owen and Casper have always had their moments. Casper's fine. I'm sure he got her out of his system in Roatán."

"Maybe. But I stopped by the Wild Harbor today over lunch, and he told me to tell you he was working late tonight. Again. That's three days in a row."

He held up the fixture, fitted it to the ceiling, and with a pencil marked the holes for drilling. "Maybe he's decided to take life seriously. I think Ned might have offered him a management position."

"Casper, a store manager? *Ho*-kay."

Darek looked down at her. "What's that for?"

"Nothing. It's just so . . . normal."

He drilled the first hole, blew away the dust from the Sheetrock. "Well, a man has to choose between his dreams and responsibility. He can't have both." He drilled another hole. Blew that dust away.

The silence that followed crept up on him like syrup, invading his pores.

Ivy was looking away, out the window, her face stoic. Her hands cradled her belly.

"Ivy?"

"Nothing. It's nothing." She ran a hand over her cheek.

Was she crying?

He started down the ladder, but she rose to her feet, held up her hand. "I just brought by your dinner. I figured you wouldn't take time to eat. I have to . . ." She turned away, then came back with a smile. Something forced if he read her expression correctly. "I have a deposition tomorrow, so I have to head back to work. I'm dropping Tiger off at his grandparents'."

The parents of his first wife, Felicity. The wife who died after Darek had all but checked out of their marriage.

He came all the way down the ladder. "Ivy, what's the matter?" He reached out for her, but the door swung open.

"Dad!" Tiger barreled into the cabin, his snow pants dampened, his woolen cap and mittens spraying flakes onto the new wooden floor. He held a wooden box made of Popsicle sticks. "Look what I made you!"

But even as he said it, he slipped, his rubber-soled boots slick on the now-wet floor, and the craft project flew into the air. Tiger slid, feetfirst, bumping the ladder.

The light fixture toppled off the top.

Ivy screamed and grabbed Tiger.

Darek lunged for Ivy, pulling them back as the fixture landed, splintering into a million stained-glass fragments.

And then everything went quiet, only the thunder of his heartbeat in his ears.

"Everyone okay?" he finally managed, his heart sinking as he added up the cost of the fixture.

"My birdhouse!" Tiger scrambled up, oblivious to the glass, and tromped across the floor to where his splintered craft project lay.

Leaving wet, blackened, salty footprints on the brand-new carpet.

"Tiger, get off that carpet right now!"

Darek didn't mean to shout—or maybe he did—but the adrenaline turned his volume even higher, and by the time he'd reached Tiger, the seven-year-old's face began to crumple.

"But, Dad, my birdhouse—" He held up the smashed milk carton–and–Popsicle stick creation.

Darek grabbed it and tossed the wreck onto the table even as he picked up Tiger and deposited him on the rug by the door. "This carpet is brand-new, Tiger, and look what you did—it's wrecked. I'm going to have to shampoo—"

"Darek!"

Ivy's voice caught him, made him breathe.

Tears streamed down Tiger's face, his brown eyes filled with hurt.

Darek exhaled, his breath shaky. Oh. He dragged a hand down his face, then crouched before Tiger, reached up, and thumbed away a tear. "I'm sorry, pal. But you can't just run in here. There's glass everywhere now, and the carpet—"

"I'm sorry, Dad." Tiger caught his lip between his teeth. He glanced at the distorted birdhouse. "I made you a present."

Darek took the project, examined it. Oh, buddy. "Did you make this for me?"

Tiger nodded. "It was supposed to be for Christmas, but the glue didn't dry, and then Mrs. White said I should take it home, but I forgot it in my cubby and then Mom, I mean Ivy, came today and said I should bring it. That you've been working so hard and maybe you needed something to make you smile . . ."

Mom. Yeah, he caught that slip. He glanced at Ivy, who had her hand over her mouth.

"Mom was right," Darek said quietly. He reached out and pulled Tiger to himself, tucking his son into his embrace. Tiger's arms tightened around his neck. "I'm sorry I've been working so hard. I promise things will get better."

Tiger released him, leaned back. "And then we'll build a snow fort?"

"A snow *castle*!"

Tiger glanced at the glass. "I'm sorry I made your lamp fall."

"It's okay, Tiger. I'm just glad you didn't get hurt. Go have fun with your grandparents. I'll see you later tonight."

He stood as Tiger ran outside.

"Mom?" Darek said, turning to Ivy. He cupped her face.

Ivy smiled, her eyes wet. "He's done it a couple other times recently. I think, maybe with the arrival of this baby, it'll sink in."

He pushed her hair back behind her ears. "I don't deserve you. I know this. And I know I've been working long hours. But it'll get better. I just have to get the resort into the black and then—"

"Then our lives will slow down?" She laughed, a sort of sweet mocking, and took his hand, resting it on her belly. "I doubt that."

He widened his fingers, feeling the baby move inside. The sense of it could buckle his knees. No, he didn't deserve Ivy.

He had to make a go of this resort—for her and Tiger and this baby.

"I'll be home later."

She patted his cheek. "I know. I'll leave the light on."

CHAPTER 7

AGGIE AND THOR WILDER lived on a farm that overlooks Lake Superior about four miles out of town. Turn on old County Road 41, then at Wilder Trail. Their house is at the end of the road about a quarter mile.

Gust's words hung in Raina's mind as her used Aveo bumped along the icy road leading back to the estate, drifts of snow just barely wider than her car guiding her through a shaggy, snow-covered forest. The pine boughs hung low and shivered as her car dragged through them and shook white powder on her windshield.

A gal could get lost back here until the thaw. She made a mental note to head home long before the five o'clock sunset. Even now, just after noon, shadows hovered over the path like disapproving sentries.

Maybe she should have waited for Gust's grandson, Monte,

but after spending three days helping Gust boot up his computer, set up e-mail and his Facebook page, and learn the rudiments of an Excel sheet, she left him to begin cataloging his inventory, including prices.

They had an eBay jackpot in their future if she could just wipe off the dust, take a few pictures, and convince Gust that his best clientele could be found beyond the tiny borders of Deep Haven.

And she could probably catalog Aggie's entire "estate" on her own. How much work could it be to sort through the few possessions of a small-town farmer?

She slowed as she eased her car over a fallen drift, praying she didn't get stuck. Casper certainly wouldn't be around to save—

See, there she went again, letting him creep into her thoughts. So he'd pulled her out of the mud, once upon a time. Right now the man probably sat on some white-sand beach, forgetting about her, just like she told him to.

And frankly, she should too. Move on. Fresh start.

As she drove out of the grip of the forest, the land began to clear and white drifts rolled away from the road, downhill. Leagues below, the lake spread out, all the way to the horizon in a breathtaking expanse of glory, the open water in the middle steel gray under a smoky sky. She imagined that, in summer, touched by the cirrus-streaked blue sky, the view could steal her breath.

The road arched and she kept her speed lest her wheels start to spin. At the top, she spotted the house.

Clearly Aggie and Thor had been more than farmers. Or perhaps just extremely successful farmers. The house, now covered in snow, rose three stories in the middle of a grove of dormant fruit trees. A mansard roof capped the third story, with a turret that jutted against one corner.

Green-shuttered windows on the second story peered over a shingled wraparound porch. Pillars made of stone, probably hand-picked from the lake, propped up the roof and added an Old World feel to the structure.

In fact, as she drove up and stopped at the end of the plowed road, where it opened into a parking area, the entire place felt old.

Or perhaps vintage. Valuable.

Raina got out, pulling her satchel onto her shoulder, and surveyed the house. Around back, she made out a dilapidated greenhouse. And behind her, a barn for livestock or vehicles.

She could imagine sipping lemonade on the porch in the summertime, watching the boats travel the lake. See children running in the grassy field, apples dripping from the trees.

The image rushed up and wrapped a hand around her neck, choking her. Her eyes burned, and she bit her lip, blinking away the tears. Shoot. Someday, please, she had to get past this.

Probably she was kidding herself. How did you forget losing a part of your soul? Or even worse, giving it away?

The hollow places inside burned as she recalled Gust's instructions: *Monte shoveled to the front door and left it unlocked, so you should be able to get in.*

She found the shoveled trail and hiked up the wide stairs that led to the front door. The protection of the porch left it clearer of snow, and she stood for a moment at the top, staring at the view of the lake, the road. The past.

She could imagine standing here in the fifties or sixties, a young girl in love, watching for her date's Mustang . . .

She'd clearly read too many historical romances while recuperating. She stamped her feet free of snow and opened the door.

Time caught her up and settled her into an era of parlors and tea, of family dinners around a dining room table, the smell of pot roasts infusing the home with the taste of welcome.

She could nearly hear the voices calling from the upstairs bedrooms.

She closed the door. A stairway ran from the foyer to the second floor, a worn red carpet waterfalling over the oak treads. Green wallpaper, the color of jade, lined the entry hallway, and behind the door, on an oak coat stand, hung a blue woolen jacket.

"Hello? Anyone here?"

Her voice echoed in the frigid air. She stepped into the octagonal sitting room to her left in the three-story turret. A sheet covered a high-backed parlor sofa with eagle claw legs; another sheet draped a chair of the same design. In the center of the room, a marble-topped coffee table with carved legs held a milk glass tea set.

She ventured into the room, found dusty black-and-white portraits, solemn descendants of the Wilder clan in silent vigil over the capsule of time. A bookcase suggested highbrow reading—she recognized hardback Dickens, Alcott, the Brontë sisters, Austen.

Only the ancient square Panasonic stereo television pushed against the far wall gave a nod toward the modern era.

Raina crossed the hallway into the living room and found herself in the seventies, with wood paneling and built-in hickory cabinetry filled with framed photographs, figurines, and yet more books. In the center of the room, a green davenport, the fabric worn nearly through, suggested hours spent there reading. Two more chairs, dressed in gold velveteen, held needlepoint pillows crafted with Christmas patterns.

The place seemed as though someone had simply shut the door and walked away. Raina wandered through the dining room to the kitchen. A hand-tatted lace runner draped the oak table, more milk glass in the corner hutch.

Dark-hickory cupboards hung in the kitchen, accented with Tiffany-style overhead lights designed in fruit patterns. A side-by-side stainless steel oven, white Formica countertops, tall orange stools at an overhanging counter, and a floor covered in a wild geometric-patterned rug in lime green and red reflected a high-style early seventies makeover.

Although the freezer box stood empty, the green General Electric fridge stirred up memories of her grandmother's frozen chocolate chip cookies hidden inside.

She opened the cupboards and took a quick visual inventory of the contents, her gaze lingering on a collection of Ranger Joe dishware, then headed upstairs.

Four bedrooms all contained double beds with eyelet dust ruffles, homemade quilts, and needlepoint bolster pillows. Papered in a print of tiny roses, each room held a writing desk and wardrobe and netted a small collection of vintage clothing. It wasn't until she examined the bedside table of what she assumed must be the master bedroom that she hit the jackpot.

In a drawer of the round table she found two books. One, a handwritten journal of poetry. The other, a diary.

She picked it up, began to page through it. Scrawled on each page seemed to be the ongoing activities of each day, like a day planner.

Raina flipped to the front. Stared at the date.

OCTOBER 1929

Arrived at the station today, 3 p.m. Met by Father's man, Duncan. He drove me to the school. It's not at all

*what Father said, and I shouldn't have believed him.
I think I might perish here, and I suppose that is what
he intends after the debacle in Paris. He says that he will
have to arrange a marriage here, to someone who would
overlook the rumors.*

   *I have ruined myself and I miss Mummy more than
I can bear.*

Raina closed the diary.

She felt like an interloper. Clearly some mistake had been made. Certainly whoever lived here must be returning . . .

Indeed, outside, she heard a car door close. She got up and peered out the window. A black pickup was parked next to her car.

Downstairs, she heard feet on the porch, the door opening.

She turned, clutched the diary to her chest. Uh . . .

"Hello the house, anyone here?" The voice, male, drifted up the stairs.

She swallowed. "Here, I'm up here."

More footsteps. She chased away her fear with the truth that anyone who might want to hurt her probably wouldn't announce himself.

Right?

She tucked the diary back in the drawer and headed out of the room just as the man appeared on the landing.

A real estate agent, maybe, a business look about him. Tall, with short blond hair, hazel eyes, broad shoulders, lean hips. Wearing dress pants, holding leather gloves.

"Monte Riggs. I think you already met my grandfather, Gust." He held out his hand and smiled at her, a dimple in his right cheek.

"Raina Beaumont."

She waited for him to make the usual connection to her aunt, but he didn't, and for some reason she liked him all the more for it.

"Grandpa says you're new in town?"

And right then, she knew. She could reinvent herself. She didn't have to be the woman with a past, a woman dogged by her mistakes. Just . . . Raina. At least until her aunt Liza returned home, and by then she'd have figured out what to do with the rest of her life.

"Yeah. I used to be a caterer, but I'm house-sitting for the winter. I'm not sure if I'll stick around after that. We'll see."

He raised an eyebrow. "Next time try to find a house in Florida."

"No kidding."

"I was a little afraid you'd get stuck. I hired a guy to plow the driveway, but I wasn't sure how good a job he did. I thought I'd better come and check on you."

Gallant as well as handsome.

"I know you want me to catalog the place, but I think there's been some mistake. The house feels lived in or, at least, would if there was any heat on. It's like someone simply went out intending to come back."

Monte shoved his gloves into his pockets, walked down the hall, peering into the rooms. "I know. I was out here once before, after Penny came in with her collection of milk glass."

"Penny?"

He turned back to her. "Yeah, Penny Townsend. She's the granddaughter of the owner, Aggie Wilder, who passed away about ten years ago. Before that, Aggie had to be moved into a nursing home. Apparently she fell and broke her hip one day and could never return to the house."

"So they just shut it up?" She followed him down the hall and up another flight of stairs.

It opened into a giant room, empty save for the buffet built into the far wall. The windows jutted out of the mansard roof, offering a breathtaking view of the lake. He walked to a window as if also mesmerized by the view. Then he faced her again. His eyes held mystery and just enough sparkle that a girl might be hypnotized by them.

"Penny lives in Minneapolis with her family, and she owns this place. Until a couple years ago, they used it in the summer for vacations, but with her kids grown, she wants to sell it. She said that we were supposed to sell it all."

Raina stared at him. "Seriously? There are years of memories here—pictures and books. Personal books."

"We'll catalog it all, but she said she went through everything she wanted." Monte walked across the floor, stood in the middle. "I wonder what they used this room for."

"Shuffleboard?"

He laughed. "So, Raina Beaumont, my grandfather tells me you have introduced him to something called the Intro-net."

"Right. It's my pleasure. He hadn't a clue how to use that computer you got him."

"I know. It's my fault. I work out of Duluth doing estate sales, and I should have been here to set it up for him. I blame the weather."

"It's been brutal."

"But that's no excuse. And I have to admit, sometimes Grandpa's stories can turn me blind."

"He does like to spin a yarn. But he means well, and just think of all the history trapped in that head."

"I think he's been in Deep Haven since the dawn of time."

He headed to the stairs, then turned and held out his hand as if she needed help. Sweet. She waved him off and grabbed the banister, but the thought counted.

"Well, we're going to bring him into this century," she said. "I set up a Facebook page for him and taught him how to use Excel. You know, if you list your store on eBay, you might have a real haul."

"You, Raina Beaumont, are a true gem." He stood on the landing. "I didn't know how I was going to get this place cataloged and ready for sale. You are exactly what I was hoping for."

Another smile. It hit her like a fresh breeze.

"I'm heading back to Duluth, but is there anything you need before I take off? I'll leave my cell phone number at the office. Grandpa doesn't have one, so don't bother. And don't worry; I don't expect miracles."

She looked around at the rooms, the furniture, the accessories. "Frankly, I don't know where to start."

He nodded. "Here's what I do. I start by going through the house and collecting all the personal items. Pictures and journals and letters—anything that would be difficult to sell. Then I box it up and sometimes it goes to the family, but in this case, you could see if the historical society wants it. Aggie and Thor made a mark here in Deep Haven. The Wilders owned the Wild Harbor Trading Post for years and ran a hotel on the harbor. I'm sure there is memorabilia the town might appreciate."

"Okay. I can do that."

"Then go room by room. We have an account with a moving box supplier, so feel free to order china boxes and anything else you might need. I know the prices on much of this, but we'll hire an auctioneer, so you don't have to tag anything."

He jogged down the stairs to the first level. "You can leave the furniture behind—we'll arrange for a tour and then pictures on the day of the sale so we don't have to haul everything out of here until later."

"Okay."

Monte reached the bottom and turned. She stood two steps higher, now suddenly at eye level. She placed him at six foot three, maybe. Strong. Capable.

For a second, a strange, enigmatic emotion passed through his hazel eyes.

She smiled, not sure what to make of it.

Then he said, "I know we just met, but . . . I'll be back in a few days, and, well, would you like to go out to dinner?"

Her mouth opened. Closed.

He made a face. "Too soon, huh?"

His words caught her—but he couldn't possibly know she'd had a baby. And perhaps a date would chase any lingering memories of the Casper nightmare from her brain.

"Just dinner?"

"Pizza, if that's easiest." Was that a press of red on his cheeks?

"How about a burger someplace?"

He nodded, warmth in his eyes. "I know just the place." He pulled his keys out. "You sure you'll be okay here by yourself?"

"Yeah. I'm going to just put together the personal things, like you suggested. Hopefully the historical society will still be open when I'm finished."

He stopped at the door, his hand on the knob. "Welcome to Deep Haven, Raina. I hope you find a reason to stay."

Casper might be able to charm a customer into laying down a thousand dollars for an Armada AR7 and Full Tilt Booters ski package, complete with Marker Griffon bindings and Völkl Phantastick poles, but his real joy came from identifying the origin of a pair of spectacles he'd found in the bottom of the first box he opened at the historical society. After examining the class pictures from the one-room Mineral Springs School, he named Lyman Woodard as the owner.

So far, he'd mapped out the town's main buildings based on sketches from Carl Linnell's journal, including the Indian curio shop and general store, the post office, the Oakwood School, and the Congregational Church. He counted a total of forty-six households and even found the location of the cemetery.

And he managed to clear from his brain for two whole hours the fact that Raina had returned to Deep Haven.

He'd also refrained from glancing out the window toward the antique shop on the off chance that he would see her leave.

See. Not stalking.

Over her.

Forgetting.

Putting the past behind him.

He set the glasses on a tray and wrote out an index card labeling the object for Edith, as well as the picture of the six students in the 1932 class.

His stomach growled and he glanced at his phone. If he didn't leave now, the grocery store would close, and he'd be eating a baloney and peanut butter sandwich.

But really, he'd sacrifice food for the opportunity to spend the evening with a slice of history. Still, he had to be at the Wild Harbor early, thanks to Ned's management training program. Apparently that included having Casper open the shop so Ned could waltz in around noon.

He got up, turned off the light to the back room, and grabbed his jacket. Edith had walked out around the time he'd walked in, but she'd left the light burning. Now he grabbed his keys and was just reaching out to flick off the lights when he heard a knock.

He opened the door. "We're closed—"

"I just have to drop off a box!"

Raina?

There she stood in her powder-blue jacket, her hair held back by earmuffs.

Her eyes widened, and had she not been holding a box, she might have turned and bolted based on the expression on her face.

"Hey," he said, drinking her in again. Shoot, but his traitorous heart resurrected the feel of her in his arms, the memory of her smile as he kissed her.

Apparently he would have to work harder to break free of this spell she had on him.

She stared at him. Looked at her box. Back to him. "What are you doing here?"

"Here as in Deep Haven? Or here as in the historical society?"

Perhaps it didn't matter because her face paled under the overhead light. He watched her breath form in the air as she considered what to do.

He couldn't take it. "Come in, Raina. I promise I won't bite."

She managed a slight smile as if he were joking. But his last conversation with her played in his mind, and yeah, maybe he'd be a little gun-shy if he stood in her shoes.

He'd worn out their conversation at the hospital, replaying it, and decided that he might have been gentler. He put that regret in his voice now as he took the box from her. "How are you?"

She stuck her hands in her pockets. Wouldn't look at him. "I'm fine. I . . . I'm working at the antique shop up the road, helping to catalog an estate, and . . . Why are you not as shocked to see me?"

Oh. He swallowed. "I saw you a couple days ago . . ." He lifted a shoulder. "You told me to leave you alone, so . . ."

She nodded. Sighed. "Thanks for that."

They stood a moment in silence, their past boiling to the surface. Then she saved him by pointing to the box. "These are personal things we found at the estate. The owner doesn't want them, so I thought I'd drop them off here, see if you—the historical society—was interested."

He set the box on the table. Opened it. Pulled out a few of the framed pictures, studying them. Family photos from the forties, fifties, and later.

"It's the estate of Aggie and Thor Wilder." She stepped up to him, reaching for a photo. A middle-aged couple sat on a green sofa, hands folded together, smiling into the camera. "Is this them?"

"I don't know. Maybe. I never met them, but they're famous. They helped build the hotel in town and owned the trading post. They had one child, a girl, but she moved away long ago. Aggie is a bit of a legend around here for her philanthropy work. She was famous for her huge summer lawn parties too."

"Apparently Aggie fell and broke her hip and never returned. The house looks like she left it yesterday, if you ignore the dust."

He pulled out a journal, flipped through it. Poetry. A letter fell out and he picked it up. Opened it. Beside him he felt Raina lean in as if peering over his shoulder.

He held it lower so she could read it with him.

"It looks like it's in a man's handwriting," she said. "The letters are choppy."

Casper read it aloud.

"Dear Aggie,

By the time you read this, it'll be too late for you to judge me, but I pray you will be gentle with my memory. I think, in fact, you've known the truth about Duncan for years. In my defense, I did what every husband would do to keep his family safe. Every day I look to the Lord for peace, and I find it in your eyes. Loving you has been the greatest reward, and I found redemption in the joy of our rich lives and in your surprising faith in the Word of the Lord. You are His light to me. Thank you for the treasure of your great love.

Thor"

He finished and glanced at Raina.

"What do you think it means?" she asked.

He read the letter again. Set it down. No, it couldn't be.

"Casper, you know something."

He looked at her. Wow, seriously, she could read him that easily? "There's local lore about this guy named Duncan Rothe." He shook his head. "Certainly Thor didn't have a run-in with Duncan Rothe. That doesn't make sense."

"Why not? What's the story?"

He tucked the letter back in the book. Set it in the box. "It's just a legend. Probably not even true, but according to the stories, Duncan Rothe was a gangster and bootlegger back in the Roaring Twenties. Some say he robbed a bank; other stories tack on

116

murder. Whatever the truth, all agree he escaped north with a million dollars of US Steel bonds in his possession."

"Did he come through Deep Haven?"

"Yes. The law came looking for him, but he'd disappeared."

"Like . . . maybe met up with Thor Wilder, who killed him?"

Oh, she had pretty eyes. They could distract a man, if he let them.

"I think that's a reach—Thor wasn't even around then. The Wilders didn't open the trading post until the forties, I think."

She smiled then, and he'd thirsted for it so long that he drank it in. "Sounds like a mystery."

Casper nodded, searching for his voice. "Actually, the Duncan Rothe mystery was one of my first curiosities. Back in the nineties, someone found an old 1920s roadster in the woods—near Mineral Springs, actually—and it set off all sorts of speculation about Duncan Rothe and where he might be. US Steel offered a 10 percent finder's fee for the bonds, and it stirred up a few treasure hunters sniffing around. One of them stayed at Evergreen Resort. He regaled me with the Rothe rumors and for three long months, all I could think of was finding that million dollars." He closed the lid on the box. "Silly, I know."

But she wasn't laughing. "Not silly. Sweet, actually." She smiled at him again. "It's nice to see you, Casper. But . . ." Her smile fell, and she lifted a shoulder. "I'm really trying to move on. It would be better if maybe—"

And then he said it. Without thinking, without letting her decide their fate. "We can still be friends, Raina. No one has to know anything."

She swallowed, a sudden rawness on her face, and he realized that in an instant, he'd opened her wounds. "I mean—I'm so sorry—I just thought, you know, maybe we could be friends."

"I don't think . . ."

"Claire and her band are playing for Valentine's Day. You remember her from last summer . . ." His voice trailed off as he became aware how close their conversation treaded to danger, to memories and hurt.

"I have a date." She looked away, her expression rueful. "Sorry."

Oh. Right. He tried to shake off the sense that he'd been jackhammered in the solar plexus. A date.

I'm really trying to move on.

And he should be too.

"That's . . . great." He forced a smile. Wow, that hurt, the words like fire in his chest. "That's really great."

"I gotta go."

"Okay. If you . . . um, ever need any help hauling things from Aggie's house or . . . Well, you know where to find me." He wanted to wince or crawl under something.

But Raina was merciful. "Yeah. Thanks, Casper." She turned, not looking at him. "See ya round."

Then she was gone. Just like that. Moving on.

And he was stuck right here in the past.

No wonder bears hibernated. Maybe Raina should go to bed for the next three months, sleep away this terrible emptiness, the cold that seeped into her bones.

Although she had a wretched feeling the cold wouldn't vanish with the advent of the sun. Like a shadow, it hovered over her soul, chilling it from the inside out. She stood by the stove, willing the brass teakettle to whistle, staring at her wan reflection in the dark window—her hair pulled back, her face freshly washed.

She knocked her spoon against the counter.

And why did Casper have to return, walk right into the debris of her life? Looking good, too, in a pair of khakis and a dress shirt under a zip-up flannel vest, as if he were respectable and not about to jump on his motorcycle and roar out of her life. He still hadn't cut his deliciously dark-brown hair, though, and it lay long and curly against his collar.

She'd nearly reached out, wrapped a finger around one of those curls as she listened—no, watched—him read Thor's letter. *"In my defense, I did what every husband would do to keep his family safe."*

Thor's words on Casper's lips strummed through her, and she pressed her fingers to her eyes, hating that after a month, the pain could still sear through her, as fresh as the moment she surrendered Layla. She'd done what she had to in order to give her daughter a good life, a real life. To keep her safe. She believed that down to her bones.

Then why did the doubt haunt her, right there on her shoulder every moment?

The teakettle whistled and she picked it up, poured the water into the hot cocoa mug. Stirred it into a frothy darkness. She tied the fuzzy oversize bathrobe around her, still wearing her jeans and turtleneck under it, and headed out to the quiet family room. Light glowed from the Tiffany lamp onto the denim sofa, and a fire crackled in the hearth.

Outside, the wind whistled off the lake, hammering the windows. The thermometer outside listed twelve below, and just the trip from her car, at the curb, to the house had nearly frozen her lips off.

Maybe she should change her mind, turn Monte down

whenever he called to set up their date. It wasn't like she would fall in love with him.

And Casper had looked—what, hurt?—when she told him she had a date on Valentine's Day. She hated the lie, but she couldn't think of anything else.

No. She refused to keep thinking about Casper. Or her daughter. Only, *not* her daughter. Not anymore. This week, finally, she'd managed to get through the day without breaking down in tears, successfully keeping the howling tucked in the back of her mind.

At least until the quiet hours of the evening, when emptiness roared to life.

Someday it would fall silent, right?

Curling up on the sofa, she pulled a knit afghan over her and picked up her book. Stared at the pages. They blurred. She put her cocoa down on a coaster and leaned back into the pillows. Propped the book on her knees.

Her eyes dropped twice before she laid her head back, just to rest for a moment.

The voices came from every direction, and it dawned on Raina slowly that she stood in the middle of a room, surrounded by a crowd. The men wore suits, the women cherry-red dresses. And they all held babies.

A cry rose from one of them, bounced through the room— a plain room without color, gray walls rising to a gray ceiling.

And the cry. High-pitched, angry, afraid. It tugged at Raina, and she turned, running to the nearest man. She tore open the blanket in his arms, but it fell to the ground, empty. She turned to the next, found that blanket empty.

The cry grew louder, shrill, clawing at her. She ran to the source, tore the baby from a woman's arms.

The blanket crumpled in her embrace.

Then a thousand cries, from the armada of faceless infants in the arms of slate-faced caretakers. And every blanket Raina grabbed fell in on itself, leaving her clutching air.

She woke with a start, her heart pounding, the wailing still in her ears. She cleared the nightmare, but the sound tightened, shrilled from the kitchen.

The teakettle. She must have put it back on a hot burner.

The steam had turned the room sweaty. She shut off the stove, then grabbed the handle. Jerked back, her hand stinging. Hot pad. She found one, then moved the kettle off the burner and ran her hand under cold water. A hot red burn crossed her palm, but it hadn't raised skin.

Still, the experience left her shaking.

Faceless, crying babies. She'd had enough of these nightmares. At some point, her subconscious would have to catch up with her decisions.

But clearly the romance she was reading needed a bit more excitement if she hoped to stay awake. Unless . . .

She walked over to her satchel and pulled out the diary of Aggie Wilder. What was the hurt in reading it before she donated it to the historical society?

She pulled the afghan over her again and opened the book. Every page was filled, and it seemed the years spanned from 1929 to the midseventies, although she spied big gaps, years without entry.

Still, fifty years of a person's life. Of Aggie's life. Raina had never thought of keeping a journal. Why, really? Just so she could look back and reread her mistakes?

Maybe Aggie had nothing to regret.

Raina found where she'd left off and read the next entry.

MARCH 1930

Four times Father's man, Duncan, has surprised me, waiting for me in the parlor, his hat in hand, to inquire after my well-being. Supposedly for Father, although I had begun to suspect he had ulterior motives. And tonight confirmed it. I admit, I didn't know what to expect when he asked permission from Mrs. Etheridge to take me to the symphony tonight. She agreed, despite her reservations, I'm sure believing it a request from my father, as did I. But when Duncan escorted me to the box on his arm, I realized Father most likely had no inkling of Duncan's attentions. And how could he, a thousand miles away?

Duncan makes me feel wonderful. Dark, wavy hair, those starlight brown eyes that seem to devour me. I've never experienced such a feeling as the one when he looks at me. Yet he is a gentleman, despite his reputation, one I am loath to believe after the way he squired me around town in Father's Rolls. I feel safe with him, as if he could protect me, give me the world. After the show, he took me to a club, fed me oysters, then repaired me home just as the sun rose over Lake Michigan.

The most perfect evening of my life. After Jean-Philippe, I never believed I could fall in love again.

But perhaps that wasn't love. Perhaps it was simply an infatuation with a boy hoping to win my father's fortune. Duncan is a man in no need of a fortune.

If I were to ever truly fall in love, it might be with a man like Duncan Rothe.

Raina closed the diary. Clearly Casper's description of Duncan didn't quite match up with how Aggie saw him.

Like her feelings for Casper. Her head said to run away; her heart couldn't seem to push him from her mind. But like Aggie, perhaps what she felt for Casper was only an infatuation ignited by the summer breezes, the sense of loneliness.

Maybe it had never truly been love.

The fire flickered against the glass. Which meant that someday she might find someone who made her feel like Duncan made Aggie feel. Safe.

CHAPTER 8

MONTE WAS GOING TO CANCEL their date. And frankly, she didn't blame him.

Raina stood at the window, peering through the frosty glass to the outside thermometer. Sixteen below zero. *Sixteen.* Even indoors, the chill pervaded her bones, despite the house pumping out heat full blast just to keep the place above sixty-five. Outside, the wind scraped up snow, hurled it into the air, and it hung there as if afraid to move.

Everything should be afraid to move in weather like this.

She glanced again at her cell phone, just in case she missed his call.

Nothing. Not even a message, which might mean that he still planned on picking her up at seven, taking her out for that burger he'd promised when he called two days ago.

Conveniently it just happened to fall on Valentine's Day, fulfilling the lie she'd spoken to Casper.

It didn't lessen her guilt, despite the wisdom of dodging any interaction with him.

Now she stared out into the night, wondering if fate might be playing at revenge.

Please, don't let Monte's car be lying upside down in a ditch. He'd called before the storm of the season hit, turning the roads into a sheer plate of ice. Every plow in town mustered up, frantically salting to keep the destination open for the flood of tourists planning to escape for a romantic weekend to the frozen—yet breathtaking—north shore.

Yes, Monte could easily be bleeding in the ditch or still trying to navigate his way here and—

Breathe, Raina.

She pressed her hands to her chest, let her worry sift out. It wasn't as if her future hung on this date. Or that she even liked Monte that much. He was handsome, yes, and solicitous—he'd called twice to check on her progress at the estate and listened without interrupting as she told him about the collection of *Life* magazines she'd found in the cabinets in the family room. And the milk glass perfume bottles in the bathroom. And the newspapers of major historical events—Kennedy's assassination, the lunar landing, the announcement of D-day—tucked into the china cabinet.

Every day seemed to unearth a new adventure. And every night she read a little deeper into Aggie's romance with Duncan, who really had known how to woo her, taking her to nightclubs and out to dinner and even for a walk along Lake Michigan. The perfect gentleman, despite their age gap.

She glanced again at her phone, then headed to her room to find a sweater. She wore her hair down, and she'd picked out a red dress, added leggings to ward off the cold, but mostly because her dress pants didn't quite fit yet. She'd stood in front of the mirror today and tried to close them around her remaining baby bulge.

No, just bulge. She refused to allow the word *baby* into her vocabulary.

For now. Maybe someday.

Her cell rang and she ran to pick it up, expecting Monte. Instead, she saw Grace's name. "Hello?"

"Happy Valentine's Day, friend! How are you?"

Raina sat on the arm of the sofa. "I'm good . . . real good." Yeah, actually, for the first time in weeks, she wasn't lying. Completely. "How was Hawaii?"

"Warm."

"Are you married?"

Grace laughed. "Not yet. He golfed, I caught up with friends, we cooked—and decided that we'd probably set a date over the summer."

"Where are you?"

"I'm in Tennessee. Max and I are here for a game against the Predators. He didn't want me to be alone for Valentine's Day. I think we're going to a private concert tonight—Brad Paisley."

Grace lived a life that Raina couldn't yet comprehend. How had her friend gone from schlepping pizza at Pierre's to private parties with country stars?

She'd found the right man. Or the right life. Or realized that she couldn't stay stuck in one place anymore.

See, going out with Monte tonight? Good idea.

"I'm jealous. It's sixteen below here."

"Sixteen." Grace's voice betrayed the right amount of sympathy. "Well, if it makes you feel any better, it's about twenty degrees here. I can admit I wish I were sitting on a beach right now. Maybe I should follow Casper down to Roatán."

Raina swallowed.

"Oh, Raina. Sorry. My mouth takes over sometimes and—"

"No, it's okay. Like I told you, I'm over Casper. But for your information, he's here."

"Here? As in Deep Haven?"

"Your family needs to communicate better. Yeah, Casper's here. Working at the historical society."

Silence. Then, "Are you sure you're okay?"

Raina got up, stared in the mirror. Smiled. She'd made an effort tonight for Monte, adding golden-brown shadow around her eyes, dark lipstick. She didn't at all resemble a woman trying to piece her life back together.

"I'm more than okay. In fact, don't worry, I'm not going to freak out every time you mention Casper's name. I know he's your brother. We had a summer romance, but that's all it was. I'm moving on. I even talked to him a few days ago."

Grace's voice came through low. "You did? How was it?"

"It was fine. And I have a date tonight."

"With *Casper*?"

"No, Grace. With Monte Riggs. His grandfather runs the antique store—I'm working for him."

"Monte. Yeah, I think I know him. He was a year or two behind me in school. Thin, scrawny blond kid."

"He's not thin or scrawny anymore, believe me."

"Really." Grace laughed on the other end. "So a hot date for Valentine's Day . . ."

"It's not a hot date. We'll probably talk about business. I'm cataloging this estate for them."

"It's a hot date, and I'll bet you look fabulous."

Raina's smile dimmed. How she wanted to share in Grace's sweet enthusiasm. "It's hard to look fabulous when you're dressed in fifty layers."

"If anyone can, you can. Where are you going?"

"Just out for burgers."

"Oh, then he's taking you to the VFW. Yum. Now I'm hungry. Gotta run—have a great time on your hot date."

"It's not a hot . . ."

But Grace had already hung up.

Raina was tucking her phone into her purse when the doorbell rang. Through the glass she spied Monte, dressed in a long wool overcoat, gloves, a gray scarf, and a black stocking hat, stomping his feet on her porch.

Silly man was wearing dress shoes. She opened the door. "Get inside right now."

His eyes widened, but he stepped in. She closed the door behind him.

He whistled, raising an eyebrow at her attire. "Wow."

She smiled, an unfamiliar warmth syruping through her. Especially when he met her eyes, nothing of business in them.

So maybe it was a hot date after all.

Except she wasn't quite ready for that, was she?

"Where are we going?" She picked up her coat, and he reached for it, holding it open. Chivalrous.

"To the best burger place in town. The VFW. Sorry, but it's just the truth."

"That's perfect." She added a scarf and gloves, then stepped into her mukluks. "I'm not brave enough for dress shoes."

"Trust me, you chose wisely. I came from a meeting with a Realtor. He keeps me in the know about local estates that need attention. And he's always trying to get me to sell the store."

"Really? You're thinking of selling?"

"We haven't made a dime on that place in years. It's my grandfather's hobby, at best. I opened the store in Duluth three years ago, and it's thriving. But this place . . . I'm thinking it's time to cut our losses." He reached for the door. "Ready?"

She gripped the collar of her coat, braced herself, and nodded.

The cold could peel the skin off her face. She hustled out to Monte's truck, and the gallant man opened her door, touched her elbow as she climbed in. Then closed the door behind her and ran to his side.

The cab held on to the slightest hint of warmth from his drive over. Still, she was shivering by the time they arrived at the VFW, only three blocks away. Cars jammed the parking lot and Monte pulled up to the door. "I'll let you off here so you don't have to walk."

Again, chivalrous. He helped her down and held the door open for her. She waited by the door, listening to the music from the band onstage.

In her memory, she always pegged the local VFW as the place the rummies hung out. But not here. Pictures of servicemen lined the walls near the door along with a plaque with the engraved names of those who served. Patrons crowded every table, digging into baskets of fries and chicken fingers or burgers, and a few lumberjacks sat at the horseshoe bar. Neon bar lights, shaped in the names of breweries, lit an alcove where a group of enthusiasts jockeyed around a pool table.

At the front, the band sang a Creedence cover. She recognized a couple of the band members—oh, wait: *all* of them.

Claire and Jensen, Kyle and Emma. Her boat mates from last summer's dragon boat festival.

Shoot. Casper had mentioned the band was playing. He just neglected to mention where. She should probably leave—

"Wow, it's cold. I had to park two blocks away." Monte came in, his cheeks red, a gust of frigid air in his wake. He surveyed the room. "Are there any open tables?"

"I . . . I don't see any."

"I'm sure we can find one." He winked, then led the way into the room. She followed him, keeping her head down. Maybe, with luck, she could sneak in. Or better, maybe Casper had decided to hibernate.

Monte found them a table next to the pinball machine and held out her chair as if they were at a five-star restaurant. He helped her off with her coat, then gestured to the menu, tucked in the condiment holder, before he took her coat to the rack by the door.

She might have lost her appetite. Instead, she focused on the band. Noticed that Claire looked pregnant. Of course.

Monte returned in a moment and sat across from her. "It really is worth it, I promise!" he said above the song.

She smiled, nodded, hoping.

Over his shoulder, she noticed others she recognized. Annalise and Nathan Decker sat with Noelle and Eli Hueston. Tucker Newman, the snowboarder, laughed with a group of friends at another table.

She'd forgotten how small this town could be. Yeah, she'd definitely lost her appetite.

"Hey, Monte, when did you get back?" Their server, a shapely blonde in her midtwenties, set down two glasses of water, a hint of intimacy in her smile.

"Signe. Hi." He shifted in his chair. "Just today." He turned to Raina. "Raina, this is Signe Netterlund. Her family runs the local waste control—"

"The dump, honey. We run the dump." She winked at Raina. "Monte's just being unusually tactful."

His mouth tightened around the edges. "Well, we junk collectors need to stick together."

Signe laughed, dropped a possessive hand on his shoulder. "What'll ya have tonight? We have a spare rib special going on."

"Burgers. Two of them." He glanced at Raina for confirmation. "Or . . . cheeseburgers?"

"A burger is perfect. Medium rare."

"And a basket of fries to share?"

"Comin' right up."

As Signe headed off through the masses, Raina made the mistake of watching her go.

Because the woman's next stop was Casper Christiansen, sitting with a buddy, nursing a Coke, his head bobbing to the band. She put a hand on his arm, flirted with her smile, her posture, then laughed as she nodded and walked away.

It would help if he didn't look good. The embodiment of all Raina's memories, wearing a red flannel shirt, the sleeves rolled up to reveal his tanned forearms. Sprawled back in his chair, casual. He held a straw between his fingers, playing with it as he listened to the music. Comfortable.

And not giving her one second of thought.

When the Blue Monkeys finished their set, she watched as Casper clapped, then got up as if to leave.

"Raina?"

Monte turned to follow her gaze.

Oops. "Great band, huh?"

He turned back, still frowning, then took a sip of his water.

She would not allow Casper's memory to haunt her date. A hum of conversation settled over the room as the band exited the stage. "I finished the dining room and packed up all the china. I think there is a couple grand, at least, there. And today I found a collection of Hummels—just a few of them, but I know they'll fetch a great price."

Monte played with his glass. Looked again over his shoulder. Back at her. "Who were you looking at?"

Oh. Uh. "Casper Christiansen. He . . . I saw him at the historical society. He . . ." She scrambled for something. "We found a letter tucked into this book of poetry that I delivered to the society. Remember, you told me to box up everything—"

"Right." He leaned back. "So what did the letter say?"

"It was from Thor, to his wife. Something he probably wrote on his deathbed. The usual—apologizing for mistakes, etc. But he mentioned a guy named Duncan, and Casper told me this story about a bootlegger—"

"Duncan Rothe. I know the story. A bootlegger from Chicago. He came up here with some kind of fortune, only to vanish."

"Right."

He seemed to forget Casper now as he leaned forward, stirring his water with his straw. "It's just a tall tale. My grandfather looked into it but could never find any evidence that it was true." He looked at her. "Did you find anything else that might corroborate his story?"

It touched her lips to tell him about the diary and Aggie's mention of Duncan on the pages, but it felt like maybe Aggie's thoughts should remain private.

Or at least between Raina and Aggie.

"No. But it does feel a little strange to go through her house. It's like she's speaking to me through her things. What she kept, how she cared for them."

"Raina! You're back!" Claire's voice parted the conversation, and Raina got up to intercept her hug. "You look great. Catering with Grace seems to agree with you."

Raina didn't know what to make of that comment, except, okay, maybe she had been too skinny before. "Thanks?"

"I wish I had your hair. It's so full and gorgeous. I heard pregnancy is supposed to make your hair thick and shiny, but mine is still sad and thin."

Raina's eyes widened. How—?

"I have to know—what shampoo do you use?"

Raina let out a shaky laugh. "Nothing special."

"Well, you look great, and . . . Oh, hi, Monte." To Raina's eye, it looked like Claire's smile fell, but she recovered fast. "Nice to you see again."

Monte's eyes, however, seemed cold. "Claire."

Claire squeezed Raina's hand, shot another look at Monte, then said, "Call me if you want. I've missed you."

Raina nodded, warmed by Claire's greeting, even if she'd seen a few heads in the crowd turn.

She sat, glancing past Monte to Casper's chair.

He'd vanished, just as she'd hoped. Except she couldn't deny the faintest twinge of disappointment. What, did she want him to see her out with another man? Stupid. Oh, so stupid, because she knew what happened when Casper got jealous.

Another good reason to forget him.

"What did Claire mean by 'you're back'?" Monte asked. "I thought you just moved here."

"I . . . I lived here last summer. But I moved to Minneapolis this past fall—worked as a caterer."

"Mmm," he said, staring at his glass.

She had the unsettling feeling that he thought she was lying.

Signe showed up with the hamburgers and fries, and Raina's appetite returned with ferocity. She cut the burger in half, dug in. "This is fantastic."

Monte smiled then, a twinkle again in his eyes. "I know, right? Stick with me, Raina. I'll bring you to all the best places."

He winked, and suddenly the strangeness in his demeanor vanished. Perhaps she'd simply read into it—after all, she did have secrets to keep, and sometimes it felt like they sat right on top of her skin.

The Blue Monkeys returned and played a set of oldies that had her singing along. She noticed Monte singing too, and at the break, he told her about crazy Nona Lillibridge, who insisted that she had ghosts living in her attic and had roped Gust into sitting up every night for a month to catch them.

"I think she just had a thing for Grandpa, but he's never gotten over losing Grandma. He's very loyal that way." Monte took a sip of his water, finishing it off. "We all are, actually."

He asked her to dance once and didn't push when she turned him down. But later, as they left, he slipped his hand into hers.

Raina let him because his hand was warm. At the door, he

donned his gloves and ducked out into the icy blast to retrieve the truck.

When he pulled up, he helped her into the cab and drove her home, walking her to the door.

"Thanks for going out with me, Raina. Can I call you again?"

See? Gallant. The perfect Valentine's date. She nodded, and he left a kiss on her cheek.

Raina pressed her hand against it as she watched him drive away. Now that was the kind of man a girl could fall in love with.

And she hadn't thought of Casper once.

In at least an hour.

Casper shouldn't let it bother him.

What was Raina doing with Monte Riggs? The sight of them dug a tunnel through him, and he'd had to leave after the Blue Monkeys' second set. He'd heard Claire greet Raina—who hadn't, really?—and Casper had to wince, just for a second, as he saw her glance at Claire's belly. But . . .

But yes, she seemed to be moving on, exactly like she'd stated at the historical society.

Moving on with Monte Riggs.

Casper had fumed in silent frustration in the shadows, watching them eat their hamburgers, watching her laugh at his jokes, and then left before he could call himself a stalker.

He eased up on the gas around an icy corner, clamping a fist over his emotions. It shouldn't bother him. Not with his anger over her recent choices. He should let her walk away before she did any more damage to his family.

To him.

Except . . .

Monte Riggs.

He pulled up to the lodge, let the fact that he had to hunt for a parking space cheer him. Maybe with the resort nearly full, Darek would stop grousing about the bills and how Casper left the lodge lights on.

Still, the frigid cold burned his skin as he got out to run to the lodge, and by the time he stamped his feet off in the private entryway, the boil had returned to his chest.

"Whoa, you sound like a herd of elk." Darek emerged from the office area carrying a cup of coffee. "What's with you?"

"Nothing."

He should have ordered food at the VFW because now his stomach clenched, empty and churning. Opening the fridge, he found leftover stir-fry Ivy had left for him—or probably Darek. He pulled out the container. "Do you mind—?"

"Have at it. I'm going to eat with Ivy."

Casper glanced at the clock. "You should take off. The roads are getting icy."

"I still have one more check-in." Darek slid onto a kitchen stool. "Then I'll go."

Casper dumped the beef and pea pods with rice onto a dish and stuck it in the microwave. "I can check them in."

Darek's silence dug into him, and Casper rounded on him. "Seriously? You don't trust me enough to do check-in?"

Darek shook his head. "It's not that. It's just . . ." He sighed. "You wouldn't get it."

"I wouldn't get responsibility? Needing to stick around? Is that what you mean?"

Darek held up a hand. "No. That's not what I mean. It's just,

I'm worried, and it'll make me feel better to know everything is okay. Listen, I'm counting on you to be here should there be any problems this weekend."

That tempered Casper's heat. "Okay. Yeah. But you know, I can handle checking in guests. You can let go a little."

Darek stared at his coffee. "So can you."

Huh? Casper frowned. "What are you talking about?"

"Ivy saw Raina in town." Darek looked up, met his eyes. "Please tell me that's not why you returned to Deep Haven. Some sad attempt to win her back?"

Casper's mouth closed, his jaw tight. "No. I had no idea she'd returned. It was just a *happy* coincidence."

He turned back to the microwave, took out the food and stirred it, then stuck the dish inside and heated it again. He stared at himself in the reflection of the glass. "I saw her tonight, though."

"Go figure."

Casper turned and Darek held up his hands in surrender. "I'm just sayin', you have angry ex written all over you. I'm seeing a flashback—"

"Don't go there, Darek. I very much regret the fight, okay? I agree I lost it, but if you knew all the details—"

"I know Owen slept with the girl you had a thing for."

"Thanks. Thanks for that." Casper opened the microwave.

"If it were me, I might have beaten the tar out of him also. But then you walked away, Casper. And now you're back, and so is she, and she's clearly not out of your system."

Casper put the food on the counter, his appetite evaporating.

"That's the problem, isn't it? You can't let her go."

"I can let her go. I want to let her go, but she's right here."

Casper pointed to his head. "And every time I think I'm past it, she shows up. With Monte Riggs."

"Huh?"

Casper stirred the food, then set his fork down. "She went out with Monte tonight—for Valentine's Day. She was at the VFW."

"And that's a disaster because . . . ?"

"Because she doesn't know Monte like I do. Like most of us do. The guy's a jerk. He always thought of himself as the world's gift to women. He did a lot of locker room bragging."

"I sort of remember that."

"Well, Monte was not only arrogant, but he's mean too. He once took a baseball bat to Rhino Johnson's truck just because the guy parked in front of him."

"Rhino did have issues with parking—no wonder his truck looked so wrecked."

"Did you hear me? A *baseball bat*—"

"Dude. We all did stupid things in high school. Doesn't make us the same people today." Darek raised an eyebrow. "You gotta stop acting as if she belongs to you."

"I'm not—"

"Yes, you are. She's not yours to control or judge."

Casper leaned against the counter, arms crossed. "I can't help but think that God put her in my life for a reason. If not, then why is it so hard for me to let her go?"

"He probably did, but maybe not for the reason you're hoping. The fact is, when God brings Christians into the lives of the hurting, it's because He intends to use us to be truth and light to them. Not fix their problems but point them to the One who can."

Casper looked away. Yeah, he'd spent most of his summer

trying to fix Raina's deep wounds with no idea that his brother was the source.

"If you really want to help her, maybe you should step back and just start praying for her. You're a fixer—I know this—and I know that you want to push your way into her life, make sure she's okay, but you can't. If you have to be anything, be truth to her. Be patience. Be light. But let all this anger and darkness go." Darek took a sip of coffee. "Trust me on this. Hanging on to the past will only eat you alive."

"So pray for her and then watch her destroy her life with Monte Riggs? Ouch. No, I'm not interested if that's God's plan."

"You seem to think that God owes you an explanation for what He does in people's lives. You want to be involved, but only if you get to choose what happens. You don't. God tells us to be light, but you can't make her choose the right path. Nor should you." He got up. "Because you're not God."

Casper pursed his lips.

Darek paused, considering him. "I think if Dad were here, he'd say something like, the thing about light is that it doesn't come from us. It's God in us that provides the light to the world. So if you want to be light to her, you'd better make sure that light is shining in you first."

Yeah, their dad would say that.

The bell rang in the office.

"Our guests have arrived. I'll tuck them in, and then I'm going home to my beautiful wife to celebrate Valentine's Day."

"I think I hate you," Casper said, smiling.

"Of course you do," Darek said as he closed the door behind him.

Casper stared at the food. He could go for a hamburger. Fries. But here he was, eating leftovers.

Fine. Clearly he couldn't shake free of Raina. So, yeah, maybe he'd pray for her. Be a true friend, somehow.

Maybe, in fact, that's what he should have been doing all along.

Darek had spent nearly the entirety of Valentine's Day helping other people find romance. He'd tucked guests into ten of the twelve cabins—a triumph, especially given the slick roads and frigid temperatures that had the northland in an icy lockdown.

But by the looks of the couples who'd arrived for the weekend special he'd advertised, the temperatures outside wouldn't put a damper on the heat inside.

He had his own romance heating up in his head as he drove to Deep Haven. Next year, he'd simply walk across the expanse of the resort to go home, but he still had to finish hanging Sheetrock, painting, and laying the floor of their new home. And with the resort's doors open and all the winter maintenance, he had his hands full keeping the place running.

Yeah, he could use some help. Should have probably taken Casper up on his offer to help him check in the last guest.

But he couldn't get past the worry that Casper would let something drop and . . . then a seventy-five-year-old legacy would disappear.

Not that Casper would forget something, but . . .

Casper *might* forget something. Darek could admit that he didn't completely trust his kid brother not to drop the ball. A deposit. Or freshly delivered firewood. Or even checking on the unoccupied cabins during the deep freeze.

Poor guy was lovesick. But so was Darek.

He pulled up to his two-bedroom rental house, the outside light shining over the icy steps. But he was surprised at the dark windows—he expected at least the kitchen lights to be blazing.

Oh no, was he supposed to bring home dinner? Or . . . roses! He'd completely forgotten anything for Ivy. No chocolates, roses, dinner—

She'd probably gone to bed, heartbroken. He eased the door open, listened.

No light cascaded down the hallway. Even for Ivy, 9 p.m. was early to turn in for the night.

He toed off his boots, trod down the hallway, and softly opened the door. In the shadows, the bed appeared unoccupied. He flicked on the light.

Empty.

Across the hall, he opened Tiger's door. Again, empty.

Huh. He headed back to the kitchen and turned on the light.

His heart fell. Rose petals were scattered over the kitchen table, a note tented on top. He reached for it and read Ivy's invitation to join her for dinner.

Reservation at 8 p.m.

So he was only an hour late. He could still make it. Tugging his boots back on, he returned to his truck. Pulling out his cell phone, he went to text her, but discovered it had died. Shoot—she'd probably tried to contact him.

Some Valentine's Day. He plugged in the phone, but it was too dead to power on, so he put the truck into drive and headed out of town to a tiny Irish restaurant down the shore.

His amazing wife knew how he loved bangers and mash.

The ten-minute drive didn't allow enough time for the phone

to charge, and his heart fell even further when he reached Mulligan's and searched for her car. Inside, the hostess told him she'd left over thirty minutes ago.

He sat in the lot, willing his phone to power up.

When it did, he found three voice messages waiting. The first had come earlier in the evening, as Ivy waited at the restaurant. The next informed him that she loved him but was going home.

The last, however, took his breath from his chest.

"Darek, I hit a deer and slid off the road somewhere before County Road 13, and the car won't move. I'm stuck. I know you're busy at work, but if you could come and get me, that would be . . . great."

The call ended and he noted the time. Over an hour ago.

He hit his speed dial, but the phone went immediately to Ivy's voice mail.

He put the truck in drive, his heart thundering in his ears. "Hang on, honey."

He drove slowly with his high beams on. Along this part of the road, the highway dropped off to the lake below, and farther, past County Road 13, Cutaway Creek had claimed a number of lives over the years.

Please, God.

He slowed, spying tracks tunneling off the highway as if the driver had spun out. The car had cut a jagged swath through the snow. As he slowed to a stop, he forced himself to breathe.

No wonder no one saw it. She'd rammed the back of her car into the bank, snow encasing it, the front end smashed, her lights obliterated, the hood crumpled where the deer landed.

Please, don't let the deer have hit the windshield.

He spied the animal then, not ten feet away, a bloodied mass on the highway, and his heart tore in two. She'd dismantled the deer—which only meant that it could have dismantled her.

He replayed Ivy's message in his head even as he got out, scrambling down the hill. *I know you're busy at work—*

"Ivy!" He fought the snow, slogging toward her in the scar she'd made, his headlights cutting away the shadows. "Ivy!"

He saw her then, sitting in the car, eyes closed. "Ivy!" He banged on her door, struggled to open it.

She opened her eyes with a start, reached over, and unlocked the door, helping him push it open. "Darek!"

He muscled his way past the door and the snowbank and dropped to his knees. "Are you okay?"

The air bag had deployed, now lying in a crumpled sack on her lap. She shivered, her face pale. "I'm sorry about the car."

"Are you kidding me? Sorry? Baby—oh, my." He unhooked her seat belt and pulled her to himself, shaking. "Shh. Just . . ." He closed his eyes. "It's okay. It's okay."

"Darek, I'm fine." She pushed away from him. "Cold, but you found me."

He put his hand on her stomach. "And the baby—?"

"Moving around. Fine." She pressed her gloved hands to his cheeks. "I'm so sorry. I wanted to surprise you. You've been working so hard, and I thought if I made reservations and left a note . . . I should have figured out that you'd have to work late." Not a hint of rancor or blame in her voice.

He sat back, leaned against the door, feeling nauseous. The noise that came out of him sounded more pained than relieved.

She shouldn't have been out alone tonight. Why hadn't he listened to her suggestion to ask Casper to fill in? He might have spared his brother the agony of seeing the woman he should forget out with another man.

And he could have treated his wife to the Valentine's Day she deserved.

How could it be that after everything he'd survived, everything he'd learned since Felicity died, he could possibly repeat his mistakes? But yeah, he was going to blow this again. Clearly he didn't have the faintest grasp on how to be a father, husband, and owner of his own business.

Ivy turned to him, grabbing his jacket. "Listen to me. I'm fine. Tiger is spending the night at his grandparents' house. It's just us. Let's get the car out of the ditch and go home. We can still have a beautiful Valentine's Day."

He stared at her, wordless. Then, "The car is totaled. The deer annihilated it."

"Oh no." She put her mitten to her mouth. "Do you think the deer is dead?"

This was why he loved her. He took her hand. Gave her a sad nod. "I'm so sorry." He got up and began to lift her from the seat.

And that's when she cried out.

"What is it?"

"Oh, ah . . ." She pressed her hand into her side, and her expression made him swoop her up into his arms.

"Hang on, baby."

Raina walked into his dream like she belonged there, her footsteps along the rocky shoreline leaving divots as the pebbles spilled out behind her. The late-afternoon sun, a simmering ember across the horizon, caressed Casper's skin, nourishing, as he walked beside her.

Her fingers laced through his, curled tight, and between them, their hands swung as if strolling down an uncharted beach at twilight was something to treasure, a rare and uncluttered moment.

Perhaps it was. Because instead of chasing the dream away, Casper leaned into it—the heat of summer on her tanned skin, the silky whisper of her hair on his shoulder as the wind caught it. Her hair was down, captured away from her face with a backward baseball cap—his—and she wore a marmalade sundress that showed off her long, tanned legs and turned her skin to a dark cocoa, almost edible.

The sense of her beside him could turn him weak, and now it only lured him further into the dream, his heart a live ember in his chest.

Then she laughed, sprinkling the dream like fairy dust, as if he'd said something right, and warmth bloomed through every cell in his body.

Oh, he loved her. That unblemished thought wound around him, and he let it take him, drank it in.

She clasped her other hand over theirs and leaned close to him, turning slightly. Her beautiful brown eyes bore a gold shine to them, bright and free of the shadow that would come.

"Is that what you want? To be a treasure hunter?"

"I'd like to find something precious, yes. Maybe Blackbeard's treasure. Or a lost artifact from the Crusades."

She hadn't laughed at him, not even a hint of the quiet ridicule he often felt from his family. She could hold him captive with her gaze, the way her eyes danced in the sunset, the waves against the shore, whispering.

"Mostly I just want to find the things hidden, the treasure that no one sees or doesn't think to look for."

"So Indiana Jones is a better description." She nodded, a smile lifting the corner of her mouth. "That seems about right—you already have the leather jacket, the motorcycle . . ."

"The pretty girl." He turned on the beach, took her beautiful face in his hands. He ran his thumbs over her cheekbones, then dropped them to her shoulders, delicate yet strong, her skin warm under his touch. "What I want to know is, how did I get so lucky as to find you?"

She leaned in, her lips a fraction from his, so close he could nearly taste them. Just lean down and brush them with his, a stolen, dangerous touch. "Because if anyone can find a lost treasure, it's you."

Then she kissed him. Sweetly, her lips on his top lip, then bottom. As he curled his hand around the back of her neck, pulling her to himself, she melted into him, letting him deepen the kiss.

The feel of her in his arms again could take him under. She smelled of vanilla and jasmine, of summer and freedom and hope, and as he kissed her, he began to drink her in.

Thirsty.

He could hear his own breath start to shudder, and that's when the dream began to splinter.

Casper held on tighter, his kiss almost fierce, possessive, as he felt her slip away, as the sun dissolved from the sky, as the taste of her turned to ash in his mouth.

And just like that, she vanished.

No.

Raina—oh. His heart thundered in his chest, and he opened his eyes to a darkened room, tasting salt on his lips. He touched his face, soggy, and wanted to be disgusted with himself.

He released a shaky breath, then ran a hand through his hair and threw off the covers, letting the bracing chill yank him further from the treacherous grip of the dream.

Sitting up, he put his feet on the cold floor, relishing the jolt, then got up and walked to the window. His entire body trembled, the power of the dream still inside him, and he ground his jaw against the terrible ache in his chest that nearly brought more tears.

He hung his hands on the windowsill, leaned his forehead against the cool glass, hoping to sear away the images. The taste of her that still lingered like a poison on his tongue.

"Why, Lord? Why can't I get her out of my brain? Why is this so hard?" He'd had other girlfriends, women who'd walked into his life and back out, but no one had stayed, hung on, Velcroed to his heart like Raina.

He couldn't place it. Jealousy? Maybe, but he'd forgiven her of her behavior with Owen, even if it was before she met him. Regret—yeah, but he didn't blame himself for fleeing, either.

"I want to forget her, be free of her. I do. But it's like You put her in my mind, in my heart, and . . . why won't You take her out?" He lowered his voice, and it emerged through the broken glass in his chest. "Please."

He listened for a moment, then stepped back and headed down to the kitchen. He found a glass, filled it with water, drank it halfway down as he moved to the sliding-glass door that overlooked Evergreen Lake. A silvery moon in a perfect sky puddled light over the expanse, turning the snow to diamonds.

His brother's voice seemed to rise from the shadows. *The thing about light is that it doesn't come from us. It's God in us that provides the light to the world. So if you want to be light to her, you'd better make sure that light is shining in you first.*

Maybe Casper couldn't let Raina go because he'd seen a better, stronger, more capable version of himself in her eyes.

And then he'd run, doing everything he could think of to fill up the empty places she left behind. Travel, adventure, even coming home to start over despite the brutal, beautiful memories.

Maybe it wasn't so much that he couldn't escape Raina, but rather that he'd never really let God in to heal that void.

If he took a long, hard look, he'd been filling himself up with everything but God. Raina, yeah, but also his quest for adventure and the need to find something—be something beyond Casper, the middle son, the one standing in the shadows. The second choice.

If he wanted to escape the engulfing darkness of this hurt, he had to reach out for the light.

And only then could he be the light that Raina needed. Not his light—God's.

He rested his forehead on the glass, closed his eyes. "Help me, Lord. Make me Yours. Fill this terrible longing with Yourself—with truth and hope and . . . love. Real love. Not the desperate, hopeless, deceitful love that tempts me to believe I can have her back, but the love that means it when I pray for her. The love that sets me free."

He looked up at the moon, glistening in the sky. "Be light in my life, Lord. Show me the truth. Illuminate my path. Ignite the man You want me to be."

Casper closed his eyes and stood just breathing in the quiet pool of moonlight.

CHAPTER 9

"Dad!"

Darek sat at the kitchen table, the computer open, his Quick-Books file up, a stack of bills littering the table. Outside, icicles hung like daggers from the roof, the sun turning the snow brittle and sharp beneath the frozen, white sky.

Not technically a snow day, but the school feared sending kids outside in negative-windchill conditions. In his day, his mother would have bundled them up and tossed them outside to wreak havoc in the yard instead of her living room.

He picked up the electric bill, studying it. How did it double last month? Maybe from the endless hours burning the wick to get cabin three back to working order. He looked at the number, then plugged it into the QuickBooks account, along with the kilowatts used.

"Dad!"

Housekeeping too? How could he have higher housekeeping expenditures than two years ago? Except, yeah, they hadn't been open in January back then. Still, he'd have to call the service, see if they'd work out a deal.

"Dad!" Two grimy hands clamped Darek's face, turning him. Tiger peered at him with wide brown eyes, his hair a curly mop. Darek realized his son was still wearing his Spider-Man pajamas despite it being long after lunchtime. "The macaroni is boiling over!"

Maca—? "Oh no!" Darek launched himself out of his chair, sending it spinning, but not before Ivy hustled into the kitchen.

"I got it!" She reached the stove, turned off the heat, moved the pan off the burner.

"No, you don't. Get back in bed." Darek crossed the kitchen and intercepted her at the sink, taking the rag from her hand. The gesture seemed a little too rough, so he softened his voice. "Please."

She could take him apart with a look, despite being dwarfed by his height. She swam in one of his flannel shirts, with the exception of her basketball tummy. With her red hair in a simple ponytail, no makeup on her beautiful face, her green eyes were luminous. If he stopped long enough, they could tear him away from the raucous mess of his worry into a place where he could believe everything would be fine. Better than fine.

Yeah, moments like this, he thanked God she hadn't walked away from him the thousands of times he deserved it. "Babe, you should be in bed . . ."

"I'm fine, Darek. The doctor said two days of bed rest. It's been four, and you should be back at work."

"He said at least two days, maybe a week."

"I'm fine. And I know you're worried about the resort."

He wiped the water from the stove and dropped the sodden,

steamy rag in the sink. Then he guided his wife to a kitchen chair. "I'm not worried—"

"You've called Casper eight—no, *fifteen*—times a day over the past four days. He's had to take off work so I could lie in bed and watch reruns of *Doctor Who*."

"At least you got caught up. What do you think of the new doctor?"

She gave him another dismantling look, and he sighed, crouched in front of her. "Listen, you might feel just fine, but I'm not taking any chances. It could have been worse, Ivy. Much worse." His throat tightened with the sudden rush of what-ifs. "You're staying in bed at least another day. And I'm not going anywhere. Who else is going to take care of you?"

"I can, Dad!" Tiger had climbed atop the table and now leaped off it, landing like a monkey on Darek's back. Darek grunted, the force knocking him to his knees, into Ivy. He caught himself—barely—on the edge of the chair.

"Tiger!" He grabbed his son, pulled him off. "You could have landed on Mom. And hurt the baby."

Tiger scrambled to his feet, then stared at his father, wide-eyed. All at once, he took off, running down the hall. Slammed his door.

"Tiger!"

Ivy touched Darek's arm. "Stop, honey. He's just trying to get your attention. It's the first stretch of time you've been home in a long while and he misses you."

"He could hurt you, jumping around like that, and he needs to know it." He started to get up, but Ivy grabbed his shirt, pulled him back down. Framed his face in her hands, forcing him to meet her eyes.

Her voice softened. "He would never hurt me, Darek. He is

exactly like you—protective and sweet—and he loves his baby brother or sister. At night, right before I tuck him in, he says a prayer for the baby and kisses my tummy. It's so sweet it makes me want to weep."

He could see it, Tiger's small hands hugging her belly, his son kissing it. And Darek was missing every moment.

"He could still hurt you without meaning to."

She nodded. "I'm fine, Darek. Please, be patient with him. Remember, he was here first, so he's bound to be feeling a little neglected with all this attention you're giving me."

"I'm not giving you enough attention." He raked a hand through his hair. "You could have died out there, Ivy! And I wouldn't have known. What if I decided to stay at the resort all night, waiting for guests? You would have sat there, maybe going into labor . . ." The thought wrapped tentacles around his chest, threatened to strangle him. He stood and stalked away from her, staring at the blue shadows of the late afternoon crawling across the yard. "I don't know if I can do this."

Silence.

Then a sigh shuddered out of her. "I'm sorry. I know the baby was unexpected. We never talked about it, and I thought that it would be a good thing, but I . . . Yeah, I should have realized . . ." Another sigh.

Her words washed over him, then dug in and left him cold. He turned. "Wait—do you think I don't *want* this baby?"

Ivy met his eyes for a terrible moment, then looked away, that same stripped expression on her face from two weeks ago when he'd broken the light fixture in the cabin. When he'd . . . when he told her that Casper had to choose between his dreams and responsibility. Oh no.

Darek crouched before her, looking into her beautiful green eyes, his hands on her knees. "Oh, Ivy, do you think that somehow I've given up my dreams for you?" He ran his hand over her belly. "For our baby? For Tiger?"

"I don't know." She swallowed, wiped her cheek. "I just know that every day the birth of this baby gets closer, you seem more tense, more . . . unhappy."

He pressed his forehead onto her knees, looked back at her, his voice wrecked. "Ivy, the only reason I'm tense is because I know I can't do this—"

Her jaw tightened, pain in her eyes.

"*This*, meaning I can't be a great dad and a decent husband and take care of Evergreen Resort. We're sinking, babe, and I can't figure it out. How did my dad do it? He raised six kids and still managed to leave a legacy. I'm drowning in bills and . . ." He got up. Shook his head. "Casper had to take off work this week so I could be the husband I should be."

"Darek—"

"No, see . . . I'm not good at this. I can barely figure out how to do our accounting, and as for guests, well, my mom had this way of making everyone feel like they belonged, with her homey fires and fresh-baked cookies, but it all feels fake to me. I march guests out to their cabins like a Sherpa, and the whole time I'm actually mad that they're taking me away from you and Tiger."

He turned away, stared at the mess of bills on the table. "When did it all get so complicated?"

He didn't hear her move, just felt her tummy bump up against him, her arms go around his waist. She leaned her head against his back. "You're not in this alone, Darek. You have me and your parents. Casper."

He ran his hands over her arms, clasped around him, even as he stared out the window to their stamp-size backyard, buried in snow. Their nine-hundred-square-foot rental house shivered in the cold, the floors creaky, the window frosty.

She deserved better.

"The resort is my responsibility. And so are you and Tiger."

Ivy rose up and kissed his cheek, then directed his chin so that he met her eyes. "Is it?"

He frowned at her words. Uh, yes . . .

The phone rang, and she stepped away as he picked it up. "Casper, what's up?"

"Open your front door. Your bell isn't working."

Darek turned and saw Casper waving at him through the sidelight. He hung up and opened the door.

Casper pushed his way in, stood in the entryway, hands in his pockets. He wore dress pants, his hiking boots, a leather jacket, his dark hair streaming out of a knit tuque. He looked more like a resort manager than Darek ever had a hope to, with his usual attire of work jeans, tool belt, and a flannel shirt. "Okay, all the guests have checked out, and housekeeping came today and turned two cabins. They'll be back tomorrow for three more, and by Friday you should be all set. I checked the heat and the pipes on all the cabins, shoveled, sanded, and lit a candle and recited the Irish prayer for travelers over each unit."

"Funny."

"More than that, I've put my phone on vibrate while I go down to Wild Harbor and make sure Ned hasn't fired me."

"Casper, I'm so sorry—"

"I'm kidding, Bro. Of course Ivy's more important, and Ned gets that. But we're clear for me to go back to work, right?"

Darek nodded. "Thanks again. You . . ."

"Yeah, I know. I saved your backside. That's what I do. Fix things. Just call me the helper bunny." He lifted his hand. "Hey, Ivy."

She waved back, and as Casper left, a smile tipped her lips. "What?"

"Nothing. How about some macaroni and cheese?"

Casper could admit that he loved working on the Evergreen property, knowing his father, grandfather, and even the generations before that had seeded the land, fished the lake, and tromped the same wintry paths, once shaggy with evergreen and whitened birch. He loved the resort, the smell of woodsmoke from the stone fireplace in the lodge, the sound of the wood thrush in the trees, the crisp silence of a snowy night. Most days he'd willingly give up traversing the world to stay home and paint walls, rebuild rafters, and yes, bellboy suitcases to cabins.

But always he had the priceless, exhilarating option of walking away.

Until this weekend. Darek's frantic call Friday night had noosed him into four days of twenty-four hours' babysitting high-maintenance guests afraid to poke their noses into the subzero freezer that the north shore became.

He'd even run into town twice for pizza, apparently donning the role of local delivery boy.

Of course, it only dredged up the memory of finding Raina stuck in the mud last summer, eating a piece of naked, destroyed pepperoni that had slid onto the floorboards. She played delivery girl for Pierre's about as well as Casper made buttermilk biscuits for their guests.

After a smidge of coaxing, she'd hopped onto the back of his motorcycle, eventually wrapping an arm around his waist, and he might have fallen in love with her a little right then.

Oh, see, she so easily ran into his thoughts. Seeing her smile in memory seemed as natural as breathing.

Easier than trying to remember all the checkout details Darek texted him. The temptation to turn off his phone nearly took him, but then Darek just might pile poor Ivy and Tiger in the car and drive up to the resort—or, worse, call his buddy Jensen to come over and start handing out pointers. Type A, overachieving rich boy Jensen would have Casper chipping ice off the dock or offering snowshoe tours. He didn't know how Darek coped with the fact that Jensen's high-end luxury homes had suffered nothing of the devastation Evergreen Resort had faced from the forest fire two summers ago.

But he didn't have to think about that. Yeah, walking away held its very attractive merits, and Casper didn't wish for any of Darek's legacy.

In fact, the entire experience made him wonder if he was cut out for staying. Darek's words sat like a burr under his skin: *How long are you sticking around?*

For the first time since he'd returned, he considered the answer might be no. Maybe he should have returned to Roatán, to treasure hunting.

"You sure you're okay to close?" Ned said, slapping the keys into his hand. "Don't forget to turn the heat down and close the shades in front. And drop the night deposit at the bank on your way home."

"Thanks, Ned," Casper said. "I know I put you in a tight spot."

"Nah." Ned shrugged on his jacket. "With the cold snap, this place is a graveyard. We'll need to figure out how to get some traffic in the door and move some merchandise before spring shows up." He pulled on his stocking hat. Stopped at the door. "By the way, my sister said she saw you at the VFW on Valentine's Day. Without a date." He pointed at Casper. "We need to remedy that, pronto."

Casper held up his hand. "I'm good, Ned—"

But Ned was already out the door, leaving Casper just a bit cold at the thought of the prospects he might dig up.

However, if Raina could move on, date someone new, so could he.

The thought pressed a fist into his gut.

Another reason to leave the moment winter eased its grip.

He vacuumed the store, checked the stock, printed and filled the online orders, then closed the till and ran the final report for the day.

At eight o'clock he shut the door, the wind like knives against his flesh. He ducked his chin into his jacket, pulled his hat down, and hustled to the truck. Tossing the money pouch onto the seat, he climbed in, shivering as the engine turned over and blasted frozen air from the heaters.

He should get home, check on the cabins, but four days away from the historical society had his brain conjuring up a slew of what-ifs about Duncan Rothe and Thor's letter. Which would probably only lead to a dead end and, worse, possessed the terrible power to rouse the image of Raina and her surprise as he met her at the door. Those widened amber-brown eyes, not unlike the moment on the shore last summer when he'd shown her the sunset over the lake. Or when he'd finally scrounged up the courage to trace his hand down her cheek, pull her close, catch her lips with his. She'd tasted of soda, and the little sound she made of delight, of surrender, could still find him, deep in the night.

Or any time of day.

Yeah, maybe he should steer clear of the mystery of Duncan Rothe.

The truck began to warm, blasting out tepid air. Casper shook himself from the memory and drove to the bank. He parked and dropped the pouch in the night deposit slot.

From across the street, the smell of baking pizza crust and garlic stirred his hunger. It wasn't like he had anything at home waiting for him. He left the truck parked and jogged to Pierre's.

Only a couple patrons lined up in front of him. He pulled off his gloves and ordered a pizza to go.

He was turning to wait when Monte Riggs walked into the lobby.

The man wore a fancy black wool coat, a suit and tie, like he might be a big shot from the Cities instead of a local junk dealer. His gaze fell on Casper for a moment, settled, something cool in his expression, then slid away.

Just walk away. Casper didn't know if the thought was for him or Monte, but he let it steel him, keep him moving forward.

Except Monte's voice slithered over Casper, low and dark. "I know all about you and Raina last summer, Casper."

Casper stilled, turned.

For a split second, he was taken back to high school, to that day when he'd found Monte and Beth Johnson alone in the weight room, Monte pressed up against her, his hands under her shirt.

He might never erase the look in Beth's eyes when she saw him or the way she ducked under Monte's arm and dashed out past Casper, not looking at him as if embarrassed.

Or . . . afraid?

Nor would he forget the gleam in Monte's eyes, something of triumph or perhaps power. Or the way he watched Beth flee, a smile twitching his thin lips.

Casper had stood there, unable to move as Monte swaggered past him. "Girls. They never know what they really want."

That smile was seared into his brain, and Casper saw it now, inching up one side of Monte's pale face. "And in case you get any ideas, she's over you. She's mine now."

An anvil landed on Casper's chest. "Raina doesn't belong to anybody." But his hoarse whisper gave him away and he pushed out into the night before he did something stupid.

Except he couldn't leave, not with that memory reminding him that back then, he'd done nothing—*nothing*.

The door jangled as Monte exited, holding a pizza. Casper's patience escaped in a hard exhale, and he rounded on Monte.

Who probably expected him because he betrayed not a hint of surprise in those cool hazel eyes. "What?"

What? Oh, he could give him what, longed to show him exactly *what* by delivering the answer right here on the frozen sidewalk.

No. He took another breath. "Raina's . . . she's fragile, okay? She's been through a lot and puts up a good front, but she's been hurt—"

"By you?"

Casper's mouth closed. He heard the word *meddling*—it perched in the back of his brain. But he refused to listen. "There's history you shouldn't start digging around in. Just walk away, Monte. She's not the girl for you."

The smile appeared again. "I think she's exactly the girl for me. And don't you worry about her being fragile. I promise I'll take very good care of her."

Then he winked.

Casper nearly lunged, nearly tackled him and his large pepper-oni onto the sidewalk. He had a very satisfying vision of slam-ming his fist into Monte's pretty face, correcting that nose, maybe emptying some of his frustration into the man's jaw.

Except, no. Because then he'd be the man he'd fled six months ago.

So he stood there, again watching Monte walk away, feeling like he might retch instead.

He closed his eyes, listening to his heartbeat thunder inside. *Let it go.* This was why he shouldn't get involved, shouldn't be so desperate to fix things.

He crossed the street, got in the truck, and drove to the histori-cal society, parking a half block away, which seemed silly, even to him, but he had to have a moment to sit in the car and just shake. Stare for a second at the stars poured out overhead in the crisp night and hang on to Darek's words: *You gotta stop acting as if she belongs to you.*

No, she didn't belong to him, and yes, hanging on to her could devour him. *Be patience. Be light. . . . Let all this anger and dark-ness go.*

He took a breath, trying to cling to his prayer. But how could he let her go when he saw the danger ahead?

Tonight, right now, he needed a distraction. He got out and crossed the street, unlocking the door to the historical society, flipping on the light, and heading to the back.

He'd deliberately waited to plow through the boxes of clothing in the storage room until he'd feasted on the trinkets, mostly to understand what manner of people he discovered. It helped him assign clothing to the right owner, even if it might be a guess.

He found nothing of historical significance in the first box, the contents more Goodwill clothing than artifacts. No formal tuxedos or, for that matter, voyageur wolf-tail caps or worn leather mukluks.

He closed the box, set it by the door, marked it for the Salvation Army, and opened the next. Baby clothes. A layette—a white knit christening gown with blue trim, a matching swaddling blanket, an embroidered cotton sleeping sack, but with it, a pair of bell-bottoms, a cowl-necked sweater, a plaid vest. He took out the layette, closed the rest up to donate.

The third box netted the same—contents that could be placed as far back as the eighties, things he might find in the depths of his mother's closet. Nothing of value.

He took another box, opened the top, saw a ratty brown wool sweater, and closed it again. Then he glanced quickly into the final box, lifting up one side.

Clearly whoever donated the collection hadn't stopped to sort the valuable from the trash, just handed it all over to the society.

He checked his watch and groaned. Pierre's had closed twenty minutes ago, his pizza now cold and locked inside.

A wasted, hungry night and his encounter with Monte still churning inside him. He'd dropped the boxes by the front door and was going back to the storage room to turn out the light when he heard a voice in the lobby.

"Yoo-hoo!" the voice sang. "Casper?"

He pulled the string to the overhead light and returned to the showroom. "Mrs. Draper, what are you doing here?"

She came in holding her keys, eyes wide. "Oh, goodness, it *is* you. I hoped so when I saw the light. I just finished a chamber meeting and was driving by and thought, my, my, that boy works late."

She wore a purple parka and a ski hat with pom-poms dangling around her ears. "Did you find anything of value tonight?"

He ushered her toward the door, turning out the light in the display room. "No. Just a bunch of throwaway clothing. I am starting to fear that the Linnell family considered us the local Salvation Army drop-off."

She stopped at the boxes. "No mysterious tuxedos?"

"I found a christening gown, but mostly a lot of plaid jumpers and bell-bottom jeans."

"I remember those days. Had myself a pair of paisley pedal pushers I still can't bear to give up. Ah, memories." She turned to the top box, tugged at it as if wanting to relive the past.

"I think my mother kept her entire wardrobe from the seventies—hey, is that a wedding dress?"

Edith had tugged silky white fabric out of the top box—the one he hadn't opened fully. "It certainly looks like it." She put her purse down, and he helped her release the dress, rolled up and shoved down the side of the box.

"It's immaculate," Edith said, holding up the skirt of the dress while Casper gripped the shoulders. "And looks lovely on you, by the way."

"I've always looked good in white," he said, winking, and draped the dress on the glass display of pictures for a better look. "I can't believe I missed this."

Edith arranged the skirt. "It looks Edwardian, given the high collar, the gigot sleeves. See how they puff out and then taper to the forearm? And this lace . . . it looks hand-tatted."

"Well done, Mrs. Draper," Casper said. "I didn't know you knew about early fashion."

"I didn't get my position as historical society president because of my good looks, sweetie." She held up the lace overlay. "The skirt is silk, I'm sure of it. And the V-shaped flounce on the bodice was to emphasize the S-corsets of the time. This is a very old dress, probably early 1900s. See if there's a tag. Often seamstresses of the time would embroider their name into the back, near the waistline."

Casper turned the dress over, opened the buttons, searching. "It's from the House of Worth."

"Oh, my. It's a Worth dress. That's . . ." She took his hands, pushed them away. "Darling, this dress could have been made by Charles Frederick Worth, a designer out of Paris in the Gilded Age. We should be wearing gloves."

"There's a name on the tag."

"Fine. Get some gloves on and we'll take a look."

Casper had to admit to some chagrin that he hadn't thought of that immediately. But he retrieved a pair of white cotton gloves and handed another pair to Edith, donned his own, then finished unbuttoning the dress. Took a flashlight to read the initials sewn into the tag. "C. A. F."

"C. A. F.," Edith repeated. "Anything else?"

"Nope."

"The dress is soiled at the hem as if it might have been worn." Edith lifted the dress, keeping the hem off the floor. "Get a padded hanger and a clothing bag and let's package it up. And then take those boxes back to the storage room. Just for one final look."

Her kind way of suggesting he might have missed something. Great archaeological work there, Casper.

After he found the clothing bag, brought it out to the front, he and Edith folded the dress inside. Then he returned the boxes to the storage room while Edith fired up the computer and plugged the initials into a search box of the catalogs and records of the historical society.

"I wonder . . ."

He came out to find her peering at the pictures in the display. "What?"

"Well, there is a story . . . You know that Naniboujou Lodge, the resort northeast of town, was built in the 1920s, right? It was built as a private club for the elite. Babe Ruth and Jack Dempsey were among the charter members."

"I'd heard that. They had big plans, right before the fall of the stock market."

"They called Lake Superior the ocean of the Midwest. Had plans drawn up that made it resemble Brighton Beach, complete with swim tents, shuffleboard, tennis courts, and a boardwalk."

"The playground of the wealthy, tucked into the north woods."

"The kind of place a debutante might come for her honeymoon?" Edith pointed to a picture in the case, one of a group of men surrounding a roadster, a couple standing next to the running board, waving. The woman wore a cloche, a long string of pearls; the man a dapper suit, his dark hair so shiny with Brylcreem it seemed fresh. "This came from the Naniboujou collection a few years ago. Just a sampling of the pictures they have donated over the years. But I do remember a picture that hung in the foyer for a long time—of a bride and groom, the first wedding at the resort. There was a tale attached to it. The story is that the bride disappeared the night of the wedding. Apparently she and the groom had a terrible row and she ran away. He went after her, and the two were never seen again. I was always mesmerized by that picture, wondering what the story could be."

He stared at the roadster, and it niggled a smoky memory.

What if the roadster was the same one discovered in the woods near Mineral Springs? The one rumored to belong to Duncan Rothe?

And right then, the flame ignited, the reason to stick around just a little longer. That and the untended hope of solving the mystery at last.

What if . . . ?

No. He needed to stop chasing after lost treasures. Lost causes.

"I wonder if the courthouse has a record of their marriage. You might check—it would certainly add legitimacy to the display." Edith turned off the computer, reached for her leather gloves. "I have to admit, I haven't had so much excitement in ages."

He laughed. And yeah, somehow digging into the past had kept his mind from turning over his confrontation with Monte. Maybe, just for now, the mystery could help him focus on something else. "I'll stop by tomorrow, see what I can dig up. And I'll go through each box with a fine eye."

Edith nodded, again with no judgment, although he deserved it. He flicked off the lights and closed the door behind them, locking it.

The chill had deepened, but it cleared the sky of any cloudy debris and turned on the sparkle, the canopy deep and velvety.

"Good night, Mrs. Draper."

"Stay warm, young man."

Casper got into his truck, waited until her car started and pulled away. Then he put his truck in drive.

He intended to take a left at the light, but the vehicle drove through, up to the next block, then turned left down the street.

Past Raina Beaumont's house, where Monte Riggs's truck sat outside. Light glowed from the front windows like a beacon, past the porch, into the snowy front yard, and he called himself a stalker.

Enough. "Lord, please bless Raina and make her wise. And safe."

The prayer loosened his chest, the tight grip of worry or maybe panic easing.

"And help her find peace from the pain of her past."

He took a right at the next road and headed to Evergreen Resort, not looking back.

The phone rang just as Monte was telling Raina a story about finding a collection of stuffed cats in a woman's attic, leaning in close to terrify her with a description of each feline. She let it go to voice mail.

He had eyes that could hold her, mesmerize her, toy with her, make her forget anything but right now—Monte and the large pizza he'd brought her for dinner.

She'd lit a candle and called it romantic as they sat on the floor in front of the crackling fire. He had stretched his long legs out on the braided wool rug, leaning on one elbow as he reclined, his shirtsleeves rolled up, his tie discarded and draped over the end of her sofa.

She'd never dated a businessman before and imagined he had important meetings with county officials. Like a politician, maybe.

Raina liked how he looked at her as though he respected her. Or at least the woman who'd spent the past week helping his grandfather organize his shop. With the subzero temperatures, she couldn't bear to work in Aggie's unheated house. Besides, she'd cataloged much of the main collections, bagged up the clothing, boxed the games and books, and bubble-wrapped the knick-knacks. Now she just had to dive into the files in the kitchen office drawers, as well as the bedside tables upstairs, where she'd discovered yet more books and the family Bible.

A big Bible, too, with names written inside the cover. She thought about donating it, then decided that she should ask Penny, the granddaughter. It seemed like something the family might want yet had overlooked, so she'd brought it home, intending to mention it to Monte.

Her cell phone buzzed again.

"Go ahead and get that," Monte said.

"Sorry." She got up, retrieving it. Frowned at the unfamiliar number on the caller ID. She glanced at Monte, who was freeing another piece of pizza from the box, then answered. "Hello?"

Monte was folding his pizza slice in half like a sandwich. He looked at her and grinned. A boy in a man's suit. She liked that, too.

"Raina? It's Dori, from Open Hearts Adoption Agency."

The voice doused any magic from the evening. Her voice fell, tight. "Is everything . . . uh, is everything okay?"

"Of course. But it's been over a month, and we like to do a follow-up with the birth mother to check in and make sure we're still on track for the formal adoption. Do you think you are ready to sign the final relinquishment papers?"

If she could, Raina would have signed the papers the first day. Just to have it all over, swift and final.

The longer she waited, the closer she came to turning back in a full-out run to snatch Layla into her arms.

To scream the words roaring in the back of her head. *No! I made a mistake! I want my daughter.*

She wondered if Dori could hear her hesitation, the hiccup of her words, failing at the end. "Yes. Of . . . of course . . ." She glanced at Monte, who'd finished off the slice.

"And you? How are you?"

Monte was watching her now. She gave him a smile, something quick and hopefully easy.

But just for a second, she nearly locked herself into a closet and begged for news about Layla. Was she healthy? Happy? And—yeah, okay, she probably just slept and ate, but suddenly the thought of little Layla bundled in a Plexiglas bassinet swept through Raina, singeing her throat.

She clenched her jaw against the swift urge to cry, but her voice still emerged tremulous and high-pitched. "I'm good, thank you."

"Feeling all right?"

She swallowed, found her breath. "Yes. I'm . . . great."

Or she would be in another month, once the final papers were signed. She wanted to tell Dori to send them now, but somehow the words lodged in her chest.

"Have you found a job?"

She glanced again at Monte. "Uh-huh." He was getting up now as if to walk toward her. Oh no—but he disappeared into the kitchen.

"You'll let us know if anything changes or if you can't make it to court—"

She heard water running in the kitchen, cut her voice low. "Actually, about that. Can you just have the papers sent to the court up here?"

"Uh, sure. I think we can work that out. Don't you want a final good-bye?"

"I had my good-bye. Thanks for calling, but please, don't

bother me again." She hung up just as Monte emerged from the kitchen.

He had untucked his shirt, his hair tousled, looking delightfully disheveled. "Everything okay?"

"Mmm-hmm," she said, nodding.

"I thought you mentioned something about court?"

She lifted a shoulder. "A speeding ticket in Minneapolis. I . . . uh . . . contested it."

"You gotta watch those cops. Especially around here. They'll arrest you for going two miles over. I swear they have it in for me." He took her hand, caught her phone, and set it on the sofa side table. "Now, where were we?"

He set his cup down, and she glanced to make sure it landed on a coaster. The last thing she needed was to mar Liza's—

Monte's hand slipped behind her neck. Raina looked up to see his eyes in hers, focused, intense. His intentions written in them.

Oh—

And just like that, he leaned down to kiss her. It took her by surprise—his smooth grip on her neck, the other hand sliding around her waist. With her arms crumpled up against his chest, she didn't quite know what to do. He was kneading her lips with his and it felt natural to yield, except nothing of desire or even warmth rushed through her.

In fact, she stood there, feeling awkward, as he made a little sound as if he might be enjoying the kiss more than she.

Suddenly he leaned back, looked at her, desire in his eyes. "You are so beautiful, Raina Beaumont."

She was just . . . scared, maybe. Or even, well, traitorous. Because while this handsome man entwined her in his embrace, all she could think about was the taste of pizza and how the last time she'd really been kissed, and kissed someone back, she'd been nestled in Casper's arms.

For a split second, she heard the waves, smelled the summer sun on his skin, felt the rub of his whiskers on her neck as he trailed kisses—

"Oh . . . uh . . ." She swallowed.

Monte leaned back again, cupping her face, his eyes gleaming, almost . . . victorious? "You're trembling. Are you okay?"

She nodded, smiled, just wanting to untangle herself from his grip. But a gal couldn't start over by running away, so . . .

She looped her arms around his neck, lifted her face.

He kissed her again, this time with more vigor, and she put real effort into kissing him back. Wanting to be here and calling her heart a turncoat for comparing him to Casper. Monte deserved better, so she even let him lower her to the sofa, press her into the cushions. Let him scoot his body close to hers as he ran his hand down her cheek, then lower.

It stopped at her shirt, the top button. That's when she came to her senses. She shook her head, levered her hand against his chest, making to scramble out of his grip.

However, he didn't quite catch up and lowered his mouth again, this time to her neck, his lips following a trail down her collarbone.

She pushed his shoulders. "Monte, I . . . uh . . . I'm not ready for . . ." She shook her head again, wishing for the right words. Love? A relationship?

A tawdry one-night stand?

All of the above.

He lifted his head and for a second appeared stricken as if he'd hurt her. He scrambled back and sat on the other end of the sofa, a blush rising in his face. "Sorry. I guess I forgot myself there." He gave her a sheepish look. "You have the ability to drive a man a little crazy, Raina."

Probably he meant it as endearing, but she only heard her sins in his words. She straightened her shirt and got up. Smiled, trying to find a voice that could put the entire thing behind them. "It's fine. I mean . . . of course, I like you and . . . but . . ." She exhaled, gathering her hair up, adjusting it into a clean ponytail. "Can we just take this slow?"

He stood, kicked the pizza box shut, and reached for his tie. "Of course." As he looped it around his neck, she felt like a tease. She must send off some unknown vibe that told men she was easy.

Other words popped into her head, but she refused them, wrapping her arms around herself. "Thanks for the pizza. You don't have to go. We could . . . watch a movie or something?"

He tucked his shirt into his pants, reached for his jacket. "Actually, I have an early meeting tomorrow, but I'll call you, okay?"

Right. She had the urge to grab his hand, apologize, tell him— what? That at the first opportunity she'd be glad to hand over her pride, herself, to him?

No. Not again.

She saw him to the door and tried to hold in the wail as he kissed her on the forehead, then hunched over and fled to his car.

Leaving her to stand in the family room, staring at the flickering firelight with a half-eaten pizza growing cold on the floor, as she tried not to call herself a fool.

CHAPTER 10

CASPER BARELY RECOGNIZED the sun when it appeared from behind the clouds, glorious and high in an azure sky, adding warmth to the crisp morning. He stood at the window, drinking a cup of coffee and staring at Evergreen Lake, watching a doe nudge her black nose out of the woods and tiptoe across the pristine stillness of the white expanse, her tawny body heavy with young.

Stillness fell in the lodge after the whir of guests, and he relished it, even to simply hear his own thoughts. To feel, for the first time, that he had broken free. Somehow, praying for Raina yesterday—on the way home and when her image slid into his thoughts later—had started to unlatch the terrible grip she'd claimed on his heart.

This morning he'd awoken with the sense that somehow Duncan Rothe and the mysterious wedding dress might be connected.

If so, maybe he had a real shot at finding the treasure of Duncan Rothe.

Now he dumped his coffee, rinsed his cup, and headed out to the truck. He'd stop on his way to Wild Harbor, see if Signe still had her day job in county records.

Turning on the radio on his way to town, Casper hummed along. *"It might seem crazy what I'm about to say. Sunshine, she's here; you can take a break . . ."*

In all his years of causing trouble in Deep Haven, never had it merited a trip to the courthouse. He pulled up to the three-story brick building, parked, and found the records office location on the directory in the lobby.

He rang the bell at the open window. Indeed, Signe, with her pretty long blonde hair and warm smile, came to the counter. "Casper Christiansen," she said as if his name were a song, and he found a smile for the girl he'd run track with his junior year. "I told you I was glad to see you the other night, but I didn't expect a visit so soon. I'm taken, you know."

He laughed. "Can't blame a guy for trying."

"You and Ned never change. He still flirts with me every time I come into Wild Harbor to rent a kayak."

"You can rent from me next time."

"Really?"

"I'm a . . . manager there." Almost. Except as the words fell from his mouth, they felt sedentary and pedestrian.

In his mind's eye flashed the silky beaches of Roatán. How had he ended up back in the frozen wasteland of northern Minnesota?

"Cool," she said. "So that means you're sticking around? I heard you were in Mexico or something, digging for treasure."

"Honduras, but yeah, I'm back. Actually, I'm working at the

historical society too. I have to dig up an old marriage certificate. I'm looking for someone who might have gotten married at Naniboujou back in the early days. Maybe with the initials C. A. F."

"Hmm." She went to the door, opened it. "Come in. This might take some sleuthing."

She gestured for him to follow her to a computer workstation. He sat on a straight chair while she typed in the search request.

"I don't see anything. You don't have a name at all?"

"How about Duncan Rothe?"

She put that request in and got a hit. "Yeah, I got one here. The license was issued to Duncan Rothe and . . . a Clara Augusta Franklin in June 1930."

"Really?"

"Yeah. Duncan Thomas Rothe—his full name. But it was never refiled, so it wasn't registered. I have a record of the signatures in the ledger, but no official marriage certificate."

"Can I see the ledger?"

"I have a picture of it, but the original is locked up in our off-site storage. Do you need it? Because I'd have to send in a special request to have a copy made."

"Can you print the picture?"

She nodded, and he heard the laser printer humming. She got up and handed him the grainy photo.

C. A. Franklin, in loopy handwriting. And tighter, in sharp, pointy strokes, *Duncan T. Rothe*.

He could taste his heartbeat. "Thanks, Signe. Come by for that kayak when the ice clears."

He headed over to the Wild Harbor, unlocked it, and had coffee brewed by the time Ned arrived.

"I think we need a winter clearance sale," Ned said as if Casper had tossed the night away puzzling over the need for customers. "Maybe a March Madness event."

"Sounds perfect." If Duncan showed up with Clara, intending to marry her, what had happened to the marriage certificate?

"I'm going to put together some specials. You figure out when to advertise."

And how did Aggie figure into the story?

"Casper?" Ned snapped his fingers in front of Casper's nose.

"Sorry. I was thinking about something we found yesterday at the historical society. An old wedding dress."

"Neat. But how about taking inventory of our current supply of winter wear so we know how much to mark them down."

Casper spent the morning surrounded by fleeces, wool socks, mukluks, and Gore-Tex. After Ned took a break, he walked over to the co-op for lunch, grabbed a cup of cauliflower curry soup, and sat down at one of the complimentary computer workstations.

He set his soup to the side, dumped in a handful of oyster crackers, and opened Google.

He started with *C. A. Franklin, 1930.*

A listing of hits came up, including a biography of Augustus and Clara Franklin. He reached for his soup.

Augustus John Franklin (1860–1930), president of American Steel and Co, 1904–1930. One of the early steel barons, John Franklin took over American Steel as president in 1904 and tripled its holdings into a $3.2 billion company at the time of his death.

Casper skipped over the early life and career information, scrolling down to the Family Life section.

A longtime resident of New York City, John Franklin kept homes in Newport, Rhode Island, and Chicago. Married to Clara Alice Franklin (née Bowman, 1880–1918) at the age of thirty-eight (1898).

He did the math. She'd been eighteen, her husband twenty years older. No wonder she'd run away—except, no. This was Clara Alice. Then who was Clara Augusta? He scrolled down, forgetting his soup as he read of Clara Alice's death in the 1918 flu pandemic.

He heard patrons enter the co-op lunch area, glanced around and saw a couple familiar faces. Turned back to the computer.

Clara Alice Franklin bore a daughter to the union, Clara Augusta Franklin (1908–1930).

Which meant she left her daughter motherless at the tender age of ten.

He opened a grainy black-and-white family picture of the trio in a separate window, stared at it. A solemn family, the father large and balding; the wife small, dark, fragile. The daughter pudgy-faced, her hair in braids tucked around her head.

A chair squeaked behind him, and he instinctively turned to look.

The patron, her back to him, set her tray of food on the table next to a leather book.

He stilled, his awareness of her so keen it could flood his pores, stop his heart. Today, with her hair in two braids under a pink fleece headband, that powder-blue jacket, and a pair of slimming yoga pants tucked into her boots, she looked like some version of a Norse princess.

He stopped his thoughts there. Closed his eyes. *Bless her lunch, Lord. Help her know that she's forgiven and that she can be set free from the past.*

Just like that, her power fled, and he breathed out the pressure in his chest. Returned to his reading.

> John Franklin died May 3, 1930, in a fire in his Chicago
> Avenue apartment. Deceased in the fire included his
> daughter and two house attendants, a valet and a
> housekeeper.

There went any leads.

Or not. Because how, if Clara Augusta died in a fire, could she take out a marriage license a month later in northern Minnesota?

He printed the picture as well as the article, then went to retrieve them and dropped a quarter in the cup. Maybe if he headed up to Naniboujou, they'd still have the picture Edith had mentioned.

He turned, and his world stopped.

"Hey, Casper," Raina said, standing in his way and smiling at him.

What would it hurt to talk to him, really? For ten minutes she'd snuck peeks over her shoulder at Casper, sitting on the high-top stool, scrolling the computer. For ten minutes she'd sifted through her emotions, testing them.

She might have been too hard on him at the historical society.

Her phone had vibrated and she'd smiled at the text message Monte had sent her. He wanted to see her tonight—so she hadn't destroyed their budding relationship with her hesitation.

She was moving on.

Which meant that maybe she could look back, see things without the pinch of heartbreak. See how she must have hurt Casper when she pushed him away—even before last week. As if he were somehow to blame for the fact that her heart so easily fell into his arms.

Casper couldn't help it that he could turn a girl to honey with his smile, the way his hair curled out from under his hat. He had an easy, let's-be-friends aura that she dearly missed, a laugh that could chase away the darkness that always seemed to threaten her.

She'd cut him off from her the way she might knock the snow from her boots, fast and hard, and now she rose above her shadowed pain to see the scars she'd left on him.

He'd run to Central America to flee her, returned with his heart plucked from his chest, and the gesture, the intensity of it, terrified her.

She simply didn't deserve that kind of devotion. But now that they were both moving on, maybe they could find a balance. Friendship. Something new and fresh. Safe.

So she'd closed Aggie's diary and gotten up, intending to simply sidle next to him, to apologize for her coldness earlier. But he headed to the printer, grabbing something out of it, dropping a quarter into the cup.

Then he turned.

And for a second, Raina rued her own impulsiveness. Trapped. Right there, in the middle of the co-op deli, surrounded by patrons eating their lunches, she was about to open her mouth and what—apologize for dismantling his life? For hurting his family, even if they didn't know it? Would never know it?

Casper stared at her, his eyes widening, the papers he'd printed held like a shield to protect him.

She came up with the only words she could muster. "Hey, Casper."

"Hey," he said. His flummoxed expression might have been cute—except for the flash of hurt that rose for a split second, only to die behind a mask of nonchalance.

She didn't want to consider that his hurt might still burn.

"What are you doing here?"

She gestured to her table. "I'm on lunch break from the shop, and . . . What are you researching? I saw the page open—"

He showed her the picture he'd printed. "Actually, I'm following up on that story I told you about—Duncan Rothe. We found a wedding dress in the boxes donated to the historical society, and it had the initials C. A. F. on it. So I went to the courthouse today and tried to track down the bride. I think I found her. Clara Augusta Franklin. But the article says she died in a fire in Chicago with her father, so I seemed to have run into a dead end . . ."

"Or not."

He frowned. "What are you talking about?"

"You have that funny tone to your voice. When you're trying to convince yourself that something is true, but you know deep down it's not. Like when you were trying to tell yourself that you should probably just quit the race last summer, when you knew perfectly well that we could win."

He gave her a slow smile, letting it slide over his face as if he'd pulled up the memory, found it pleasing.

"Okay, yeah." He gestured to the computer. "According to the article, Clara Augusta Franklin died in the fire in Chicago. But what if she didn't? What if she got out and ran away with Duncan Rothe? What if she and Duncan did get married at Naniboujou?"

"Did you say Naniboujou?"

"It's a resort—built in the 1920s, about fifteen miles northeast of here."

"Stay right here." She went back to her table and grabbed her tray, piling the book on it. Returned to the counter and slid onto a stool.

"Listen to this." She opened the diary.

"May 1930. The most wonderful day and the most terrible night. Duncan finally declared his love for me and proposed as we walked along the boardwalk of the lake, the oak trees stirring in the fragrant breeze. Of course I said yes, and then to my delight, he took me to the apartment with the bright news that Father had arrived in town."

Casper had slid onto his stool. "What are you reading?"

"The journal of Aggie Wilder." She glanced up, saw him watching her, and could see in his expression the old, easy friendship, the camaraderie. Yes, see, now that she had Monte, she could allow herself to put Casper in the right, permanent place in her heart. Friend.

"We arrived to the terrible discovery that Father had been murdered. Duncan found his body at his desk, shot, and although he bade me wait, I too impulsively ran in behind him to witness the horror. In my grief, Irina put me to bed.

"I awoke to the apartment in flames. Had it not been for Duncan, I would have perished. He tore me from the house in my nightclothes and we escaped death in Father's roadster."

Raina looked up and smiled at Casper's openmouthed expression. Without thinking, she reached over and touched his arm. "I know. But there's more."

She kept reading.

"He is taking me north, to a retreat where he says I can recuperate—his friend Jack's place, an Indian lodge of some sort. We will marry there, and someday I will forget all I have lost."

She closed the book.

"Where did you get that?"

"Aggie's estate. It was in her bedside table. It goes all the way to 1982, when Thor died. I've only read the first few entries, but . . ." She took the picture. "What if this is her? Aggie—that could be Augusta, right?"

"You are brilliant, Raina Beaumont."

"But if she married Duncan, how did she end up with Thor?"

And right then, it happened again, just like last summer. He lifted his blue eyes to her, gave her a look that could grab her up, make her feel shiny and bright. She couldn't help but grin back.

"I want to go to Naniboujou and see if they have any old pictures or records, just so we can get a confirmation, and then figure out what happened from there."

"I want to go with you." She said it quickly, before the urge, the courage, died.

"You do?" Casper frowned, ran his hand over his forehead as if working out a knot. "I don't understand. You said you were trying to move on—"

"I know. But . . . well, I realized that maybe . . . You were a good friend to me last summer, and I probably shouldn't have been so—anyway, I was a little afraid you were going to say something about . . ." She nearly said her name aloud. Layla. But she bit it back.

"It's not my secret to share."

She looked around at that, but no one picked up on his words.

"To that point, though, if you do ever need anyone to talk to, I . . . I can be that friend."

Yes. She believed he could. She held out her hand, and after a quick blink, he took it. Shook it. She tried to ignore his touch, the feel of his skin on hers, how it sank into her pores and warmed her. Memories, nothing more. "Deal."

"I'll pick you up on Saturday morning."

"Aye, aye, Captain," she said. It slipped out. But she didn't take it back, just grinned as she slid off the stool, carrying her tray to the counter. Then she returned and picked up her book, heading for the door. "See you Saturday."

Casper wasn't sure what really transpired at lunch, but by the time he returned home—bypassing the historical society for a take-out burger and fries from the VFW—he'd decided that maybe he should stop dissecting his conversation with Raina and just . . . be her friend.

The impulse, the thought, solidified inside him. And it seemed she longed for it also because she'd shaken his hand and even acted like she meant it.

Aye, aye, Captain. Her friendly moniker dredged up tangible, heartbreaking memories of last summer's nickname. *Captain, my Captain.*

If he didn't watch his heart, this could really hurt. Unless . . . he kept praying for her.

Lord, help her to see that You love her.

Casper pulled up to the lodge and got out, cheered by the sight of his father's truck in the lot. Indeed, when he opened the door, the smell of his mother's homemade spaghetti met his nose.

So much for the burger and soggy fries. "Mom?"

Ingrid Christiansen came around the corner, so much joy on her face it turned him into a child. Thirteen or maybe five and wanting to leap into her embrace.

"Casper!" She threw her arms around him, pulled his head down to her shoulder. "You're home."

He held on. It seemed she'd lost weight, but she still had that softness to her, the sense of belonging that made him feel that no matter what sins he committed, he could find forgiveness in her smile. "Mom."

She squeezed him a bit longer, then stepped back and held him at arm's length. She wore jeans and a long-sleeved blue thermal shirt, a fleece headband in her bobbed blonde hair, as if she hadn't just gone tromping off like a hippie, backpacking through Europe.

"When Darek wrote that you'd come home, I told your dad we had to cut our trip short—"

"And I told her that you needed time to get on your feet again." John Christiansen came from the next room, wearing jeans, a green woolen shirt, a baseball cap on his bald head. "Son, it's so good to see you."

He reached out to shake Casper's hand, then pulled him tight. Clapped him on the back. "You look good."

Casper nodded, a little unsettled at the emotion in his chest. "Thanks, Dad. I got a job at the Wild Harbor."

"That's what Darek said."

Ingrid took the take-out bag, looked inside, and made a face. "I'll put this in the fridge for later."

He followed her to the kitchen, sliding onto a stool. "So how was Europe?"

Ingrid looked at John, and something in their exchange had Casper frowning. Then she said, "Good. Interesting."

"Casper! You're home."

He stilled, then turned to see—Amelia?—trotting down the stairs.

No, gliding. The girl who'd left Deep Haven in a pair of yoga pants and a sweatshirt arrived home in a deep-blue dress, a gold belt, her red hair long around her shoulders. She looked . . .

Grown-up.

"It's so lovely to see you!"

Lovely . . . ?

She reached the bottom, walked over to him, slipped into his embrace. "I missed you!"

"Sis—hi. Wow. You look great."

She smiled, but it didn't touch her eyes. In fact, she'd lost weight, her face finely etched, and a slight edging of shadow darkened her green eyes.

"What are you doing home? Are you okay?"

She nodded. "Of course. It was just . . ." She exhaled a shaky breath and glanced at their mother. "Time. Just time. I missed everyone."

A lie hung in the air, but he didn't chase it. Yet.

"Are you home on break?"

"Nope. Just . . . home. For a while." She lifted a shoulder and slid onto a stool, crossing her legs. "Tell me everything about the dig. Did you find a lost treasure?"

Since when did Amelia wear dresses? And there, on the inside of her wrist—he actually reached for it.

A dove tattooed in red and yellow.

She frowned and pulled her arm away.

"Would you set the table, Casper?" Ingrid said quietly.

Oh, he was missing something, and by the way Amelia tightened her jaw, swallowed, it couldn't be good.

Casper got up, and like he'd traveled back in time to a year ago, he reached into the cupboard and took out the dishes. A fire crackled in the hearth while the snow piled against the sliding-glass door on the deck, the night already dense and murky.

Yeah, it could be last summer, with Darek and him working side by side on the cabins, back when he, like Amelia, had secrets to hide. Like the fact that he'd quit school. And didn't know where he belonged.

Back before he'd met Raina and thought he'd found the answer.

He finished setting the table as his mother laid out the spaghetti, garlic bread, and salad.

"Wow. I've been living on takeout, Darek's leftovers, and ramen noodles for a month."

Amelia cracked a soft smile, this one real. "The first month I was there, I think I ate ramen noodles every night."

She pulled out her chair and sat. Their father took her hand, squeezed it, something protective in his eyes. "Not anymore. Now you're home."

Safe. Casper could nearly hear the word on his father's lips.

"Let's pray," John said.

Casper listened to his father's voice, thought of his own prayers.

"So tell us everything about Roatán," his mother said. "I have to admit, when you didn't make it home for Christmas, my only consolation was that you were on a beach instead of enduring this deep freeze."

He watched Amelia out of the corner of his eye. How she played with her food, stirring it around her plate.

How his mother leaned over and said, "Eat, Amelia."

Amelia offered another brittle smile and nodded. But continued to worry her food.

"When did you make it home?" his father asked.

"Middle of January. I was here when the pipes burst in cabin three. Helped Darek repair it."

His father went silent. When he glanced at Ingrid, Casper wanted to grab those words back, maybe run them by Darek before outing him.

Clearly Darek had kept a few secrets from his parents.

Amelia sighed and pushed her food away. "I . . . I'm not hungry."

"Amelia—"

But she got up, shook her head, dropped her napkin on the table. "If you'll please excuse me . . ."

Casper had never heard her use so many manners in one sentence.

His gaze fell on his mother, who was watching her go. He was a little surprised that Ingrid didn't trail after her. Especially when his sister stifled a sob as she climbed the stairs.

Casper raised an eyebrow.

"She . . . needs some room," John finally said.

Casper glanced at his mother again, pushing her noodles and sauce around the plate. Right. Okay. "Hey, Dad, what do you know about Thor Wilder?"

John glanced upstairs, toward Amelia's room. Sighed. "Um, I don't know. I mean, he owned the trading post for a long while. His family tree goes back to the early traders in this area. One of his ancestors—I think it might have been an uncle—owned the fish house in town. Why?"

"Well, you remember the old Duncan Rothe mystery?"

John chuckled low. "I know it put a lot of dreams in your head—probably what started your love of history."

"I'm working for the historical society now and—"

"That's so wonderful, honey." Ingrid's hand went to his arm. Squeezed. Her eyes were wet, and even as she did it, she glanced upstairs. Then back to him for a smile. Forced.

Oh, boy. Something with Amelia had managed to tie his parents into a knot.

"Yeah. Edith Draper is beside herself with joy."

His dad laughed at that.

"So—I found this wedding dress from a collection of artifacts from Mineral Springs, and it had the initials C. A. F. on it. I did some sleuthing and found a connection to Duncan Rothe and Aggie Wilder."

"Really. How do you do that?" His mother looked impressed, and it sent a spark of warmth into Casper. Maybe, for the first time, his parents didn't think him a complete dreamer.

"Raina has this journal she got from Aggie's estate, and it mentions Duncan in it . . ."

The silence around the table could slice his words, leave them lying in pieces on the table.

His father put down his fork. Exhaled.

"Did you say Raina?" This from Ingrid. She flicked a glance at John. "She's back in town?"

Oops. Casper nodded. Suddenly the magnitude of Raina's secrets—and her absence over the past six months—rolled into a smoldering, inescapable ember in his chest. What a fool to think he could somehow keep her pregnancy, their grandchild, the adoption, hidden from his parents. From Owen.

Casper just might be walking around with the truth tattooed on his face for the way he felt himself going white.

His father even noticed. "Casper, are you okay? You look— listen, I know you had a summer fling—"

"It was more than a fling, Dad."

He didn't know where that came from, but hearing *fling* on his father's lips made what they'd had sound tawdry and trite.

That was Owen. Not him.

"I really cared—*care* about her."

"Oh, Casper, please tell me you're not mixed up with her again," his mother said.

For a moment Casper, too, had lost his appetite. But yeah, maybe they had a right to be worried. "It's all good. I'm over her. We're friends—"

"Casper," his dad started.

"Dad, really. Sure, I had feelings for her. I thought I loved her." He felt his mother's hand on his arm. Wanted to shake it away but decided not to hurt her. "But I realize that maybe I'm not supposed to be in her life like that. Maybe I'm supposed to be . . . I dunno . . . light to her."

"Light?"

"You know—patience? Kindness? Prayer?"

His dad considered him so long that Casper examined his own words to see if he meant them.

Yes, of course he did. Friends. Light.

His mom squeezed his arm again. "If anyone can be light to her, Son, it's you. I like Raina; I really do. But she is a hurt and broken soul, not a little lost."

"I'm not trying to save her, Mom. Nor fix her, I promise."

She patted his arm once, then let go. "I'm so glad to have you back. I missed you."

"I missed you too. Now tell me about Paris."

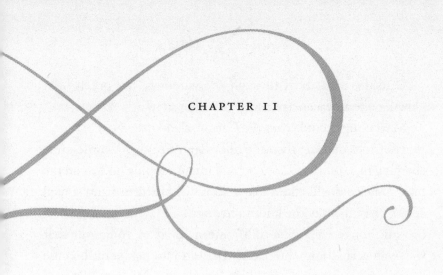

CHAPTER 11

GRACE WOULD BE so proud of her. Raina opened the oven, the fragrance of bubbling mozzarella, basil, and tomato sauce seasoning the kitchen. She donned hot pads and pulled out the sizzling pan of lasagna, setting it on the stovetop.

See, she could open the fridge and concoct something wonderful too. Just like Grace Christiansen.

And just like Grace, she had a beautiful man to cook for. She peeked toward the door, then the clock. Maybe she'd misheard Monte.

She covered the casserole with tinfoil to retain the heat, then walked over to the kitchen table and blew out the flickering taper candles. The smoke twined into the family room, leaving behind an acrid scent.

Outside, night bled through the windows, her porch light glowing like a beacon against the swirling snow.

Maybe she should cover the Caesar salad—

Footsteps outside; then the door handle turned. Monte came charging in, closing the door behind him, stamping his feet on the mat. "The cold will take a man's skin off." He turned and smiled at her, chasing away the knot in her gut.

"Hi. You're late." She didn't mean for it to come out that way—an accusation—but clearly he read into her words because he frowned as he shrugged off his jacket.

"Yeah, and—? I was working, Raina. A man has to do that." He hung the coat on the rack behind the door.

"I'm sorry. I just meant I was worried."

"Don't worry about me, sugar." He winked at her, his scowl gone. "You just worry about supper. Wow, that smells good."

She grinned as he crossed the room.

How had she landed such a handsome gentleman? Wide shoulders under a cream sweater tapering down to a thin waist, a pair of crisp jeans. He came up to her, caught her face in his cold hands, lifted it to his. His hazel eyes held hers. "Miss me?"

She nodded, and he pressed a kiss to her lips, something solid and urgent as if he'd been waiting all day to kiss her.

She kissed him back and tasted the faintest hint of something tangy—beer?—on his breath. But his eyes seemed clear and she guessed she'd imagined it.

"You are so pretty when you're wearing an apron." He winked again, then moved past her into the kitchen.

"Lasagna."

"I love lasagna." He leaned over the stove, lifting one edge of the tinfoil. "My mother used to make us lasagna. Never did meet a woman who could compare." He smiled, a hint of challenge, maybe even delight, in his expression. "Until now, hopefully."

Her heartbeat quickened. "I didn't follow a recipe—it's something I learned from Grace Christiansen. She has this ability to open a refrigerator and just . . . cook something. I've always wanted to do that."

"Let's hope it tastes good." He laughed and tweaked her cheek as he walked into the other room. "By the way, I know about you and Casper."

She was lifting the casserole dish with the hot pads when he said it and didn't know why the comment strummed unease in her. She brought the casserole to the table.

Monte was looking through the mail at Liza's rolltop desk, his back to her.

She frowned at him, trying to shrug away the invasion of her privacy. Probably he was just killing time. "That was a long time ago."

He didn't look at her.

"Really, Monte. Casper is . . . he's just a friend now."

He put the mail down, came up to her. "I know." He looked at her, his eyes calm, cool. She felt his hands at her waist and realized he was untying her apron. Then he tugged it over her head and tossed it to the floor near the stove.

She went to retrieve it, but his hand on her arm guided her to the chair he'd pulled out for her. "Sit. I'll get it. Do you want a Coke?"

She nodded. "But I can get it—"

"Sit." He moved toward the fridge. "I got it."

She sat, her hands folded in her lap, watching as he picked up the apron, wadded it onto the counter, then retrieved two cans from the refrigerator. He stopped as he closed it to consider the pictures tacked under magnets—pictures of Liza and Raina and one of the dragon boat team from last summer. She'd forgotten about that.

They wore matching lime-green shirts, grinned at the camera, paddles in hand. In the picture, Casper's hand touched her shoulder, a shine in his eyes under his crazy red bandanna.

If she wanted to, she could too easily return to the smells of summer, the triumphant warmth of the sun, the moment before everything dissolved with a positive pregnancy test.

Monte returned and set a can in front of her. Sat down and smiled. "So what have you been up to today?"

Raina picked up the knife and drew it through the casserole, then reached for the flat spatula. "I cleaned Aggie's house, then went over to the store and helped your grandpa clean and package a wire basket filled with old milk jugs he sold on eBay."

He held up his plate for her. "This looks perfect. I'm so hungry. I drove from Duluth today, after spending the day at an estate sale."

"How was it?"

"Fantastic. I sold a walnut dining room set for twice what it was worth, and—what is this stuff?"

He had cut a piece of the lasagna and put it in his mouth. Now he grabbed a napkin and emptied the bite into it. "That's horrible."

"It is?" She took a bite. The basil and tomato sauce sank into her tongue, perfectly seasoned, the eggplant decadent and rich.

She swallowed, not sure . . . "Did you get a bad piece?"

He made a face. "What kind of lasagna is this?"

"Eggplant."

"Seriously?" He drank his Coke down. "Wow. Maybe we should just leave the cooking for the local pizza joint, huh?" He rested his hand on her arm, his eyes soft. "Nice try, though. Next time you decide to root around in the fridge, look for the peanut butter and jelly, okay?" He laughed. "How about if I order us a pizza while you throw this out."

Raina watched him, her chest hollow, as he stood, pulled out his cell phone. She retrieved her hot pads and brought the dinner to the kitchen. Debated throwing it in the trash.

Glancing over her shoulder, she saw him in the next room, pacing, ordering.

Tucking the tinfoil around the pan, she opened the fridge and set it inside.

Not everyone liked eggplant, no big deal.

By the time she'd returned, Monte had dished himself a Caesar salad. "This is fantastic."

Raina decided not to mention that it had come from a prepackaged bag. "Thanks for ordering pizza," she said quietly.

"No problem, sweetie. That's what I'm here for—glad to save the day." He gave her a warm grin. "So what's the latest on your search through Aggie's things? Any more connections to Duncan Rothe?"

At her silence, he looked at her. "Raina?"

But she had tucked herself back in her moment with Casper, seeing his blue eyes, hearing his voice calling her brilliant.

"Raina?" Monte put down his fork. "You do know that anything you find at Aggie's belongs to me." He wiped his mouth.

She came back to herself, looked at him. "I . . . I haven't found anything."

He sighed. "Good. You'll let me know if you do, right?"

For some reason, her upcoming trip with Casper suddenly felt . . . deceitful. "I did find a connection to Aggie and Naniboujou . . ."

"Really?" He leaned forward, touching her hand. "What kind of connection?"

Why had she said that? She tried to shrug it away. "I don't know; I just . . ." She watched his fingers tracing her knuckles.

"Listen. I'm not stupid. I know Casper has some kind of reputation as a treasure hunter—the rumor around town is that he was trying to find Blackbeard's gold or something down in the Caribbean. Now he's back and he's stirred up this Duncan Rothe garbage." He took her hand. "You know it's not true, right?"

She frowned at him, nodded fast because his eyes told her to.

"Good. I just don't want Casper finding a reason to spend any time with you." He squeezed her hand, maybe a little harder than he'd intended. "Not with my girl."

The doorbell rang and he got up, met the pizza delivery, paid. Raina cleared a space at the table, his words sinking in.

His girl.

Monte's girl.

He opened the pizza box on the table. "I'll get us clean plates."

Maybe she shouldn't jeopardize anything with Monte by chasing after a silly rumor with Casper. After all, was his friendship so important that she needed to mend it? And what happened when he left on another adventure? She'd be here, building a life with Monte.

He returned to the table, set the plates on it. "Now this is dinner." Scooping up a piece, he handed her the plate. "I'll take you up on that movie tonight." He put his arm around her and kissed her forehead. "Is that *slow* enough for you?"

She laughed, her voice just a little uneasy. "Yeah, perfect."

A movie. A pizza. The perfect date.

Monte sat on the sofa and patted the spot next to him. Raina settled in, drew her legs up. He smelled good—sandalwood and a hint of vanilla in his cologne. He reached around her, put his arm across her shoulders, pulling her to himself as he turned on the television and clicked on the pay-per-view movie choices.

My girl.

He pressed a kiss to the back of her head, then picked up his piece of pizza.

No, she didn't need Casper or a silly adventure. Not when she had the amazing Monte Riggs.

Casper deliberately took the main road home from the Wild Harbor. Deliberately did not drive by Raina's house. Deliberately did not wonder if she was spending her Friday evening with Monte Riggs.

And deliberately did not wish that instead, Casper and Raina might spend the evening bent over a game of Sorry!

Most of all, he deliberately kept his thoughts from straying too far ahead, to tomorrow, when he would show Raina that they could be friends.

To prove it, he prayed that tonight, as the temperature dropped to negative ten, she would be safe and warm. And find a measure of happiness.

He pulled up to the lodge, got out, and ducked against the bracing wind churning off the lake. Overhead, the night turned to pitch, and he smelled a storm in the air.

He stamped his feet in the entryway, then toed off his boots and headed upstairs to wrestle off his dress clothes.

What he wouldn't give for summer—his cargo shorts, a T-shirt, and the feel of sand mortared between his toes. He put on said cargo shorts, adding a sweatshirt, and went back down to the kitchen.

The light of the refrigerator creased the wood floor as he searched for sustenance. With his mother home, he'd never have to tote home a cold, greasy burger again. He found a container of wild rice soup, heated it in the microwave, then plated it and headed to the den, where he heard the low tones of the television.

The paneled room, once his father's resort office, had become the family retreat when his parents banished the television from the family room. At least they'd upgraded to a flat-screen; it hung on the wall surrounded by an assortment of hand-me-down furniture—a denim sofa, an oversize green velvet chair, a suede recliner. Magazines and newspapers were scattered across the top of a faded, dinged oak coffee table. The room smelled of popcorn and laughter, the family pictures on the far wall a history of their legacy.

Dressed in leggings and an oversize flannel shirt, her hair braided down one side, Amelia sat on the sofa with her legs stretched out, eating a bowl of dry Cap'n Crunch. Now this kid sister he recognized.

She glanced at Casper and moved her legs, making room for him on the sofa. "Hey."

At closer inspection, it seemed red rimmed her eyes. He sat, picked up her feet, and put them on his lap. "Where're Mom and Dad?"

"A hot date. Snowshoeing."

Yeah, that would be a hot date to his parents. "Have you been crying?"

She ran her hand across her chapped, reddened cheek. Her smile appeared, wet and unsteady. "It's just the movie."

He glanced at the television. "Yeah, *Transformers* always gets to me too. So sad, the destruction of all those machines."

A bare smile, then it vanished. She stared into her Cap'n Crunch. Sighed.

"I'm a pretty good listener."

"I know. It's just . . . it's so embarrassing."

He lifted one eyebrow.

She swirled her finger around in the cereal. "I fell in love with the wrong guy."

A darkness stirred in him. "What kind of guy?"

"The kind of guy you think is perfect until you find out he was using you. Making a fool out of you."

He kept his voice low, tamed. "What . . . kind of fool? What happened?"

She closed her eyes, bit her lip, looked away. Her voice emerged shaky. "It's just . . . it's so awful, Casper. I just want to forget it."

He took her hand, a fist tightening in his chest. "Amelia, help a brother out here. What kind of awful? You didn't . . . do anything you'd regret?"

"I regret everything!"

He sucked in a breath. "Do I need to track down this guy who hurt you and take him apart?"

Amelia looked at him, startled. Then a smile edged up one side of her mouth. "No. I mean . . . I only regret how stupid I was to believe that anyone like him could fall for me."

A tear dripped off her chin.

"Aw, Sis." Casper reached out, thumbed it away. "Listen, this guy's an idiot if he didn't realize how amazing you are. Beautiful and smart—it's his loss."

She wiped her chin with her arm. Shook her head. "No, you don't understand. He's a really nice guy. I just . . . I read into everything. He didn't lead me on or promise me anything. I just thought that I meant something to him. But he walked away from me as if I were . . . junk."

He read her face, and the expression arrowed inside, landing with devastating precision. "Yeah. I know how that feels."

She blinked, catching her lip with her teeth, and considered him a long moment. "I know you probably don't want to talk about it, but . . . is everything okay with you and Owen?"

He looked at the television, watched Optimus Prime battle with another bot. "I regret the fight. And no—we haven't talked since that day."

She nodded, her mouth a grim line.

He eased the cereal bowl from her grip. Handed her the soup. "This is better than Cap'n Crunch."

"Hardly. You're just trying to steal my cereal."

He laughed but then dug in. Crunched.

She picked up the bowl of soup and blew on it before dipping in her spoon and stirring it. "You loved her, didn't you?"

He knew who the *her* was in that sentence. "I . . . Yeah, I think so. But not anymore. We're friends now."

Huh. That only hurt—well, just a pinch, really.

"Friends." She shook her head. "I don't know how you do that. Maybe I don't know what love feels like, because I don't think I could ever be friends with . . ." She sighed. "I hate love. I don't understand it. Why does it hurt so much?"

He had nothing for that, his own throat tight.

"But maybe it was just infatuation. I don't know, but I can't seem to get Roark out of my mind."

He understood that part too.

"How did you get over her? I mean, you two seemed so perfect for each other this summer, and then one day . . . nothing. What happened?"

Her green eyes met his with the power to unravel everything that flooded to the surface. He opened his mouth, aware of the fact that he might have Raina's secret written on his face.

Owen's baby. Even the adoption.

He stared at the cereal before the words scooted out.

"Casper?"

"She just . . . she didn't really want me. I was her second choice."

And that was it, wasn't it? He'd never really voiced it, made it real, but the truth tumbled out, lay there, naked and raw before him.

He hadn't realized how deep the thread of rejection ran, how it tangled his insides. He almost couldn't breathe with the swift immensity of it.

Raina hadn't wanted him once she realized she carried Owen's baby. How blind did a guy need to be not to get that? She'd only told him a thousand different ways. *Leave, Casper.*

Probably she'd been hoping that Owen might come back. And Casper destroyed that, too, with his jealousy.

He hadn't given his brother a chance to hear the news, to show up in his daughter's life. And because of Casper, Owen would never have that chance.

No wonder Raina could walk up to him and declare herself a friend. Because she'd never loved him like he'd loved her.

As usual, he'd acted as a stand-in for one of his incredible brothers.

"Casper . . . that's not true," Amelia said softly. "Of course she wanted to be with you."

"No, actually, that *is* the truth, and I'm an idiot for not figuring it out sooner." He took a breath, fighting against the crushing knot in his chest that threatened to work its way up his throat. He laughed it away. "And really, why not? Because she had Owen, so why settle for me?"

Amelia lifted an eyebrow. "Seriously? Casper, you are sweet and funny and . . . I'd choose you over Owen any day."

"Owen is dark and misunderstood. The perfect catch."

"You've got to be kidding me. Owen has been nothing but a jerk since his accident. He's arrogant and angry—"

"And the father of her child! Of *course* she wants him!"

Oh.

No.

Amelia's eyes widened, her breath caught. She pressed a hand over her mouth.

Casper winced and scrubbed his hand down his face. "I . . . Wow, I really . . ." He made another face, looked at Amelia. "You can't tell anyone, Amelia."

"Raina is pregnant?"

He sighed. Swallowed. Shook his head.

"Did she lose the baby?"

He shook his head again, his expression as terrible as her response.

"She had a baby? Owen's baby? I don't . . . I don't understand. Does Owen know?"

He shook his head again, apparently unable to form words, so he exhaled hard. "She gave the baby up for adoption."

Amelia just blinked at him. Again.

Then she stared at the television screen, her expression blank.

"Amelia—"

"I heard you. I'm just trying to wrap my brain around the idea that we have a nephew—"

"Niece, actually."

She looked at him. "A little girl. Owen's little girl, somewhere out there in the world, and we'll never see—" She closed her eyes for a second. "That's not right."

He set down the cereal. Leaned back, his head against the wall. "That's what I said, but Raina . . ."

"I can't believe her. How could she do this? To us. To Mom and Dad. You know how much they love Tiger and are looking forward to Ivy and Darek's baby. The thought that they will never know they have another grandchild . . ."

"It's her prerogative—"

"No, it's not!"

"Yeah, it is. She's the mother—"

"And Owen is the father!"

"But he doesn't know that."

Amelia closed her mouth, gathering in his words. Then, "She never told him that she was pregnant?"

"No. And now it's too late."

Amelia set down the soup. Pressed the meat of her hands into her eyes. "And I thought falling in love and having my heart broken when Roark cheated on me was tragedy enough."

Huh? "He cheated on you? Okay, so remember that bit about me tracking him down, taking him apart?"

She got up. Handed him the bowl.

"Where are you going?"

She rounded on him, nonplussed. "To talk to her, of course. To tell her that she can't do this—"

He grabbed her arm. "It's done, Amelia. We can't make her choices for her. We have to accept it."

Her mouth tightened into a dark line, her eyes stormy. "This is so utterly selfish of her."

"To her defense, Ames, she believes it's for the best for her child. She looked devastated in the hospital—absolutely overwhelmed."

"You saw her in the hospital?"

"And Grace agreed with her."

"Grace knows?"

"Yeah. Raina lived with her while she was pregnant. I told Raina that we'd all help her, but she's probably right. Owen isn't going to be overjoyed with the knowledge that a one-night stand netted him a daughter. It's not like he's going to show up and suddenly become father of the year. She had no choice—"

Her eyes widened, and it stopped him cold. "You still love her."

Her declaration stilled him. He shook his head, then again. Frowned.

"Oh, my . . ." She knelt in front of him. "You totally do because you've already forgiven her."

"Because *I had to*. Because if I didn't, she'd keep creeping into my head at night, and . . . Don't judge me," he said a little sadly. "But now you see why we have to be friends and nothing more. I can't love her anymore. At least not like I used to. Now I'm trying to love her the way God wants me to."

But she had pity in her eyes. "Why are you so crazy about her?"

Why . . . ? The question pinged inside him, bringing up all the feelings, the sweet memories of last summer. He came up with one word. "Belief. She believed in me. Made me feel like . . . when she looked at me, I could save the world. I was someone . . . valuable."

He looked away, wrinkling his nose, wishing he could take those words back.

Her voice turned soft. "I have this feeling that Raina didn't reject you because she didn't want you. She rejected you because she *did*, but she knew how wrong it was to want you and have Owen's child. She rejected you because of shame."

"I don't think so."

She touched his face. "I wish you could see what an amazing guy you are."

He caught her hands, pulled them away from his face. "Not so amazing, Sis. Trust me on that. Especially since I've added 'can't keep a secret' to my list of failings. You have to swear to me that you won't tell Mom and Dad."

She sat back on her haunches. "Oh, don't do that to me."

"I have to, Ames. You have to promise. She is trusting me with her secret."

"She doesn't deserve you or your *friendship*." Then she sighed, held up three fingers. "Scout's honor." She crossed her heart and poked at her eye in the classic children's gesture.

He reached out and grabbed her in a hug. "That guy is a fool."

"Mmm-hmm," she said.

He put her away from him then. "You really loved him?"

"I don't know. Maybe."

She picked up the cereal bowl. Considered it for a moment, then stood.

"Where are you going?"

"To the kitchen for more cereal."

He took the remote. "You might as well bring the entire box."

CHAPTER 12

RAINA RUMMAGED AROUND her bathroom drawer searching for the eye drops, glancing again in the mirror at the disaster staring back.

She looked like she'd pulled an all-nighter—her hair stringy and limp, her skin sallow, her eyes—oh, her eyes. Cracked and angry.

Next time Monte decided to watch all three Lord of the Rings movies, she'd curl up on the other sofa or suggest they watch them, say, over three days.

Not until 4 a.m.

She held up the eye drops, blinked in the moisture. A drop trailed down her cheek, and she caught it with her hand, then stared again at the mess in front of her.

She'd scare Casper right off the porch.

But maybe that would be best for both of them. Monte obviously didn't want her hanging out with Casper—and she didn't want to upset Monte.

Because if Monte hated Casper so much, perhaps Casper felt the same about her new boyfriend.

Boyfriend. She rolled that word around in her head even as she pulled back her hair, braiding it. He'd held her all night, cocooned in his embrace, and when he'd left—after suggesting that he should just stay on her sofa—he'd caught her in a long, lingering kiss.

She couldn't name the emotion it ignited. Probably she'd simply been too sleepy to respond. Still, disappointment hung in his eyes when she closed the door behind him, clearly sad to leave her.

As if she mattered to him.

Which, of course, accounted for why he didn't want her to spend time with Casper. A little jealousy over past boyfriends seemed healthy.

She found a pair of jeans, a pink thermal shirt, a white fleece sweatshirt. Added a thermal headband to her hair. Then she returned to the bathroom, leaning on the marble counter, surveying any repairs she might make.

She attempted some mascara, but it only made her eyes stand out, bright, shocked. Wary.

And why not? A day spent with Casper, stirring up the past? Despite their friendly moments sleuthing out Aggie's story, she could nearly hear the horns blaring, alerting her to danger.

She walked over to her bed, cast a wistful glance at her pillow, and pulled up the comforter. Smoothed it, fighting the urge to flop down on top.

A knock jerked her out of the moment, and she walked to the window, spied Casper's truck parked outside at the curb.

He was stamping his feet at the door, dressed in a black parka, red stocking cap, jeans, and boots.

Raina took a deep breath, searching for the right words to turn him down, and went to the door.

He peered through the glass, and shoot, but he could wake a girl from the dead with that grin, those blue eyes that felt like pure sunshine to her soul. She opened the door, bracing herself, digging up the resolve that had fled at his smile.

"Hey, Watson, ready to go solve a mystery?"

She could ache with the power of his words to wrap around her, separate her from wisdom. She hung on to the door, not inviting him in from the cold. "I can't."

He'd been clapping his hands together; now he shoved them into his pockets. "Oh, really? Are you sick?"

She probably looked sick, so she forgave him for that, and yeah, she felt a little rumble inside but . . . "No, I just . . . I don't think it's a good idea."

She let that hang there, let him decide what she meant on his own.

He seemed to take it in, and his smile fell to a grim line. "Okay. Well, I understand. I just . . ." He lifted a shoulder, glanced at his truck. Back to her with a smile, nothing of blame in his expression. "You make a good sleuthing partner."

She felt the response building inside, the urgency even as he turned to leave. "Wait!"

Casper stopped, glanced back at her.

"Wait, Casper. Yeah, I want to go. I'm tired is all. I stayed up late last night. Come in, and I'll get my jacket."

He hesitated a moment, however, testing her. "Are you sure? If you want to stay in and sleep . . . Winter is made for hibernating, after all."

The last thing she wanted to do was sleep now, because she'd simply stare at the ceiling, thinking about Casper digging up photographs and clues and fearing that if she did sleep, images of Layla might crawl into her head.

At least, after six weeks, she'd started to sleep through the night without waking in a cold shudder.

"No, I'm not that tired. Really." She ducked into her room, grabbed Aggie's journal off her bedside table, tucked it into her bag, then returned to the foyer.

Casper's gaze had fallen on Monte's sweater, the one he'd taken off after the fire toasted her family room to a sauna. He'd worn a T-shirt underneath and forgot to grab the sweater when he left.

She made to offer an explanation, but Casper turned suddenly, again wearing that smile, bright, not a hint of accusation in his expression. "Ready?"

Shrugging on her jacket, she grabbed her hat, shoved her feet into a pair of UGGs, and tucked her bag over her shoulder. "Let's go, Sherlock."

"The game's afoot," he said, and she laughed as he held the door open for her. The sky overhead hinted at a watery blue, the sun high and bright. Snow and ice silenced the harbor, and the wind curled the drifts into foamy sea shapes.

Casper held open her door but didn't help her into the truck, although he did wait to close it behind her.

She noticed a file folder tucked into the well beside his seat. She glanced at it and found what looked like a number of printed Internet articles on Augustus Franklin and his daughter, Clara.

He got in. "Breakfast?"

Her stomach suddenly sat up and roared in agreement.

"Wait until you have some of Naniboujou's sour cream coffee cake." He pulled out, headed down the road, turning onto the highway out of town. "They also have a sweet bread pudding and rum sauce that will make your eyes roll back into your head."

Okay, now she was ravenous. She pressed a hand to her stomach, remembering the pizza from last night. "Yum."

"Do you miss cooking? Or are you liking your job at the antique shop?"

Nice that he didn't call it the junk place. "I miss cooking. I made an eggplant lasagna last night."

He made a slurping sound. "I have no doubt it was delicious."

It touched her tongue to invite him over later, offer him a piece.

Wow. How had she gone from "No, this is a bad idea" to "Hey, wanna catch dinner together?"

And what if Monte finished his estate sale auction early? She didn't want him traveling all the way back to Deep Haven to discover Casper at her table.

So she didn't comment on the disastrous results of dinner. "I really loved working with Grace. She is an incredible cook."

"Max is a lucky guy, but I happen to know that Grace depended on you. She told me you were her secret weapon."

Truth or not, she appreciated the words. But she couldn't turn around and flee to the Cities. Not yet, at least. Plus, Grace had already filled her position with Aliya, the culinary student.

No, she had to keep moving forward.

They drove along the big lake, the evergreen and birch thinning out to reveal chunks of aqua-blue ice that lay like jewels along the shoreline. Casper must have noticed her surveying the landscape.

"That happens when the temperature warms enough for the

plate of ice along the shore to crack, and the natural waves and currents toss it onto the beach. Then it refreezes into this beautiful display of arctic color."

"They say it's the coldest winter ever up here."

"Not the coldest, but yeah, you're getting a good dose of chill."

"I'll bet you wish you were in the Caribbean right now."

Silence. Then, "Not right now."

Oh.

He took a breath. "So what's the latest on Aggie and the journal?" They passed a bridge over a frozen river, the rocks shiny in the sunlight.

"Not much. Aggie arrived at Naniboujou, and apparently Duncan left her to go back to Chicago, promising to return and marry her. What I don't get is, how did Aggie end up with Thor?"

They rounded a corner and he pointed to a lodge now appearing through the trees. "That's Naniboujou."

Trimmed in red, the two-story lodge appeared straight out of a storybook with its wood-shingled siding; the turreted roof; the tall, plate-glass, peaked windows; the red lampposts standing sentry along the exterior. Two giant wreaths hung on double-paned doors in the middle, and from the roof jutted a stone chimney.

"It's gorgeous."

"It was built in the 1920s as a private club. One of the founding members was Babe Ruth. They envisioned a hunting lodge on the shore." He turned at the drive, winding down to the lodge where it sat on the rocky, ice-cast shore. "Imagine flappers and roadsters—"

"And gangsters from Chicago?"

"Maybe. All escaping to this secret luxury resort in the woods."

"Scandalous."

The parking lot was filled with cars, but he found a spot. "I know the owners. They've been running the place for about thirty years, and now their kids run it. I called ahead and they said we could take a look at their old photographs and some of the scrapbooks, see if we can find what we're looking for."

"But—" She reached out and grasped his jacket. "Food first, right?"

"Yikes. The woman is hungry." He got out and she met him at the front of the truck. He was every bit as tall as Monte, maybe, but with his curls twining out of his hat and the hint of whiskers—as if he'd slacked off shaving today—he carried a rangy, almost-roguish aura.

Her own personal Indiana Jones.

No. Not hers.

Maybe Monte's fears had merit.

"You okay?" Casper said, looking at her with a hint of a frown.

"Like you said, hungry," she said and headed toward the double doors.

He held one open for her. She pulled off her gloves as she walked inside, taking in the grandeur of the dining room. Gloriously brilliant, not an inch was spared of paint. From one end to the next, a dizzying pattern of red, green, blue, and orange geometrics and zigzags spanned the ceiling. Images of totem-type birds, capped with Native American–inspired designs, rose two stories on columns bracing each wall. They stood between towering windows, flanked by green linen shades and capped by canopies in the same material. At one end, a fire in the lake stone fireplace, big enough to hold a sofa, flickered welcome. On the other end of the room, high up on the wall, the visage of yet another Indian-inspired image peered over the diners, rays of green light issuing like a halo from his head.

"The paintings are all original Cree Indian designs," Casper said, putting his hand on Raina's shoulder. She noticed how quickly he removed it, however, when he caught himself. "Some people call it the Sistine Chapel of the north woods."

The room hummed with the morning crowd, all seated at tables covered in indigo-blue tablecloths and dainty table lamps. The smell of bacon, maple syrup, and frying eggs could turn her knees to butter.

A hostess came over, greeted Casper like an old friend—of course—and ushered them to their seats.

Casper ordered coffee; Raina asked for juice.

"Like I said, it was built in the 1920s, but after the stock market crash, it floundered. I think some hotel chain might have bought it in the thirties, but later it went through one private ownership after another. One of the owners lost a couple of their adult sons in that river we drove over."

"Oh, that's horrible." She imagined moving up here to the woods, raising a family . . .

"I think my dad knew them. They were older than him, but the resort owners all stuck together. The family sold and moved away a couple years after that."

Their waitress brought their drinks and took their orders. Casper picked the Dempsey omelet. Raina chose the Three Bears porridge.

Casper had taken off his jacket, draped it over his chair, but kept the hat on. He wore a maroon long-sleeved UMD Bulldogs shirt that hugged his body, accentuated his wide, sculpted shoulders. She wondered if he still had any remnants of his Caribbean tan.

She shooed the thought away. Not the kind of musing a friend should have.

Her gaze did linger a moment on a lanyard with a copper coin around his neck. "Is that a souvenir from the Caribbean?"

He frowned.

"The necklace. It looks like a pirate coin or something."

His hand moved to touch it as if he'd forgotten he had it. "Uh . . . yeah. It's a British East India Company coin. Fitz, my dig director, gave them to everyone who worked on the dig. It's probably worth about twenty bucks." He lifted a shoulder.

"It's cool," she said.

He smiled at that, something sweet in his eyes. "Thanks."

"How is your resort? I remember Darek hoped to have it open for Valentine's Day."

"He opened it early, for the New Year. But . . ." He made a face. "This winter's been brutal. And we had a pipe burst in one of the cabins. Unfortunately it was one I worked on, so Darek thought it might be my fault."

"He does like to blame you—" Oh. "Sorry. I shouldn't have said that."

His mouth lifted in a smile, however. "That's okay. I sort of liked how you defended me last summer."

"He was always poking at you, criticizing you. If I remember correctly, it was you, Captain Casper, who led our dragon boat team to victory."

It swooped to her mind then, the memory of him standing in his shorts, holding a paddle high, the wind in his hair, his shirt rising a little to show off his tanned, sculpted stomach.

He looked away from her, toward his coffee, as if he too remembered it. "That was a good race," he said quietly.

She sipped her orange juice, soothed her suddenly dry throat.

He lifted his gaze, latched it on to hers. "How are you?"

The quiet of his words, the way he didn't flinch or break away as if her answer meant something to him, pushed her heart into her throat, raw and aching.

See, this was why she should have turned him down, begged an excuse. Because the man simply knew too much about her, knew how to find her frailties.

Her eyes burned. "I'm . . . fine."

She saw his hand move as if he might touch hers. But suddenly he pulled it back. She glanced up, and his expression could take her under. Kindness, nothing of accusation.

"Are you? Because . . . you did a brave thing, but I know it isn't over. It must sort of feel like you're walking around with this emptiness inside, your heart on the outside of your body . . ."

She caught her lip, reached up, and wiped the wetness on her cheek.

Casper frowned at the gesture. "I'm sorry—I didn't mean—"

"It's worse than that. Because I've actually given my heart to someone else and have no idea how . . ." Her breath shook and she drew it in, found solid ground. "How she might be doing. If she's okay and happy and healthy."

Raina closed her eyes, the words so freeing that it seemed a band had released around her chest. When she opened her eyes, he still wore that expression. Kindness. Friendship.

"I really believe what I did was right." She said it without her voice shaking.

"I agree."

She blinked at him. "You do?"

He nodded. "I think what you did was loving your baby the best way you knew how. I know it took incredible courage. And I . . . I understand."

She stared at him, testing his words. "But you wish I hadn't."

His mouth twisted and he shrugged a shoulder, shook his head. "My feelings don't matter. And frankly, I don't know what I wish." He swallowed. "Actually, I do." He sighed, then met her eyes with a sad expression. "I wish that I had been braver and not so easily hurt."

Oh.

"I wish that you'd felt safe with me and my family. Safe enough to tell us what happened with you and Owen. And safe enough to know that you deserved more from us. From me."

He seemed to struggle over his next words, whether trying to dredge them up or—no, trying to deliver them without embarrassing them both. His eyes turned glossy, but he kept them on hers. "I'm so sorry for the way I treated you."

Raina drew in a breath and, on the edge of it, found a smile emerging, a warmth spreading through her. "I forgive you."

Casper nodded, looking away fast. Blinking.

Then the waitress arrived with their food.

"I'm starving," Raina said. "I feel like I have a hole right through the center of my stomach."

Casper laughed, so much warmth in it that it lifted the shadow between them. "Thanks for helping me today, Raina. I'm glad you came with me."

"Me too."

Casper hadn't realized how sorry he truly felt until Raina started talking. Or until she sat down. No, before that, when he met her at her front door and realized she was backing out on him.

He didn't know why, didn't want to consider it might be because she was afraid of spending time with him.

As he'd turned to go, he felt the tug on his spirit. *Pray for her.*

The thought pulsed through him. Of course. After all, he'd hurt her the last few times they'd been alone together. So he'd lifted it quickly. *Please help her to feel safe, Lord.*

With him, yeah, but maybe there was something more. Then she'd changed her mind and invited him in. His gaze had fallen on the sweater hanging over a chair but he said nothing, because really, it was none of his business.

But the impulse to apologize grew as she sat at the table, and the whole thing came crashing down on him when he realized he *should* have made her feel safe. Last summer, she had confessed that she longed for safety—and he'd just been trying to figure that out when he'd discovered her past. When he'd turned on her.

He'd given her anything but safety.

The apology felt natural and honest and freeing.

For himself, it was as if with the forgiveness, light sifted into his dark wounds.

He was aware of Raina close behind him now as they followed a Naniboujou employee into the basement under the lodge and to the vault that housed artifacts and remnants along with other items.

Judy, the front desk woman, tall and thin, wearing a green sweater emblazoned with the lodge's emblem on the shoulder, pointed at the boxes of pictures—three cartons of them and books and books of old hotel registers. "We keep them for posterity. We never really know when we might need them, but we have no room for them upstairs, so we keep them down here. Feel free to look through them or even bring them up to the solarium if you'd like."

"What was this place?" Casper asked.

The vault, six feet by six feet, forged out of the stone foundation and lined with cedar, emitted a musty, ancient smell. "We think it must have been an old bootleggers' hideout, although the lodge was built at the very tail end of Prohibition, so maybe that is our imaginations talking. We use it for storage now. Make yourselves at home."

She left them, her feet echoing as she walked up the stairs. The heating units, water pumps, and other mechanical devices housed in the basement rumbled to life.

"Wow, look at this stuff." Casper took down a box and opened it. Inside, shoe boxes piled high contained pictures in neat rows. Polaroids, black-and-whites, some large, others small. He took out a box and sifted through it. "It looks like this is from the MacNab era. From the attire and the cars, it might be 1938–1939."

"That's too late," Raina said.

"But look at this." He handed her a picture. It featured the front of the lodge and two women linking arms, wearing hats and sensible dark dresses, one holding a bouquet of lilacs as if they'd been on a picnic. Neither of them smiled. They stood in front of a Model T.

He started riffling through more pictures, handed another one to her. "That is most definitely the fifties."

The photo featured a couple. The man in jeans, a white T-shirt with rolled-up sleeves, slicked-back hair, long sideburns. The woman wore pedal pushers, her shirt tied at the waist, brown hair under a bandanna. They sat atop a 1957 Thunderbird.

"I might have enjoyed living back then," Raina said. "It seems so carefree."

"I don't know," Casper said, taking out another. "They had a war and problems just like us. But here on the north shore, people could sneak away from their trials in life with their families, find a place to hide, just for a moment."

"Not everyone is hiding," Raina said.

He glanced at her.

"Well, some of us are, I suppose."

He laughed. "I might have been hiding out last summer, but going to Roatán made me miss Deep Haven."

She handed the picture back to him. "So you're not leaving again?"

"I don't know," he said. "My boss likes me, and I'm busy at Wild Harbor. We're having a sale next week."

"Wow, that's . . . normal."

"Don't judge me. I know it's not Indiana Jones, but a guy can't exactly make a living hunting for treasure. He has to grow up—"

"That sounds like your father talking."

"Maybe he's right." He stood, closed the box, dusted off his knees. "I never did find anything in all my days of treasure hunting. I know I cleverly disguised it as studying archaeology, but the fact of the matter is that I just wanted to—"

"I know—find something priceless. Something that others have missed and only you have figured out."

He looked at her sharply, then frowned. "You remember that?"

"Of course I remember." A smile lifted one side of her mouth and the slightest shade of color pressed her lips. She pointed past him to another box. "Try that one."

He opened the lid. "Envelopes this time. Manila." He pulled one out, removed a stack of pictures. "We might be getting closer here. This looks like a shot from the 1920s."

The photo displayed a couple dressed in swimsuits—his more of a short tunic, hers a long one-piece dress with flounces at the hips and stockings and a matching ruffled headpiece.

"Oh, my," Raina said. "Fetching." She reached for the pile.

"Give me half and let's see what we can find." She began looking through the pictures.

Casper sat next to her, the hum of the furnaces like a serenade.

"You know, I . . . I named her. Just for myself. Nothing official."

He stilled. She looked up, her eyes, big and brown, falling on him. Testing him. Then quickly went back to the pictures.

"You named her—"

"Layla. I thought it was a good name. It means 'dark beauty.'"

Trying to act casual, not wanting to scare her with how much he cared, he picked up a picture of what looked like Babe Ruth and two other men. "It's a beautiful name."

"I think about her every day."

"I figured that."

"Do you . . . do you think she'll be mad at me?"

Oh, Raina. He put down the pictures, tried to catch her eyes. "I can't answer that, Raina. I think if she understands love, she'll understand what you did."

That seemed to resonate because she swallowed and let the silence, the hum of the basement, fill the moment.

He picked up the pictures again.

"Thanks, Casper, for letting me talk about it."

He kept sifting through, not really looking. "I told you, anytime. And I meant it."

More silence. Then, "You know, when I first got pregnant, I thought I would keep her. I had this crazy dream that somehow I'd live in Deep Haven in a cute little house—not Liza's house, but my own, and I don't know—I . . . I would raise her and we'd take picnics on the shore and I'd teach her about cooking and how to . . ." She sighed. "How to garden. But there was no one else in the picture with me, so . . ."

No one?

The words edged his lips, but he held them back, fighting off this sudden spurt of disappointment.

No. He wouldn't let his thoughts go there. *Lord, help me be a friend to her.*

So he stayed silent, letting her have room.

"You know my mom died when I was nine."

"I didn't know that. I knew she died, but I didn't know you were only nine."

"She had cancer. She'd had it for a few years, but we thought she'd beat it. The end came too fast. My brother was six, and my father was so angry, he began to drink and go out on the road for long periods of time . . ."

She picked up a picture, squinted at it, put it back. "One year he just dropped us off at my grandmother's house. She lived in Iowa, on a pig farm—imagine that. I'd never been around pigs. She was a large woman, four hundred pounds, hair black as coal, fat fingers. Her house was . . . quiet. And small. Dainty, with china. But she loved me and my brother. For all of her fussing at us to keep her house clean—on a pig farm, of all places—she fed us and tucked us in at night and sometimes sang to us. And I thought . . . what if I could be that kind of mother?"

Casper saw it then, her tucking in Layla, pushing back her dark hair, singing softly, and the image made him ache. He found words, however, to move them past it. "Do you remember your mother?"

"Sure. Fuzzy memories. I remember her making us frosted graham cracker treats after school. We lived outside town in a trailer house, but she was there every day. She worked the second shift at the hospital, so we'd come home and she'd kiss us and then leave and we'd eat the graham crackers. Daddy would come home an hour or two later, and if he didn't, it was okay . . . because she'd leave dinner and I'd tuck in Joey and climb in with him and we'd wait, chasing the shadows from the room until we heard her car drive in. Usually she was home by midnight. But always by morning. Making me pancakes."

He came upon a picture of a pretty girl in what looked like the gown he'd found at the historical society, standing outside the lodge, next to a roadster. He looked at it closer. It could be the same dress.

Raina held out a picture. "What about this one?" Similar to the one he held, but this one was formal, the man sitting on a chair, the bride beside him, her hand on his shoulder, staring resolutely at the future with a grim look. "I didn't see any pictures this young in Aggie's house, but it could be her. Does that look like the same dress?"

"Maybe." He thumbed through the folder of research he'd downloaded off the net, found a grainy picture of Duncan Rothe. "Do you think this picture looks like him?"

"Maybe, yes."

"And this picture has him in front of the roadster. Maybe they're going on their honeymoon."

"So she *did* come here and she did marry Duncan Rothe. Or she planned to. What do you think happened?"

"I don't know . . . What does the diary say?"

She reached for her bag, but he touched her hand.

"Just for the record . . ." He took a breath, softened his voice, unable to stave off the words another moment. "You would have been—and you will be someday—a *fantastic* mother. You will be the mother who makes frosted graham crackers and waits for her child after school and tucks her in at night and sings her songs."

"I don't know." She sighed. Her voice was so soft, he had to lean in. "I remember the night my mother died. I remember going in to kiss her and . . . she might have been already gone, but when I did, nothing happened. She didn't move, didn't breathe, didn't take my hand . . . and I remember the disappointment. That maybe I wasn't enough, that I should have been more—"

"Raina, you were nine."

"No, see, my mom told me right before she got so sick that I was responsible for Joey. She had no one else—Dad drove every week, and her mom had died. Grandma was Daddy's mother. Mom told me I was supposed to take care of Joey, but . . ." She swallowed hard and glanced at him. "My brother died when he was fourteen. A drug overdose—meth. I should have been paying attention, but I was seventeen and I wanted my own life. And he was a pain. He came home that night and fell asleep on the sofa, and I was angry at him—he'd left a trail of his shoes and jacket and socks everywhere, his dishes in the sink, and he'd thrown up on the carpet. I walked into the family room and yelled at him. I stood over him and told him that he was worthless and I was sorry I ever took care of him and that he made me ashamed. And he . . . didn't move. Just . . ."

Casper put down the picture, longing to take her in his arms.

Her voice fell. "He was dead and I was yelling at him. See, I shouldn't be a mother." She stared at the picture. "I didn't sing him songs."

"Raina." His voice emerged wrecked, his throat filled with fire. "I don't think you know what kind of mother you are until you are one. You weren't his mom—you were his sister."

"My mom asked me to take care of him—"

"I know, but you were just a kid yourself. Nine years old."

"And then I was seventeen, my mother was dead, and some-where in there, I blew it."

"No." Now he did take her hand and touch her chin, lifting her eyes to him. "No, see, we all have to make our own choices and live with our own mistakes. Your brother's mistakes are not yours."

A tear dripped off her chin. "But he probably paid for mine."

"That's how families are . . . We pay for each other's mistakes." The words fell on soft soil in his own heart, settled deep. "But that doesn't mean you're to blame for your brother's death. And it doesn't mean you won't make an amazing mother someday. Actually, it doesn't even mean that you weren't *already* an amazing mother to Layla."

When she looked at him, the urge overwhelmed him to pull her close, wrap her tight in his embrace so no one could ever hurt her again.

But he drew back, tried to hide the way he trembled, and tucked the rest of the pictures back in the envelope. "What do you say we take a closer look at those pictures you found at Aggie's house?"

Raina was already slipping the pictures back into the envelope. "That's a great idea," she said, way too brightly.

He replaced the envelope in the box, shoved it onto the shelf.

"Let's see if we can find their names in the register," she said.

Maybe fifty books lined the shelves. Raina found the right year, paged the book open, and located the right month. "I think we have something here. Look at this," she said, pointing to the scrawled, sharp signature of Duncan Rothe. "And here's another." The loopy signature of Aggie Franklin.

"You're a genius, Watson," Casper said.

"We make a great team."

He closed the book. Tucked it back in its spot, turned off the light.

"Oh, it's dark."

"It's okay. Here, take my hand." He said it without thinking, and she slipped her grip into his as if it belonged there. He felt his way out of the vault, toward the stairs, and led her up.

He let go as soon as they reached the landing, but the moment lingered all the way out to the truck. He climbed in beside her as she pulled out the diary.

"I think I found something," she said a few moments later. "Look. If I follow the entries correctly, Duncan left, and Aggie expected him back in June, but he didn't come back. There's an entry here in early June that says she is waiting for him to return, and she's getting lonely."

"No wonder the marriage certificate wasn't signed. They didn't get married then."

"Not yet. I'll keep reading tonight, and if I find anything, I'll let you know."

He believed her. And tried not to let that spark any more than it should be: two friends, Sherlock and Watson, sleuthing out a mystery.

"That would be great."

"You can come to Aggie's house if you want. It might be interesting for you to see how she lived. I'll try to find more pictures. I don't know—maybe you'll find clues to those missing bonds from that story you told me about the legend of Duncan Rothe."

He glanced at her. "Yeah, I'd like that."

She smiled, and it lit up her whole face, so beautiful it could turn his heart inside out. They'd had a good day, a really good day, without treading too far into their past. A safe day. The kind of day he'd hoped to give her.

And she seemed to know it also because she stared out the window, her profile to him, and hummed.

Her music died as he pulled up to the house. It took only a moment for him to connect the sight of Monte's truck to her quickening of breath, the way she swallowed, her face falling.

"Monte doesn't want you around me." Of course, he knew that—but nothing like what he saw on her face.

She shook her head. "Let me out here."

"A half block from your house? No, Raina, listen, I'll explain to him—"

"Let me out, Casper!"

He slowed, aimed for the curb, had barely stopped before she opened the door. "Whoa—Raina, seriously? C'mon, he can't be that jealous."

She frowned, sharp and fast. "No. There's nothing to be jealous of."

The words hurt, a spear through his heart, but wasn't that what he wanted? "Of course not," he agreed. "Okay, well . . ." He glanced at the house, and darkness coiled inside him when he saw Monte emerge from inside to stand on her porch.

The man crossed his arms over his chest, his eyes bouncing off Raina, skidding over to Casper.

The whole thing felt . . . unsettling.

But Casper couldn't scramble up the words to—what, warn her? Or . . . just ask her if she needed help before she said a quick "See ya, Casper," and slammed the door.

Casper waited, though, watching as she quick-walked up the

road toward the house. Watching as she bounded up the steps, met Monte's embrace.

He drove away slowly, Monte's eyes on him until he turned, his arm clamped around Raina's shoulders as he escorted her into the house.

And Casper prayed for her again because it was better than turning around and repeating the past.

Lord, please protect her.

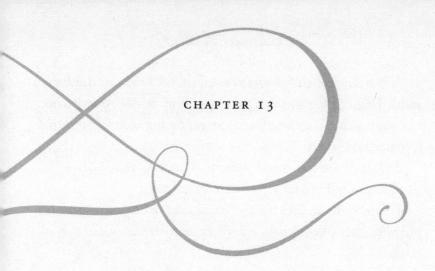

CHAPTER 13

Darek couldn't help glancing at his watch.

"Tiger, you want to see the baby?" Ivy lay on the table, her stomach glistening with gel. She gripped Darek's hand, the residue of worry in her eyes lingering despite her words to the contrary. Maybe she'd finally figured out how close he'd come to losing her, losing their baby, and she'd stop lecturing him on his hovering.

She gestured to Tiger, who sat in the chair, reading a book. "Come over here and take a look."

"No."

Darek frowned. For the past week, Tiger had seemed withdrawn, almost angry. "Tiger, your mom said to take a look—"

"I don't wanna."

When Tiger kept his eyes trained on his book, it lit a flame inside Darek. He glanced at Ivy to see if the words wounded her, but she watched Tiger with such an expression of gentleness that it tempered his fury.

Still, he wanted to march over, grab his son, make him—

"Do you want to know what the gender is?"

Darek glanced back to the ultrasound technician, a pretty girl with short brown hair, maybe in her twenties, wearing pink scrubs.

His wife raised an eyebrow, smiled at him. "Well?"

He shook his head. "I . . . I think I want to be surprised."

Ivy squeezed his hand. "Then me too."

The technician nodded and wiped Ivy's skin with a towel.

As Darek helped Ivy sit up, she groaned, made a face.

"Labor?"

She pressed a hand to her belly, blowing out a breath. "No. Braxton-Hicks."

"It's normal," the technician said. "Your baby's heartbeat seems strong. I'll show the pictures to the doctor—she'll call you if there is anything to worry about, I'm sure."

Ivy slid off the table. "We need to get to the conferences at the school."

"Oh, Ivy, I have to get back to the resort. I've barely been in the office since my dad came home, and if he takes a look at the pile of bills . . . Can . . . ?" He glanced at Tiger, back to her.

She caught his hand. "No problem. Drop me off at home and take Tiger with you. I'll meet you later."

He tried not to let the image of her sitting in the frozen, smashed car while the cold closed in on her creep into his brain but—

"I promise I'll call you before I leave the school. And I'll use the four-wheel drive."

He'd purchased her the best car he could find for this area—a used GMC Yukon with four new snow tires—after the insurance company deemed her little tin-can compact totaled. Still, it added another dent to his budget, money he didn't see coming in anytime soon. "Okay. But if it's too slippery, stay home. I'll bring home dinner."

She grabbed his jacket, tugged him down for a quick kiss. "You worry too much. About everything."

But if he didn't, who would? Ivy seemed to wear a perpetual smile as the birth of the baby approached. But Darek could only see the lean, muddy spring months ahead, stretching the lodge budget thin, with his unfinished house waiting on the far edge of the property. He heard sleepless nights with the baby crying, and Ivy exhausted, Tiger jumping from furniture or worse, argumentative and sullen, and Darek's father staring at him with questions as he held their overdrawn checkbook.

The truth about the cabin three repairs had sat like a boulder on his chest, nearly choking his words when his father asked for a report on the resort. He'd offered a quick and too-cheery answer that summed up the high points and omitted the cold snap, the rebuild of cabin three, and most important, his complete abandonment of the operation after Ivy's accident.

A lie by omission still felt like a lie.

"C'mon, Tiger," he said, reaching for his son, who slid morosely off the vinyl chair and trudged out after him and Ivy. Darek settled his hand on Tiger's shoulder, but he shrugged away from it, ran ahead, and took Ivy's hand.

She smiled at Tiger, eliciting a pang of envy in Darek. Since when had he turned into the bad guy?

He dropped Ivy off at home, waited for her to start the Yukon, then headed to the lodge in his truck.

Tiger sat in the second-row bench seat, buckled in and staring out the window.

"You okay, buddy?" Darek kept his voice light, glancing at him in the mirror. His son needed a haircut, his blond hair poking out the back of his hat, and it looked like he wore his hot-dog-and-ketchup lunch on the collar of his sweatshirt.

Tiger shrugged.

"Anything bothering you?"

Tiger stared out the window.

"You know, when this baby comes, she's going to be lucky to have you for a big brother."

"I don't want a sister."

Darek frowned. "Maybe it's a boy. A baby brother to wrestle with you when he gets older? And build snow forts?"

"Dylan has a baby brother and he breaks his LEGOs."

"We'll keep them out of reach, then."

Another shrug.

"Are you mad at me, buddy? I know I've been working a lot but . . ."

Tiger said nothing and the silence stirred an ache in Darek, rushing him back to those days after Felicity had died when Tiger fled into himself, not eating, not sleeping. He'd only fall asleep on the sofa with his stuffed tiger nestled between him and Darek.

"I promise it'll get better," he offered, but the words seemed feeble.

He sighed in tune with Tiger.

A layer of fluffy snow had blanketed the shore overnight and clung to the shaggy fir on the south, untouched-by-fire side of the road. He turned at his drive and pulled up to the resort. Sometimes the vastness of the flames' destruction could still blind him with disbelief. But now snow settled grace upon the charred forest beyond the rim of evergreens they'd planted to wrap the resort in an enclave of protection.

If only he could wrap Ivy and Tiger in the same kind of enclave. But God had given them a husband and father to stand in the way of the storms. And he wasn't going to let them—any of them—down.

Darek turned to see if Tiger needed help unbuckling, but he was already opening the other door and jumping down. He slammed the door shut, running inside.

Darek walked into the resort's tiny front office, attached to the main house through a side door. A tall counter in gleaming oak portioned the reception area from the workstation, and a rack on the counter held local brochures, coupons, and an activities chart. In the corner, one of his father's chain saw–carved creations—a black bear—held a *Welcome to Evergreen!* sign in its outstretched paws. The scene only lacked a plate of his mother's fresh-baked snickerdoodles.

He circled the counter, noticed the machine had three messages, pulled out the rolling chair, and booted up his laptop.

The mail accumulated in a metal in-basket beside the computer, and tucked next to it were a daily diary and an old-fashioned guest book—something his mother insisted on retaining for legacy—that kept the activities and testimonials of their guests.

One of Ingrid's tricks for remembering everything that happened, year after year. She considered her guests friends rather than customers.

Darek heard Tiger greet his parents behind the door to the house, knew that his mother had probably swung him around and then invited him in for a cookie.

Darek's stomach growled, but he opened his e-mail.

The messages poured in—spam and a few requests for lodging information.

His pulse quickened at a message from his buddy Jed Ransom. The image of his old fire boss flashed into his brain—his blackened face, white teeth grinning as a wall of flame rose behind him. Like battle, fighting the flames was exhausting, backbreaking work—digging trenches, lighting backfires, and felling trees.

Exhausting and exhilarating, and Darek thrived under the heat of a forest fire. He knew how to read a fire, how to attack it. How to win.

He could almost feel the soot in his eyes, the sweaty moisture of a handkerchief over his mouth and nose. Hear the ruckus of the chain saws, the roar of a greedy fire.

Wow, he missed it.

He opened the e-mail.

Darek!

We've been watching the temperatures—frozen much? I don't know if you're open yet, but if not—or even if you are—we could use your help here in Arizona. The season hasn't officially started, so we're lean on teams. I could use you for a couple weeks just until we're fully staffed.

Old times, huh?

Jed

Darek read it again. Just a couple weeks. Working again with Jed and the team.

The thought sparked inside him, tasted of hope. But really he couldn't get away, despite the fact that they had no revenue on the books yet for March.

He could use the month to finish his interior walls, maybe get the kitchen cabinets hung, the bathroom roughed in.

Build the house his family needed.

He was moving to reply to the e-mail when he heard the door behind him open.

"Hey, Son." His father's voice entered a moment before he did. Darek closed the e-mail, turned.

His father wore a denim resort shirt and jeans, his head freshly shaven. The way a resort manager should attire himself, instead of Darek's work pants and sweatshirt. But he'd planned on shoveling and cutting firewood after he wrangled the books into submission.

"How did Ivy's appointment go?"

"Good. The baby looks fine, thank the Lord."

His father looked leaner after his trip to Europe, a new light in his eyes. And from the pictures he'd shown Darek of their Paris leg, it seemed the vacation had turned out to be the second honeymoon he'd hoped.

Except for their strange stopover in Prague to pick up Amelia. Nothing but closed-lipped secrets behind her return, but based on the way she'd holed up in her room or the den over the past few days, Darek suspected it might have been boy-related.

"I'm so glad." His father sat on the old straight-back chair. It creaked under his weight. "You want to tell me about this?" He handed Darek a folded piece of paper.

Darek took it, frowned, his breath catching at the total.

"In my recollection, that's the largest propane bill this resort has ever seen. I'll be honest, Son, that's one too many zeros there."

Three thousand dollars. For one month's gas and oil?

"Now," John continued, "I called the company and they said that propane prices have doubled, which only makes me wonder if staying open in the winter is a good idea."

Darek's idea.

"And then there's the matter of the cabin three repairs. Did you ever think of mentioning that?"

Darek set the bill in the basket.

"Darek, when I gave you this resort to run . . . I believe in you, Son, but—"

"Save it; I get it. I'm blowing this." Darek got up, stalked away. "I understand what's at stake here. Seventy-five years of legacy going down on my watch."

"Darek—"

He rounded on his father. "But the fact is, maybe I'm not cut out for this. I'm a . . . I'm a carpenter. A lumberjack. I'm not good at numbers and schmoozing with the guests and figuring out what ads to run in the local papers—"

His father rose, frowning.

But Darek couldn't stop. "You know what, Dad? You're wrong. You *shouldn't* believe in me. Because I'm not you. I can't run this place. And frankly, I don't want to."

His words stripped all expression from John's face.

"I don't want to spend every waking moment running this resort, catering to guests. I hate it. I want to do something that actually accomplishes something. Like . . ." He tried to shake the word *firefighting* from his head, but there it lodged, burning inside him.

He ground his jaw, staring at his dad, and couldn't help it. "Sometimes I wish I never had a family. I just let them down."

"Darek—"

"Get Casper to run this place. He's the one who's good with numbers and wooing the guests. I'm just . . . the guy who cuts firewood."

He pushed past his father into the next room. Tiger sat at the high-top counter, eating a Rice Krispies bar. Ingrid stood on the other side, arms akimbo, her eyes on Darek.

So she'd heard.

As had Ivy, who stood in the entryway, her face white. She still wore her coat as if she'd just walked in.

"Ivy, I—"

She held up her hand. "It's fine, Darek. It's fine." She looked at Tiger, Ingrid. "The conference had to be rescheduled. I think Tiger and I are ready to go."

Tiger slid off the stool.

"Ivy, please don't go." Darek reached out to touch her, but she jerked away from his grip, and he felt it like a knife in his chest.

"I'll see you at home," she said, her jaw tight. Tiger had slipped on his boots, and Ivy added his hat. He took her hand.

Darek watched her leave, unable to move from the cold entryway.

John stood in the doorway of the office. Darek didn't look at him as he stalked back into the office.

He stared at the computer for a moment, then closed it and headed outside, letting the bracing wind cool him as he escaped to the woodpile.

Casper had unpacked enough Gore-Tex rain suits, cargo shorts, thermal shirts, Teva sandals, and day packs to wish himself into spring. He could nearly feel the sunshine on his skin, smell the piney scent of an awakening forest on the breeze as he crunched across trails littered with amber needles. He'd take out his dad's old canoe—the one he kept tied to the dock—find some remote lake, and spend the day chasing walleye.

Except one look outside told him that any hope of spring might have slunk out in surrender to the gusts of icy wind that piled winter in haggard drifts along the roads, the shoreline.

He might never escape the cold.

"Two more boxes just arrived, Casper!" Ned called from the front room, his voice echoing all the way into the upstairs storage area. "I think these must be jackets—Windbreakers. Yeah, here's those convertible pants. They zip off at the knee—"

"I'll be out in a second." After he figured out where to stack this last box of hiking boots. "Next time you decide to order spring supplies, you might consider doing it after the winter clearance sale."

Nothing. He shook his head, trying to find a space—anywhere—in the crowded room. He'd labeled every box, tried to keep it ordered, but the place was packed, with a tiny aisle to crawl through to reach the camp chairs, lanterns, and collapsible bowls and camping utensils in the back.

"Just be glad I put the kayaks in the shed," Ned said, leaning into the room. He surveyed the clutter. "Why aren't you using the overflow storage?"

"Huh?"

"The old fish room." He reached for the box of boots and Casper handed them over, climbing out of his prison.

"The fish room?"

Ned was already descending the stairs but glanced over his

shoulder. "It used to be an old fish house. The fishermen would bring in the catch, clean it, and then store it here, in the coolers."

Casper followed Ned to the room, stepping through time into the cleaned yet ancient space. The briny odor of fresh fish still embedded the rough-hewn walls, the ceiling low, a window cut into one side that peered out over the lake. A locked door led outside.

"You sure you want to put the boxes in here?"

"Just for a week, until after the sale. It's weatherproof." Ned set down the box of boots. "Look, you can see the initials of the first proprietor right here." He pointed to a gold plaque by the door, then left to get the next load of boxes.

Casper walked over to the plaque, peered at it. *D. T. W.*

"Ned?" He came out of the room, jogging up to the front. "Are you sure that's right? I thought the Zimmermans were the first owners of the trading post."

Ned hoisted a box, handed it to Casper. "They were. But Dalton Wilder ran the fish house. He used to run supplies up and down the shore in his skiff. Actually, I think his kid Thor did a lot of it. Would run supplies between here and Mineral Springs. Thor opened a curio store there but probably bought this place when the Zimmermans passed and Mineral Springs closed down—took over the trading post and used the old fish house for storage."

Casper fell into step behind Ned. Thor ran supplies to Mineral Springs. Which meant he might have occasionally stopped at Naniboujou on the way? Where he would meet Aggie Franklin?

He set the box on the floor, and Ned turned the light off as they exited.

He had to tell Raina. The thought rushed at him, and he even made to reach for his phone.

Except Raina hadn't called him—not once—all week. He tried

not to let the image of Monte on the steps unsettle him, but twice he'd driven by her house, spied the truck, and decided that Monte spent way too much time alone with Raina.

"I think we need a little fun before the big clearance sale this weekend," Ned was saying. "The ski resort is having a mountain bluegrass festival and you're going out." Ned held out Casper's jacket, apparently retrieved from the office.

"What? No, Ned. I have stuff to do—"

"No, you don't." Ned went over to the till, locked it, and grabbed the money bag. "You're not spending one more night alone over there at the place time forgot."

"If you're referring to the historical society . . ."

"The has-been sanctuary, yeah." He grabbed Casper by the shoulder. "You're young and single and you haven't had a date in months. That changes tonight."

He'd dated . . . Just last weekend, he'd gone out with Raina. Except that wasn't a date exactly.

Although it felt like a date. Or more, maybe. Deeper.

The kind of moment real friends shared. But that was all they would be. So . . . "Okay, fine, but listen, I don't need you to set me up. I can find my own girl."

"I know exactly what you need," Ned said.

Two hours later, with the bluegrass music winding around him and Ned leaning against the bar, sweet-talking a couple of out-of-towners into dancing with him, Casper harbored his doubts.

His brain kept traveling back to Thor, Aggie's journal, and the other pieces of the story, now floating to the surface of his mind. Like the fact that Aggie's father had died. Or as Aggie said, been *murdered*. And what about the missing US Steel bonds? Did they actually belong to Aggie?

What if she still had them tucked away somewhere?

But if she truly was a wealthy debutante, why would she hide in the woods, married to a local fisherman-turned-merchant the rest of her days?

Thor's letter pulsed at him. *"I think, in fact, you've known the truth about Duncan for years. In my defense, I did what every husband would do to keep his family safe."*

Casper had a feeling he knew exactly what Thor might have done—

"Casper!"

He turned to see Signe sidling up to him. She wore jeans, a low-cut black shirt, a white faux fur–trimmed vest, looking every inch a snow bunny. "I was hoping I'd see you."

"Hey, Sig. I thought you'd be working at the VFW tonight."

"Nope." Her long blonde hair was down and she flipped it. "Remember when I told you I had a boyfriend?" She reached for his drink, pushed it aside, and climbed onto the stool beside his. "We broke up."

Movement beyond her caught his eye, and for a moment his gaze landed, stayed on a brunette, her hair piled on top of her head, a few curly tendrils escaping. Then she turned, and his entire body went numb. In fact, maybe he'd never be able to breathe again. She wore tall black boots that only showed off her legs, a black dress that hugged the outline of her body, tracing all her curves—the ones that having a baby had left behind. A red scarf draped her neck, accentuating her red lipstick, and when she smiled at Monte, sweetly, trusting, Casper wanted to launch himself across the room and tackle him.

But he couldn't move. Couldn't breathe.

"So if you're still interested, wanna dance?"

He reeled himself back, followed the voice, and found Signe grinning at him, reaching out to touch his shirt. "I like your necklace." Her fingers closed around it. "Where'd you get it?"

"From a dig I worked on." He saw her eyes sparkle as she examined it and thought, *Why not?* He'd hardly be giving it to Raina, and he wasn't sure why he hung on to it. "You can have it."

"Really?"

He untied it and reached around her, tying it around her neck.

"What is it?"

"A pirate doubloon," he said, not sure why.

"I like it." Then she leaned over and popped a kiss on his lips. Fast and tasting of beer.

Oh. Uh.

"Now do you want to dance?"

But the kiss had somehow slid shadows into his mood. "No. I think . . . I think I need to go." It didn't help that when he glanced again at Raina's table, he saw Monte seated across from her, his hand on the table, holding hers. Caressing it. She laughed, and Casper thought he might shatter right there.

"No, Casper, stick around. I'm sorry—"

But he pulled away, slid off the stool. "It's fine. Nice to see you again, Sig. Another time."

Or never.

He pushed through the crowd toward the door and had almost reached it when he felt a hand on his jacket.

"Casper!"

Ned.

"I gotta get out of here."

"But I saw you talking to Signe." Ned had consumed a few

beers and probably didn't realize that the way he clamped his arm around Casper's neck might cut off his air.

He unwound Ned's grip. "Please tell me you didn't send her over."

"She's lonely, man. On the rebound. Eddie cheated on her, and she needs a little attention."

"Not from me. Ned, do you have a ride home? Because if not, I'm taking your keys and calling you a cab."

Ned laughed and gestured to the two girls at the bar. Nice.

"Okay, great. Listen, if you need a ride, call me. Otherwise, I'm heading home." He couldn't help it. He glanced again toward Raina but shouldn't have because he saw Monte take her hand and lead her to the floor as the band churned out a country slow dance.

Yeah, maybe Casper had been harboring some delusional hope that last weekend's outing would spark something between them, something better, deeper. Something that would heal old wounds.

Except maybe it had. Maybe it had healed them too well.

At least for Raina.

"Stay out of trouble," he said to Ned and ventured out into the cold. Whatever clues they'd dug up, he'd sleuth out the rest of the mystery on his own.

It took him the entire ride home before he could muster up a prayer for her.

"You're so pretty, Raina. We had such a fun night. Are you sure you want me to leave?"

Monte stood just inside her door, one hand braced on the wall behind her, the other playing with her scarf, running it through his fingers, his eyes caressing her. Probably he didn't realize how the scarf tightened around her neck.

She'd dressed up for him tonight because he'd asked her to, although her simple black dress still felt tight. However, the gleam of appreciation and the way he'd treated her—pulling out her chair, leaning in to give her his full attention, dancing with her, introducing her to his friends, his hand on the small of her back— all felt so . . . official. As if he wanted her to be a part of his world.

Which, after the debacle with Casper last weekend, she should welcome. Poor Monte—of course he should be jealous after she'd lied to him and snuck off with Casper as if it were a date. Of course he didn't want her to spend time with her old flame, and when he explained, put it to her plainly, she saw that.

He'd had every right to raise his voice, to slam his hand against the wall in frustration. And then he'd actually teared up like she'd hurt him—really hurt him—and she'd pulled him into her arms.

He'd probably gotten the wrong idea about her, but thankfully she'd resurrected some boundaries before she found herself repeating the past.

Clearly she had problems drawing lines—Monte even told her that she didn't know her own powers, that she drove a man beyond himself.

But not tonight. Monte had been the perfect gentleman, helping her into his truck, complimenting her, telling her jokes. He regaled her with a story about the estate he'd just landed, including a barn filled with old signs, a 1938 Ford tractor, and a player piano. "We'll make a killing if we can find the right buyers."

For a moment, her thoughts had flashed to Casper and what he'd say about the old car, the piano. The story he'd weave about the person who'd owned them, and maybe how he'd restore them.

She'd even mentioned the idea of restoring the piano to Monte. But he was right—why hang on to the past?

Now she ran her hand down his dress shirt. "It's late, and I'm tired. But you could come by tomorrow night. I'll make you dinner—"

He made a face. "Sweetie, I hate to tell you this, but . . . maybe you should let me do the cooking."

"Oh."

"I mean, of course, you're so precious for offering, but I can bring over some takeout." He slid his hand around her neck and kissed her softly, then with more ardor, his mouth tasting of the cabernet he'd had with his steak. She sank into him, trying to relax. He deepened his kiss, his hand now leaving her scarf. She caught it before his fingers could travel and pushed him away.

Monte frowned. Sighed. "Okay, Raina. Have it your way. This time." He winked, added a smile.

She found a smile back, trembling a little.

Probably just from the way he made her feel. Wanted. As if he couldn't get enough of her.

He reached for his coat. "What are you doing tomorrow?"

"We got more orders into the shop, and Gust asked me to help him package them up."

"As long as you're not meeting Casper for more frivolous treasure hunting."

She swallowed. "Nope. Of course not."

"Good. I'll be out of town for the day, but I'll be back in time for dinner." He pressed his lips to her forehead. "Sleep well." Then he closed the door behind him.

She bolted it. Watched him drive away.

Then she turned out the porch light and headed to her

bedroom. Ten minutes later, dressed in her pajamas and a robe, she plopped down in the family room with a cup of hot cocoa and Aggie's diary.

Only a month ago, she'd longed to do anything but read her evenings away. Now, with Monte at her house nearly every evening, watching one series after another—the Bourne movies, the Mission: Impossible movies—she longed for a quiet night.

Besides, Aggie and her mystery tugged at her. She'd tried to go to the house all week, but with the new snowfall, her car couldn't make it through, and Monte hadn't offered to clear the trail.

She might have to wait until spring to track down more pictures of Aggie. Without Casper.

She opened the page to where she'd last read, caught for a moment in the memory of Casper smiling at her like she'd uncovered something rare and precious.

JUNE 6

Duncan has been gone a month, and I feel as if my heart will stop beating with the pain of missing him. I know our courtship was fast and born in secret, but his attention soothed the loneliness I have felt since Mother's passing and the shame of Paris. He wants to take care of me, to love me and protect me.

The hotel feels like a prison, despite the delicious foods, the attention of the staff, the daily games of shuttlecock and pinochle. At night, the wind rustles the shaggy pine trees, whispering, and it is then I feel my father return to me, see his blood pooled on the desk. By day, the sunshine fights to find me, wrapped in a blanket in a chair by the beach. I fear I will never be warm again.

Please, please return to me, Duncan.

JUNE 8

Today, as I sat outside in a chair, searching the sea as if Duncan might return to me over it, a deliveryman came to the resort. He brought smooth, juicy oranges, and he delivered one to me by the sea.

He is a northern man. Tall, with broad shoulders that bear the evidence of hard work, and blond hair—so blond it seems almost white. He wears it shorn in back, a long fop of it in front, leaking from his fisherman's cap, and under it, the palest-blue eyes, like the sky at dawn. He wore a white shirt, suspenders, and a pair of dark trousers and smelled of the north woods that surround us. Piney. Solid.

He offered me the orange, said he'd plucked it from the sky because it told him to.

Funny man. His name is also peculiar—Thor.

JUNE 17

Thorsen Wilder. This is his full name, the blond man from the woods. He works for a local merchant, driving his delivery vehicle, but today he came in a skiff over the water. He wore his hat, the brim shading his eyes until he got to shore.

He strode right up to me and asked me if I wanted a tour by sea.

I told him I'd already seen the sea, had crossed it twice.
He told me that I'd never seen his sea.

Indeed, I have never seen the sea like Thor showed me.
He sails with his face to the winds, eyes on the horizon,
expectant, even alive with the anticipation of the next
wave. It stirs in me an odd longing, as does the rugged,
uncut wilderness, the jagged rock jutting into the water.
It is untamed and yet, sitting in the boat under Thor's
watchful attention, I feared nothing.

It was then I realized it was the first time since Mother
died that I truly wasn't afraid.

July 1

My dreams are simple. I want to have a family.
A stable life. Someone who loves me.
A home.

Thor took me on a picnic two days ago and told me
that he too wants a home, a family. Children. To make his
way in the world as a merchant. I suppose he is not unlike
Father with his aspirations.

How strange my tailored world must seem to him—
a woodsman, lumberjack, sailor.

When I told him of Father's death and how Duncan
rescued me from the flames, he fell uncharacteristically
quiet. For the first time, listening to my words in the
wind, against his silence, I heard my secret fears. But
certainly Duncan is innocent of Father's blood.

Then Thor asked the most peculiar thing. He asked, if
I had the choice, would I choose my manicured life or one

Susan May Warren

of uncertainty. *Foolish question, of course, for everyone longs for the surety that life will be without blemish.*

Thor listened through it all while sprawled on the blanket, the sun turning his hair to gold, his skin to bronze. He has a way about him that makes the world seem small when he walks into it. And when he touches my hand, my entire body goes limp as if I am a handkerchief left in the sun.

It is nearly two months since Duncan has left me, and I fear he is not returning.

Deep inside, I am also beginning to fear that he will.

JULY 10

Today we hiked to the falls behind the lodge, a roaring kettle of frothy water. Thor took my hand, and we climbed to the higher falls, where he spread out a picnic, perched above the ruckus, and we lay on our backs and traced the clouds. He says God is out there, and when we fix our eyes on Him, so is our future. He has a funny way of talking about God—easy, unafraid. I mentioned it, and he says it is because fear is a result of looking at ourselves.

Thor's large hand took mine, and he told me to look up at the largeness of God. He said that God's favor depends on His greatness, not our smallness. His great love, showered upon us. He says that a small life is lived by staring inward, but a large one is lived by diving into God's love.

I am not sure. It seems that God's love should be more tame, more reasonable. Expected and attained.

Thor walked me home, and in the soft glow of the

lamplight near the back door, he pulled me into his arms.
He searched for words in my eyes and then kissed me.
Gently, yet with the taste of the wilderness, untamed, bold
and free in his touch.

It was only after he let me go that I realized what I'd
done and fled to my room in shame. This is why I know
Thor is wrong. Because how can God not love a man like
Thor? And likewise turn away from a sinner like me?

CHAPTER 14

"Don't be afraid, Raina. Nothing down here will bite you."

Gust stood at the top of the stairs, one hand on the cord of the overhanging light, the other on a makeshift banister that led down to the dungeon below the store. The room was black as pitch, with the odor of rust, oil, and dirt rising from the darkness.

"What's down there?" She glanced back at the shop, where the gray wash of light turned everything to shadow. The sun fought to burn away the clouds this morning, a valiant attempt at cheer despite the biting cold.

He turned on the light and it bathed the stairs, puddling at the bottom. "I want to show you something."

She wanted to reach out and steady him as he ventured down one delicate, feeble step at a time. He wore a pair of dark wool pants, gray suspenders, and a bow tie today, like he might be a shopkeeper out of the fifties, and had shown his age this morning by his consternation over starting his computer.

"Confounded thing just keeps beeping at me."

But when she'd put in his password—which she pointed out to him again, taped to his metal filing cabinet—she discovered they'd sold the entire collection of milk glass on eBay.

They'd spent the morning boxing it up. "The window looks so empty," Gust had said, staring at the vacant window, something of melancholy in his expression. Based on the dusty circles etched into the glass shelving, the figurines, vases, cups, and perfume bottles hadn't been moved in fifty years.

Purposely, no doubt.

In fact, over the past month, the junk shop—as Monte put it—had been transformed into a clean, uncluttered antique shop with the sale of miscellaneous vintage signs, a set of four red-vinyl stools from the teardown of the malt shop, a malt maker, and two penny-operated grocery store rides—one a boat, the other a zebra. Raina had sold an Underwood typewriter that Gust used to type receipts and an orange Zenith record player from the 1960s, along with a small vinyl collection still in the wrap, as well as a box of drive-in movie speakers.

"Where do you get this stuff?" she'd asked as she packed up a stack of 35mm film reels.

"Here and there," Gust said, handing her the tape. "When I see someone throwing out something perfectly good, I can't bear but to save it."

His words rattled around in her now as she descended the stairs behind him. "Please don't tell me there are more . . . antiques . . . down here."

"Undiscovered treasures, my dear." Gust reached the bottom of the stairs, edged out into the darkness, and found another hanging string. He pulled it as Raina reached the dirt floor, and fluorescent light flooded the basement storage room, bouncing against the grimy cement walls.

"Oh, my." Under the bright glow of the room, an aisle of sorts tunneled through rows of crates and boxes filled with cables, greasy machinery parts, old stage lighting, mason jars, and books. Gust had attempted a meager organization by building shelving against one wall—she spied a box of soapbox derby cars and a clear plastic bin of what looked like comics. Metal alloy toys and wooden lawn art and—

"Is that an apple peeler?" She picked up the brushed metal object. It resembled a vise at one end, with a large gear attached to a handle and a three-pronged fixture to hold the apple as a blade filleted off the skin. "My grandmother had one of these."

"It was my mother's," Gust said, rooting around in a section of boxes.

"What are you looking for?" She came over to him and peered into the crate he'd just uncovered. "Are these headlights?"

"Oh, those." He picked one up, found a rag from a nearby crate, and wiped off the dust. "This came off a 1928 Hispano-Suiza H6C boattail roadster someone found in the woods by Mineral Springs. I had to have myself a look-see, so I tracked it down. Beautiful car, destroyed by the elements, but quite the looker back in the day. Probably just a pile of rust now."

"Is it still there?"

He lifted a shoulder. "Dunno. Not even sure I could find it again. But these headlights are beauties."

She tried to see them the way he did, attached to a sleek convertible roadster with running boards and spoke-hub wheels.

Not unlike the famed Duncan Rothe's car.

"Gust, have you ever heard the story of Duncan Rothe?"

"Of course. Everybody in these parts has. It's an old legend."

"How did it get started?"

"Oh, I reckon it didn't help that the law come up here looking for Duncan. Said he killed a man down in Chicago, but by the time they got here, old Duncan was long gone."

"I've been doing some research, and I think Duncan might have known Aggie Wilder."

Gust raised an eyebrow. Then he shook his head. "Don't know how. Aggie was a gentle soul—full of compassion. She would have never been mixed up with a murderer."

"People find themselves in unexpected places. Life just happens."

Gust put the headlights back, but Raina made a mental note to retrieve them later, take some pictures, and put them up on eBay. "Nah. I never met a kinder, more giving soul than Aggie. No one would have blamed her for shutting herself up after her son died—"

"What son? I thought she only had a daughter."

He frowned. "Nope, although he was born quite a bit before Ginny was. Otto died when he was ten. He fell through the ice up near Mineral Springs."

"Sad."

He continued to shift crates around. "Aggie and Thor moved to Deep Haven not long after. A few months later, Ginny was born."

He sighed, a smile tipping his lips. "When Aggie died, Deep Haven hosted the biggest funeral we'd ever seen—before or since.

Packed house, and we had it at the Lutheran church, despite her being an Episcopalian." He picked up a shadow box of medals, set it aside. "Did you know that when she opened the hotel, she had no set rates—just a *Pay what you can* sign?"

"Really?"

"Yep. See, we find here in Deep Haven that people show up to start over or even just escape. And when they do, Aggie wanted to make sure they had a place to stay." He glanced at Raina. "It probably helped that Thor footed the bill with his trading post, but Aggie cooked and cleaned and ministered for nearly twenty-five years at the old East End Hotel."

Raina had seen pictures on the bookshelf of Aggie standing in front of a rickety two-story hotel at the edge of the harbor, on a porch that wrapped around the building to face the sea.

The words from Aggie's journal filtered back to her. *"My dreams are simple. I want to have a family. A stable life. Someone who loves me."*

"A home."

And she'd gotten that. With Thor.

"Grab the end of that box." Gust gestured to another crate filled with what looked like copper, and Raina made another mental note as she helped him move it to the floor.

"Aggie also started the first crisis center in town," he said. "It was called Haven House, and she often took in women, no questions asked. Gave them jobs at the hotel. My wife, Noreen, volunteered there. She said Aggie had a way of making each woman see her own worth. She always said the best days were ahead, and she wanted to give them the gift of their future. . . . Oh, here they are."

He crouched next to an uncovered crate filled with odd-looking glass bowls. Grimy, covered in a lifetime of dust and dirt, they looked like misshapen knobs. He held one to the light.

"What are they?"

Gust smiled. He had a lean face, and sometimes she could see his features reflected in Monte, but when he smiled, an unfamiliar warmth touched her heart. "Wait and see." He grabbed one end of the box, Raina took the other, and they wove their way through the channels to the stairs.

"I can carry this, Gust," she said, seeing him labor.

He put up a fuss, but she managed to fight him for it and win. She carried the crate up to the store and set it on the counter.

In the light, she recognized different colors of glass—blue, green, clear, brown—but the filth that covered them rendered them unimpressive.

Gust shuffled his way upstairs, huffing by the time he reached the top. He held up a finger as if to say, *Wait*.

Then he went into the tiny bathroom. She heard running water, and he returned with a bucket and a washcloth. He rolled up his sleeves, then took one of the blue knobs and dunked it in the water.

"These are glass insulators. Back in the early day of the telegraph, linemen used these to connect the electrical line from pole to pole. Later, they were used for telephone and electric lines." He leaned close to her. "I had a buddy who worked as a lineman. Gave me crates and crates of these."

He pulled the knob from the water, cleaned it. Then he dried it with another rag. "The insulators used a lot of cullet, or recycled glass, in them, and you get different colors depending on the cullet. If it wasn't mixed well, you'd get ribbons of color, like this thread of white."

As the store light caught it, the insulator turned from a deep cobalt blue to an array of blues, rich indigo to lighter turquoise. It refracted the light and sent the color through the store, washing everything in a delicious ocean of blue.

"Wow."

"See? This is why I never throw anything away." His hazel eyes warmed as he smiled at her. "Other people might consider it junk. But you just have to clean it up, hold it up to the light, and suddenly it becomes breathtaking."

His gaze lingered on her and she had the strangest curl of affection for him, as if he were trying to tell her something.

Raina turned away. "I'll wash these and take their pictures, get them listed on eBay."

"No," he said, touching her shoulder. "Let's put them in the window. No need to sell them right away. Let's just enjoy them for a while."

"Gust, I think you're a romantic."

He winked at her and handed her a rag.

An hour later, with the washed insulators lining the window—honey amber, royal purple, aqua, apple green, white with red swirls—the overhead lights transformed the front window into a prism of color.

"Just imagine how radiant it will be when the sun finally comes out," Gust said. "See, you just never know when something seemingly ordinary might become rare and precious."

He might just hate people.

Casper stood in line, eyeing the last piece of pepperoni being offered to the person in front of him, and nearly did something irrational.

Like tackle the patron, steal the pizza, and run for the hills.

Or rather, the impulse to run might be from the onslaught of bargain hunters storming Wild Harbor, trying to lay their hands on the deals of the season. The door busters had lined up at 6 a.m., despite the early morning fog, and emptied the 75-percent-off racks in the first hour.

He tried to convince himself that these early morning shoppers weren't so different from him—they recognized something priceless in a $1.99 teal fleece pullover with raspberry trim.

But the fight that broke out over a pair of ski pants for six bucks? Yeah, he just about chucked the tourists right off the premises.

Maybe he didn't hate people. Just . . . customers.

"Casper? What'll you have?" Claire gestured him to the counter.

"Freedom?"

Claire raised an eyebrow. "The retail world feeling constrictive to your ramblin' man genes?"

"Large pepperoni and mushrooms, deep-dish, to go."

She laughed, keyed in the order. "Should I charge this to Ned's account?"

He nodded, ordered a drink, paid for it, and moved over to the soda machine. There he leaned against the door to wait, peering into the waiting area.

The residents of Deep Haven appeared as tired of winter as he. Pale as the dour sky, most still wore parkas, glistening with the residue of the fog off the lake. It covered the town, a ghoul that seeped between the buildings, hovering over the bay as if it were a haunted moor.

The door jangled, and his gaze flitted over to catch the customer, his stupid heart leaping as Raina came in, hands in her pockets, wearing her cute pink hat over her long dark hair. She looked up and, for a second, met his gaze.

And if it were possible, went just a little more pale.

Huh?

He frowned at her, not sure why seeing him should elicit that response.

Then she nodded at him, dismissive, before getting in line.

The gesture lit him up. That and his too-early morning and the fact that last time they'd talked, he actually—foolishly—thought they were friends. And worse was the realization that she'd so easily forgotten him, moving on with Monte . . .

Monte. In a flash, he saw her expression as she got out of the car that Saturday night. If he didn't know better, he'd call her afraid.

He moved over to her, standing next to her in line. "Are you okay?"

She glanced at him, frowning, then stared ahead. "What are you talking about?"

And that stirred him even more. Because he saw her swallow as if nervous. "You're not allowed to talk to me, are you? That's why you didn't call."

She shook her head. "Don't be silly. I've been busy, is all."

But he wasn't quite buying it, especially not after seeing the tightening of her jaw.

"It's Monte. He told you not to call me." He lowered his voice. "Is he *threatening* you?"

Raina jerked to look at him, her mouth in a perfect, tight knot. "Leave me alone, Casper." But the way she peered past him toward the dining room as if checking for prying eyes made him hold his ground.

"Raina, you don't have to be with him—"

"You know, I don't think I'm hungry." She turned and headed toward the door.

Shoot, but something about this woman just made him . . . well, care. Because he'd seen Raina with fire and passion and courage and somehow she'd vanished almost before his eyes.

"Raina. Stop." He had her by the arm and turned her. They stood on the sidewalk, the mist twining around them. She glanced at his hand on her arm and he let go.

She kept moving down the street.

"Raina, come on." He scrambled after her, hating the way his pride lay in pieces on the street. "What happened? I thought you were going to call—you said we'd go to Aggie's—"

"What is your problem, Casper? So I didn't call. Get over it."

Ouch. He recoiled, stung, but rebounded fast. "I thought we were better friends than that."

She stopped, her eyes hard, bright. "We're not. We're *nothing*."

He didn't mean to flinch.

Then—and this was even more painful—she softened her tone as if regretting her words. "Besides, Aggie's place is snowed in. I can't get there." She'd shoved her hands into her pockets and now continued quick-walking away.

And he was just curious enough to start after her. "Done. It just so happens I drove the resort truck into work today, and it still has the plow on it—"

"No." She stopped, her voice shaky. And her eyes—yeah, he'd called it right. Fear. Or something like it, rooted deep inside. "Listen, I should have never gone to Naniboujou with you. I shouldn't have said there is nothing between us. *Of course* there will always be something between us. But that's the problem. How am I supposed to move on? We need to let our friendship go and try to forget."

He stood there, struck, but he refused to let her words find a soft place. "No, I won't let it go. We *are* friends, Raina. Maybe you don't want to search for Aggie's story anymore, and if that's the case, yeah, I'll walk away. But if this is because of what I saw the other day—Monte standing at the door like he owns you—"

"He doesn't own me." She gave him a terrible, dark look. "But we are dating, and I don't want to jeopardize that."

He understood that—or should. Maybe he had let Monte's behavior stir his jealousy. Because, yeah, with her words, he could nearly taste it, the acrid poison of envy lining his throat.

He refused to be that guy.

"Okay, fine. You're right. I don't want to come between you and Monte." A lie, but what choice did he have?

Casper shoved his hands into his pockets, hunkering against the cold. "I just thought you'd be interested to know that I figured out how Thor and Aggie met. He was a delivery boy for the trading post, back when it was owned by the Zimmermans."

She seemed to relax, glancing past him, then nodding. "I read it in Aggie's journal. They met that summer."

"Do you think she ran away with him?"

"I don't know but—"

He lowered his voice. "I understand that you're dating Monte. And if you're happy, then that's great."

See, he could say that in one even flow without a hint of rancor. "But . . . if you're still serious about hunting up old pictures of Aggie, I'd be happy to plow so you can get in there."

Her gaze softened, and she seemed to be considering his words.

"What if Aggie is the heiress of those missing US Steel bonds,

Raina? Wouldn't it be amazing if we found her living an ordinary life in the woods?"

"Aggie wasn't exactly ordinary. She ran one of the first women's shelters. And did you know that her funeral was the largest attended in Deep Haven history?"

He listened as she told him about her conversation with Gust.

And watched as the tight knot of panic inside her seemed to loosen.

In fact, for a moment, she seemed to glow.

"Raina," he said, "I get off work in a couple hours. Let me pick you up and take you to Aggie's. We can look for clues to what happened between Duncan and Thor. Maybe find some hint about the bonds."

The shadow reappeared across her face.

No, Casper didn't hate people. He hated Monte Riggs.

He shook the thought away. Especially when she nodded. "I'll walk over to the Wild Harbor."

"I'll be the one breaking up a fight over mukluks."

A smile edged her face, and he let it sink in, feasted on it the rest of the afternoon.

Raina arrived just as he started to wonder if he should drive over, track her down. She climbed into the cab. "I stopped at home to pick up Aggie's diary."

She read him passages about Aggie meeting Thor, ending with an entry about Aggie fearing that Duncan would return. She closed the book. Stared out the window at the fog over the lake.

"What?"

"I don't know—it's what she said at the end. I know she loves Duncan, but when she talks about Thor, it's like she's alive."

"Duncan doesn't truly love her," Casper said, trying to keep his thoughts from veering too close to the present. Really, it wasn't his business. "He's not a good guy."

"But maybe he's good enough. He can give her a home and a life. Safety."

"Maybe that's not what she truly wants."

She looked at him, frowned. "Of course it is."

He pulled into the driveway, lowered the plow. "It's a bit icy out, so hang on. It could get bumpy."

He drove slowly, pushing curls of snow onto the side of the road, through the jagged, icy trees that scraped his windshield. He finally parked in front of the house.

Raina made to get out, but he stopped her. "Let me shovel a path to the door." He got out, grabbed his shovel, glad he'd stored a pair of Sorels in the car, and cleared a path to the stairs.

Then he turned off the truck and helped her out.

"Such a gentleman," she teased, and the sudden change in her demeanor could knock him over.

He followed her up the path and into the house. A chill hung in the air as he closed the door behind him.

"It's been unoccupied since Aggie went into the nursing home over a decade ago, and since then, it was only used as a summer vacation home for the family," Raina explained. "I don't think anyone really did any packing up. Her granddaughter finally hired Monte to clear it out and put the estate up for sale."

She moved from the foyer into a large living room. "I've already been through all the drawers in the built-ins and packaged the pictures and books." She gestured to the empty shelves. "And I worked my way through the upstairs, with the exception of Aggie's closet. I found a bunch of vintage clothing and a number of boxes on a shelf. Maybe they have some old pictures."

She led the way upstairs, leaving him to marvel at the oak detailing of the banister, the molding, his inner carpenter appreciating the handiwork. Darek would love this place.

Casper followed her up and found her in a dark closet. He turned on the penlight on his key chain and shone it in.

"Aren't you a Boy Scout?" she said, reaching up to grab a stack of boxes.

"Always prepared—" He caught two of the top boxes before they fell on her. "Careful."

She brought the boxes to the bed, set them on the bare mattress. The light of the day had begun to dim, casting shadows in the room. She opened the top box. Postcards, a shiny medal on a blue ribbon, a pair of dainty white gloves.

"This looks like a World War II medal," Casper said, picking it up.

"Could be Thor's?"

He put it back, reached for another box. This one held letters, all addressed to Aggie and sent from Paris.

Raina took the letters, bound together with ribbon, and ran her thumb over the script. "She was ninety-five when she died. Which meant she lived through two world wars, the Korean War, Vietnam, the Cold War, and even our war in the Persian Gulf."

"She saw the advent of telephones to cell phones."

"Television to computers." She put the letters back in the box. Opened another one. "Pictures. Black-and-white." She held one up. "This is Aggie and a little girl."

He picked out another one. "And in this one, she's sitting on the beach, laughing." He put it away. "I'm freezing. Let's take these back to town, grab a bite, and we'll look at them there."

She put the handful of pictures she'd grabbed back in the box.

"I have the fixings for pad thai at home that I've been dying to make."

"Let you cook for me? Any day."

She smiled, something shiny in her eyes. He boxed up the pictures and the rest of the collectibles and carried them outside.

A bluish hue from the setting sun hung over the forest. The snow crackled when he walked and he could sense her behind him, quiet.

He put the boxes in the cab, and she climbed in, shutting the door.

Still quiet.

Casper fired up the truck. "You okay?"

She sighed, nodding. Then suddenly shook her head. "It's not fair."

"What's not fair?"

Her voice dropped so low he could barely hear it over the car engine. "Why do some people get to live happily ever after and others don't?"

"Raina—"

"She fell in love or something in Paris—she wrote about it at the beginning of the diary. Her father called her tainted and sent her to Chicago. Then she fell in love with a man history calls a gangster. Except how could she be so wrong about that? It seems more like a legend than a fact. But she still married the man of her dreams and it all worked out for her. Why did she get everything—her home, her family? Her dreams?" She pressed a hand to her mouth.

Casper had the terrible urge to pull over, take her in his arms. "I don't know. But I do know that just because you make a mistake doesn't mean you have to live in it for the rest of your life."

She turned to him, narrowed her eyes. "Spoken like a man who is working in a job he hates because he's too afraid he'll fail at what he loves."

His mouth opened. He closed it. "I'm not afraid of failing."

"Then why are you still here, Casper? Why aren't you on some remote island digging up treasure? Why are you still stuck in this cold, miserable, dark forest?" Her voice had risen now, and it cut through the motor noise, sliced clear through to his heart.

You.

The word filled his chest, rose into his throat.

You, Raina.

He'd never seen it so clearly before now. But looking at her, her beautiful brown eyes glistening, her lips pursed and tight, he knew the truth.

Oh, how he loved her. And instead of going away, that truth had only deepened over the past few weeks as he thought about her, prayed for her, knew her grief. Her courage, her sincerity, her sacrifice—it all made him love her past his hurt. Wow, he wanted her to be happy. Whole.

Even if that meant without him.

His hands tight on the steering wheel, he stared ahead, trying to scrounge up an answer that didn't require him to pluck his heart from his chest. "I'm helping my family get back on their feet. The resort is . . . floundering."

Lame, but he had no other words.

"Oh," she said softly as if his answer had unseated her. Then she wiped her cheek, stared out the window.

"But I'm leaving as soon as the summer season starts."

"Good," she said. "You should."

They drove in silence, the excitement of the pictures—and the dinner awaiting—vanishing. Casper hadn't a clue how to resurrect it. Or if he wanted to. Because a guy could only handle so much pain.

Still, as he stopped at her house, Raina sat in silence, not getting out, her hand on the boxes. He finally put the truck in park.

"For what it's worth, you're going to live happily ever after, Raina. I know it. You will find someone who deserves you and loves you and you'll have the family and everything you want," he said, his heart breaking with each word. "I know you will because that's what you do best. You keep hoping, keep believing, keep loving, even when life lets you down."

He touched her hand on the seat. "You just have to get past this fog to the sunshine."

She turned her hand over in his, and he felt her squeeze it. Then she met his eyes with a smile. "Still want some of that pad thai?"

Casper sat in the breakfast nook, weeping.

"Really, you had to give me the onions?" Tears dribbled down his face as he took another napkin and wiped his cheeks.

Raina laughed, something sweet and freeing after her crazy breakdown in the car.

Somehow, seeing Aggie's happy life spread out in a handful of pictures had reached down, fisted her heart, and twisted.

But maybe Aggie deserved her happy ending.

And then she'd blurted out the question that pinged inside. *Why are you still stuck in this cold, miserable, dark forest?*

She probably had no right to ask—and especially no right to want the answer to be *her*. No right to wish he'd pulled over on the side of the road and taken her in his arms.

No right to ask him to keep driving out of Deep Haven and show her a world like Thor had shown Aggie. Maybe not a safe life, but one that radiated joy and laughter.

A strange, almost-horrified relief had washed over her, though, when he didn't. Because then she wouldn't have to tell him how wrong he was in still caring for her.

She wasn't a fool—no man in his right and clear mind would want to be with her after . . . Well, the baggage simply seemed insurmountable. Probably that included Monte too. But with him, she got a fresh start. He didn't have to see her the way Casper always would, look at her and see the destruction she'd caused.

"Do you need a hankie?"

"Leave a man alone when he's crying," Casper said, finishing the onions. "Next, O cruel one?"

She threw him a towel and picked up the cutting board with the onions. "That's enough for now." On the stove, sesame oil sizzled in the wok. She tossed in a handful of chicken, stir-fried it, then added carrots and onions. In a moment she'd add the bean sprouts, red pepper, and crushed peanuts.

Water for the rice noodles boiled on the back burner.

"I love to watch you cook," Casper said. He leaned back on the bench, arm over the top, his legs extended on a chair, crossed at the ankles. He had hung his black parka by the door, toed off his boots, and now sat in his socks, his black tailored dress shirt unbuttoned at the neck and rolled haphazardly over his elbows to reveal strong forearms. His curly hair hung below his ears, and a thick five o'clock shadow on his chin suggested he'd risen early to shave. Professor Jones, in the flesh. He opened a shoe box on his lap, casually flipping through the photos.

She'd forgotten how easy he was to have around, how he

radiated a sense of peace, even humor, his smile like a balm to her tired sorrow. *You just have to get past this fog to the sunshine.*

She dearly wanted to believe that. She stirred, and the fragrance of the onions could make her weep too. Her stomach reminded her that she'd eaten barely a piece of pizza after returning to Pierre's to fetch it for Gust.

It only added to the turmoil inside from Casper's words about Monte. She couldn't bear for them to be true. *Monte standing at the door like he owns you—*

Monte didn't own her. Like she said, she just didn't like to make him mad. And she'd told Casper—clearly—that she and Monte were together.

So having him over for dinner meant zilch. Friends poring over clues to an old mystery.

She added fish sauce to the stir-fry. It sent up a decaying, acrid odor.

"I think I found it." Casper set the box on the table. Got up. "Here's a picture of Aggie and Thor—I think this must be at the trading post in Mineral Springs. She's holding a baby in a christening gown—it looks like a gown we have at the historical center."

He walked over, stood beside her, so close she could feel him, his body warm and solid, as he held the picture up for her.

She grabbed a towel. Wiped her hand and reached for the picture. "Stir."

"Aye, aye, Captain."

She took the picture, moving away from him and the way he made her pulse ratchet up. The grainy picture showed a young woman standing on the steps of a rough-hewn store, holding a baby, her husband behind her. He was dressed in what looked like a pair of breeches, the woman in a simple shirtwaist and skirt. Her hair up, she smiled at the camera, a shine in her eyes.

"She looks happy here."

"As opposed to . . . ?"

"Well, that's certainly not the same man from her wedding photo." She set down the photo. "Add the peanuts and cilantro. I'll be right back."

She went into the next room, retrieved the Bible, brought it back to the table.

"What's that?" he asked, glancing at her.

"Aggie's Bible." She flipped to the front. "Here it is. Otto T. Wilder and his birthdate. May 1931." She closed the Bible, then took a stack of pictures from the box. "This picture is of the curio shop in Mineral Springs."

"I was thinking the lean-to attached to the store could be their apartment."

She found another, this one of a man standing in front of a winterized delivery cart on skis. He wore a fur hat, a thick coat, leather moccasins.

Another showed a little boy, maybe age four or five, riding bareback on a horse, a beaming father holding his leg.

"Hey, I think this is one of early Deep Haven. This is the antique shop." She brought it over to Casper, and he glanced at it, lowering the heat on the stove.

"Yeah, that's the old smithy shop, before Gust and Noreen turned it into the junk place."

"Collectibles and antiques," she said.

"My bad," he said and winked at her. "I'm sure there are plenty of finds."

"There are." She set the photos in the box. Closed the lid.

"Like today—Gust dragged out a box of glass insulators. They used them on old—"

"Telegraphs and railroad lights."

"Yeah." She pulled two plates from the cupboard, then set them on the table in the kitchen. "Gust washed them and put them in the window. They were beautiful . . . like a stained-glass window."

"I have no doubt," he said. "Actually, Gust was one of the culprits who got me into treasure hunting. He used to sponsor the great Deep Haven medallion hunt every year."

She drained the noodles and added them to the wok. "Medallion hunt?"

Casper was paging through the Bible, examining it. "He was on the chamber of commerce, and I think he made it up to draw tourists, but the tradition stuck. Every year, the chamber hides a medallion during our annual Fisherman's Picnic, with clues posted in the paper. The winner gets a check for $100."

Raina brought the wok over, and he put the Bible away, grabbed his plate. She dropped noodles onto it.

"You're looking at the medallion champion of 2003 and 2004," he said.

"Two years?"

"Yep. Even got my name and picture in the paper. My mom cut it out and taped it to the fridge, next to all of Darek's and Owen's hockey headlines and Eden's article about some variety show she was in. I think Mom still has it."

Raina pulled up a chair. "I have a feeling you could find the Holy Grail if you put your mind to it."

He scooted in his chair, giving her such a disarming look that a blush rose in her face. "What?" she asked.

"That's about the nicest thing anyone ever said to me."

Raina picked up chopsticks, handed him a pair. And of course he knew exactly what to do with them. She lifted a shoulder. "It's true. You say I always believe in love—you always believe there is something worth finding out there."

He frowned a little as if her words touched him, settled inside. Her throat tightened, her words resounding back to her, too raw, too intimate.

Then he saved her. "You know there really is a lost Knights Templar treasure. They were sort of military priests who protected people in their travels to Jerusalem. People paid tribute to them, and they got so rich that kings borrowed money from them. But they were forced out of the Middle East, along with the treasure." He leaned forward, his eyes sweet, his voice low. "And they were never heard from again."

She giggled.

He leaned back, stirring his pad thai. "Actually, I'd be happy with figuring out the mystery of Duncan Rothe and whether he left a million dollars of US Steel bonds behind. I don't even care about the money—just the fact that I wouldn't be the family laughingstock anymore."

"Oh, Casper—"

He made a face. "Sorry. It's fine."

Except it wasn't fine, because probably she was to blame for his escape to the Caribbean, to find something that might make him feel accomplished and heal the wounds she'd created. "I certainly hope your treasure hunting days aren't over."

Again, that look, a slow smile that infused his entire face. "Not yet."

She took a bite of the pad thai. "This is fantastic."

"You're the cook." But he took a bite, made a loud, slurping sound that had her entire body turning warm. "Whoa. Divine."

She heard the door open, the voice barging in before she could jump up to intercept. "Raina? Who's here with you?"

She glanced at Casper, who frowned, and met Monte just as he came into the room.

He took one look at Casper, his face darkening.

She pressed a hand to her stomach. "Monte."

Inexplicably he smiled. Extended a hand to Casper. "Hey. That looks good."

Casper considered Monte's outstretched hand maybe a second too long before he stood, shook it. "It is."

"Mind if I have a plate?"

Really? "Of course not," Raina managed. "I'll get you some."

"Thanks, Raina, hon." Before she could turn, Monte grabbed her hand, his grip tight, and pulled her to him, landing a fast, hard peck on her lips. "You're a doll."

She managed a smile but turned away, tasting the sharp bite of blood.

CHAPTER 15

Ivy's voice drifted from the bedroom as Darek came in.

"'Now the little boy, who had been keeping very quiet, had another good idea. He said, "Why couldn't we leave Mary Anne in the cellar and build the new town hall above her?"'"

Darek pulled off his boots and hung his jacket on the hook. A half-eaten tuna casserole congealed, cold and sticky, in the middle of the kitchen table, next to an empty plate and a glass of milk.

He should have called. But the chain broke on the splitter and he'd spent half the evening welding it together. It would have been better to take it to Wade's machine shop, but he didn't have extra cash for repairs.

He walked down the hall to where light streamed from Tiger's bedroom. Ivy sat on the bed, leaning against the headboard, a book open on her lap. Tiger curled up next to her, holding a LEGO truck, driving it up and down his leg as she read.

Darek crossed his arms and leaned against the doorframe, soaking in the scene. The quiet power she had to heal him could leave him weak.

Sometimes I wish I never had a family. I just let them down. How he regretted his words and the wounds he'd inflicted on their marriage. No amount of apology or her forgiveness could erase from his memory the shocked, broken look on Ivy's face. Nor did it change their dire financial straits.

Ivy looked up and smiled at him, her eyes gentle.

"Hey," he said.

"Hi. We're just finishing here. There's tuna casserole left on the table."

"I saw it. Mom gave me some soup."

"Oh, that sounds better. One day I hope to cook like your mother."

"You're a great cook. I'll put it away." He walked into the room and leaned over her, kissing her forehead. Then he reached out for Tiger. "How you doing, champ?"

"Fine." Tiger didn't meet Darek's eyes.

Okay.

Ivy caught his hand as he turned. "I'll be just a moment."

He nodded and returned to the tiny galley kitchen, where he covered the casserole with tinfoil and shoved it into the fridge. Then he drank the milk, cleared the dishes, and added the glass and plate to the dishwasher. Started it and turned off the light.

Ivy was in their bathroom when he returned, washing her face. He came up behind her, caught her hair back, and held it as she rinsed. Then he handed her a towel.

She patted her face dry before turning to him, so much trust in her eyes that he wanted to slink away. Especially when he cradled her face with his hands and noted that despite his scrubbing, they seemed dirty.

"I love you," he said and bent down, pressing his lips to hers. Softly, because he treaded on the edge of hating himself for what he'd decided. But he'd thought it through. Really wrangled it around in his head since his fight with his father and . . .

He didn't see any other choice.

"I love you too," she said, her eyes shiny. "And I know you're worried about Tiger." She caught his hand, put it on her belly. It had seemed to double in size in a week—or maybe he hadn't noticed how cumbersome pregnancy was before. He certainly hadn't been around much when Felicity carried Tiger.

Apparently old habits ran deep. But this time he wasn't running from the future. He would run to save it.

"I think he's just got big brother syndrome," she was saying. "I've never had a sibling, but I remember every time some new foster kid arrived, for about two weeks I fought jealousy. It didn't help that I got moved around so much, but . . . well, Tiger's bound to feel like he's being replaced."

"I don't think so. I think he's mad at me for being gone so much."

Disagreement touched her brow in a frown. Then she took his hand, led him into the bedroom. "Sit. I have something to show you."

"What?"

"We need to talk. At the conference, Tiger's teacher said he hadn't turned in any of his assignments in about a month. I thought, what kind of assignments does a first grader have? But

I guess he had worksheets and art projects and permission slips and they were all supposed to be brought home, signed, and returned."

"What happened to them?"

Ivy walked to their closet, opened it, and pulled out a plastic bag bulging with wadded paper. "This. I searched his cubby at school, and his backpack, and found nothing. But then I started to think—when I was in foster care, I usually found a hiding spot for food or treasures in every home I lived in. So I came home over lunchtime today and searched his room while he was at school." She handed him the bag, sitting next to him. "I found this in the back of his closet, in his toy chest."

Darek picked out one of the crumpled papers, opened it. A Valentine's Day card. He smoothed it on the bed and reached for another. A picture of a groundhog. "Why would he do this?"

"I don't know. But it makes me want to cry for him."

He set the bag down, turned to her, dreading the words forming. As usual, she could read his face. "What is it?"

"I need to go to Arizona." He said it without emotion, without betraying the twist in his chest.

"What?" She wore the appropriate expression.

He got up, not sure how to explain his tumble of thoughts over the past few days, but—it had to be the right decision.

"I got an e-mail from Jed Ransom, my old fire boss with the Jude County Hotshots. They're fighting a fire in Arizona, and it's so early in the season, they don't have a lot of help. He asked—"

"Are you out of your mind?"

Just like that, his quiet, patient wife vanished, and in her place was the assistant county attorney, angry, resolute. She kept her voice low, however—a dangerous trick that told him to brace himself.

"Ivy, listen to me. I can earn money—we *need* the money. So far we have no revenue for March or April on the books. And if past seasons are any indication, we won't see any traffic until May or even June. I have mountains of bills to pay—"

"And a baby on the way." She held her hands over her stomach as if to protect the child. "I know I have more than a month left, but what if I go into early labor . . . ?" She exhaled hard as if to relieve the pain written on her face and looked away. "Yeah. Right. I get it." She lifted a shoulder. "No problem."

No problem?

"Ivy?"

"I'll—we'll be just fine, Darek. Go."

"I don't know what else to do. This feels like a solution that I can't pass up." He knelt in front of her, took her hands.

With the gesture, the lawyer vanished and his wife returned. Solid, unwavering. "Darek, I know you're overwhelmed and that we're a burden to you, but . . . but leaving us isn't the answer."

A burden? Oh—her eyes had filled, and now a tear spilled over his thumb. She blinked hard, shook it away, and got up, stepping away from him. She wiped her cheek, angry. And like he'd been slapped, he got it. He'd walked right into her wounds, ripping them open.

"I'm not abandoning you. Or pushing you away. This is not me rejecting you, Ivy. Or our family. I need to do this. We're *broke*. I swear to you I'll be back before the baby comes."

She nodded as if that made perfect sense, but he could spot a lie from his wife, despite not being the one with the law degree.

"Ivy—" He took her arm. She stilled and he turned her. Yeah, tears ran down her face, and they tore a hole through him. "I love you. But . . ."

Shoot, now he felt like crying. Like the world had opened up around them, taken him under, and he floundered, suffocating, not sure how to reach the surface.

They *were* drowning, and he just hoped—no, prayed—that this could save them.

"I'm in over my head here. And I'm trying to be a good husband. A good father—"

She reached up, laid her hand over his mouth. "I know. I just wish you could see that you already are."

"But I'm not, and I get that. My son is hiding from me and already, in first grade, failing school. My father is trying to figure out why he trusted his resort to me. And my wife—"

"Your wife loves you."

"My wife is too good to me." He pressed a hand to his eyes, hating the tremble in his voice. He barely noticed as she backed him up to the bed, made him sit. Settled her bulk on his lap, looping her arms around his neck.

Then she bent his head to her chest, holding him. "When do you leave?"

He clung to her. "As soon as I can. I need to talk to Casper and my father, of course. But . . . maybe on Monday."

She kissed the top of his head, and he didn't want to move, ever.

Raina stood at the window, her hand pressed against it as she watched Monte leave, the morning sun bleak behind the clouds.

According to Monte, he had wanted to propose, and she'd wrecked it.

He'd come home to surprise her and found Casper sitting at her kitchen table, her betrayal so sour that he'd thrown her pad thai out the back door.

Of course, he'd waited until Casper left, the meal tense and awkward despite Monte's attempts at conversation. He'd just wanted to know what they were doing with Aggie's photos. If only Casper hadn't turned strangely, morosely, tight-lipped.

So she'd filled Monte in on the details—how Casper found the wedding dress, then the license, how they'd tracked down the picture at Naniboujou, which he knew. But then she'd dug out Aggie's picture from the trading post in Mineral Springs.

She told him about the diary too, despite the frown on Casper's face. But she didn't want to keep anything from Monte—that seemed underhanded and sneaky.

She'd had enough of secrets and lies.

Monte listened, asked a few questions, even probed into Casper's memory of the Duncan Rothe story.

Casper turned downright stingy with his information. What, did he think Monte might steal the crazy legend from him, actually compete with him for the so-called treasure?

Watching Casper as Monte quizzed him, his mouth a dark line, his furtive glances in her direction, maybe that's exactly what Casper thought.

Casper finally left, again shaking Monte's hand, but the smile had long faded from his face.

Raina ran her hand over her arm, feeling the bruise from where Monte had grabbed her, pushed her against the wall. Kissed her a little too passionately. But he'd been holding back all night—had driven two hours to surprise her, to tell her that he wanted to propose. She'd wrecked his perfect moment, and now . . . who knew when he'd trust her again?

So yes, she understood when he returned to the kitchen, took the rest of the dinner, and threw it outside in the snow. And the way he scooped up the plates, dropping them into the sink.

He didn't apologize for breaking them until later, but maybe he didn't notice, the way his shoulders shook. As if he might be crying.

She'd run her hand along his back, trying to ease him out of his fury. He'd stalked away from her—she thought for a moment he might be leaving. Then he returned and took her hand, pulling her with him to the sofa.

There, he drew her onto his lap and told her how much he cared for her. Really cared. So much that he couldn't bear to share her with anyone else. In fact, he'd said, "I want a future with you, Raina. A home. But I'm not sure you want that too." His red-rimmed eyes betrayed the depth of his emotion.

She clung to those words, letting him weave his hands into her hair. Pull her to himself.

And tried to reassure him that, yes, she was his.

She'd let him stay on the sofa because of the icy roads, and he curled up with his head in her lap, finally sleeping.

She wove her fingers into his hair, a strange swirl of anticipation inside she couldn't quite read.

A future, a home.

A home for Layla. The thought sprang to her mind the moment he'd suggested a future, and she couldn't shake it away.

She could give Layla security. A family.

It didn't matter that she didn't love Monte. He was a good enough man. The man she probably deserved. And he wanted a future with her. That was more than . . . anyone else . . . offered.

Icy rain pinged against the window, glazing the trees. She had called in sick today, fatigue making her ill. Now she rubbed her arm as she went to her bedroom, changed into her pajamas, and climbed into bed.

The sun barely dented the weepy palette of the day. She pulled up her covers, her head thick, stuffy, her body achy.

She picked up Aggie's diary, thumbed to the next entry. Yawning, she found her place.

JULY 25

I can admit now that the feeling I had for Jean-Philippe couldn't have been love. Nor could the sweet excitement of dancing with Duncan be more than infatuation. Because love feels like the sun on your face after a cold winter, smells like lilacs and wild roses, sounds like the lilting song of the bluebird in my soul. It's Thor bringing me oranges, or recently, fresh-cut strawberries, and curling up against him as we trace the stars that canopy the magnificent lake. It is his eyes finding mine as I tell him my dreams, our fingers laced as we tread along the rocky shoreline.

It is the way he kisses me, his hands cupping my face gently as if I might break, his own desire for me tightly coiled even as he trembles. He is so strong, and yet I feel only freedom when he lifts me over the waves to his sailboat or lends me his arm as we stroll down the paths around the hotel. He even drove me into Deep Haven, a tiny fishing village settled upon the marshy bay of the grand lake, and introduced me to his father, a local fisherman. They fed me trout caviar and smoked whitefish.

Thor said to me, as we floated in the big lake, that richness is a state of mind, that money can't buy safety or even happiness. I know he is hinting at marriage, waiting for me to believe his words, "to live large," as he puts it.

He doesn't have to. I see my life with him. A life so different from what I expected, but right nonetheless, because I never felt more myself, the person free from the trappings of Father's commands and even Duncan's designs.

Thor hasn't asked, but I see it in his eyes. Perhaps he is simply waiting for me to be free. Thus, I penned the truth to Duncan in a letter and am posting it today. If he never returns, it would be for the best.

Raina yawned again, the gray sky seeping into her bones, the wind on the pane moaning.

AUGUST 7

Duncan is here. He showed up last night, late, burst into my room, and threw my mother's wedding dress at my feet. He informed me that I'd made him a promise.

Apparently he means for me to keep it.

Raina closed her eyes for a moment, fatigue a blanket pressing her into slumber. The moaning seemed to flow over her, soak through her.

Then, thudding.

"Augusta, hurry up; everyone is waiting." Not Augusta. *Raina.* She tried to say that, but the words clogged in her throat.

She couldn't breathe, her ribs constricted, and she touched her stomach, discovering it encased in a hard bodice, her dress—no, a gown, silk that flowed through her fingers like ice. White.

She found her image in the bureau mirror.

A long veil draped down her back, her hair pinned up to show her thin neck.

"Augusta, now. We must take pictures before the magistrate gets here." The door handle rattled.

She looked around and identified a dressing room. Wood paneling lined the walls, the scent of summer folding in on the breeze from the window, bracketed in lace eyelet curtains. A steamer trunk sat propped open on the floor next to an empty dress stand.

Just a dream. Yes. But somehow Aggie's words imprinted in Raina's mind and now she'd dreamed herself into Aggie's story. Or perhaps her own nightmares—she didn't know. Just heard the racing of her heartbeat as she ventured into the next room and found a suitcase open on the bed. Inside, an envelope lay tucked on top. She eased it out, opened it. Bonds. Made out to Clara Augusta Franklin.

"Augusta!"

She tucked the bonds back in the suitcase.

The door swung open.

It seemed she recognized the man in the frame—solidly built, slicked-back dark-blond hair, handlebar mustache over thin lips, angry black eyes. He wore a gray pin-striped suit, an ascot at his neck, and carried a bowler.

She stood frozen, her mind blank, as he stormed over, hooked his hand around her arm. "Don't give me any trouble, now."

She struggled for words as he dragged her into the hallway, then righted her and held out his arm. "You'll feel better once this is over." He'd lowered his voice, but she found no comfort in his tone.

She took the stairs down to the foyer and recognized it at once by the bright tapestry of colors adorning the walls—the green-lined draperies, the zigzag orange-and-crimson pattern on the ceiling, the eyes of the totem birds watching as her escort directed her toward a photographer. He stood with his camera and pointed to a chair. "Mr. Rothe, take a seat; Miss Franklin, behind him."

Duncan Rothe. The name came to her lips and might have tripped out because he glanced at her, trouble creasing his brow.

She stood behind him, solemn, and he took her hand, placed it on his shoulder.

The bulb flashed, the smoke acrid in the air.

"Now by my roadster." Duncan put his hand on her arm, one foot propped on the running board as he positioned her in front of him.

She shivered in the piney breeze.

"I need—" Her brain seemed snarled as if she couldn't break free of the cotton webbing her thoughts. "I need—"

"Inside, my love," Duncan said, his hand gripping her elbow. "A moment of rest before the ceremony." He directed her back upstairs, yet his smile faded as he pushed her inside her room.

She heard the turn of the lock.

I need . . . Thor.

The thought pulsed, clear, rich, beyond the moaning, into the free.

Yes, she needed Thor, and the more she said his name, the more he materialized in her mind. Thor, with his ruddy outdoorsy aura, blue eyes, the way he made her feel free and whole.

Unafraid.

"Thor!" She heard her voice, a rumble, deep inside. "Thor!"

She beat on the door. Her body shook, her voice hoarse, her eyes burning. *Thor!*

Then voices outside. She ran to the window, looked out. Spied Duncan glad-handing a man in a suit.

No. She held on to the window frame, crumpling to the ground in her silk. Buried her head in her arms, breathing hard.

A buzzing trickled into the room, wound around her beating heart like a bee or a wasp. She looked up, searching—

The door banged open, slamming against the bureau, and she jerked, her gaze caught on the man in the frame.

Dark hair, long around his ears. Blue eyes—the kind that could take her apart and rebuild her in a glance. Dressed in boots, leather breeches, a white cotton shirt open at the neck. Tanned where his shirtsleeves were rolled up to reveal his thick, sinewed arms, and an expression on his face that swept all thought but one from her mind.

Casper.

No, that wasn't right. She frowned. "Thor?"

"Run, Aggie." He gripped her arms, pulled her to her feet, and laced her hand in his. Then he pressed a hard kiss to her forehead. "My car is out back. It's time to go."

She gathered her skirt, but it seemed endless, the swaths and layers tangling around her knees. His hand loosened on hers, and his voice echoed, growing distant in her ears. "C'mon, Aggie! Run!"

The buzzing again.

She fell, fought to free herself from the dress, clawing at it, tangling herself, her breathing tight, short, gasping—

"Oh!" Raina opened her eyes, still struggling as the afternoon pressed shadowy ghouls into her room. The sheets noosed her legs, her waist. Her heart pounded with the fading dream.

So terribly real, she could still smell the lilac on the breeze.

Her cell phone vibrated on the stand by her bed. She slapped at it, knocked it on the floor, then rolled over, groping for it under the bed.

It had stopped buzzing by the time she curled her grip around it. Voice mail had already caught the message.

She flopped back on the pillow, breathing hard, waiting.

Casper had no place in her dream. No right to her unconscious musings.

Aggie's diary lay on the pillow next to her. She picked it up, read the last lines of the entry.

> *Duncan says we are to marry in the morning. He has locked me in my room. I have no hope of getting a message to Thor.*
>
> *And yet I wonder if perhaps Duncan is right. He has told me that the north woods are no place for a debutante. More, that Thor has simply been dallying with my affections.*
>
> *And he has reminded me that, after Paris, perhaps Thor wouldn't want me anyway.*
>
> *My stubborn heart refuses to believe it, and yet as the night grows long, I wonder if I am trading safety for a summer love that holds no true promise.*
>
> *I will marry Duncan in the morning.*

Raina closed the diary. Untangled herself from her bedsheets and got up. She dialed her voice mail as she went to the bathroom and drew a bath, sitting on the side of it, stirring her hand in the clear, warm water.

When the message started, the voice slogged through her.

"Raina, it's Dori. Just a reminder that the court date to finalize the adoption is Monday. It's imperative that you sign the final relinquishment papers. Your local court administrator has them and you can sign them there. We'll take care of everything else. Call me if you have any questions."

Questions.

She had too many questions—the kind of questions Dori couldn't begin to answer.

Like, would it really get easier as time went on? Because two months later, the peace she'd hoped to find had only turned into a haunting wail.

And would Layla really be better off? Especially now that Raina could give her a family?

Monday, she could finish it. Sign her baby over and walk away. Try to forget. To heal.

Or . . . she could say yes to the only man who offered her a future.

"I have an announcement."

Casper looked up as Darek propped his fork on his plate and sighed.

Everyone at the Sunday dinner table, with the exception of Tiger, stopped talking. Ingrid set the mashed potatoes down beside her plate as John handed Casper his plate of roast beef.

Out of the corner of his eye, Casper saw Ivy's mouth tighten into a grim line.

Amelia glanced at Casper, an eyebrow raised. True to her

promise, she hadn't mentioned a word of his secret to their parents—or at least, neither Ingrid nor John had tracked him down for details.

To get Amelia's mind off her broken heart, Casper had dragged her to the Wild Harbor, putting her to work helping fussy women try on Keens. Ned roped her onto the staff in a blur that still had Amelia trying to unravel how she'd ended up wearing a Wild Harbor uniform.

Yet being gainfully employed seemed to buoy her spirits. And it helped keep Casper's grim thoughts from traveling to his own tragedy—namely Raina and her gut-wrenching choices.

"What is it, Son?" John said now to Darek.

Darek took another breath as if bracing himself. "I'm going to Arizona for a couple weeks to work for the Jude County Hotshots."

Silence, this time so thick Casper could slice it with the blunt edge of his butter knife. He glanced at Ivy, who set her fork down, her mashed potatoes, gravy, roast beef, and green beans growing cold. She sighed, offering no comment.

Next to her, Tiger gnawed on his dinner roll as if ignoring his father's news.

Darek glanced at his father, then at Casper. "I'm hoping Casper can fill in for me while I'm gone."

"Casper has a job," John said, his tone soft.

Casper frowned, not sure why the words prickled him.

"Tiger, how about I fix you that plate in the den—I think we have one of your Scooby-Doo shows taped," Ingrid said. Mom must have figured out how to work the DVR. She scooped up Tiger's plate, grabbed his milk.

He slid off the chair and followed her. "Does it have Scrappy-Doo too?"

"Darek, what on earth are you thinking? Ivy's about to pop—"

Darek held up his hand to Amelia's words, glanced at Tiger, still exiting, then cut his voice low. He reached across the table to take Ivy's hand as he spoke. She closed her grip around his. Gave him a sad smile.

"It's just for a couple weeks—and it's good pay for once," Darek was saying. "Jed needs me, and we need the money. Someone has to pay that propane bill, and with no more business on the books until May . . ." He shook his head. "I don't know what else to do."

Casper couldn't identify the knot forming in his chest. Or the way it tightened when his father said, "Darek, your place is here, running the resort, like we talked about. You can't just dump it into Casper's lap."

"I don't mind," Casper started.

"You've spent almost two years rebuilding this place. It's just as much yours as it is mine now. You can't abandon it."

Outside, the sun finally escaped the swaddle of clouds, and water dripped from the jagged icicles hanging from the roof.

"I'm not abandoning it, Dad. Casper will check the cabins, and you and Mom can take any calls to the office—it's only for two weeks."

"Two weeks, and the thaw is just beginning. Who knows but we'll have flooding or icefall on the roofs or even sewer problems. That's what running a resort is all about, Darek—sticking around in case—"

"I'm useless here!"

Casper stared at Darek, who had pushed his plate away, shaking the table. Even Ivy frowned at him.

He exhaled hard, hauled in his voice to a low, schooled volume.

"Sorry. Listen. Ivy will be fine. I'm leaving as soon as I can, Monday morning. Casper, I'll make sure you have an exhaustive list, *in case* the world falls in."

He got up, heading to the office.

Casper studied Ivy's face as she watched him go, trying to interpret her expression.

"He's a good man," Ivy said, directing her words to John. "He's just overwhelmed with the baby and Tiger's issues at school and now the resort. He'll work it out." She folded her napkin, tucked it under her plate. Worked herself to her feet. "I'll get Tiger—"

Amelia touched her arm. "Sit, Ivy. Eat your lunch. I'll come over after work and help with Tiger. Darek is a great brother—the best. I know he'll figure it out."

But Casper had found his feet almost without realizing it. "Not like this."

He tracked down Darek at the desk, booting up the computer.

"Have you completely lost your mind?"

Confusion creased Darek's brow. "No. In fact, it's the first sane idea I've had in years. I probably should have done this after the resort burned, realized the place had seen its last heyday. Should have figured out that I needed to get a real job—"

"Oh yeah, I'm here to testify that a real job is *just* what you need." Casper shook his head. "Dude, do you have any idea what it feels like to spend your day trying to find angry women a size 8.5 wide Keens?"

Again, confusion.

"Trust me on this, you've got a good gig going here. Ivy and Tiger, a job building on what Mom and Dad built—"

Darek stood and rounded on him. "And what *you* don't get is that I'm failing at it. How would you like that on your shoulders—the brother who brought down seventy-five years of family legacy?"

"I get it—I know what it feels like to leave a scar on the family tree. But running isn't the answer."

"That's rich, coming from you."

"Exactly. That's why you need to listen to me. I wish more than you can know that I'd stuck around, that I'd forgiven Raina last summer. That when Owen showed up, I didn't let my pride destroy any hope I had with the woman I love."

Oh. Casper hadn't meant to let his voice thunder, to hear it echo into the rest of the house.

Darek stilled. "I thought we talked about this. I thought you were trying to get over her."

"I am. I was . . ." Casper tunneled his hand through his hair, blowing out a breath. "I can't. And frankly, I don't even think I want to."

He walked over to the window. Pressed his hand against the cold pane. "We're good together. When I'm with her, I feel like I'm not the second choice, even though I'm probably just fooling myself."

"What are you talking about? Second choice?"

"Oh, c'mon, Darek. I'm not Dad's first choice for this resort and clearly wasn't Raina's first choice of brothers. Even now, she chose someone else. But for some reason, I forget that when I'm with her. She makes me believe that I can . . ." He shook his head because *find the lost treasure* sounded so lame. "She makes me feel like I'm not a failure."

Nothing from Darek's side of the room, but he didn't expect it. Not with Darek looking at the same visage in the mirror.

"And to grind salt into my wounds, she's dating Monte Riggs, of all people."

"You make it sound like she's dating Satan," Darek said.

"She is. I swear it. He looks at her like he owns her."

"So why don't you do something about it? It's not like she has a ring on her finger, right?"

Casper considered him. "Seriously?"

Darek lifted a shoulder.

"For one second, track back with me to Owen. And our fight. Now picture Raina and me together. Can you imagine *that* family Christmas dinner?"

"Seems to me that you don't owe Owen anything."

But he did. Or Raina did. Maybe more than anything else, the ever-present agony of the secret, burning deep inside them, would be enough to drive them apart.

He'd always believe Owen deserved to know the truth. And she'd always consign him to secrecy, to betrayal.

Casper turned to stare out the window overlooking the resort, the cabins, and the glistening, melting snow. "I think as soon as you get back, I'm leaving. This time for good."

The words simply slipped out from where they'd been hibernating in his thoughts. Now he saw them, knew the decision had been fermenting for weeks. He couldn't stick around and watch Raina make one disastrous decision after another. "I don't know what else to do. What do you do when the person you love doesn't love you back?"

"That depends. Is your love dependent on her love for you? Or not?"

Casper startled at his father's voice behind him. Darek shrugged, like, *Sorry, dude; I didn't realize he'd walked in.*

John stood at the door, one hand on the knob. He closed it behind him. Looked at his sons, first Casper, then Darek. "Sit down, boys."

Oh. It was one of those moments. Casper lowered himself onto the chair. Darek folded his arms, leaning against the desk.

"I've just been remembering . . . You might not know that I never wanted this resort." John pulled out the desk chair, sat on it. "When I was a teenager, the last thing I wanted to do was return to the postage stamp–size town of Deep Haven and run my dad's place."

Casper glanced at Darek, who frowned.

"I even told him so—right out there on the lake. I told him I didn't want his resort, that I had a bigger life planned. And then I left to play football at the University of Minnesota. Even after I graduated and didn't get drafted, I refused to come home. I played arena ball of all things, refusing my father's phone calls until it was too late. He died during one of my games. I never said good-bye."

Darek's jaw tightened.

Casper looked down at his hands, his throat thick.

"I came home, and after the funeral, I found that old canoe I keep tied up at the dock. Dad and I made it together, and I took the canoe out onto the water and wept. I felt sick with my own regret, my own selfishness. And then I remembered the last time we'd taken out the canoe—the very day I'd told him that I'd never run this place. He sat in the bow of the canoe, not arguing with me, but humming."

John began to hum, and Casper's memory picked up the tune, the words. *"O Lord my God! When I in awesome wonder consider all the worlds Thy hands have made . . ."*

"It was my dad's favorite song. He'd sing it when we went fishing and while he was nailing down roof tiles and shoveling and cutting firewood." John's low, dependable tenor voice broke out. "'When through the woods and forest glades I wander and hear the birds sing sweetly in the trees, when I look down from lofty mountain grandeur and hear the brook and feel the gentle breeze . . .'"

He paused, letting them fill in the rest. *"How great Thou art! How great Thou art!"* His gaze fell on Darek. "My dad told me, after I'd spurned everything he wanted to give me, 'I have no doubt you'll be a success at whatever you do.' I had no idea that he was giving me a glimpse of success in the humming of his song."

He looked at Casper then. "See, I was my own worst enemy back then. My pride told me I deserved better. A bigger life. But my dad figured it out—there is no life bigger than the one lived, every day, in awe of God. God showing up in our lives to love us despite ourselves. That is a treasure we can find every single day."

Casper frowned, glanced at Darek.

John got up and put his hand on his oldest son's shoulder. "Darek, there are many different definitions of success. I'm not sure that any of them are stamped with the Evergreen Resort logo. I'm sorry if I made you believe otherwise."

Darek unfolded his arms, his expression slackening.

Casper looked up to find his father's gaze on him. Solid, kind. "How do you keep loving someone who doesn't love you back? Like Jesus did, Son. Faithfully praying, faithfully abiding, faithfully loving anyway."

"Hey, I gave him that advice," Darek said, nodding, a slight grin creeping up his face.

Casper rolled his eyes. "Thank you both, but you don't understand. I am praying—all the time. And it hurts more every day because my prayers are accomplishing *nothing*. I can't fix her. I can't save her. I just have to stand by and watch. I wish she could see that she's going to really get hurt."

"You don't think Jesus sees our choices, our decisions, and wants to run out in front of us with semaphores?" John said. "He does, in fact, warn us over and over of the ways we're destroying ourselves. But we don't listen. And what does love do? Forgives. Comforts. Protects. Saves. Renews. *Loves.*"

John moved toward the door. "If what we call love doesn't take us beyond ourselves, require more of us than we ever dreamed, then it's not the unconditional, divine love God intends for us. God's love is not cautious, not wise, not sensible, and not remotely conservative. In fact, loving another person the way God loves them is the greatest adventure we can have." He winked at Casper. "The greatest treasure you can find."

His eyes seemed to glisten. "I am thankful I raised better sons than I was. I believe in you both, and I know you're good men. I'm very proud of you."

John gave Darek a nod. "Stay safe, Son." Then he looked at Casper. "And you, be wise. You can be your own worst enemy sometimes. Maybe it's time to get out of the way and let God be in charge of your heart."

Then he walked out the door.

CHAPTER 16

RAINA WORE THE BLACK DRESS to her appointment at the court-house. Finally it fit her.

She'd lost her appetite three days ago. Somehow the physical ache served to distract her from the howl inside, the one that cracked free every time she thought of the finality.

Good-bye.

This was crazy. She'd already made the decision two months ago. Already accepted the wounds, the scars. Now, with Monte's supposed upcoming proposal, her mind lay in knots. She should have signed Layla over a month ago instead of waiting. She thought it would get easier—it only turned the act excruciating.

As Raina walked into the courthouse and found her way to the county attorney's office to sign the paperwork, every step seemed to revive Layla's tiny cry, tucked away in her memory.

She wrapped her hand around the railing, forcing herself up the stairs.

How, really, did a mother separate herself in two pieces and give the best part of herself away? Forever?

She found the office, breathing through the burning in her chest, and knocked.

"Raina, good, you're here."

"Dori—what are you doing here?" She hadn't expected her adoption coordinator in person. Dori once again wore the green jacket, this time with a short black-and-white wool skirt, and looked younger than a person who talked people into life decisions should.

"I came because we have a new development in your case," Dori said. She opened the door wider, and Raina recognized Ivy— a very pregnant Ivy Christiansen—sitting at her desk.

Oh. No. She hadn't considered, when she asked to have her case moved here, that Ivy, Casper's—*Owen's*—sister-in-law, might be the one to do the paperwork.

She stood there stricken.

"Don't worry, Raina," Ivy said, waving her in. "I'm bound by confidentiality."

Raina tried to read her expression, found it enigmatic. Judgment? Compassion?

Dori gestured her to a chair and shut the door.

Ivy sat behind a desk that overlooked the harbor, sunlight cascading through the window onto her desk, piled with files, a laptop on the pullout arm. She shifted as if trying to make herself more comfortable.

Yeah, Raina well remembered those days.

The balmy day—a temporary and unseasonable forty-two—had

left the air soggy. She'd talked herself into needing the cool, spring-sweet air, but now sweat slicked down Raina's back from her walk to the courthouse.

"Is everything okay with . . . the baby?"

Dori sat down. "She's fine. Healthy. But her adoptive parents . . . Well, there's a new development. The mother is pregnant."

"What?"

"This happens occasionally—somehow, with the adoption, the pressure of conceiving seems to be lessened, and parents inexplicably find themselves expecting."

"But . . . I don't understand. She's pregnant? How does that affect . . . ?" She might as well say it. "Layla."

Dori didn't even seem to blink at her name. "The mother is very ill. She's bedridden and on medication. But she's nearly three months along, and the baby is still alive and growing. Unfortunately, they've decided that they would rather decline the adoption in favor of preparing for the birth of their own child."

But Layla was supposed to be their own child.

Except, no, she wasn't. Layla was *Raina's* child.

Her child. "What . . . what happens now?"

Dori glanced at Ivy, back to Raina. "It's up to you. We can put Layla in the system. I have no doubt we'll find new adoptive parents for her. She's a wonderful baby."

"Or . . . you can keep her," Ivy said, leaning forward. She wore a strange smile, her eyes bright. "You can raise her yourself."

Raina had no words, nothing for the feeling of relief inside her as the knot in her chest loosened, as the long-accustomed ache released.

Except . . . "I don't know. I mean, I haven't prepared for . . ."

Only, maybe she had. In fact, until January, she'd held on to the feeble, tenuous hope that Casper might return, that somehow he'd forgive her. Crazily hoped that they'd scrabble past the wounds, betrayals, and fears of the past nine months and come out the other side, a family.

Which meant that yes, she'd thought about being a mother. Longed for it, in the place she refused to voice.

"When do I have to decide?"

Dori caught her hand. "Take a few days. But soon. They are delivering her to the home tomorrow, and we'll place her with a temporary family. But we have other parents who might be a good fit."

Other parents.

The thought could unravel her. She looked at Ivy. "Please don't—"

"This is all confidential," she said, but a question remained in her eyes.

"The baby is Owen's," Raina said quietly.

"Oh." Ivy's eyes widened. But then she nodded, saying nothing.

Raina got up. "I'll call you with my decision," she said to Dori and walked from the office, her thoughts ahead of her, down the road to her daughter in her arms, a hand clasped around her finger, her tiny body curled into Raina's embrace. She saw a little girl with black pigtails chasing seagulls on Deep Haven's rocky shoreline, laughing as her mother pushed her on the swing set. She saw her tucked on the sofa, reading one of the Frances books, and making cupcakes and . . .

Swinging up into her daddy's arms. Only, the image that swept through her mind had dark hair, blue eyes. Not Owen. Not even Monte . . .

Raina stood in the middle of the sidewalk, her cheeks wet, her throat hollow.

Oh, she still loved him, and denying it only turned her inside out, made her moan.

She shoved her hands into her pockets and headed toward the harbor, water running under the snowpack along the gutters.

It didn't matter how much she longed for Casper. They had too much between them, and her silly daydream had no happy ending.

Still, she wanted to call him. Needed to talk to him. Just . . . as a friend, of course. Because despite everything, he'd been kind to her. Light, in a way that pierced her dark heart.

Yet what, exactly, would she say? He'd demand she tell Owen and . . .

What about Monte? He'd said he wanted a future with her. She tried to fit him into the picture like a puzzle piece.

The sun hung bright, the sky so blue she could drink it in, the snow crispy and fragile, melting, the scent of woodsmoke lingering in the air from the nearby fish house. She stopped in at the Java Cup, bought a latte, and took it outside.

Clarity. She just needed someone to tell her what to do.

If Liza were here, she'd know. Her aunt always mustered up the right answer, tapped into her deep faith, her unwavering assurance that God had a plan.

Maybe He did for people like Liza. But not for people like Raina who kept making one bad decision after the next.

Maybe she wasn't selfish—just afraid. After all, others might have God, but she had no one but herself to depend on.

Except what about Thor's words? *"A small life is lived by staring inward, but a large one is lived by diving into God's love."*

And sitting alone on the bench now, the lake water breaking free from the clasp of ice and washing debris to shore, what choice did she have? She lifted her face to the wind like Thor. *God, if You're up there . . . if You care in the least about Layla . . . help me know what to do.*

Raina waited.

Silence.

It was a silly prayer, and she didn't harbor the faintest hope God would really hear her. Or answer. She took a sip of her latte and remembered her outburst to Casper right after Layla's birth. *But God—no, He doesn't love me. God doesn't even notice me. I am* nothing *to Him.*

She'd pegged that right.

Raina watched the shadow of a tanker drift along the horizon. Took another sip of coffee, listening to traffic, the ruckus of the water churning the ice on shore. And the expected silence from the heavens.

"Raina, are you okay?"

She turned and her brain reeled as Casper's shadow fell over her. With his hands tucked into his down-jacket pockets, he stood, wearing jeans and hiking boots as if he might be headed out for a trek in the woods.

She blinked at him. Opened her mouth.

"I was driving by and saw you sitting here and . . . You looked like you needed a friend."

She closed her mouth, swallowed as unexpected tears filled her eyes.

"Hey," he said softly, moving onto the bench beside her. "What's the matter?"

Oh, she couldn't . . . Not really. Because she might think she needed to talk to him, but actually speaking the words of her failure out loud to Casper—no. She shook her head.

He slid his arm behind her, turning toward her. She looked down, picking at the coffee cozy, seeing him out of the corner of her eye.

He wore a loose stocking cap, his curls long and tantalizing, worry in his blue eyes. Just his presence beside her made her want to lean into him.

She looked out at the harbor, blinking hard against the sunshine and the fragrant springlike breeze, trying to scrounge up words.

As usual, he saved her. "Listen, I don't know if you're in the mood, but I'm heading to Mineral Springs." He gestured behind her to his truck, a snowmobile propped in the back. "I downloaded a map of the area, and I thought maybe it would be interesting to check out where Aggie and Thor lived."

He made a wry face. "I know it's probably stupid, but I've been thinking about your question—why would she end up with Thor when she believed Duncan offered her everything?" He lifted a shoulder. "Maybe it's because, despite what Duncan could offer her, she longed for something bigger, the grand adventure of true love."

Raina nodded, hungry for his truth.

"And Thor's letter, the line that mentions the truth about Duncan . . . I think Aggie ran away with Thor on her wedding day—we did find that dress in the Mineral Springs collection. And if she did, maybe Duncan came after her," Casper said.

"But what does that have to do with the bonds?"

"If Duncan stole them from Aggie's father, maybe he had them with him. Once she was married, all her worldly goods would pass to him. Who knows what nefarious plans he'd made? What if . . . ?"

Something . . . a memory pressed against her. Or maybe just her crazy dream, but—

"What if Aggie found them and took them?" she finished. "Duncan would surely go after her. Maybe that's why he and Thor fought?"

Oh, she liked it when they brainstormed ideas, when she ignited that fire in his eyes.

"Right. And maybe afterward, Thor took the bonds and hid them."

"But why?"

"To protect her? To keep someone from looking her direction?"

She frowned. "Where would he hide them? Mineral Springs?"

"At their old store?"

"I like it." More than she wanted to admit. Because right now, just right now, she couldn't think another moment about her future. About the choices before her.

Just for this moment, she didn't want to be afraid. She wanted to stop looking at herself and look ahead. To live large.

"Enough to take a drive?"

She took a breath, feeling the sunshine on her face, the fresh air in her lungs. "You just can't let this treasure hunt go, can you?"

His smile dimmed for a second. Then he shrugged. "Not if there's the slightest chance . . ."

That, probably more than anything, was what she longed for. Hope. "Let's go treasure hunting, Sherlock."

"Give me a kiss, Son. I won't see you when you get out of school."

Darek stood at the door, holding it open as Tiger climbed out of the truck. A caravan of other vehicles—parents dropping their kids off at the Deep Haven elementary—lined up behind him.

He bent down to wrap Tiger in a hug, but his son put a hand on his shoulder, pushed, turning his face away.

"Tiger."

"I don't care!"

He took off at a run, his Power Rangers backpack bumping against him.

"Tiger!"

But Janelle Ingstrom was frowning at Darek from her Chevy Blazer, so he watched until Tiger disappeared into the building, then climbed into his truck. Closed his eyes.

Lord, I don't know what else to do. He didn't really mean to pray; it just trickled out. In fact, he hadn't prayed much over the past few months—so wrapped up in frustration, fatigue, and anxiety that he didn't have time for it.

But what could he do? He put the truck in gear and pulled away from the curb before Janelle started honking.

Just a quick stop for his gear and he'd be on his way. If he drove all day and through the night, sleeping at truck stops, he might get there by tomorrow night.

Two weeks. He promised that to Ivy this morning as he kissed her good-bye. She had two weeks left until her maternity leave anyway, and then it was just sit around and wait.

Maybe he could stay a week longer—after all, Ivy didn't really need him.

Maybe Tiger didn't either.

In fact, Ivy and Tiger seemed to be moving forward without him, adapting to his decision to leave as if he were already gone.

He pulled up to the cubicle rental house, parking his truck in the drive, climbing the cracked steps to the house. The snowpack on the roof had melted into the gutters, trickling down the side of the house. Before he left, he'd make sure the sump pump in the basement was running.

He'd packed last night, so he grabbed his bags from inside the door and loaded them into his pickup. Then he toed off his shoes and headed to the kitchen to make a sandwich.

He got out the bread, then turned to the fridge.

Ivy had dug Tiger's artwork from the bag, smoothing it and taping it onto the cool green surface. He paused, looking at Tiger's handprint, colored the hues of the rainbow. On a piece of construction paper, yarn formed a stem and seeds created a flower.

And below that, a picture, words scrawled under it. He removed the magnet that held it to the fridge and read the paper.

My Favorite Superhero

He studied the picture, realization coming slowly. A man wearing a green shirt, a yellow hat, holding a hammer. Behind him, the log structure of a house. Pine trees.

For a seven-year-old, Tiger had sketched a recognizable likeness of his father.

In large, misshapen letters, it was labeled *My Dad*.

Darek braced himself with one arm against the fridge as he read the essay.

My dad is my hero.
He is happy.
Silly.
Stinky.
Good.
Old.

Muscley.

Funny.

And most of all he loves me.

"Most of all he loves me."

Oh, Tiger.

The page was stapled behind another, now turned over, so Darek flipped it forward. Apparently this was one of those pieces of artwork he was supposed to sign.

More than that, it was an announcement about career week, the teacher asking for volunteers.

He looked at the dates.

"Most of all he loves me."

Yes, he did, except maybe he'd forgotten, a little, how much.

The school was locked, but he pleaded his case with the school secretary and she issued him a pass. He found Tiger's classroom already in session. He'd met Mrs. White—a short woman with dark hair and kind eyes—on the first day of school, his hand laced with Ivy's as they toured the classroom, helped Tiger find his desk. Animal-themed alphabet letters ran around the top of the room, and a sum chart hung on the wall next to a computer station. A reading nook with beanbag chairs and baskets of early-reader books encouraged a time-out inside the pages.

He spotted Tiger sitting with his back to him, bent over a workbook, writing. Stepping into the room, he caught eyes with Mrs. White, who looked up from where she helped a child with her letters and came over to him.

He put his finger to his lips and gestured her into the hall.

"Hello, Mr. Christiansen."

"Darek, please, and I'm wondering if I'm too late to sign up?"

He held out the pink flyer. Then gestured to his red Nomex helmet, his Pulaski ax.

She appeared impressed. "I think we can make time for you. Stay here."

He watched as she walked to the front of the classroom and brought the students to attention.

Tiger sat in his chair, his feet barely touching the ground, his blond hair tousled—oops, Darek had been in charge of combing it today.

"I have a surprise for you, children. One of our parents is here to talk about his career. Mr. Christiansen, please join us."

Darek smiled as he walked to the front of the room, wearing his hat, his ax over his shoulder. "Hey, gang. My name is Darek Christiansen, and I'm Ti—Theo's dad. I'm also what they call a hotshot. Which means that when there are wildland fires, I join a team of other firefighters and we try to put the fire out using tools like this one." He held up his Pulaski.

Only then did he look at Tiger.

He expected a smile or at least something of fascination. But Tiger's eyes had filled, his bottom lip quivering.

Darek frowned, trying to continue. "We have to wear these hard hats, and they have this liner inside called Nomex that protects us—"

Tiger put his head down on his desk.

Darek's heart fell. He glanced at Mrs. White, who leaned over her desk, then started toward him.

But he couldn't help himself. "Tiger, buddy, what's the matter?"

Every head turned to look at his son, and he wanted to wince at his mistake. But evidently Tiger didn't care because he lifted his head and stared at Darek. Shook his head, his brown eyes wet.

"You're saying it all wrong. Tell them about the new tire swing. And the basketball court. And . . ." Tiger looked around the room. "And the big fire and how I got to go up on the roof and hammer. And then Dad let me use a chain saw—"

"No, actually, I didn't—" He glanced at Mrs. White, who seemed to be hiding a grin.

But Tiger had risen now. "Then we made this giant box and poured cement into it—"

"For the foundation of cabin twelve—"

"I stirred it with a long stick and then put my hand into it. And it made a mark."

Darek smiled at that, remembering how he'd held Tiger over the foundation wall, how he'd pressed his hand in beside Tiger's.

"We signed it, too," Darek said. "'Theo and Dad.'"

"And then we went fishing!" He was climbing on his chair now. "And I caught a fish." He held his arms out as if he was regaling them with a whopper tale. "And then Butter tried to eat it . . ." He frowned. "Except Butter died."

Tiger caught his lip in his teeth. Glanced at Darek.

He walked over to his son, meeting his eyes. "Yeah, Butter died. But . . . Theo is getting a brand-new brother or sister any day now."

"Yeah. My mom's tummy is this big." He held out his hands, and the class laughed.

So did Tiger.

The sound wrapped around Darek, weaving through him, stealing from him his breath, his resolve.

Oh, God, what have I done? He saw it then—the times he'd crawled in so late, so many days in a row, that he hadn't seen Tiger for over a week. And the moments he did, he'd barked at him, annoyed.

No wonder Tiger crumpled up his artwork. Because every time he turned to his father, he got hurt.

Darek, there are many different definitions of success. I'm not sure that any of them are stamped with the Evergreen Resort logo.

No, they weren't. They were stamped with Tiger's smile and Ivy's kisses and their sweet baby moving under his hand.

He'd forgotten that with the stiff brutality of the winter. By trying to simply survive, he'd lost sight of the reasons he wanted to.

"But Dad's building us a new house," Tiger was saying, still talking. "And I'm going to get my own bedroom and a swing set and maybe even a dog!"

Oops, he'd better pay attention. "Whoa, let's start with the baby and go from there."

But Tiger had turned to him, such a wide smile on his face that Darek could deny him nothing. "But probably."

"And we'll name it Scooby-Doo!" Then Tiger launched himself off the chair.

Darek should have expected it—did, really, and his instincts caught up in time to catch him. "Whoa, Tiger—"

But his son flung his arms around his neck, squeezing. He put his lips right up to Darek's ear and whispered loud enough to be heard in Canada, "I love you, Dad."

Darek didn't care that every kid in the room might be watching. That he looked like a fool with tears edging his eyes. He wrapped his arms around Tiger, buried his face in his neck, breathing in the sweetness of his brilliant son. "I love you too, buddy."

He leaned back as Tiger took Darek's face in his hands, his own face solemn. "Don't go, Dad. Please don't go."

The room hushed then. Darek could hear his heartbeat as he nodded. "Don't worry, pal. I'm not going anywhere."

He set him down, tousled his hair.

"Mr. Christiansen—Darek—would you like to stay for lunch? I think we're having fish patties."

"Yum," Darek said, winking. Except his phone vibrated in his pocket. He pulled it out and read the text. "But actually I think I have a prior engagement."

Casper could admit harboring an unreasonable joy with Raina riding behind him on the snowmobile, her arms wrapped around him, just like she had that day when he'd pulled her out of the mud, nearly a year ago.

He didn't know the reason for the sadness that shadowed her eyes, but he could light a fire with the sudden flash of passion at his suggestion. He couldn't exactly account for why he'd stopped earlier, either, driving out of the Java Cup with his morning jolt. He'd turned onto Main Street and the person on the bench caught his eye.

He stopped without a thought as if his inner psyche was so in tune with her, he couldn't help it. And as he did, he prayed, an act so habitual now, it embedded his thoughts. *Please, Lord, ignite joy in her.*

He didn't exactly mean to invite her along on his quest. The words simply spilled out.

Or maybe he recognized too well the expression on her face. Lost? Discouraged? Yeah, he'd lived with that feeling long enough to understand the compassion that rose in him.

Faithfully loving anyway.

His father's words lurked inside and he heard them again,

embracing them, perhaps: *And what does love do? Forgives. Comforts. Protects. Saves. Renews.* Loves.

Regardless of the cost.

Except, right now, he didn't know what price he might be paying, with the sun high, turning the snow into a texture perfect for snowball fights and ice forts. He followed the dirt road that led back to the old town, the evergreen trees low and treacherous, conspiratorially forcing Raina to hang on to him as he ducked and dodged their grasp.

Under the thaw, the forest seemed to come alive, a rebirth in the air with the trickle of water flowing down rocky streams and birds scattering at the roar of his machine.

"Do you really think we'll find something?" Raina shouted over the motor. She had braided her hair when they stopped by her house for her to change, adding the pink fleece headband that only softened the amber-brown in her eyes. She'd clearly regained her figure, her ski pants clinging to her in a way that brought back images of last summer and her tanned legs. She wore the powder-blue jacket and a pair of woolly mittens and might be the prettiest treasure hunter he'd ever seen.

Do you really think we'll find something?

He already had. And lost it. However, maybe over the past few weeks he'd put enough of it back together that she'd listen to him. He didn't hope for more than that—just a chance to warn her away from Monte and suggest that she wasn't alone. He might even go for the gold and remind her that God loved her.

He slowed, cutting the engine noise. "I think most of the town has decayed, but I did read that Thor's curio shop still stands, along with the attached apartment. Maybe they left something behind. Hold on."

She tightened her mittened grip around his waist, and he gunned the machine. He'd tracked his mileage, the map tucked into his pocket, but guessed correctly when they happened upon the ghost structures on the outskirts of a main thoroughfare. He slowed the machine again, searching for his bearings.

The town sat in a depression in the forest, a valley under the shadow of Eagle Mountain, which rose in the west. The high afternoon sun crossed shadows through an overgrown swath of what must have been the main street. The skeletal foundations of brick and wooden structures betrayed the former prosperity, with a few buildings still standing. At one end, a tiny church's steeple caved in a wooden roof. Next to it sat a log schoolhouse, the timbers rotted and one wall collapsed.

This side of town, he recognized the scars of tiny cabins, a dilapidated boardwalk. He motored the snowmobile into town, spied a false-front building with saggy windows.

"How big was this place?" Raina asked.

"According to my research, about forty-six families lived here. They had a post office and a general store, a school, a couple churches. It was originally a lumber town, but I think someone might have found gold here too. Anyway, the government bought it and absorbed it into the Indian reservation, and the families moved away. I think that's when Aggie and Thor bought the trading post in Deep Haven."

Raina pointed to what looked like a cemetery, just on the outskirts of town through a wrought-iron arched entrance. "I wonder if we'd find Duncan Rothe in there."

Casper glanced over his shoulder, and she waggled her eyebrows at him, the shadows gone from her eyes.

"I think he's probably buried deep in the forest, if at all, if he really came after Aggie like Thor suggested. I can promise you if anyone came after the woman I loved, I wouldn't leave his bones behind."

Oh. He didn't quite mean that.

Really.

Especially when she frowned. But then, "Yeah, I know what you mean."

"I think that's the curio shop," he said and pulled in front of the building. He parked, and she got off. "Be careful. I'm not sure how sound the structure us."

Raina moved onto the boardwalk, and he followed. Water flowed beneath it. A sign hung over the main door: *Ten and One, Wilder Curios*. Light-green paint, the color of the sea, peeled from the wooden door in jagged curls.

On either side, broken glass-paned windows still displayed taped adverts from bygone years. One advertised a dance at the nearby VFW. Another was for Dr. Swett's root beer.

"This one is for a Viewtone television. Half-radio, half-television." She leaned down. "The screen looks about as big as an iPad."

"And only sixty-five years old." When he grabbed for the door handle, it came off in his grip. "Oops."

"You break it, you bought it," she said.

"Funny." He reached around, pried open the store door. It whined on its hinges.

"It smells like animal in here," Raina said as she stepped forward.

"Wait." He grabbed her arm.

She flinched, recoiling as if he'd hurt her, and the response stopped him cold.

"Raina—"

"I'm fine. Wow, look at this place." She ventured inside.

Casper stood there, frowning. No, please . . .

But she waited for him inside, surveying the place, unfazed, so maybe he was reading too much into it.

"It's clearly been vandalized," she said as she crunched across the litter of glass, empty display cases torn from the walls. The branches of a dead birch poked through the partially collapsed rear wall.

The place did smell of animal, raw and feral.

She walked into a back room. "This looks like the cold storage," she said, her voice echoing. "In a curio shop?"

"I think he ran it more like a general store, with curio items for sale. Please, be careful—"

"Look what I found!"

He turned and glimpsed a head with painted blonde hair, one side of her face caved in, emerging from the room. "What—?"

Raina poked her head out from behind it. "A mannequin. Sort of. Mannequin parts."

"Any secret doors?"

She made a face. "Just Mabel here. Holding down the fort."

"Leave Mabel behind. I think this is the door to the apartment." The tiny apartment leaned against the store like an afterthought, but when he opened the door, he saw the charm inside.

Raina came in behind him, peering over his shoulder. "Wow. Creepy." She pushed past him, and he trailed behind as she surveyed the remains of the tiny apartment. A low ceiling with a long beam held up plaster, and the chinking between the logs had begun to crumble onto the painted wood floor. Two broken windows had let in leaves that littered the floor, forming a pile of debris at the front of the room. Along one wall, a brick fireplace still housed the cast-iron stove, ash spilled on the hearth. A broken cane chair sat at a built-in table. Rosebud wallpaper peeled from the walls in wide swaths, and a chipped Formica counter ran against the far wall, a porcelain sink betraying its age. The door of an icebox hung ajar.

Small. Primitive.

Raina stood at the bottom of rough-hewn stairs, looked up.

"Maybe not a good idea," he said, pointing to a hole in the ceiling.

She wrinkled her nose at him and climbed up anyway, peeking through the top. "It's empty. And the roof is exposed."

He stood below her, ready to catch her if the stairs gave way. When she turned, he held out his hand. "Scare a guy, will ya?"

Raina came down the stairs. "Aggie was an heiress. Worth millions. And she chose this?" She walked around the room, kicking aside debris.

"Maybe she loved Thor."

Raina looked at him. Nodded. "A lot."

Was that her fascination with Monte—that he had money?

He hadn't thought about it before, but yeah, a woman who'd grown up in poverty without a home might find that kind of security alluring. Even if it came attached to a shyster like Monte.

She ventured to the room in back. "Hey, you gotta see this."

Casper followed her and found her standing in a small bedroom, light streaming in from a window. A door to the outhouse in back stood ajar.

"Look." She walked to a beam running at eye level across the back of the room, ran her fingers along etching there. "'Aggie and Thor, 1930.' And here is 'Otto, 5/1931.' Gust told me he drowned when he was ten."

"So sad."

"Yeah. Maybe that's why they moved—they couldn't bear to face the past."

She ran her hand along the beam, and the action stirred up his brother's words. *It's not like she has a ring on her finger, right?*

Raina turned and, in the soft glow of the afternoon light, looked so pretty it could silence him. "Sadly, I don't see any hidden treasure."

Yeah, but he did. Sure, maybe he'd never find the treasure of Duncan Rothe—but he didn't need it. Not really.

She walked past him again, and he couldn't help it—he reached out and took her arm.

Again she winced, and that shook him right out of his moment. "Are you hurt?"

She frowned, jerked her arm away. "No. I'm fine." But she'd answered too fast and he saw the lie in her eyes.

"He hurt you, didn't he?"

She stared at him, her face flushing, her breath quick. "No." But her hand went to her arm. "He didn't mean it—"

"He didn't *mean* it?" Casper's voice rose and echoed in the tiny room. He cut it in half, repeated his statement, his heart thundering. "He. Didn't. Mean. It."

"Casper, you don't understand—"

"Here's what I don't understand: what a beautiful, smart, courageous, strong woman is doing with a guy like Monte. And please, don't tell me it is for his money."

She flinched, her eyes sharp. "You're a jerk."

That slowed him a little, but—"I guess I am, but you deserve better, Raina. Monte is—"

"Monte wants me, Casper. He doesn't see my sins every time he looks at me. And yeah, he might be sort of bossy, but it's just because he is so into me. He . . . wants me."

She turned away, pressed a hand to her mouth. "Just leave me alone."

So they were back to that.

Or not, because he'd had enough of leaving her alone. "*I want you.*"

Oh. He sucked in a breath. "Seeing you with him is killing me, and the idea that he hurt you . . ."

She didn't move and he turned away, stared out the window, shaking.

He could hear her breathing behind him.

Then, "You . . . want me?"

Casper closed his eyes. *You can be your own worst enemy sometimes.*

He turned. "Yeah. I want you in my life. I think about you all the time. I can't seem to do anything without the thought of you in my head. I tried—wow, I tried. I went two thousand miles away and still . . ." He swallowed, took a step toward her. Her eyes widened. "Still I couldn't get you out of my mind. I . . . I love you, Raina. I never stopped. I don't think I can."

He was breathing hard, his heart right there in his hands.

Her expression, the way she drank in his words as if she wanted to believe him, could make him weep. "I love you too, Casper. I—"

But he didn't care what she was about to say—in fact, didn't want to hear it, just in case it might resemble her pushing him out of her life.

So he kissed her. Just wrapped his arm around her waist, pulling her to himself, his mouth full on hers. Hungry.

Oh, he'd missed kissing her. She tasted like sweet coffee, memories of summer, freedom. She moved into his arms, wrapped hers over his shoulders. Kissed him back. In fact, her response seemed so utterly Raina, so full of life, of passion, that he realized how completely she'd gone into hiding.

Out of shame, probably. Except, not anymore. He could burst with the joy of kissing her, moving both arms around her waist to mold her against him, picking her up, twirling her around. She made a little sound in the back of her throat as if another barrier collapsed, and he set her down, cradled her face, softened his kiss.

She smelled so amazing, and he wanted to peel back time . . .

Yes.

Casper broke away and pressed his forehead to hers. Caught her beautiful eyes. "Raina . . . let's just forget about everything—the past and what happened and . . . let's start over. I don't care anymore. Not about any of it. Not Owen . . . or . . . the baby. Oh, please, can't we—?"

She stiffened. Put her hands to his shoulders and pushed.

He backed away. "What—?"

But she raised one hand to her mouth. Shook her head.

"Raina—"

"I'm sorry, Casper. I'm so—I'm so sorry." Her face crumpled. "I think you need to take me home."

Then she turned and fled from the cabin.

No—"Raina!" He chased after her because what else could he

do? But she had already exited the building, already charged out to the snowmobile.

He sat on the sled, facing her, took her face in his hands. "What is it?"

Her breath whispered out in a sigh. "I got some news today. I . . ." The look she gave him then could reach down and tear him asunder. "The adoption fell through. I think I'm going to raise my daughter on my own."

He blinked at her, her words settling inside.

And then he got it. Owen's baby. She planned on *keeping* his brother's baby.

Talk about reliving the past, every single day.

"Oh."

"See." She wiped her face, gave him a sad smile. "This is why you don't really want me, Casper."

He had no words for that. In fact, he hated himself when he turned and fired up the sled.

She didn't lace her arms around him as they motored home.

CHAPTER 17

RAINA DIDN'T KNOW WHEN—or why—the decision had taken root, burrowed into her. Maybe during the ride into the woods, as her head cleared and she realized . . .

Layla belonged with her. Sure, she could find a safe, loved life with adoptive parents—Raina had no doubt that many adopted children did. But Layla would have a family. Her. And yes, the Christiansens. She shouldn't have kept their grandchild from them, despite her shame. And Owen.

She would tell Owen. Eventually.

More than that, her future could never include Monte. Not when Casper still embedded every heartbeat.

She had wrapped this around her brain before Casper took her into his arms, before she imagined them in a house in the woods, like Aggie and Thor. Before she'd had them inscribing their children's names on the walls.

But she definitely saw him in her picture of happily ever after.

So what that it was primitive? Walking through Aggie's place told her just how valuable loving the right man could be.

Aggie chose the unknown and lived large in love. For a second, Raina did too. Breaking free of the past, embracing the wild adventure that was Casper.

Then his words took her apart, back to the beginning. Back to reality. *Let's start over. I don't care anymore. Not about any of it.*

She stared out the window as they drove toward town, the sun baking the truck. "For the record, I don't expect you to want to raise Owen's child. That's not why I told you about the baby. I just felt you deserved to know."

Casper seemed as if he might be trying to hold himself together based on his clenched jaw and the way he held the steering wheel with a whitened hand. Not angry, just . . . Well, he appeared as if he might shatter, so she didn't add to her words, just let them simmer.

She touched her lips, still feeling the way he'd kissed her—as if he ached for her, as if he'd held back desire for the past seven months, only to suddenly have it break free, rich and consuming.

I'm sorry, Casper. She wanted to say it again but for the first time didn't really know what she was apologizing for.

She couldn't look at him, her disappointment raw despite her compassion.

He finally pulled up to her house. She reached for the door handle, but he stopped her with a hand on her sleeve.

His eyes were red rimmed. "I . . . I need some time . . ."

Her heart turned over then, seeing the fight in his eyes, and she couldn't bear it. She pressed her hand to his on her arm. "I didn't tell you about the baby so you could show up and save the day. Let yourself off the hook, Casper."

Then she got out, breathing in the fresh air, holding herself together until she reached her house.

He drove away, and she watched him, her forehead against the cold glass. After all, what did she expect? Clearly her destiny with the Christiansen men included watching them leave.

Despite his friendship, Casper was still an adventurer, his heart set on leaving her. She should have seen that in the beginning.

She went to the shower, turned it on. Let the steam fill the bathroom, then undressed and climbed in.

It seemed the safest place to cry.

Her phone was vibrating on the sink when she finally got out, her skin wrinkled and seared. "Hello?" Shoot, her voice still trembled. She shivered a little, pulling on a sweatshirt, her yoga pants.

"Raina! It's Grace."

She put the phone on speaker, then grabbed a towel to dry off her hair. "Grace! How are you?"

"I'm actually on my way north. Ivy's in labor; she's been ambulanced to Duluth."

"Oh no . . ."

"Yeah, I know. I'm with Eden—"

"Hey, Raina!" Eden's voice came across the line.

"I know this will sound weird, but . . . have you seen Casper?" She stilled. "Why?"

Silence, then, "Because Amelia seemed to think he might be spending time with you."

Amelia was home? "I thought she was in Europe."

"Long story—I think. I haven't gotten all of it, but . . . um, why did she think that?"

Raina sighed. "Because we've been . . . we're friends again." Or they were. Until today. "Actually, he just dropped me off. We were working on a project together."

More silence.

"Don't worry, Grace. The whole thing is too complicated. Trust me—this time Casper won't be sticking around."

She heard a sigh on the other end. "I'm not worried about Casper. How are *you*?"

That was all it took. Grace's gentle prodding, the memory of her friendship, her willingness to keep her secrets. Raina picked up the phone, climbed into bed, and told her everything.

Landing the job at the antique shop.

Discovering the diary.

Meeting Monte.

Finding Casper at the historical society and letting him woo her into the mystery.

Or maybe she'd wooed him.

Monte's strange jealousy.

Their trip to Aggie and Thor's.

And finally, the adoption.

"You told him you were keeping the baby?" This from Eden, who had listened with the same compassion Grace showed.

"Yeah. He completely freaked out. And I don't blame him." Maybe she shouldn't have told them about the kiss.

"I do," Eden said. "Because if anyone could step in and be an awesome father to this baby, it's Casper. No one knows how to forgive, how to fill in and save the day, like Casper. He's loyal and sweet and frankly, the one who cares the most about keeping the rest of us out of trouble—"

"It doesn't matter. Casper would be a great dad. But he doesn't want the job." Raina got up, stared at herself in the mirror. Her hair had thinned again after the baby, and she looked gaunt and pale. "But I do—"

"Raina, are you here?" The voice emerged over the sound of her front door opening.

"I gotta run," she said to Grace. "Don't tell anyone—"

Monte appeared at her door, wearing work pants and a sweatshirt, his face drawn in a scowl. "Don't tell anyone what?"

She dropped the phone on the bed and found a smile for him as she walked over to hug him. "Hi."

He narrowed his eyes, backed away from her kiss. "I know you have a secret, Raina. And I want to know what it is. Where are the bonds? I know you and Casper are hiding them from me. I've been through all Aggie's things and up at her house all day. Where are they?"

She stared at him. "I don't know where the bonds are. I'm not hiding—"

"I've been calling you all day! Where were you?"

He reached out and in a second had grabbed her phone off the bed. She watched him disconnect it, a sliver of horror twining through her that perhaps Grace had heard everything. But she stayed still as he scrolled through her recent calls, frowning at the last one, then held up the list. Seven missed calls.

Because she'd been out of range.

"I'm sorry." She swallowed, debating. But he deserved the truth, at least the one that mattered. "I had a court meeting today . . ." She took his hand. "I need to tell you something."

He didn't close his grip, just frowned, one lethal eyebrow dipping.

"I had a baby in January."

His frown deepened.

"I gave her up for adoption. But . . . uh . . . the adoption fell through."

She could see him trying to keep up, replaying her words in his head. Then he turned and stalked away from her, into the next room.

"Monte, I was going to tell you—"

"When?" He rounded on her. "You don't think I deserved to know?" His face darkened. "All those times you pushed me away. I thought maybe you were just nervous or a prude. But no—you gave it up for someone else. Who—?" His mouth opened, eyes widening. "Casper Christiansen. He's the father of your child, isn't he?"

"No. He's not."

Monte closed the gap between them. "Then who was he?" He stood over her, fury radiating off him.

"It doesn't matter—he's not in the picture anymore." She put her hand out to touch his chest, but he slapped it away.

"Tell me."

She swallowed. "Owen. Owen Christiansen."

A strange smile slid up his face. "Nice. So you sleep with one brother, then tease the second."

"No, I didn't . . ." But his words turned her to ash.

"So now what? Don't tell me you're going to keep the baby?"

At her silence, he shook his head. "Seriously?"

"I thought—well, I am her mother."

He laughed, something sharp and brutal. "Right. You, a mother? You would make a terrible mother."

She closed her mouth, her words vanishing.

"You have nothing, Raina. You *are* nothing. You barely have a job—if I decide to keep you employed after today—and can hardly take care of yourself. Do you seriously expect to be able to raise a child?"

She frowned. "I . . . Yes. I . . . I practically raised my brother—"

"Yeah, and where is he now?" He looked at her, lifted an eyebrow.

Raina bit her lip, letting the blood fill her mouth, wishing she hadn't told him about Joey's death.

Monte sighed. "Fine. Okay. So you wanted to raise this kid. I get that. You have a lot of foolish ideas. But listen." He came over to her, cupped her face in his hands. "I'm willing to forget all this. Put it behind me." He ran his thumbs over her cheeks. "You made a mistake. It's not the end of the world."

Then he smiled and she didn't know what to do with her feelings, the way they tumbled around inside her. "Really?"

"Yeah. Of course. I can forget the Owen thing and the kid. I mean, I'll try." His mouth lifted in a half smile. "You might have to work at it a bit, though, to help me."

And then he kissed her. Not gentle, but with possession in his touch. He pushed her up against the doorframe, his hands on her waist. His mouth moved to her neck. "And here I thought I was dating a good girl."

She stiffened, but his hands moved to her shoulders to pin her to the wall. He lifted his head, his eyes in hers, dark. Angry. "How many other men have you slept with?"

Her mouth dried. "Monte, I'm not that girl anymore."

"Oh yeah, you are." He kissed her again, pulling her to himself, rough. She wrestled against him as he pushed her to the sofa. She fell over the arm, landing in the cushions, Monte standing over her.

He unzipped his sweatshirt.

She rolled off the sofa onto the floor, finding her feet. "Monte—I think you should leave."

"You do, huh?" He advanced toward her.

She backed up, her hand out. "I know you're mad, but—"

"Oh, honey. I'm not mad." He leaned in, his finger at the base of her neck, tracing the well of her throat. "I'm going to make you forget all about Owen—and Casper—Christiansen."

Yeah, well, she didn't want to forget Casper Christiansen—or Owen, for that matter. Because he'd given her a child, and even if their union had been wrong, Layla wasn't. And even if Casper wasn't in her life, he'd made her believe in herself, taught her that a girl could make mistakes, but it didn't mean she didn't deserve a happy ending.

It doesn't mean you won't make an amazing mother someday. Actually, it doesn't even mean that you weren't already an amazing mother to Layla.

She *would* be a great mother. They might not be rich—they might struggle—but what if she chose to lean into the hope that God did see her? Did love her? What if she embraced Thor's words, like Aggie had, and looked at God instead of at herself, believing His love for her because of who He said He was, not disqualifying it because of her mistakes, her sins, her shame? Not telling herself that she deserved less—but wildly reaching for love?

Her grip closed around the Bible—Aggie's hardcover family Bible that she'd returned to the living room.

Monte closed his hand around her neck, tightening.

In one quick move, Raina raised the book and, with everything inside her, slammed it against his head.

He howled, and the act loosened his grip, knocked him into the fireplace.

Raina didn't stick around. She dropped the Bible and opened the door to run.

And right there stood Casper.

Casper had nearly gotten home, nearly been out of reception again when his cell phone rang.

Grace. Breathless. Upset. And not about Ivy going into labor, or the fact that Darek and his entire family had left for Duluth. But about Raina.

"Something's not right," she said, her voice taut after she delivered the family news. "We were talking—"

He didn't ask about the topic.

"—and suddenly someone came in. He sounded angry and accused her of hiding something—"

That was all Casper needed to disconnect and turn his truck around.

Probably he should have turned it around two—no, seven months ago when he'd left, but he couldn't change that.

Maybe it's time to get out of the way and let God be in charge of your heart.

He loved Raina. The depth of it could knock him over, and he'd battled that thought the entire drive home from Mineral Springs.

He loved her. And he should have stuck around to fight for the woman he loved instead of letting his pride decide for him.

Sometimes he did stand in his own way. His pride—his fear of getting hurt. Yeah, loving Raina would cost him something.

A lot.

But the reward—oh, the reward.

He could choose in this moment to follow his heart—God's heart—for Raina and Layla. So what that she wanted to raise Owen's child? He wouldn't love Layla any less because she was Owen's—and really, even if Owen decided to show up and wanted to be a father, it didn't mean Casper had to surrender Raina.

In fact, if he stepped back and looked at the signs, maybe he could admit that God brought him back to Deep Haven not to escape Raina . . . but *because* of Raina. The Almighty hadn't taken her out of his heart because . . . because she *belonged* there.

Which meant that Casper wasn't going to stand back and let anyone hurt the woman he loved.

He landed on her doorstep without remembering how, exactly, he'd gotten there. Fast—he remembered taking the Third Avenue corner on two wheels. But the moment he hopped out of his truck, heard the howl as he barreled up the sidewalk . . .

He reached the porch just as the door flung open.

Raina ran full tilt out of the house, smack into his arms.

He caught her, his heart in his throat. "Raina!"

Then, behind her . . . Monte.

The man bled a little from a scrape on his forehead, and oh, Casper dearly hoped she'd put it there.

Casper read the fear in her expression, and something snapped. "Are you okay?"

But Monte had barely slowed, and maybe the sight of Casper only ignited him because he launched himself at Raina.

Casper pushed Raina out of the way, catching Monte, and

they flew backward off the porch into the sodden snow. Slush embedded his clothes, but it couldn't cool the fury as he rolled and landed on Monte, his knee in the man's gut.

His first punch exploded Monte's nose. Monte got one punch of his own in before Casper's second cracked his jaw, and Casper would have just been getting started if he didn't hear sirens.

And if Raina didn't grab his jacket. She must have run back inside, because now she held a rolling pin raised above her head.

Fierce, her eyes on fire.

Casper bounced off Monte—hot, pumped, wanting to dive back on top of him. But Raina still had ahold of his jacket. "No, Casper!"

Monte just lay there, moaning, swearing, and the words he called Raina made it a good thing that she tightened her grip on Casper's coat.

When a Deep Haven cruiser pulled up, Deputy Kyle Hueston stormed out.

Only then did Casper begin to breathe.

Monte groaned, pushing himself to his feet. "Kyle, arrest him. Casper attacked me—"

"Seriously?" This from Raina. She turned to Kyle, yanking up her shirtsleeve to show where bruises in the shape of a hand stained her arm. "This is from him." She pointed at Monte.

Casper wanted to take him apart again.

Would have, if Kyle hadn't clamped his hand on Casper's shoulder. "I got this." He turned to Raina. "Are you saying Monte attacked you?"

"Yes. He tried to rape me." Only then did her gaze go to Casper. He winced, feeling like he was going to be ill. "And I'd like to press charges."

Attagirl. But he had his hands on his knees, bent over, gulping in air.

He couldn't drive her stripped, vulnerable expression from his mind, even as Kyle cuffed Monte and his partner settled him in the cruiser.

"And by the way—I'm a great cook!" Raina said, still holding the rolling pin.

Huh?

Casper could still feel the heat in his veins an hour later as Raina poured out her statement. He'd stood at the window, staring out at her front yard, clenching and unclenching his fists at the image of Monte forcing himself on her, and listening to some abbreviated, G-rated version of their fight—he knew she'd cleaned it up for him.

"I should have never let you date him," he muttered under his breath as Kyle left and she shut the door.

"What?"

Casper drew in a breath. "Sorry. I realize how stupid that sounds. But I knew—I just knew—"

"Stop." She put her hand on his mouth, looking at him. Her lip was swollen.

He reached out, rubbed his thumb over it. "That needs ice."

"So does your hand." She lifted it, examining the bruising. "Why did you come back?"

Oh. That.

He opened his mouth, wanting to find an easy answer, discovering none. But maybe it *was* easy if he sorted through the clutter.

"Because I'm still completely, utterly undone by you, Raina. And if you'll let me, I want to be your family. I mean, I get that Owen will always be in our lives. He is my brother, after all. But

I've seen Ivy and Tiger. I know that I could—*will* love Layla as if she's my own. She's a part of you, and that's reason enough. But I—maybe I'm supposed to be in her life. Maybe that's why I met you on the road that day, because God knew that she would need a . . ." He blew out a breath, suddenly weak. "A dad."

She looked at him, swallowed, the fear back in her expression. "I don't—"

"I get it. I really do. I know I'm not Owen—"

"Are you kidding me?"

He recoiled at her words. But she refused to let him, reaching for his sleeve.

"I don't want Owen. I want you, Casper. You're the brother I'm in love with—have always been in love with. Owen was nothing to me. I gave my heart to you. And I never took it back."

It took him a second—two—to catch up, but when he did, he wove his hands behind her neck, his gaze soft in hers. "So that's why you're always on my mind."

She smiled then, reeled him in, and he had no choice but to taste that smile, capture it with his lips. Gently, as if kissing her for the first time.

Raina.

She surrendered into his arms like she belonged there.

Finally.

She kissed him sweetly, then met his eyes. "Casper, I don't understand it, but when I'm with you, I feel . . . well, as if I'm alive. And . . . at peace. I don't know what the word is—"

"Beautiful? Precious? Amazing?"

She smiled. "Found. That's how I feel when you look at me. Found."

He tipped his forehead to hers. "What was it that Thor said

to Aggie? 'Every day I look to the Lord for peace, and I find it in your eyes.'"

"'You are His light to me,'" she said, quoting from the letter.

Casper leaned back. "Wait one second." He let her go. Pressed a hand to his forehead, turning away from her. "Oh, I'm an idiot. It's been right there in front of me the entire time."

"What?"

"The Bible." He found it on the floor next to the fireplace.

"I hit him with it," Raina said as Casper picked it up.

"Good. I think everyone needs to be hit by the Word of God." He sat down, opening the cover. "I kept thinking the other night— the cover feels thicker than it should be, the binding rough."

He ran his hand over the back cover, then turned it on its side. "Do you have a knife, something thin and sharp?"

She disappeared into the kitchen and returned with a fillet knife.

Casper held the book open and began, very gently, to pry the endpaper up. "What did you mean by you're a great cook?" He looked at her. "You're an amazing cook."

Raina just smiled, and for a moment he forgot what he was doing. Then—

"There's something under there." She knelt, held the book as he pried up the paper, folding back the parchment.

And there, in a well dug out of the cover, sat folded US Steel bonds.

Casper eased them out, counted them. "Five bonds. I'll bet the front cover has five more."

She took them, stared at the papers, then at him. "You did it. Casper, you found the treasure of Duncan Rothe!"

He set the Bible aside, on the sofa next to him, then reached out, pulling her into his lap. "Actually, I think Thor ended up with the treasure of Duncan Rothe. We just found the savings bonds he secreted away."

"But look—they're written to Aggie. And I think Aggie did find them and hid them so that no one would ever know what Thor did—or why."

"She could have been rich, the heiress to the Franklin fortune. Why didn't she spend the money?"

Raina looped her arm around his neck. "Because she was already rich. She'd found the man who made her feel like she was priceless. She didn't need the money."

"So are you saying she loved the man who had nothing?"

"Aw, he didn't have nothing. He had everything." She lowered her voice, her eyes shiny. "He had her."

Casper smiled, his hand on her cheek. "He had her."

CHAPTER 18

HE'D NEARLY MISSED the birth of his daughter.

That thought pulsed inside Darek, relentless like a heartbeat, as he watched the neonatal doctor checking the Apgar score of his squalling little girl under the bili lights.

What if he'd been halfway to Arizona by now? He wouldn't have made it home in time to ride to the hospital with Ivy, wouldn't have held his wife's hand as the doctor performed the C-section.

And what if something had happened to either of them? After a few hours of labor, Ivy's pulse had dropped, along with the baby's heartbeat, and the C-section happened so fast—

"Darek, you look white. Breathe." Ivy's voice from the delivery table, where the obstetrician was stitching her up, shook him out of himself, back to the quiet concentration of the nursing staff cleaning the table, checking Ivy's vitals, the team washing and swaddling the baby.

And then, suddenly, from the doctor: "Darek, do you want to hold her?"

Wait—

But the doctor settled the flannel bundle in his arms. Tiny, old face, wrinkled, red. Wisps of dark hair, blue eyes fighting to open, failing. Her baby doll fingers played a silent tune as she reached for him. Her mouth opened, fragile lips forming unuttered words.

Perfect.

His chest was so full, he simply stood there, staring at her, drinking her in.

He'd nearly missed this.

This was God, right here, reaching down into his life, telling him to be still. To wonder. To embrace joy.

Oh, God, I'm sorry I exchanged worship for worry. I let my fears overwhelm me instead of standing in awe of You every day.

His eyes ached and he blinked, letting the moisture drip onto his cheek.

"Let me see her," Ivy said.

"I'm sorry, of course." He bent down to show the baby to Ivy. His wife wore a blue surgical cap, her body draped as the doctor finished his sutures. She reached over and touched the baby's face, her fingers running along her tiny, perfect nose, her cheeks.

The baby yawned.

"What do we name her?" Darek asked.

"I don't know. I have a list at home, but we haven't talked about it—"

"We haven't talked about much the past few months."

A nurse eased the baby from his arms. "We need to put her back under the bili lights, so she'll spend some time in the nursery."

"My parents are probably here," Darek said to the woman. "And my son will want to see his little sister."

The nurse set the baby in a bassinet. "When Ivy is moved to her room, we'll bring the baby back."

Darek watched her wheel the bundle out, fighting the impulse to run after his daughter, pull her into his arms again.

Ivy's hand found his, squeezed.

"We're all done here," the OB said, and they began removing the draping around Ivy. Darek ventured a look and spied the bandages before averting his eyes. Wow, he hadn't remembered any of this from Tiger's birth—his sweaty palms, the weakness that buckled his knees when the doctor whisked Ivy to the delivery room. The light-headed surrealism of holding his daughter in his arms.

"Do you need a gurney too?" one of the nurses asked, and she didn't look like she was kidding.

He shook his head and took Ivy's hand, holding it as an orderly wheeled her to a room and lifted her onto a bed. "I alerted the reception area to okay visitors, but I think my parents might be lost." He kissed her on the forehead.

"They're here." She pointed past him, and he turned to see his mother at the door.

She carried her parka, wore worry in her eyes. "Can we come in?"

"It's a girl," he said.

Ingrid threw her arms around his neck. "A granddaughter." She kissed his cheek, then let him go and moved to Ivy.

His father came in behind her, caught Darek's hand, then pulled him into a hug. "A girl. Oh, boy."

Darek laughed.

"Dad!"

John stepped away just as Tiger ran into the room, breaking free of Amelia's hand. He launched into Darek's arms, and Darek caught him. "You have a little sister, pal."

"Where is she?" Tiger looked around as if she might be lying on the floor like one of his toys.

"Sleeping. She'll be here soon."

Amelia pressed a kiss to Darek's cheek. "Well done, Bro."

He heard laughing from down the hall, warm, rich, and by the time Grace and Eden reached the doorway, he knew his daughter's name.

To be born into this family—to share this love, this legacy—only one name seemed right.

Grace came into the room first, saw Darek, and wrapped her arms around him. "I was worried."

He kissed the top of her head. "Where's Max?"

"On the road to Boston, the last stop in a ten-day trip. He'll be back tomorrow night."

Which meant that Eden's husband, Jace, was gone too.

Eden followed with another hug. "I'm so proud of my big brother." Beautiful and wise, Eden always had exactly the right word to cheer him on.

"Where's Casper?" Darek said. "Not that he has to drop everything and—"

"We're the drop-everything kind of family, Dare," Grace said. "He's on his way. He called about a half hour ago, said he had a surprise for us."

No one mentioned Owen, though they felt him in Ingrid's

sigh. But she took Ivy's hand, smiling at her. "And when do I get to see my granddaughter?"

Ivy rang for the nurse.

Darek walked to the window. The hospital overlooked the thawing harbor and the blue-gray outline of ships, the aerial bridge twinkling against the velvet of night. The sun had long vanished, a crystal moon now hanging over the dark waters of Lake Superior.

He heard the sweet sounds of his family meeting his new daughter as the nurse brought her in, and of course his mother scooped her up. "Oh, Darek," she said, her blue eyes glistening. "She's beautiful." She smiled, so much pride in her eyes he might burst. "What's her name?"

Darek glanced at Ivy, and she frowned, just a twitch of confusion in her brow. Then he said, "I was thinking . . . Joy."

A slow, sweet smile slid over Ivy's face. "Joy Ingrid Christiansen."

His mother's eyes filled as she looked down at her granddaughter. "Joy. It's perfect."

John cupped his big hand over Joy's head, kissed his wife on her cheek.

Ingrid set the baby in Ivy's arms, and Ivy kissed her daughter's forehead. "Welcome to the family, Joy."

Footsteps echoed down the hall. Darek looked up to see Casper standing at the door.

"Is that a shiner, Casp?"

His brother just grinned. Nodded, like, *Yay, a shiner!* And then Darek spotted Casper's companion, the one holding his hand.

He remembered Raina from last summer, of course—everyone did after the debacle with Owen. She looked older, perhaps, dressed in jeans, a blue jacket, her hair long and wavy, a tentative expression in her brown eyes. Yeah, he could admit she might be pretty enough for Casper's unexplainable obsession.

"Raina?" This from Grace, who flew at her, her arms closing around her. Raina, too, looked a little beat up, her lip swollen.

Darek glanced at his father, who wore the expression he felt.

Casper came into the room and headed for the baby, running his thumb across her cherub cheek.

Okay, so whatever crimes Casper might have committed today, he had a soft, flannelly place in his heart for babies. His expression turned all tender and even a little sappy.

"For cryin' in the sink, Casper, you two look like you've been in a fight. What gives?" Amelia said.

"It's a long story," Casper said. "And now's not the time." He turned to Ivy and the baby again.

"Isn't she sweet?" Ingrid said.

"Miraculous," Casper said, pressing a kiss to the baby's forehead, a soft smile on his face.

"Ivy, good job," Casper said. "Bro, you came out lucky—she doesn't have your crazy nose."

"Hey—"

Darek broke off when Tiger climbed up on the chair, then onto Darek's back, his arms around his neck.

"So what's her name?" Casper asked.

"Joy," Eden said. "Joy Ingrid Christiansen."

Casper leaned close, lowered his voice. "Listen, just a couple things about your father you should know. First, he's all bark and no bite."

"Not true," Darek started.

"True!" said Grace and maybe even Amelia.

"And second, I know all your daddy's secrets, so when you turn sixteen and maybe one day happen to take the car without asking and accidentally wreck it, you call me first. I have the goods that will keep you out of trouble."

"Casper!"

"Shh, you'll frighten the baby," Casper said, grinning. "You done good, Ivy Christiansen. My brother clearly doesn't deserve you."

"Agreed," Darek said. He lowered Tiger to the floor. "So what's with the shiner, Bro?"

Casper looked at Raina, took her hand. "How about if I order a couple pizzas. And then I have to tell you something."

Casper had spent two hours running the rough draft of his announcement through his head, and thankfully, the ordering and waiting for the pizza allowed him time to put words together. When the three large pizzas arrived, he forked over the cash and brought the food upstairs, Raina carrying the Cokes, plates, and napkins.

"Are you sure now's the right time?" she said. "With the baby and everything?"

"They're all here, and I'm not sure how long Grace and Eden are sticking around. I thought you'd like them here for support. Besides—" he leaned over and kissed her quickly—"it's time we put the past behind us. I need to apologize for my behavior at the wedding. To Eden and Jace, yes, but also to everyone. I think today's the day for new beginnings."

She nodded, but fear shadowed her smile.

"Pizzas!" He entered the room. His mother helped him set up dinner, serving slices to the family. Eden rocked baby Joy as Darek arranged Tiger's dinner on the bed table.

Finally his mother sank into a chair, and as Grace slipped her hand into Raina's, Casper knew it was time.

"I love Raina."

That shouldn't be a shock to any member of his family, but he paused there and let his words settle on them. He glanced at Raina, connected with her beautiful amber eyes. "I love her, and I knew that last summer, and . . . that's why Owen and I had our fistfight. Because . . . I was jealous."

Darek looked at the floor. His mother's expression betrayed compassion. His father darted a glance at Raina.

"Mom. Dad. Eden. Everyone . . . I'm so sorry I put such a black mark on Eden's wedding day. Please forgive me."

Eden met his gaze. "It's over, Casper."

"Thanks, Sis. But it's not quite over yet. See, I had to also forgive, even though neither of them did anything against me. I harbored so much anger I thought it would devour me. It was always with me—this jealous thing. It followed me to Roatán, then back to Minneapolis, and finally home. I thought I had it licked, but when Raina showed up, it came to life again, prowling through me."

Baby Joy yawned, and Eden delivered her into Ivy's arms.

"And then Darek suggested I start praying for her, so I did, and . . . the short of it is, I think God kept her in my heart because He wanted us together. Because He knew that Raina . . . well, that . . ." Oh, wow, he wasn't sure how he was going to say this.

Raina touched his arm. Looked in his eyes, so much love in hers that words left him.

Then, as usual, she rescued him. "Because God knew that I'd need him to raise my child." She smiled. "Our child."

Silence. So thick it could descend, suffocate.

"What are you telling us?" John said in a tone rife with suspicion.

Oh, oops. "Raina's not pregnant," Casper said.

"Then what is she talking about?" Darek said.

Casper saw Amelia leaning against the wall, arms akimbo, looking at the floor.

"Owen is a father." This again from Raina, and she turned to Ingrid and John. "Owen and I . . . we had a night together and I got pregnant. I had his baby in January."

Casper wanted to wrap her in his arms for her courage, the way she blamed no one, simply stood in the truth.

Then her gaze dropped to Ivy. "I had a girl and named her Layla."

"You named her?" Grace said and every eye turned to her.

"You knew about this?" John asked.

"Of course she did, John. Raina lived with her for months." This from Ingrid, who'd risen and now came over to Raina. "Honey. Uh . . ." She frowned. "Is . . . ?"

"I gave her up for adoption."

Ingrid's mouth opened. Then closed, her hand going over it. She shook her head even as her eyes turned bright.

Casper slid a hand over his mother's shoulder. "But the adoption fell through. Raina is going to raise the child herself."

He watched as the news played over Ingrid's face. She frowned, then looked at Raina, back to him. "I don't—I don't understand. You knew about the baby?"

"He showed up on my doorstep the day Raina gave birth," Grace said.

"You knew about this the entire time, and you never said a word?" Their father's voice dropped, dark and dangerously quiet.

His gaze landed on both Casper and Grace. Then it stopped on Raina.

Casper's grip tightened in hers. "It wasn't my secret to tell," he said.

"He and I had a terrible fight about it. He said it wasn't fair to Owen not to know—"

"Owen doesn't know?" This from Darek, and Casper gave him a sharp warning look.

"I was going to tell him . . . I mean, I should have. But then he left and I . . ." Raina swallowed, and Casper squeezed her hand. "I don't love him."

"But he's the father of your child," John said, and Casper transferred his warning look to his father.

"What?" John asked him. "Owen is the father of her child. We can't get away from that. I mean, I understand—" He sighed, his voice softening. "I know you love her. But it's more complicated than that. What do you think is going to happen here, Casper? That you'll marry Raina and adopt Owen's child?"

When he put it like that, it seemed . . . tawdry. Like they lived in some seedy soap opera. "No—yes—I don't know. But we already learned from Darek's experience that two people who make a baby together don't necessarily belong together—"

"Hey! Really?" Darek leaned down, grabbed Tiger's hand. "Buddy, how about we get a teddy bear for your sister?"

Tiger's eyes had gone wide at the entire conversation, and for the first time, Casper saw it the way his father seemed to. Tawdry.

Darek stopped at Ivy's bed, kissed her. Then he turned to Raina. Smiled. "The one thing we're forgetting in all this is . . . congratulations, Raina. Every child is a gift."

He pressed her shoulder, glared at Casper, and took Tiger from the room.

Which left only Casper and his words lingering in the room. He exhaled. "That didn't come out right. What I should have said is, Owen and Raina don't love each other. We do. Which means that yeah, Owen is Layla's biological father, but he isn't even around—nor does he want to be—to be her real father. I want to be that."

He waited for a response. His father continued to frown, and his mother's face appeared drawn as if she was sorting through her options, her words suddenly haunting him. *I like Raina; I really do. But she is a hurt and broken soul, not a little lost.*

Not anymore. He planned to be around to help her find her way back and into the future.

"What about Owen?" This from Amelia, who spoke quietly from the corner. "Doesn't he deserve to know?"

"He does," Raina said before Casper could jump in. "That's why Casper's next great treasure hunt is to find him."

She squeezed his hand, nodding at him.

Yes. "Are you sure?" he asked quietly.

"I think the only way you or your family will have peace is to know he's okay. And . . . to tell him about the baby. Find your brother, Casper. And then come home to me."

He couldn't help it, and he didn't care what his family said or thought—he bent down to kiss her, softly, purposefully. He met her beautiful eyes as he leaned away.

"Nice, Casper," Grace said. He looked at her, and she winked.

Raina laughed, and he felt it all the way through to his bones. Sweet and buttery rich.

"Hey, Mom! Look what I got for Joy!" Tiger scampered into

the room, holding a stuffed rabbit, a bow at the neck. He shoved it toward Ivy, who took it.

"I think she'll love it."

Tiger leaned in, peering at the bundle. "She's really wrinkly."

They were laughing when Darek walked in. He glanced at Casper, eyebrow up.

"It's all good, Bro," Casper said.

Suddenly, from Raina—and he couldn't miss the sound of pride in her voice, sweeping over him, soaking him with heat—"By the way, everyone . . . Casper found the treasure of Duncan Rothe!"

Casper's words tossed in Raina all night, finally pursuing her out of bed and into the lounge area of the Beacon Pointe hotel to watch the sun rise over the far edge of Lake Superior. Passion red, indigo, and lavender all mottled against a ceiling of tufted clouds, the sun's glorious, rose-gold rays like arms pushing against the gray swaddle of night.

Light defeating darkness.

And then Darek suggested I start praying for her, so I did, and . . . the short of it is, I think God kept her in my heart because He wanted us together.

God wanted them together . . . She sat in a leather club chair and drew up her knees, wrapped her arms around them, tried to let those words settle somewhere that didn't hurt.

She opened Aggie's diary, flipping past the details of her marriage to Thor, the skipped-over years after Otto's birth, her grief over his death and how she gave his christening gown to the Linnells after the birth of their son, her daughter's arrival, the move from Mineral Springs, the opening of Haven House, a drawing of her house on the hill, the happy decades that must've required no reflection, and then, finally, to the last entry.

JULY 1982

I said good-bye to my beloved Thor today. We stood at his grave, Ginny and me, holding hands, her husband, three children, and grandchildren gathered behind her. The sky overhead arched in a triumphant cloudless blue, the sun warming a breeze through the pine trees.

A day when I would have found Thor outside, tending his hobby tomatoes or even under the hood of his old Ford, tinkering. But at the end of the day, he would have enticed me onto our deck to lounge in the Adirondack chairs facing the lake, taken my hand in his, and made me breathe in the moment. The largeness of our life.

God has been good to us. Even the cancer became a gift because it allowed me time to tell him, finally, the truth of that tragic night when he saved me from Duncan. I found his note, of course, wedged into the Bible at Job 42:5, his favorite verse, and realized he never knew the truth of that day.

Of course he didn't. How could I tell him that I killed Duncan Rothe? It was my bullet shot from my father's Colt revolver that found his tuxedoed breast. My father, for all his chagrin at my renegade behavior with Jean-Philippe, might have looked with approval at the lessons he gave me, especially after my vision cleared and I came to realize the truth. Duncan killed my father, stole his bonds—my bonds—and intended to marry me, and perhaps cause me harm, to obtain them.

He would have gotten away with it had Thor not shown up, had he not convinced me to follow my heart. To leap out in faith.

And had I not returned to the room for the bonds, which I found in Duncan's case—along with Father's revolver. Thor and Duncan were already engaged in fisticuffs outside the lodge, Thor more than a match for Duncan, except that Duncan had his brass knuckles. Although Thor met him without flinching, the beating hurt my soul.

Except for Thor's brute strength, Duncan might have killed him. But Thor wrestled him to the ground, held him, forcing his breath from him.

Thor would have left him there, half-alive, had it not been for Duncan's friend Jack, who found them both. While Duncan lay unconscious—dead, to Thor's eyes— Jack attacked and knocked my beloved Thor out with two professional punches.

That is when I stepped out of the shadows and shed my fear. When I picked up Father's weapon.

Sometimes the details blur, but I remember threatening Jack, piling Thor into his truck, driving away toward Mineral Springs, Thor's home.

It was to my great horror that Duncan followed us. But I was no longer the shrinking debutante who fainted at the sight of Father's blood.

I stood in the road. Confronted him. And when he came to me, blood in his eyes, I didn't flinch.

I hid him and his roadster in the woods and escaped to Mineral Springs, hoping for absolution. What I received was a life of unmerited forgiveness from God, who gave me much more than I deserved, although, as I explained to Thor as he lay in his sickbed, I tried to be worthy of it.

He took my hand and told me what he'd said so many years earlier: we will never be worthy. But that is the point. The more I've come to realize this, the more I am grateful for it. The largeness of God. His grace. The love He gave me in Thor.

Yes, I have been rich beyond my wildest dreams. As for the bonds—they remain my offering to the Lord, my surrender, tucked safely away in the belief that God has more for me than I can imagine.

Thor was right. Before I knew God, I had only heard of Him. But to love Him, I needed to see Him. He showed up when we lost our dear Otto and then in the joy of Virginia's birth. He showed up as we prospered in Deep Haven and opened Haven House. And He appeared every single day in Thor's devotion, his leading, his affirmation to look forward, into light.

I have lived large with Thor. And now I will live large without him.

Because I have so much to look forward to.

So much to look forward to. Raina let the words echo, remembering the way Casper had stood beside her yesterday.

She reached for the Bible on the nearby side table, a Gideon edition, and flipped it open to Thor's verse, Job 42:5.

"I have heard of You by the hearing of the ear, but now my eye sees You." Yes, perhaps she had seen Him.

"So this is where you're hiding."

Raina turned to see Ingrid easing up to her, holding two cups of coffee. Casper's mom always looked so put together—cute today in a purple fleece jacket, jeans, and running shoes.

"I'm not hiding," Raina said.

"Mmm-hmm," Ingrid answered, handing her a cup. "I hope you like vanilla lattes." She sat in the other club chair. "I stopped by the room, hoping Eden might be up reading the paper, but she and her sisters apparently think they're still in high school. I had to knock three times before Grace appeared. They had no idea where you were."

"Eden snores," Raina said, trying a smile. But Ingrid's chill toward her yesterday, despite a stiff hug, lingered, setting her defenses on high.

"Yes. She always has. I hope Jace has figured out a way to sleep through it."

Raina took a sip of the latte, letting it nourish her. The sun had advanced higher, turning the entire lake to lavender.

"I've had a night to think about this, Raina, and I've come to a conclusion."

Raina braced herself. After all, she had damaged the lives of two of Ingrid's sons, sent them both on the run.

"I think God handpicked Casper for this task." She smiled then and reached out, catching Raina's hand. "I can't wait to meet my granddaughter."

She hadn't expected that and, for a second, nearly pushed her away, the affection too overwhelming, too intimate.

"Really?"

"Yes. See, from the moment Casper was born, he lived to be a brother to his siblings. I would walk into his room and he'd be standing in his crib, watching Darek. He followed him like a puppy. And then Owen arrived. I am convinced that Casper put the first hockey stick in Owen's hands. And cheered him on, even when Owen started beating him out for playing time. Casper has an unequaled heart. But his light has always been a little eclipsed by his bookend brothers. They can steal the show, you know."

Or tried to. Raina nodded, watching the sun turn the snow along the shoreline to gold.

"But Casper has this sunshine about him. He's funny and sweet and loyal, and he loves to be the guy who shows up just when you need him."

A couple of early morning runners jogged by on the boardwalk.

"Even if it hurts him."

Oh.

Ingrid touched her arm. "More than anything, Casper needs to be needed. He has so much to give. If anyone can bridge the gap between you and Layla and Owen, it's Casper."

Raina saw him then, kissing baby Joy—the tenderness in his eyes, the way he ran the back of his finger over her downy cheek. She smiled. "Yeah."

"And, Raina—you were also made for Casper."

She glanced at Ingrid, who nodded, an enigmatic expression on her face.

"Casper needs someone who believes in him. Who can see the genius in his ideas. Who can stick by him when he fails—and wins."

"I'm sorry I hurt him—"

"Oh, sweetie, we're so over that. Casper is a big boy; he just needed time. And let's not forget Owen's part in all of this." She stared out at the lake. "By the way, although I'm so thankful that we'll get to be Layla's grandparents, I can appreciate the courage it took to offer her up for adoption. It's a true act of love."

Raina didn't know why, but somehow hearing that confirmation from Ingrid balmed her still-open wound.

"I tried to forget her, but I couldn't."

"Forget her? Oh, Raina, a mother would never forget her child, even if someone else raised her. She'd always be in your heart."

Like Casper had said about her. "Do you think . . . do you think Casper meant what he said? About praying for me?"

"Of course I did." Casper came up behind her, settled his hands on her shoulders. Leaned down to kiss her cheek. "Hey, Mom."

Ingrid got up and gave Casper a kiss. "Just talking to your girl here. So glad you two finally worked it out." She patted him on the cheek. "I'm going over to the hospital with your father to pick up Tiger. Darek will stay here until Ivy and Joy are discharged in a couple days. How about if we meet you back at the resort?" She leaned down and caught Raina in a quick embrace, then backed away, smiling. "*Both* of you."

Casper sat down opposite her, in his mother's seat. He looked—and smelled—freshly showered but unshaven, his hair in wet curls. "I prayed for you all the time, that you would see how much God loves you."

"Even after what I said to you?"

"About God not loving you? Or noticing you? The crazy idea that you are nothing to Him? Yeah, I remember that because it burned a hole in me. Nothing could be further from the truth, Raina."

She studied his face, those blue eyes so earnest, and a bud of hope opened in her. Maybe God *did* notice her. After all, He'd sent this amazing man into her life, refused to let him leave.

"See, what you don't know is, I'm only following in God's footsteps, picking up the clues He's dropped for me," Casper said, taking her hand, his thumb running over it, curls of warmth weaving up her arm.

"'For the Son of Man came to seek and to save the lost'—it's from the Bible. God is all about finding lost treasures, and He took me on the quest with Him. Raina, God loves you, and He's not willing for you to think for one moment He has forgotten you. You are always on His mind."

Her throat tightened, but . . . maybe . . .

"You thought you could use your mistakes—and even your anger—to hide from God. But we can't hide from God—nor should we. Because why should we hide from Someone who wants so much joy for us? So much light?"

Light. Yes, that's what Casper had made her see—light. Hope. Forgiveness.

Love.

She saw it now—the relentless pursuit of a God who believed her valuable enough to put Layla—and Casper—into her life.

Not forgotten.

Seen.

"And He appeared every single day in Thor's devotion, his leading, his affirmation to look forward, into light."

She made to run her fingers under her eye to catch the tear, but Casper's thumb did it for her.

"I love you, Casper. And I think . . . I think God put you in my life to help me see that I don't have to be lost. Not anymore."

"I promise I'm never going to let you go." He pulled her onto his lap, cupped his hand on her cheek, turned her face to his, and kissed her. He tasted of coffee, smelled of home, and yet had enough wildness in his touch to remind her that their great adventure was just beginning.

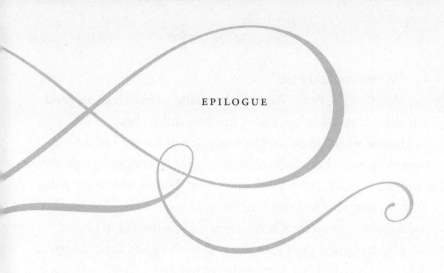

EPILOGUE

MELTING ICICLES DRIPPED like tears from the roof of the lodge to the deck, sparkling against the sunshine, the bright blue of the day. The thaw had dented the snowpack along the walk to the lake, and the fragrance of spring hung light, faint hope in the air.

Somehow Deep Haven had survived the deep freeze of the century.

"She's late," Casper said from where he stood at the fireplace, staring at the flames.

Raina watched him. Already a pensive father, awaiting his daughter's arrival. His dress shirt stretched against his wide shoulders, although he rolled up the sleeves. And he probably needed a haircut, his curls long and scraping his collar.

Nah. She liked how he tucked his renegade self behind the tailored facade of a manager. For now.

"Where could she be?"

"Dori will be here," Raina said, walking over to take his hand. He drew hers to his lips, kissed it, worry in his eyes.

Except what did he have to worry about? Casper had a natural way with kids. Even infants, who seemed to coo and giggle the moment he took them in his arms. But Raina—well, what if she hadn't a clue what to do with a three-month-old infant? She couldn't exactly show up on the Christiansens' doorstep at 2 a.m., right?

Her expression must have betrayed her because Casper dropped her hand, cradled her face, and met her eyes. "You'll be great." He gave her a quick kiss despite the fact that his father sat there in a recliner, reading the paper, his mother in the kitchen. She could hear Jace and Max talking hockey in the den, the crew from Minneapolis having driven up together after the Blue Ox's last home game.

Tiger sat at the counter, coloring, Grace occupying him so Ivy could get some sleep. She'd dozed off on the sofa.

Eden held baby Joy, rocking her quietly in the corner. Raina gave it six months, if that, before Eden and Jace announced their own happy news.

The door opened, and Raina looked up, her heart falling when she spotted Darek in the entryway, stamping his feet. "We had a logjam on the road, but I got it cleared. It's a bit of a muddy soup out there."

"First thing we do when I get the Rothe check is pave the lot," Casper said.

Raina expected protest out of Darek at the idea of taking the money from the finder's fee Casper offered, his pride maybe getting in the way, but he simply nodded. "We could put a new roof on the lodge too. We still have some cinder damage."

She could still reel in disbelief at the reward distribution from Aggie's bonds. One million nearly a century ago had multiplied to $20 million today, and 10 percent still made for a hefty, generous addition to the Evergreen purse and Casper's own checkbook.

Better, however, was listening to Casper regale his family with the story, every step of the mystery, and watching their faces as they realized Casper's brilliance. Which, of course, she'd known all along.

Casper, in his generosity, even set up an account for Raina and Layla, although she planned on keeping her job at the antique shop, at least part-time.

And sure, Monte had shown up, tried to claim the bonds as his, but Penny Townsend shut him down so fast it would have made her grandmother cheer from the grave.

Monte vanished from Deep Haven then, and Raina hadn't seen him since.

Darek kissed his sleeping wife on the forehead, then went over to Eden.

The doorbell chimed, deep and resonant, and Casper took Raina's hand.

"I'll get it," Grace said, heading to the door. Raina couldn't help but start to follow.

She stopped as Dori came in, holding a baby carrier. The social worker handed it to Grace. "Sorry. The drive took longer than I thought."

But Raina had forgotten her, watching as Grace brought in her daughter. Layla lay asleep, strapped in and dressed in pink, her head covered by a bunny hat with fuzzy white ears.

Grace set the carrier down, and Raina knelt before it, began to undo the straps.

Layla woke, yawned, her perfect little mouth sideways. She

stretched, her back arching as Raina took her out and held her to her shoulder.

"She'll probably be hungry soon," Dori said, handing Grace a baby bag. "There's some formula in there, along with fresh diapers."

Layla began to fuss, wriggling in Raina's arms, tiny snorts and hiccups of unhappiness coming from her body. Suddenly she lit out in a howl.

"Oh!" Raina held her as she struggled, Layla's body writhing as she worked herself into a lather.

On the sofa, Ivy stirred, and from across the room, Joy began to mimic Layla.

Raina glanced at Casper. See? What was she thinking—?

Suddenly Ingrid's hand landed on her shoulder. "Just tuck her in close and bounce her a little. Babies like that." She kissed Layla on the forehead even as Raina tried not to give in to the urge to pass her off. "I'll fix her bottle."

Raina turned Layla in her arms, swaying her body back and forth, walking to the window. *Please, don't cry. Don't cry.*

She could hear Dori behind her, talking to Casper and the family, discovering Raina's plans. How she might move into cabin one to be close to the family and child care, but separate, at least until Casper returned from finding Owen.

He left that last part out when talking to Dori, but she knew that as soon as she and Layla felt ready, he planned on leaving.

She refused to think about it. But yes, she agreed that Owen deserved to know about his daughter, and Casper wanted to be the one to tell him. And as he put it, ask permission to marry the mother of Owen's child.

Layla had stopped howling, but she whimpered in Raina's arms, gearing up for another outburst.

"Here you go," Ingrid said, handing Raina a warm bottle. "Sit over here." She pointed to a rocking chair that faced the deck. "It's where I fed all my babies."

The rocking chair held a knit blanket that Ingrid settled over Raina's lap as she sat, propped up Layla, and gave her the bottle. Her daughter slurped it down as if ravenous.

"See, you're a natural," Ingrid said to Raina. Then she leaned over the baby. "And you are precious." She tweaked Layla's little foot. Layla met her eyes and smiled around the nipple of the bottle. Blue eyes. She had the rich blue eyes of the Christiansen clan.

But the black hair belonged to Raina.

Layla reached up, curled her hand around Raina's thumb.

Raina's eyes filled, and she began to rock, a song filling her chest. Something sweet she couldn't yet name. *"Hush, little baby . . ."*

Casper knelt beside her, met her eyes. "She's beautiful, Raina."

Yes. A dark beauty.

"I think you're all set here, Raina," Dori said.

Casper got up and shook Dori's hand as if he were making a deal, a little flummoxed.

Yeah, well, life had them all off-kilter with joy.

Raina finished feeding Layla, burping her on her shoulder.

"Can I hold her?" Casper asked, and she handed over her package, caught in the sweetness of his expression as he cradled the baby.

Yes, this was a moment with no regrets. Large. Light.

"Oh no, Dori left her scarf," Eden said, picking up the orange knit scarf from the entryway. She set it on the counter.

Amelia came down the stairs, wearing a dress, leggings, tall black boots. She stopped at the landing, her expression bright as her gaze landed on Layla. "Wow, really? I missed it?"

"That's what you get for primping. What happened to sweat-shirts and yoga pants?" Grace said as Amelia walked over to Layla, held out her finger for the baby to grasp.

"I'm trying to class up the joint," Amelia said.

"She has a hot date," Eden said from the kitchen, where she was now mashing the potatoes. Jace, her husband, walked from the other room, gave Amelia a low whistle, then eased the masher from Eden's hand.

"No good, pal," Max said. "Let the master work." He retrieved cream cheese and milk from the fridge and bumped Jace out of the way.

"I don't have a hot date. It's just me and Seth hanging out. He's home for spring break and wanted to get together. Don't set me a place—we're going out for burgers."

"I think he's still carrying a torch for you, honey." This from Ingrid, who carried plates to the table.

"I always thought you two would end up together," Grace said. "You were so cute when you dated in high school."

"Maybe someday, but I'm not ready for another relationship. Not yet." She left the rest unsaid, but Raina caught Amelia's exchange of glances with Casper. Amelia dumped her purse on the counter, ran back upstairs.

John got up and walked over to look at Layla. "She has Chris-tiansen eyes," he said. He winked at Raina, his expression tender.

The doorbell rang and Grace went to answer it. "Probably Dori."

Ingrid added silverware to the table. But as she looked up at Grace, she stilled.

Grace was backing into the room, still holding the orange scarf. Behind her followed a man about Casper's age, although taller, with curly dark hair, a two-day layer of whiskers, and piercing blue eyes. He wore a white oxford, a suit coat over faded jeans.

And then he opened his mouth. "I'm looking for Miss Amelia Christiansen." Crisp British vowels, sharpened to an aristocratic point.

Clearly not from the hamlet of Deep Haven. The entire family stared at him.

Amelia appeared at the top of the stairs, her hand gripping the railing. "Roark." Her voice emerged as a thin wisp.

Casper handed Raina back the baby. She glanced at him—something had his burr up.

Amelia came down the stairs, a little white. "What are you doing here?"

No one moved as Roark turned to her. "Amelia, darling, I'm so sorry for the way I bumbled everything. But I believe I have it sorted now and . . ."

Casper took a step closer, stood next to his father. Raina had the eerie sense that redcoat Roark might have just walked into the heavily armed camp of revolutionary patriots.

But he apparently paid them no mind as he moved to the bottom of the stairs. "I've come to ask for your forgiveness."

Amelia took another step down the stairs. "What are you doing here?"

Raina ducked the crazy urge to wave him off.

Then stopped as he reached into his suit coat and pulled out a small box. "Just a token, darling, but I came to say that I can't get you off my mind. I love you terribly. Please, won't you give us another chance?"

A NOTE FROM THE AUTHOR

WHAT DO YOU do when you love someone who seems bent on self-destruction? Worse, when they seem incapable of listening to reason?

Pray. Hope. Love anyway.

I came upon this story idea after hearing about a woman who had inadvertently walked into an abusive relationship. She didn't exactly know how she got there—just that one day she opened her eyes to the truth. But she'd told herself so many lies that tracing her path toward this abuser seemed almost natural. She accepted abuse because of her inability to believe she was worthy of anything else.

Those outside the horror warned her. Wanted—tried—to wave her off. And watched with torn hearts as she entwined herself in a situation that nearly cost her and her children their lives.

Eventually the abuser hurt someone else—someone less afraid, less intimidated, less willing to believe lies—and was imprisoned. Justice finally.

So often, believers are like this woman: we stand in our mistakes, our sins, our regrets, and determine that we don't deserve love. So we accept less—even abuse—because we can't lift our eyes off ourselves and onto truth.

Jesus stands outside the lies, waving at us to stop our self-destruction, to believe Him for freedom, to reach out for His love, to trust His justice. And He asks us, as Christians, to stand in the darkened pathways and shed light.

I wanted to write a story about a man who couldn't escape the pull of love God had for the broken, the lost—and yet depict the agony of seeing them run away into destruction. Just as God must feel when we push Him away and stubbornly head into darkness. Casper seemed exactly the right person to shoulder this task . . . even though it could have cost him so much.

That kind of love cost Jesus even more . . . cost Him everything.

But Jesus, like Casper, is a treasure hunter who has come to seek and save the lost. I love the fact that He believes we are worth the search.

And Raina—who lived always looking behind her—had to learn to look ahead, outside her comfort zone, into faith. I love the message that when we look at ourselves, we get afraid. After all, it's true: how can such a wretch be redeemed? We can't if we depend on ourselves. But if we depend on God . . .

Well, as John Christiansen says, "What does love do? Forgives. Comforts. Protects. Saves. Renews. *Loves.*"

Friends, look forward, your face to the wind, and live large in God's love. Jesus says you are worth the search, worth His outrageous, unwavering love for you, despite the cost.

Thank you for reading Raina and Casper's story. With Casper off to find Owen . . . well, it's time for Amelia to come up with an answer, don't you think? Can she forgive the man who broke her heart? More, will she choose her high school sweetheart, Seth, or this European blue blood? Which would you choose?

In His grace,
Susan May Warren

ABOUT THE AUTHOR

Susan May Warren is the bestselling, Christy and RITA Award–winning author of more than forty novels whose compelling plots and unforgettable characters have won acclaim with readers and reviewers alike. She served with her husband and four children as a missionary in Russia for eight years before she and her family returned home to the States. She now writes full-time as her husband runs a resort on Lake Superior in northern Minnesota, where many of her books are set.

Susan holds a BA in mass communications from the University of Minnesota. Several of her critically acclaimed novels have been ECPA and CBA bestsellers, were chosen as Top Picks by *Romantic Times*, and have won the RWA's Inspirational Reader's Choice contest and the American Christian Fiction Writers' prestigious Carol Award. Her novels *You Don't Know Me* and *Take a Chance on Me* were Christy Award winners, and five of her other books have also been finalists. In addition to her writing, Susan loves to teach and speak at women's events about God's amazing grace in our lives.

For exciting updates on her new releases, previous books, and more, visit her website at www.susanmaywarren.com.

DISCUSSION QUESTIONS

1. Ingrid describes Casper, a middle child, as "the one who is neither the oldest—the responsible legacy bearer—nor the youngest, pampered and cherished just because he is the last." How does his role as the middle son affect how Casper sees himself? Where do you fall in your family's birth order? How might that define your role?

2. Though Casper feels like a failure in comparison to his siblings, each Christiansen struggles with his or her own inadequacies and failures. Why does Casper set such high and perhaps unrealistic standards for himself? Do you ever find yourself comparing your strengths and weaknesses to those of your siblings, friends, coworkers, etc.? Is it more often helpful or damaging?

3. As her due date grows closer and even after her baby is born, Raina agonizes over whether to keep her daughter or give her up for adoption. Do you think she ultimately makes the right decision? What would you have said if she'd come to you for advice?

4. Darek faces enormous pressure to keep Evergreen Resort afloat and maintain the Christiansen legacy. How does this affect his relationships with Ivy and Tiger? When faced with a big responsibility, do you ask for help or shoulder the burden yourself?

5. When Casper suggests that Raina turn to God for help, she argues, "God doesn't love everybody, despite what Sunday school says. . . . He doesn't love me." What brought her to this conclusion? Have you ever questioned whether God loves everyone—or whether He loves you?

6. Even though Raina tried to keep her baby a secret from the Christiansens, several family members eventually find out. Did they deserve to know from the beginning? Did the siblings do the right thing in keeping the news from John and Ingrid for so long? Have you been asked to keep a secret when you weren't sure it was right? What did you do?

7. Casper and Raina are both intrigued by "undiscovered treasures," whether found on an archaeological dig, among the historical society's donations, or in Aggie Wilder's abandoned home. Do you share their love for antiques or relics from the past? What are some of your "treasures"— whether family heirlooms or just great finds?

8. Once she finds Aggie Wilder's diary, Raina gets caught up in her story. Why does it hold such fascination for her? In what ways does Raina relate to Aggie, even without realizing it?

9. Darek challenges Casper on his relationship with Raina, saying, "The fact is, when God brings Christians into the lives of the hurting, it's because He intends to use us to be

truth and light to them. Not fix their problems but point them to the One who can." How does this change Casper's perspective on Raina? When someone in your life is hurting, do you find yourself wanting to fix their problems? How could you bring truth and light to those situations?

10. Raina continues dating Monte despite some twinges of doubt along the way. What red flags did you see in Monte's behavior? Why do you think Raina stayed blind to them for so long? Have you ever continued a relationship you knew was unhealthy? What was the result?

11. In her journal, Aggie records Thor's belief that "a small life is lived by staring inward, but a large one is lived by diving into God's love." How did Aggie "live large" once she believed this to be true?

12. When Casper questions how he can continue loving Raina, John answers, "How do you keep loving someone who doesn't love you back? Like Jesus did, Son. Faithfully praying, faithfully abiding, faithfully loving anyway." Has God called you to love someone this way? Where does that relationship stand now?

13. As the resort continues to struggle, Darek seizes an opportunity to rejoin his hotshot firefighting team. Did you agree with his decision? When have you been tempted to run away—literally or figuratively—from a stressful situation? What did you do?

14. Near the end of the story, Casper and Raina bring their secrets into the light and arrive at a plan for their future. If you were a member of the Christiansen family, how would

you have responded? What do you think the future holds for Casper and Raina? For Owen?

15. Do parents' roles change as their children reach adulthood? If so, what life events typically signal that transition, and how should children and parents go about establishing new boundaries? Do you think John and Ingrid have managed this transition well?

MORE GREAT FICTION
· FROM ·
SUSAN MAY WARREN

THE DEEP HAVEN
NOVELS
Happily Ever After
Tying the Knot
The Perfect Match
My Foolish Heart
The Shadow of Your Smile
You Don't Know Me
Hook, Line & Sinker: A Deep Haven novella

TEAM HOPE
SERIES
Flee the Night
Escape to Morning
Expect the Sunrise
Waiting for Dawn: A Team Hope novella

THE PJ SUGAR
SERIES
Nothing but Trouble
Double Trouble
Licensed for Trouble

THE NOBLE LEGACY
SERIES
Reclaiming Nick
Taming Rafe
Finding Stefanie

STAND-ALONE TITLES
The Great Christmas Bowl

www.susanmaywarren.com

CP0790

TYNDALE HOUSE PUBLISHERS IS CRAZY4FICTION!

Inspirational fiction that entertains and inspires

Get to know us! Become a member of the Crazy4Fiction community. Whether you follow our blog, like us on Facebook, follow us on Twitter, or read our e-newsletter, you're sure to get the latest news on the best in Christian fiction. You might even win something along the way!

JOIN IN THE FUN TODAY.

 www.crazy4fiction.com

 Crazy4Fiction

 @Crazy4Fiction

CP0021